"I TRUST YOU ENJOYED THE LIBERTIES YOU TOOK WHILE I WAS RESTING?"

"Liberties, my lady?"

"How *dare* you touch me," she snapped, "let alone remove so much as a slipper from my foot!"

"Ahh," he said. "*Those* liberties. You would have preferred to sleep in cold, wet clothes?" His gaze raked appreciatively down the shapeless form of the cloak and left no doubt as to what he recalled seeing beneath. "I thought it a convenient opportunity to assess the precise value of the goods I am holding to ransom. Had I done so earlier, I heartily believe I would have put a much higher price on returning them undamaged."

"Then . . . you did not—" Servanne bit her lip, resenting the flow of ruddy colour that made his smile widen further.

"If I did?"

"If you did"—she searched his face in vain for a trace of humanity—"then you are a lower, viler creature than ever I could have imagined. Will you or will you not answer my question truthfully?"

The Wolf laughed. "Truthfully"—he said the word in such a way as to raise a spray of gooseflesh along her arms—"had I seen to my own comforts as well as yours, you would not now have the shield of a blank memory to hide behind. Nor would there be a need to ask what manner of liberties I had taken, for your body would still be singing their effects loudly and clearly."

Advance praise for Marsha Canham's
Through a Dark Mist:

"Ms. Canham writes a medieval novel with rare authority, weaving a rich tapestry of atmosphere, action, and romance. This book is a wonderfully satisfying love story that I would recommend to anyone."　　　　　—Anita Mills

"Canham captivates. Swashbuckling adventure. Sweeping pageantry. Lusty passions. Clever dialogue. A thoroughly engrossing love story."　　　　　—Nan Ryan

"Infectious characters, witty dialogue, thrill-a-minute intrigue and intense conflicts of the heart—Marsha Canham gives you all this and more. If you like romance; if you like adventure; if you like first-rate fiction, you'll love *Through a Dark Mist*."
　　　　　—Elaine Coffman

Other books by Marsha Canham

China Rose

Bound by the Heart

The Wind and the Sea

The Pride of Lions

The Blood of Roses

THROUGH A DARK MIST

MARSHA CANHAM

A DELL BOOK

Published by
Dell Publishing
a division of
Bantam Doubleday Dell Publishing Group, Inc.
666 Fifth Avenue
New York, New York 10103

If you purchased this book without a cover you should be aware that this book is stolen property. It was reported as "unsold and destroyed" to the publisher and neither the author nor the publisher has received any payment for this "stripped book."

Copyright © 1991 by Marsha Canham

All rights reserved. No part of this book may be reproduced or transmitted in any form or by any means, electronic or mechanical, including photocopying, recording, or by any information storage and retrieval system, without the written permission of the Publisher, except where permitted by law.

The trademark Dell® is registered in the U.S. Patent and Trademark Office.

ISBN: 0-440-20611-1

Printed in the United States of America

Published simultaneously in Canada

November 1991

10 9 8 7 6 5 4 3 2 1

RAD

This one is for me—
a fantasy I have always had about walking into
the heart of a misty forest and
meeting Errol Flynn midway across a
narrow footbridge . . .
Now, of course, it's Kevin Costner
wearing the lincoln green . . .
but do you hear me complaining?

PROLOGUE

Voices!

She could swear she heard voices—not just one, but several—and she struggled painfully to her feet, her back scraping the length of the rough stone wall. The cell was small, cold, and damp. The air stank with a combination of mould and salt spray, echoed with the sound of waves crashing furiously against unseen ramparts of rock.

Servanne slid her hands up through the slime that coated the rotted wood of the narrow oak door and reached for a fingerhold on the ledge carved high above her head. A natural chink in the stone passed for the only window and was her sole means of determining if it was day or night. Even then she had to rely on her instincts to know if it was hazy sunlight or bright moonlight penetrating the tangled mat of moss and lichen that grew over the outer wall.

Scarcely average in height, she could do no more than curl her torn fingers over the lip of serrated stone and pull herself up on tiptoes to judge the source of light. Was it daylight, moonlight, or firelight? Was it voices she had heard, or was it the surf and the wind playing games with her sanity? *Someone* was playing games with her sanity, that much was a certainty, for between the incredible cold, the dampness, the incessant pounding of the waves, and the complete isolation, she feared the strongest of minds could not long resist the lure into madness.

Was this what De Gournay hoped for? Was he hoping

madness, or the threat of it, would wear away her resistance and make her succumb to his demands like a sheep succumbs to slaughter?

Servanne's eyes were dry and burning, and she realized she must have slept for a time despite her vows against it. She could not distinguish much in the murky half-light that permeated her cell, but she could hear enough furtive rustling in the mouldered straw to know she was not the solitary inhabitant of the stone cage. The terror of waking up to find rats gnawing on her flesh had decided her against seeking refuge in sleep, but after having wept a pool of tears, her eyelids had simply grown too swollen to resist any further.

With an anguished sob she slumped against the uneven stone wall, the tears stinging hot and sudden in her eyes. There were no voices. No one had come to rescue her, no one had even come to see if she was alive or dead since she had first been flung into the cell. There were guards out there somewhere; she had heard the occasional clink of armour as they paced back and forth to warm themselves. And one of them seemed to take special delight in pausing outside the door to describe in lurid detail what he and his companions intended to do with her to relieve their boredom.

Servanne suppressed a moan as she clasped her small hands around her upper arms and hugged herself through a violent bout of shivering. Sweet Mother Mary in Heaven, but she was cold! Cold clean through to the marrow of her bones. The pale yellow silk of her tunic was no protection against elements that were causing discomfort to coarse, sweat-stained men who stood about in bullhide armour and full overlays of Damascan chain mail. Petite, slender as a willow, regal as befitting a gentlewoman of noble birth, Servanne de Briscourt had appeared before the gawping, staring guardsmen like a sylph, her gown and surcoat frothing about her ankles with the airiness of sea foam, her long blonde hair left unbraided, free of its confining wimple, and cascading in a wealth of glossy curls to her waist. For the duration of her week-long stay at Bloodmoor Keep, she had felt their hot eyes devouring her, and until this morning, she had been able to return their hungry stares coolly and disdainfully, confident they would not dare to lay so much as a fingertip to the heel of her slipper.

The yellow silk was torn in a dozen places now, soiled with the filth and muck of her stone cell. Her face felt puffed, and she knew it was bruised and badly discoloured. Her slim white arms were marbled black and blue from the steely grip of uncaring hands; she had lost one dainty silk slipper and the jewelled girdle of gold links she had worn about her hips had long been broken up among her captors to compensate them for their troubles.

Her cell measured four paces in length, three in width. The only entrance was through a low-slung oaken door, the planks of which were studded and bound in iron that was badly corroded from the sea air. Servanne had been semiconscious when she had been dragged from the castle tower, only dimly aware of the cold bite of the air and of lewd hands pinching at her breasts and buttocks. There had been talk of putting her in the donjon beneath the keep, but De Gournay had obviously believed the stone cage might be more effective in winning her cooperation.

Vague images of being pushed, dragged, and carried through the dank and cramped passageways that tunneled through the underbelly of the sprawling castle brought further distorted recollections of exiting through a postern gate in the outer walls. She remembered screaming and drawing back, for the gate opened onto a jagged ledge etched into the sheer face of a cliff. There had been only empty sky above and beyond, the angry crash and thunder of raging seas below. She had thought it was to be her end then and there, a wisp of yellow flung into the rising sheets of spume, and indeed, had it not been for the sturdy grasp of her guard, she might have quickened her meeting with fate—would surely have done so if she had known the hell of uncertainty and fear that awaited her.

Led down a hair-raising spiral of rock to a point midway along the wall of the cliff, she had scratched runnels of blood from the guard's face and arms as he had pushed her into a cell eroded naturally out of the stone, sealed unnaturally by oak and iron. She had been given neither food nor water since. Neither screams nor pleas nor bursts of pounding rage had had any effect on the thick iron bar that had been slammed across the outer surface of the door.

Lucien had tried to warn her. Dearest God, Lucien had warned her not to trifle with forces she did not understand, but she had not listened. She had . . . dear Christ . . . she had doubted Lucien instead. Doubted, questioned, even been half-convinced of *his* madness.

Servanne stiffened, her wide blue eyes flicking up to the window slit again. She hoarded her breath, her ears straining to hear over the booming thunder of the sea. Something *was* happening outside her small, dank prison cell. Someone *was* out there, talking to the guard . . . *laughing*!

Servanne scrambled back into the farthest corner of the cell, shocked numb by the unexpected sound.

Laughter? In a world that held only darkness, pain, and terror? Was it another of De Gournay's ploys to strip her of her sanity, or was this simply the beginning of the end? Had he finally reached a decision as to what to do with her? Had something happened to make him believe he no longer needed to keep her alive to fulfill his greedy ambitions?

Something bumped against the door once, twice, and a muffled cry was bitten short before it was fully formed. Servanne covered her mouth with her hand and tasted the metallic bitterness of blood as she tried in vain to stifle the scream rising in her own throat. She heard the iron bolt scraped slowly back out of its slot, and she watched in horror as the door began to creak open.

Her hair, filthy and matted beyond any semblance of its former beauty, whipped across her face on a gust of icy, mist-drenched wind, blinding her as effectively as the sudden glare of the torch that was thrust through the narrow entryway. The figure holding the torch had to bend almost double to clear the low doorway, and in those first searing seconds, revealed nothing more to Servanne than the bulk of his coarse gray monk's cowling.

The intruder straightened to his full height, the top of his hooded head coming an inch shy of the moss-covered ceiling. His eyes were squinted against the smoking pitch, and as they swept around the confines of the cell, a curse marked their discovery of the pale splash of yellow silk cringing against the corner.

Her hand raised to shield her eyes against the glaring torchlight, Servanne choked back another scream as she caught sight of the steel daggar clutched in the monk's hand, its blade slicked wet and red to the hilt. A further horror greeted her eyes as she identified the huddled black bulk at his feet: the guard who had apparently shared the monk's laughter but a moment ago now lay sprawled across the threshold of the door. The head, with its conical steel helmet, was almost completely severed from the neck, and blood was gouting in thick, steaming pulsations to form a slick red pool on the stone.

"Servanne?"

She jerked her gaze upward at the same instant the monk pushed back the gray horsehair hood to reveal, not the tonsured baldness of an almoner, but a full, gleaming mane that fell thick and gloriously unkempt to the broadest pair of shoulders in all of Christendom.

"Lucien?" she gasped. "Is it . . . really you?"

"Name another man fool enough to chase after you on a

night such as this," he said, grinning with the heartbreakingly familiar slash of strong white teeth.

"I thought you were dead," she whispered, not believing what her eyes were seeing. "When no one came . . . when I heard nothing . . . I thought you were dead."

"Did you think you could be rid of me so easily?" came the softly chiding rejoinder.

Her eyes flooded with tears, Servanne flung herself across the width of the cell and felt the long, powerful arms sweep her into a crushing embrace. The blood-slicked poniard dropped forgotten onto the ground and his hands raked into the tousled mass of her hair, holding her against him, tilting her lips up to his for a kiss as passionate and consuming as a physical act of love.

"Lucien!" a voice hissed from the doorway. "Can you not celebrate later, when we have the time and leisure to do so?"

Servanne could not withhold the cry as the hungry caress ended abruptly on a ragged curse. The taste of him, the feel of him, the scent of the courage and *freedom* that lingered on his skin drowned her senses and she was not aware of the hurried exchange that passed between the two men, she only knew Lucien was alive. He was here with her. He had come for her despite the treachery, the betrayal, the deceit, and the lies!

The second cowled figure crowded the doorway and for the briefest flicker of torchlight, his lean hawklike features glowed in the saffron light.

Alaric! Sweet merciful Virgin Mary, they were both alive: Lucien and Alaric!

"My lady." Alaric's easy smile belied the concern in the soft brown eyes as he swiftly assessed her battered, deteriorated condition. "Are you well enough? Can you walk?"

"I shall run as fast as the wind if need be," she assured him without hesitation, her own beautiful smile shining through her tears.

Lucien took Servanne's hand in his and, cautioning her to duck low, led her out of the dank stone chamber and into the brisk night air. Wind snatched instantly at the shreds of her skirt, sending the silk swirling around her ankles in a yellow corkscrew. As eager as she was to flee, Servanne stumbled across the width of the rocky ledge and froze. Where the path continued down the cliff, it was barely three feet wide; the slightest misstep would send them hurling into the black and boiling frenzy of the sea two hundred yards below. The moon was on the downward slide of its journey across the sky and offered no relief from the heavy shadows. What light it shed fell mainly on the mist-shrouded walls and ramparts of the castle at the top of the cliff.

Bloodmoor Keep, perched on the very edge of the precipice above them, loomed like a black and monstrous predator, the tall battlements and jutting barbicans silhouetted against the night sky, impregnable, cold, and silent as death.

Servanne shuddered involuntarily and Lucien, noting she was as blue from cold as she was from the abuse she had endured, stripped himself of his robes and handed her the woolen garment.

"Here, put this on," he ordered. "We have a way to go yet and—"

"Lucien—" Alaric called softly. "Come quickly."

Lucien followed Alaric's outthrust finger and saw a line of bright orange dots spilling out of the postern gate at the base of the castle wall. A dozen guards carrying a dozen torches were making their way down the side of the cliff, lighting the way for a dozen more armed with swords and crossbows.

"Go!" Alaric shouted, ridding himself of the hindrance of the monk's robes. "I'll loose a few arrows their way to discourage them long enough for you to get Lady Servanne below."

Lucien hesitated, the desire for blood and revenge warring with the need to see his love to safety.

"In God's name"—Alaric had to shout to penetrate through the fog of Lucien's rage—"we have not come this far to lose to them now! Go! I will join you in a trice, have no fear. I have no more intention of perishing on this godforsaken eyrie than I have intentions of walking back to Lincoln."

Knowing there was no time to argue, Lucien took Servanne's hand tightly in his and began leading her carefully down the steep and uneven pathway. Behind them, Alaric cursed wholeheartedly as he armed himself with the crossbows of the dead sentries. An expert marksman, he struck the first two targets he aimed for, sending both to a screaming death over the lip of the cliff. He could easily have dealt with the rest, each in their turn, but a quick count showed only seven bolts in the one quiver, and three in the second, ruling out the luxury of too long a delay or of an ill-timed miss. He rearmed both bows and sat back on his haunches, his eyes wandering upward to the eerie silhouette of the castle. Was it his imagination or was the blanket of darkness giving way under the threat of dawn?

The path from the postern gate to the stone cell had been a wide, paved road in comparison to the crumbling, fragmented sill of broken stone Servanne and Lucien descended along now. Forced to travel singly and to keep one arm and hip pressed painfully against the cold rock, Servanne's boast of being able to run like the wind was mocked at every gap and eroded toehold that kept her heart lodged firmly in her throat. Her one slipperless foot seemed to find every sharp needle of rock on the path, and the monk's robe weighed her down, snagging on brambles and granite teeth, twice shunting her back and needing to be torn out of the grasp of the greedy talons of stone.

A pale wash of blue-gray along the horizon hinted that

dawn was not far away, but the false light made navigation even more treacherous—at times, impossible. Lucien seemed to be guided by instinct alone and, on those occasions when the blackness erased all trace of solid footing, prayer.

The fleeing pair was soaked in sea spray when they finally rounded the face of the cliff. There, to Servanne's further astonishment, the path spread and leveled out, and in the blossoming flare of dawn, she could see the glittering swath of a small bay sheltered behind a break of boulders. Even though the air still vibrated with the tremendous roar and crash of the sea, the inlet was relatively calm—enough for a small boat to have maneuvered to within twenty feet of the shore.

The last stretch of the escape had to be made over a sharp, cutting bed of shale. Lucien, hearing Servanne's painful cry as the first step drove a shard of glasslike stone into the pad of her bare foot, swept her into his arms and, without missing a step, plunged into the knee-deep water. The sound of a second pair of splashing footsteps behind them brought the wolfish grin back to Lucien's lips as he turned and saw Alaric swerve away from the shoreline and follow them into the surf.

In the next breath the smile vanished. Alaric was waving, shouting, pointing to the score of conical steel helmets that lined the shore.

It was a trap!

Water began to plop and spout on all sides as a hail of crossbow bolts chased them deeper into the surf. Lucien commanded every ounce of strength he possessed into his legs, but the water, now waist-deep, hampered him and even though the breaker of rocks helped cut the force of the sea, there was still a wicked undercurrent that pulled and shifted the sand beneath every footstep.

Less than ten paces from the longboat they went down under a slapping wall of black water. Coughing and spluttering oaths, Lucien struggled upright again, managing to maintain his grip on Servanne, sodden clothes and all.

One of the two shadowy outlines crouched in the gunwales of the boat vaulted over the side and began swimming toward the labouring couple. The other figure, tall and slender as a reed, her short-cropped hair glinting red in the moonlight, nocked an ashwood arrow into a tautly strung longbow and calmly began to return the fire of the guardsmen who were now running in a parallel line along the shore. At intervals they paused to fit their stubby quarrels into their crossbows and knelt to release the triggers. The need to remain in one place long enough to rearm their clumsy and cumbersome weapons gave ample opportunity to the lithe shadow in the longboat to choose her targets carefully and with deadly accuracy. Many of the guards heard the singsong hiss of arrows arcing gracefully out of the darkness toward them and did not rise from the shale again. Others ran for the cover of nearby rocks along the shore and dove behind them to escape the quivering *fff-thunk* of the steel arrowhead punching through surcoat and armour. But they were still well within the ideal range for firing their own weapons and they did so continually, their rage fueling and improving their aim.

Servanne heard a cry and glanced over Lucien's shoulder in time to see Alaric slew sidelong into the water, an iron-tipped bolt embedded in his upper chest. Lucien shouted and released her, shoving her toward the longboat before he started back to where he had seen Alaric go under. Servanne's scream of warning went unheeded. One of De Gournay's knights, running along the shore close to where Lucien thrashed through the water, took aim with his crossbow and fired, the bolt tearing a ribbon of raw flesh from Lucien's right temple.

Stunned, he heeled sideways, the pain and blood blinding him even as his feet continued to churn toward Alaric. The knight armed his bow a second time, but before he could fire, he heard a thud and felt the hot sting of an arrow pierce cleanly through his leather breastplate. The arrowhead burst his heart and split through the vertebrae of his spine, killing him before he had time to roar his surprise.

The dead knight was no sooner swept into the foaming wash of the surf than another stepped boldly forward to take his place, seeming to rise like a Goliath out of nowhere. His sword was drawn and his face, catching a stray beam of moonlight, was a mask of pure, malevolent hatred.

Recognizing both the face and the intent in the slitted eyes, Servanne screamed again, this time to beat away the determined arm that had snaked around her waist and was dragging her toward the longboat.

"No!" she screamed. "No, let me go! Let me go to him! Lucien! Lucien . . . *behind you*!"

The arm remained fast around her waist even though she kicked and writhed and fought to be set free. Salt water was in her eyes, blurring her vision; her hair was a sodden mass wrapped around her throat, choking her. Her hands, flailing wildly about, tried to strike at the unseen force that was carrying her away from her love, her life, and smashed into something solid and wooden—the boat! A streak of white-hot pain lanced up her arm, causing her to temporarily cease her struggling and to look at the man holding her.

It was Eduard! Eduard, so badly wounded himself, yet straining valiantly to lift her into the violently rocking longboat. He grunted in agony as his wounded leg was driven by the current to smash against the leaded keel. Servanne felt his grip loosen, saw him claw desperately for a hold on the gunwale, lose it, and begin to slide under the rolling waves. Instinctively she reached out to help him . . . and screamed again.

It had not been the side of the boat her hand had struck. Rather, she was the one who had been struck, and not by a wooden plank, but by a twelve-inch-long crossbow bolt. The barbed iron head had split through the padding of flesh between her thumb and forefinger and embedded itself in the wooden side of the boat, pinning her there helplessly.

A wave washed over her head, filling her eyes, nose, and mouth with salt water. Without the strength or ability to resist, she was swept along with the boat as it was pushed relentlessly toward the waiting danger on the shore. The sandy bottom fell away from beneath her feet and she was dragged downward by the current, sucked into a void of muted sound and roiling darkness. Before the pain and numbness overtook her completely, a moment of absolute clarity flung her back through time, back to where it had all begun . . . the heaven . . . the hell . . .

1

Her eyes were green and bright and perfectly round. Her body was squat and somewhat ungainly compared to her more streamlined relatives, but she had speed and cunning, a predator's vision keen enough to detect the slightest movement in the carpet of trees hundreds of feet below. The air was crisp and clean, drenched in the pungent musk of spring. Her wings, stretching to a span of over four feet when outthrust, carried her through the blue vault of the sky with an effortless grace that left the less blessed of God's creatures gaping upward in envy.

Soaring, gliding, testing the flow of the currents, the hawk banked into a steep left turn, and pitched into a swift spiral that brushed her so close to the tops of the trees, the slow-moving column of humans below was startled by the faint hiss of wind on her wings. The hawk had seen them long before the sharpest of their sentry's eyes could have detected the black speck in the sky. Curiosity, scorn, amusement bade her swoop low across their path; a sense of haughty superiority made her stiffen her wings and arch her hooded head as if to mock their very earthbound inadequacies.

"Blood of Christ," someone grunted, catching the splatted evidence of greenish-white disdain smack on the back of a leather-gauntleted hand. He flicked off as much of the slime as he could and wiped what remained on the pale blue saddlecloth. One of ten knights and thirty men-at-arms, he rode escort for the cavalcade that was wending its miserably slow way through the forest.

The knights all wore full armour—dull gray hoods and hauberks of oiled chain mail, the iron links closely fitted to resemble snakeskin. Overtop lay a gypon—a sleeveless tunic of sky blue embroidered with the Wardieu crest and coat of arms, identifiable at a glance by the rearing dragon and wolf locked in mortal combat. Leather belts cinched the bulky layers at the waist and held scabbards for both the longsword and the short, wickedly sharp poniard. Each man wore the conical Norman helm with the steel nasal descending almost to the top of the uniformly grim lips. Half rode with their flowing blue mantles slung back over one shoulder to reveal crossbows held across their laps, the weapons armed and cocked. The other half formed the protective inner guard for the bright splashes of colour who rode securely in their midst.

"So this is the fearsome forest of Lincoln we have heard so much about," one of the bolder maidservants giggled. "Imagine: grown men ready to shoot at every leaf or branch that rustles lest there be devils lurking behind. How many skewered trees do you count now, my lady? Ten? Twenty?"

The captain of the guard ignored the comment and its tinkling reply. He would have liked to turn around and address the insolent dabchicks, but the tightness of the formation on this narrow stretch of road, combined with the stiffness of his mail and armour prevented him from offering more than a grinding clench of jaws.

Half the royal forests in England seethed with villains and outlaws, none of whom were laughing matters. With King Richard crusading in the Holy Land, and his brother Prince John taking full advantage of his absence, the country had fallen to lawlessness and disorder. Bands of renegade foresters were springing up everywhere. Thieves, cutpurses, traitors, and murderers alike were congealing together in pockets of scabrous vermin to challenge the rash of levies and taxes the prince had instigated. Parties of ten, twenty, even thirty knights were necessary to escort travelers safely from one point to another, and at times even so blatant a threat did not discourage a reckless attack. Only a month ago, in these very woods, a bishop and his party, traveling under the protection of Onfroi de la Haye, Lord High Sheriff of Lincoln, was waylaid, ten good men killed, another half dozen wounded, and the rest stripped of their weapons and armour and tied to their saddles like sacks of grain. The bishop, third cousin to the king himself, was relieved of the gold he was carrying to the abbey at Sleaford and, together with fourteen of his priests and acolytes, was sent on his way in a hardly less humiliating condition than his guard.

Nothing and no one was sacred to these thieves and wolf's heads. Any and all were fair game, and—the guard risked a glance over his shoulder as another burst of laughter echoed off the treetops to announce their presence—the fairer the game, the more determined the predators. But it was not only the threat from outlaws that caused the skin to shrink around the ballocks of Bayard of Northumbria at every unnecessary shout or feminine exclamation. Harm to one stray hair belonging to Servanne de Briscourt, recent widow of Sir Hubert de Briscourt, and intended bride of the powerful Lord Lucien Wardieu would mean a slow and agonizing death to the men responsible for her safe arrival at Bloodmoor Keep.

The object of the captain's pointed observation, oblivious to his concerns for her welfare—and his own—sat very straight and slim upon the back of her snow white palfrey. Awed by the pure, quiet stillness of the greenwood surrounding them, her startling blue eyes moved constantly this way and that, drinking in the beauty and majesty of the tall oak trees, some of which measured a full twenty feet around the base. A tilt of her lovely chin followed the streaking rays of flickering sunlight to their source high above where branches were tangled together in a thick basketweave, their leaves a still higher suggestion of misty green. The sun broke through in sporadic bursts, the beams splintering into a thousand foggy darts of light that shimmered to shades of palest green in the darker, musty shadows below.

How the captain of the guards would cringe if he knew what was passing through the mind of the future baroness. How shocked he would be if she dared give way to her urge to spur her mare into a caracole, to dance and prance along the earthen road to the end of the forest—if indeed there ever was an end to it. Moreover, she longed to remove the linen wimple that demurely covered her head, ached to shake her long golden hair free of its braids and confining pins, and feel the wind tug and pull at its thickness. As well, she wished she could fling aside the stiff, encumbering surcoat of samite she wore over her gown. Six depths of sky blue silk had gone into the weaving of the rich cloth, but to Servanne, who was uncomfortable from so many long hours in the saddle, it felt more like armour than the chain links worn by the guards. If she attempted to alter the positioning of her legs and rump, or shift more comfortably in the saddle, it was done without the cooperation of the heavy outer garment. If she turned too hastily, she was nearly choked by the stiff collar, which did not budge and threatened her with an awkward loss of balance.

Still, she endured the discomfort in silence. She was eager to reach her destination, eager for the first time in her eighteen years to see what the future had hidden around the next corner.

Orphaned as a child, Servanne had been placed under the wardship of England's great golden King Richard, known by the soldiers who loved him as Lionheart. When his obsession with the Holy Wars had forced him to look beyond the limits of the strained royal purse for financing, Servanne had been

married off to the aging Sir Hubert de Briscourt for a sub-
stantial consideration. Barely fifteen at the time, wed to a
man fifty years her senior, the succeeding three years had
been a trial of boredom, loneliness, and frustration. It was
not that Sir Hubert was mean or miserly—indeed, near the
end, she had acquired a genuine affection for the gallant old
knight—it was just that, well, she was young and full of life,
and impatient to do more than spin and sew and weave and
be attendant upon her lord in his twilight years. His death
had been a terrible blow, and she had truly mourned his loss.
And when the missive had arrived bearing the king's seal,
she had broken it with grave apprehension, guessing correctly that she had once again been sold in marriage to the
highest bidder.

The name of the prospective groom had leapt from the
page like a bolt of lightning. Lucien Wardieu! Young, handsome, virile . . . the kind of husband one dreamed about
and envisioned behind tightly closed eyelids while a lesser
truth fumbled and groped about in the dark.

Shivering deliciously, Servanne glanced down at the jewelled broach pinned to the front of her mantle. Bloodred rubies delineated the body of a dragon rampant, emeralds
and diamonds marked the snarling body of the wolf. A betrothal gift from the groom, it branded her as his property
and she wore it proudly for all the world to see.

"Biddy, tell me again what you have heard of my lord the
baron," she whispered under her breath. "I fear, as the miles
shrink between us and the hours to our meeting grow fewer
and fewer, my nerves grow ever less steady."

The elderly woman who rode by her side had been nurse
and maid to Servanne's mother, fiercely protective guardian
to the orphaned daughter through the subsequent years. A
face as round as a cherub's and as softly crinkled as an overripe peach turned to Servanne with a feigned look of surprise. "Surely your memory has gone the way of your morn-

ing ablutions, for did I not spend most of the hours after Prime reciting the long litany of your betrothed's accomplishments—both in the tourney lists and in the widows' beds? It grows tiresome, child, to have to repeat every gasp and gurgle you yourself uttered when you first saw the man, let alone recall the exaggerations and imaginations of every weak-limbed fancy who crossed his path."

Servanne blushed scarlet, warming under the smothered round of laughter her maids could not quite contain.

"I have heard," one of them tittered bawdily "that as a lover, Lord Lucien is inexhaustible, often going days and days without a pause for food or drink or . . . or anything!"

"I saw him once." The youngest attendant in the group gave a sigh so plaintive it caused the captain of the guard to roll his eyes and exchange a smirk with the knight who rode alongside. "In all of Christendom," she continued, "there cannot be a taller, handsomer knight. Even Helvise admitted that to see him standing beside our glorious liege lord, King Richard, a maiden would be hard-pressed to choose between the two as to which one was the more godlike in countenance and bearing."

"I said that?" a dark-eyed companion asked with a frown.

"You most certainly did," the accuser, Giselle, said earnestly. "Do you not remember? The very same night you said it, you said you also had to take two of Sir Hubert's guardsmen and—"

"Never mind! I remember," Helvise snapped, aware of the sudden attentiveness of the nearby guards.

Servanne's flush was still high on her cheeks, even though she was no longer the focus of the good-natured jesting. If anything she had grown warmer knowing she had not been the only one left with a searing impression of power and animal maleness. True, she had only glimpsed her betrothed across a crowded hall, and true the lone glimpse had occurred many months ago, but what healthy, warm-blooded woman could not have recalled his every stunning attribute, down to the last thread of flaxen hair, on much less than a half-stolen glance? Eyes the bold azure of a turbulent sea; a face that was lean and finely chiseled; a body splendidly proportioned from the incredible breadth of his shoulders to the trim waist and long, tautly muscled legs. One of the king's champions, Lord Lucien had never been bested in the lists, never emerged from any tournament less than overall victor. His skill with lance and sword was legendary; his exploits in Europe and on the Crusades had earned him the respect of kings, and wealth beyond any mere knight-errant's wildest dreams.

Comparing Lucien Wardieu to Sir Hubert de Briscourt was like comparing a gold, jewel-encrusted sceptre to a charred stick. Servanne was under no illusions as to why he had petitioned the king for her hand—indeed, she thanked God with every breath that a portion of the vast fiefdom she had inherited upon Sir Hubert's death, was coveted arable adjoining the baron's own landholdings in Lincoln. To him she was undoubtedly just a name and faceless entity; a pawn in the game of politics and economics. He would have petitioned for her hand even if she were fat, balding, and prone to passing wind from both ends simultaneously. And did she care? Not one whit! If it was her lot in life to serve as cat's-paw to the king's obsession, it was a much easier task to suffer in the arms of a golden champion than in the bed of a feeble old man.

Servanne stroked the neck of her beautiful mare, Undine, and smiled. Her mount had been among the many extravagant gifts sent to her by Lord Lucien by way of offering apologies that he could not ride to meet her himself. He was forgiven. Besides her own snow white palfrey, there were three pairs of matching roans to carry her maids. All were furbished with white trappings, the saddles bleached to bone-coloured leather, trimmed with silver bosses and tassles that glittered like fringes of diamonds. Blue silk ribbons were braided into the manes and tails; plumes dyed to the same sky-blue shade danced on silver headpieces. The Wardieu dragon and wolf were emblazoned on saddlecloths, shields, and pennants; the Wardieu colours of blue and silver rippled from one end of the cavalcade to the other.

In the rear, flanked by the servants and pages who traveled on foot, were three wagons groaning under their burden of chests containing silks, velvets, and samites woven in every shade of the rainbow; brocades so stiffly embroidered they were unbendable; pelts of ermine, fox, and sable for trimming cloaks and gowns. There were stockings of sheer, gauzelike silk from the East, girdles crusted with gold and silver, slippers to match any whim, pearls of the finest size and colour strung on threads of pure gold. Three dressmakers accompanied the cortege. They had worked day and night for two weeks to prepare the bridal clothes and even now, as the miles and hours to their destination diminished, their hands moved in a blur with needle and thread at each rest called by the captain of the guard.

Would the baron be surprised or disappointed when the procession entered the bailey of Bloodmoor Keep? Surprised, she hoped. Possibly even . . . pleased? She knew she was no frog-faced behemoth; her delicate blondeness would compliment his towering sun-bronzed presence perfectly. Nor was she just an ignorant piece of pretty finery to be displayed and admired, and useful for little else than the breeding up of heirs. She could read and write with a fair enough hand to be able to cipher what she had written some time later. Groomed to fulfill a certain role, she had also learned to keep accounts and run a competent household that had numbered near to a thousand immediate dependents. Her new husband could not help but be pleased. He simply could not.

"Please, Captain," she ventured to ask, "Where are we now? Is my lord's castle much farther?"

Bayard of Northumbria contemplated his answer a moment before turning to respond. "With luck, my lady, we should reach the abbey at Alford by nightfall. From there it is but a half day's journey to Dragon's Lair."

"Dragon's Lair?"

Bayard bit his tongue over the slip. "Many pardons, my lady. I meant, of course, Bloodmoor Keep."

Servanne leaned back against the support of her saddle-tree, a small frown puckering her smooth brow. It was not the first time such slips of the tongue had occurred, and by no means the most discordant one. On one instance she had overheard two of the knights ridiculing the methods by which the sheriff of Lincoln coaxed information out of unwilling guests of his castle. The same information, they claimed, could have been extracted by the baron's subjugator in a tenth of the time, with none of the mess and bother of red hot irons and molten copper masks.

The use of torture in questioning prisoners was not unheard of, but it was a method usually reserved for political prisoners, and those suspected of hatching plots against the crown. It was said Prince John never traveled anywhere without his trustworthy subjugator in tow, mainly because he imagined assassins and traitors lurking behind every bush and barrel.

But what use would Lucien Wardieu have for the permanent services of a professional torturer? From all she had heard, Bloodmoor Keep was impregnable to threat from sea or land. Just to reach the outer walls—twenty feet thick and sixty feet high—one had to cross a marsh nearly a mile wide, or scale the sheer wall of a cliff that rose six hundred feet above the boiling seacoast. Moreover, it was said he did not rely only upon the services of his vassals, part of whose oath of fealty was to pledge forty days military service per annum, but preferred to hire mercenaries to guard his property and his privacy year round.

Servanne glanced slantwise at the men who comprised the bulk of her escort. They all looked as if they broke their nightly fasts by chewing nails, and as if they could and did slit throats for the sheer pleasure of it.

Which raised another question, and another icy spray of gooseflesh along her arms. Why were such fearsomely huge and bestial men flinching at every snapped twig and crinkling leaf they passed?

Servanne did not have to wait long for the answer. A faint hiss and *whonk* broke the silence of the forest; a gasp, followed by an agonized cry of pain sent a guard careening sideways out of his saddle, his gauntleted hand clutched around the shaft of an arrow protruding from his chest. A half dozen more grisly *whonks* struck in close succession, each resulting in a grunt of expended air and a bitten-off cry of pain.

Shouting an alert, Bayard of Northumbria cursed loudly and voraciously at the ineptness of the scouts he had dispatched ahead to insure against the possibility of just such an ambush occurring. In the next wild breath, he reasoned that, without a doubt, they must be as dead as the ox-brained incompetents who had allowed their concentration to wander to the curves and smiles of a flock of tittering women rather than remain fixed on the deadly dangers of the forest.

A second round of curses forced Bayard to acknowledge how efficiently the trap had been laid and sprung. Four of his best scouts had been silenced, seven guards already dead or dying, the rest of the cavalcade corralled and surrounded in a matter of seconds, with no real or visible targets yet in evidence.

"Lay down your weapons!"

The command was shouted from somewhere high up in

the trees and Bayard's gaze shot upward, rewarded by nothing but swaying branches and splintered sunlight.

"Bows and swords to the ground or you shall all win the privilege of joining your fallen comrades!"

The breath hissed through Bayard's teeth with impotent fury. His keen eyes searched the greenwood but he could see nothing—no pale flash of skin or clothing, no movement in the trees or on the ground. A further lightning-quick glance identified the arrows protruding from the chests of the dead soldiers. Slim and deadly, almost three feet long and tipped in steel, they were capable of piercing bullhide or mail breastplates as if they were cutting through cheese. Moreover, the arrows were shot from the taut strings of the Welsh contraptions known as longbows. In the hands of an expert, an arrow shot from a longbow could outdistance the squatter, thicker quarrels fired from a crossbow by a hundred yards or more. Many a train of merchants had been waylaid and fired upon from such a distance that they could not even distinguish their attackers from the trees.

As was the case now, Bayard thought angrily. He and his men were like ducks on a pond and, unwilling to fall helplessly to a slaughter, he had no choice but to reluctantly give his men the signal to lower their weapons.

"Who dares to challenge our right of way?" the captain demanded, his voice a low, seething growl. "Who is this dead man? Let him step forward and show his face!"

A laugh, full and deep-throated, had the same effect on the tension-filled atmosphere as a sudden crack of thunder.

Servanne de Briscourt, her hand tightly clasped to Biddy's and her shoulders firmly encircled by the fierce protectiveness of a matronly arm, was startled enough by the unexpected sound to twist her head around and search out the source of the laughter.

A man had stepped out from behind the screen of hawthorns and had moved to position himself brazenly in the middle of the road. His long legs, clad in skintight deer-hide leggings, were braced wide apart; his massive torso, made more impressive by a jerkin of gleaming black wolf pelts, expanded farther as he insolently planted one hand on his waist and the other on the curved support of the longbow he held casually by his side.

Standing well over six feet tall, his body was a superb tower of muscle that commanded the eye upward to the coldest, cruelest pair of eyes Servanne had ever seen. Pale blue-gray, they were, twin mirrors of ice and frost, steel and iron. Piercing eyes. Eyes that held more secrets than a soul should want to know, or, if knowing, would live to tell. They were strange eyes for so dark a man—hair, clothing, and weathered complexion all combined to make it so—and it was with the greatest difficulty that Servanne relented to the tugging pressure of Biddy's hands and turned her face away, burying it against the muffling shield of ponderously soft bosoms.

"I bid you welcome to my forest, Bayard of Northumbria." The villain laughed softly again. "Had I known in advance it was you daring to venture across my land, I should have arranged a much warmer welcome."

The knight's eyes narrowed to slits behind the steel nasal of his helm. How, by the Devil's work, did this outlaw know his identity? And what did he mean by *his* forest, *his* land? Most tracts of forest, most measures of land that comprised the vast demesne of Lincolnwoods had been part of the Wardieu holdings since their ancestors had crossed from Normandy with William the Bastard.

An invisible hand clawed sharply down the length of Bayard's spine, all but tearing the breath from his body.

By God's holy ordinance . . . it couldn't be! No! No, it couldn't be! The man was dead . . . dead on the hot desert sands of Palestine! Bayard himself had seen the body, had given it an extra kick with a contemptuous boot before leav-

ing the corpse to swell and burst in the searing sun. There
was no earthly way a man could have survived such wounds
as Bayard had witnessed. Flesh peeled from the bone, an arm
half ripped from the socket, ribs crushed to bloody pulp . . .
it simply was not possible. Even if the sun had not blistered
him to rot, the vultures, ants, and packs of wild dogs would
have finished the job.

And yet . . . those eyes! Where in Christendom could
there be another pair so like them?

"So. You do remember me, Bayard of Northumbria," the
outlaw said quietly, noting the intense scrutiny.

"I—I do not know you apart from any other scum who
roams the forest with claims of renegade sovereignty. As for
giving warm welcome—" The captain raised the crossbow he
had not quite convinced his fingers to relinquish into the
dirt, and, with the speed of many years' practice governing
his action and aim, Bayard squeezed the trigger and sent a
quarrel streaking past his horse's ear to the target who all
but filled the roadway ahead.

The outlaw neither jumped nor flinched out of the way.
With a controlled swiftness, he raised his own bow and
snapped an arrow, the aim carrying it straight and true to
the eye socket on the left side of Bayard's helm. The impact
of the strike jerked the knight's head back, causing his arms
to be thrown upward, and the quarrel to be launched harmlessly into the trees. Bayard could not know this, for by then
he was dead, sliding off the back of his mount with the same
sluggish lethargy as the viscous flow of blood and brains that
leaked from beneath his helmet.

Almost simultaneously a second disturbance erupted
along the line of guardsmen. One of the knights, wearing not
the Wardieu gypon of pale blue but the De Briscourt colours
of scarlet and yellow, shouted for his men to attack and drew
his sword. The shout became a scream of agony as one of the

outlaws loosed an arrow that punched through the knight's thigh and pinned him to the leather guard of his saddle.

"Sir Roger!" Servanne cried, but her protest was smothered instantly and violently against Biddy's heaving breast.

Undaunted, the wounded Sir Roger de Chesnai made a second attempt to raise his sword and this time, was stopped by the bearlike hand of yet another outlaw—a huge, barrel-chested Welshman who grinned with enough ferocity to suggest he would enjoy crushing a skull or two for sport. Sir Roger's fingers flexed open, releasing the hilt of his sword. The Welshman nodded approval while behind him, the outlaw who had fired the arrow stepped out of the greenery, nocked another shaft in his bow, and swept the armed weapon slowly along the row of ashen-faced guards, his brow raised in askance.

As one, the escort of mercenaries and men-at-arms lifted their hands away from any object that might be misconstrued as a threat. Only their eyes dared to move, flinching side to side as branches bent and saplings sprang apart to bring a dozen more armed outlaws out from behind their places of concealment. A dozen! Expectations of seeing at least two or three times as many attackers brought renewed flushes of anger and outrage to the faces of the humiliated knights. Seeing this and knowing the prickly honour that governed these men, the wolf-clad leader moved to forstall any rash attempts to launch a counterattack. He turned his bow in the direction of the huddled group of women and coolly took aim at the nearest soft breasts.

"Now then, gentlemen. If you will be so kind as to step away from your weapons and mounts, my men will happily instruct you on what is required of you next." The leader paused and smiled benignly. "Any refusal to obey will, of course, result in one less lovely lady to escort to Bloodmoor Keep."

The men exchanged hostile glances, but in the end, their

stringent code of chivalry left them no choice but to do as they were told. They unbuckled belts and baldrics to remove any further temptation presented by knives and swords. Disarmed, the knights were separated from the rest of the cavalcade and herded to a clearing alongside the roadway where their purses were systematically removed along with any inviting bit of silver or gold adornment. Surcoats, tunics, and shirts of chain mail were also ordered removed and tossed onto one of the carts which had been emptied of its less practical cargo of feminine underpinnings. The squires, pages, servants, and wagoners who traveled on foot at the rear of the train did not require more than a barked command to scramble en masse to the base of an enormous oak tree. There they were similarly stripped to their undergarments, bound together, and left clinging and quivering in the pungent forest chill.

This left only the women, who were still mounted, still crowded together in the middle of the road.

"Do not say a word, my lady," Biddy whispered urgently. "Not one word to draw attention, and perhaps these filthy scoundrels will send us peaceably on our way without further mischief."

Until the very instant of Biddy's warning, Servanne had not given a thought as to what "further mischief" might entail. She had never been waylaid or robbed before, but knew full well of those who had been abused, raped, or even murdered in the name of outlaw justice.

"Keep your head down, child," Biddy spluttered. "And your eyes lowered."

An easy order to issue, Servanne thought. Impossible to obey, however, especially when Biddy's own words triggered the need to search out the man who now held their fate in his hands. And what hands they were—strong and lean, with long tapered fingers that held the oversized bow with savage authority. He spoke in clear, unbastardized French, which must mean he was no common, illiterate thief. For that matter, not a man among his troop looked desperately twisted by corruption or squint-eyed with greed. Not at all like the half-starved, ragged bands of peasants who usually took to hiding in the woods to escape the administrators of the king's laws. Indeed, had they been in armour instead of lincoln green, one would be hard-pressed to distinguish between thief and guard.

Drawn by the lure of forbidden fruit, Servanne disobeyed Biddy's adamant grip and studied the bold, calmly purposeful outlaw who had so casually slain Bayard of Northumbria, and who now shamelessly threatened the life of the dark-eyed Helvise. His hair was long, curling thickly to his shoulders in rich chestnut waves. His face defied description, being too swarthy to fit the Norman ideal of golden handsomeness, too squared to imply noble birth. A Saxon? But for the eyes and the demeanor, she might have agreed, but he was no ordinary outlaw, no plow-worn peasant.

He was, however, dressed to fit the role of forester, garbed as they all were in greens and browns, the exception being the outer vest of wolf pelts. Beneath it, his loose-sleeved shirt of green linsey-woolsey opened in a carelessly deep V almost to his waist, revealing an indecent wealth of wiry sable curls matted thickly over hard, bulging muscles.

The weapon he held appeared to be nothing more than a six-foot length of slender wood forced into an arc and held taut by a bowstring of resined gut. Far more graceful in design than the stubby, iron-bound crossbow, it was also far superior in range, swiftness, and accuracy. Bayard had been a full ten paces from her side when he had been cut down, yet there were tiny dots of crimson splashed across her mare's forequarters attesting to the power that lay behind the grace.

Her attention was briefly diverted to the dead captain and the rest of his subdued guards. Servanne could not help but wonder at the audacity, and in turn, the lunacy of the men who dared risk the ire of Lucien Wardieu, Baron de Gournay. Ambushing travelers was no small crime by anyone's standard, but raising a sword against the blazon of one of England's most powerful barons was . . . sheer madness! De Gournay would spare no effort, even to burning down every last square inch of forest in Lincoln, to respond to the insult. And his revenge upon those who had committed the offense . . . !

As it happened, Servanne was in the midst of contemplating—in hideously graphic detail—the many possible forms her betrothed's retribution would take, when the piercing gray-blue eyes began scanning the frightened faces of the women. An oddity in the group caused them to flick sharply back to the only gaze that was not instantly and contritely shielded behind tear-studded lashes.

If he was surprised to see instead the small, tight smile that compressed her lips, the outlaw leader did not show it. If she expected him to be rendered speechlessly contrite, or to become paralyzed with fear over the sudden realization of the enormity of his crime, Servanne was sadly disappointed.

"I had heard the Dragon had snared himself quite a beauty," he murmured speculatively. "Ah well, messengers have been known to err before on the side of generosity."

Infuriated by his insolence, not to mention the derision in his comment, Servanne pulled out of Biddy's embrace and squared her slender shoulders.

"I beg your pardon, m'sieur," she said, the chill of untold generations of nobility in her voice. "But do you know who I am?"

A swift, fierce smile stole across his face and left again without a trace as he moved forward several measured paces. "Has the excitement caused you to forget your name, Lady de Briscourt? If so, I humbly crave your pardon for our methods, but alas, stealth and haste are among our most effective weapons."

Two hot stains blossomed on Servanne's cheeks as she stared into the rain-gray eyes. "Since you obviously know who I am and where I am bound, you must also be aware of whose protection I travel under, and against whose honour you give insult."

This time the grin lingered noticeably. "My heart does palpitate with the knowledge, my lady."

"It will palpitate with a good deal more if you do not stand aside at once and let us pass on our way unmolested!"

"I am afraid I cannot do that. Why, to have gone to all this trouble to stop you, only to stand aside and let you go on your way again . . . surely even someone so pure and innocent as yourself can see there would be little profit for us in that. As for molesting you"—the smouldering eyes took a lazy inventory of her finer points, and there were not many readily visible through the bulk of the samite tunic—"I regret to say I have more important matters to contend with at the moment. But before you puff up with more righteous indignation, be informed that neither you nor any of your lovely ladies will come to any harm while you are under my protection. On that you have my most solemn word."

"*Your* protection? *Your* word?" she scoffed. "And just who might *you* be, wolf's head? *You* who dare to challenge the authority of Lucien Wardieu, Baron de Gournay!"

The outlaw moved closer, taking the mare's bridle in his hand to guard against any attempt by her rider to bolt.

"The name the sheriff has chosen to give me in explaining the lax condition of his spine is . . . the Black Wolf of Lincoln." He paused to watch the effect of his words ripple through the ranks of his rapt audience. "The name given me by God is . . . Lucien Wardieu, Baron de Gournay."

2

Servanne no longer saw the beauty of the greenwood. The air
no longer felt crisp and clean; rather it was cold and damp
and chilled her to the bone even through the heavy layers of
her clothing. She no longer paid heed to the tall, stately oaks,
nor did she admire the dancing shafts of sunlight or the
silvery burble of a meandering stream. She sat erect on Undine's back, her face a mask of outrage and disbelief. Relieved of the reins by the outlaw leader who now led her
horse through the forest, her hands were clasped together
over the frontpiece of her saddle, the knuckles white and
straining with repressed anger.

She had been stunned speechless by the outlaw's preposterous claim. Lucien Wardieu indeed! But before she could
recover her faculties and demand explanations, his curt commands had set the scrofulous band of followers into motion.
Within moments, she and Biddy were culled from the others
and led into the forest. Everything of value had been stripped
from the wagons and transferred onto the backs of the pack
horses, as had the bulk of the guards' weapons and armour.
The outlaw had given the wounded Sir Roger de Chesnai a
small, canvas-wrapped packet and a message to be delivered
to Bloodmoor Keep—obviously a demand for ransom and
proof that the hostage was in safekeeping.

The effrontery of the man was not to be believed! Periodi-
cally Servanne's gaze would stray from the path ahead to
launch unseen poisoned darts into the broad back of the

wolf's head who dared to call himself Lucien Wardieu. She had already given him a host of truer appelations—madman, poseur, traitor, charlatan, impostor, bedlamite, crack-brain . . .

Each seething glance resulted in a new term to describe an audacity that was beyond belief. Who, in all of England, did not know the great golden countenance of the *real* Baron de Gournay? What man or woman in possession of all their senses could believe for one instant that this coarse, ill-bred, unkempt, murderous creature of the forest belonged at the same table with kings and queens? The mere notion of such a ruffian even being permitted into the *servants'* gallery was preposterous. The stables, perhaps. The pigsty or the muck pit where the refuse from the castle latrines was collected . . . maybe. But as liege lord of the castle itself? As baron lord of Bloodmoor Keep?

The snort of disdain she was unable to repress caused the dark chestnut head to turn slightly. A wry smile suggested he had felt every barb and intercepted every thought that had passed through her head over the last two hours, and the sight of it fueled her anger a notch higher.

"The scenery displeases you, my lady? You see stretched before you nature at its very peak. She offers here a tranquil-ity and solitude found nowhere else; a wild purity shared only by other virgins who have not yet experienced the taint of man's interference."

"She bears your taint, wolf's head," Servanne remarked dryly. "And that must surely spoil her for all others."

"Ahh. Spoken with the true sentiment of wedded bliss. Might I assume your previous marriage left something to be desired?"

Servanne's eyes flashed blue fire. "You may *presume* noth-ing whatsoever. My marriages—past or future—are no con-cern of yours. How dare you even speak to me of them, or of anything else for that matter. There is nothing your twisted tongue could say to me that could be of the least interest, and I insist you do not insult me with it again."

The outlaw's broad shoulders shrugged beneath the black wolf's pelts. "A greater hardship on you, I fear, for I have yet to encounter a woman who could maintain as good a silence as a man. Especially not when her brain is overtaxed with righteous fervour."

Servanne opened her mouth with a ready retort, saw the mockingly expectant brow arch in her direction, and pressed her lips tautly together again. She averted her gaze and stared straight ahead, but the resentment that bubbled within her could not be as easily diverted.

"I have seen Lord Lucien with mine own eyes," she declared stridently. "How dare you presume to mock him."

"Do I mock him, my lady? I thought you would be flattered I envied his choice of brides."

"Flattered!" Her voice was brittle with anger. "You could flatter us both by dropping dead this instant and saving the baron the trouble of rooting you out later! As for envying his choice of brides, I would sooner win the praise of a crimp-kneed, foul-breathed Saracen infidel than possess one attribute the likes of you would find appealing! I would sooner an arrow pierce my heart and rend it in two than find myself the object of a wolf's envy!"

The Black Wolf studied the stubbornly flushed features of his hostage a moment longer before dropping the reins of her horse and unslinging his bow from his shoulder. With her tongue stuck fast to the roof of her mouth and the echo of Biddy's shrill screech reverberating along her spine, Servanne watched in horror as the outlaw braced his long legs wide apart, swung the grip of the bow from hip to shoulder, and sighted along the shaft of an arrow. At the last possible instant he corrected the aim so that when he snapped his fingers to release the missile, it did not pierce the wildly beating thing that sought to escape her breast, but

hummmm-ed in a long, sweeping arc over Servanne's head
and disappeared somewhere in the trees beyond.

The silence that followed was complete enough to hear the
low droning of a swarm of bees in the distance. It was complete enough to hear the swish of Undine's tail as she chased
away an annoying gnat. Complete enough that when a clean,
sharp *fff-bunggg* left the quivering shaft of a returned arrow
buried in a nearby tree trunk, both women nearly lifted off
their saddles in fright.

"If ye'd asked," drawled the burly Welshman as he ambled
by, "I would have given the signal myself, milord, and saved
ye the bother."

"No bother," the outlaw replied smoothly, reslinging his
bow, his eyes still locked fast to Servanne's. He took up the
fallen reins and gave way to a faint, wry smile as he led her
horse forward again.

Servanne's heart was still pounding against her breast-
bone, her senses still recovering from the shock of the outlaw's twisted sense of humour. They were recovering from
something else as well, an oddity she had not noticed earlier
in the excitement of the ambush.

The wolf's head shot with his left hand!

Confirming the startling discovery, she saw that he wore
his sword slung on his right hip—giving ready access for the
left hand—and wore his quiver of arrows tilted to the left
shoulder.

A child of Satan! Bastard spawn of the Devil himself! *Everyone* knew a left-handed man was born with the curse of
Lucifer on his soul—as if she had needed any further proof
of his perfidiousness!

"Not much farther to camp now, my lady," he was saying.
"From the smell of it, I would guess we are having fresh
venison in honour of your presence."

Servanne smelled nothing except an admission of blatant
guilt from a boastful poacher: another crime to add to his

growing list. A man's life was forfeit if he was caught killing one of the king's deer. He was first blinded, then tortured over a slow fire until his skin blistered and fell off in great black flakes. He was then hung, drawn, and quartered by way of an example to others. A fitting demise for such a barbarian as this wolf, she mused.

"You may be assured, sirrah," she declared evenly, "I would rather waste away to a shell of skin and bone than defile the king's law by eating his royal due. You and your men may well choke on your treasonous repast if you so choose, but Mistress Bidwell and myself should die first."

Biddy gave a ram's snort of approval; the outlaw scoffed derisively. "Another sight mine eyes would ransom kingdoms to see: a dimpled cheek without the sheen of sweet grease upon it; a slender hand not first into the pot of roasted pheasant; a dainty belly not groaning with complaint after being stuffed to the chin with capon, pasties, and pies."

An unsubtle and prolonged rumble of agreement stirred in Servanne's stomach, reminding her she had not eaten since early morning, and that an unsatisfying meal of black bread and sour ale.

"And then there are the sweetmeats," contributed a voice from the staggered band of outlaws. "Our own goodwife Mab prepares some of the tastiest creations that have ever crossed these lips. What say you, lads?" The question was aimed generally over his shoulder. "Has Mab any equal this side of the Channel?"

"Bless the stars that found her for us," came a jovial reply. "Or mayhap just bless Gil Golden for bringing her out of Lincoln with our last purchase of arrowheads!"

A round of solid backslapping sent Servanne's gaze across to the man who had perfunctorily shot an arrow into Sir Roger de Chesnai's thigh. He had a smooth, aquiline profile that suggested a far easier life lay behind than the one ahead. His shoulders were square and straight, if a little sparse of

bulk; his legs were long and agile enough to swallow the
wooded miles without visible effort. Copper-coloured locks
capped his head like woolen fleece, cropped short beneath
the jaunty green felt hat he wore slouched forward over his
brow. His eyes were a blend of greens and golds and spicy
brown flecks, and a webbing of fine lines at the corners inti-
mated a man of easy nature and good humour. The long,
ragged scar that distorted his left cheek implied it was not
always so. The disfigurement in no way detracted from his
handsomeness, but it did confirm the fact he was a branded
thief, and would have as easily aimed for Sir Roger's heart as
his thigh.

Servanne was distracted from further observations by a
sudden burst of sound and activity from the woods up ahead.
From high, high up in the boughs of a tree came a swoosh of
air and a curled knot of flying hair and shrieking laughter.
Detaching itself from the swinging vine with a whoop, the
tiny figure splayed arms and legs wide, his clothes pocketing
the wind to break the impact of his body slamming into that
of the Black Wolf of Lincoln. As it was, the outlaw was
jolted back off his feet and required several paces to reclaim
his balance. Servanne's horse balked indignantly; Biddy muttered an oath which earned stares and grins from the nearby
foresters.

"Sparrow!" spat the Wolf with a not altogether feigned
grimace of displeasure. "By Christ's pricking thorns, one of
these days I will step out of the way and let you sail clear on
past into perdition!"

The squirming bundle disentangled itself from the torso of
the outlaw and sprang onto the ground beside him. The man
. . . dwarf . . . child . . . was barely tall enough to see
the top of the Wolf's belt. Thin as a reed, as tanned as a
roasted nut, he . . . or she . . . had huge, shining black
eyes that seemed at once too large for the round, elfin face,
and far too knowledgeable for such a mischievous grin.

Servanne blinked, and blinked again. She had heard fables of such creatures living in the forests; wood elves who were several centuries old, kept young and childlike through pagan rites and rituals. She had never truly believed in such tales of magic and witchcraft, of course. Magic was only for the eyes and ears of the superstitious, and as for witches and warlocks . . .

She found herself staring at the outlaw leader again, her mouth as dry as parched wheat.

"So so so." Sparrow's voice was as delicately pitched as a woman's. "So this was to be the Dragon's new plaything. There is not much to her, is there? But then I suppose such a child would be a welcome change from being clamped between the iron thighs of Nicolaa de la Haye. You sent our demands on ahead?"

"We accomplished what we set out to do," the Wolf responded. "And you? You found the sheriff?"

"He was waiting at the fens, just as you predicted," Sparrow nodded, grinning. "He and most of the guard from Lincoln Castle. Slutching fools! Another half league into the forest and they might have upset our plans."

"They might have tried," the outlaw replied lightly. "But I am inclined to think a few well spent arrows would have had De la Haye and his men bolting for cover regardless if it had been Richard's intended bride, Berengaria, he had been sent to meet."

"The sheriff should know by now to leave such matters to his wife. The Bawd Nicolaa would have stayed and fought us with pleasure."

"The rest of our men? They made it back without incident?"

"Bah! Old Noddypeak did not even know we had him in bowshot. Mind, he kept scritching and scratching at the back of his neck"—Sparrow gave an imitation of the sheriff scratching nervously—"and shaking off the waterfalls of sweat he leaked"—he shook himself all over, like a dog emerging from a pond—"so I suspect he was not entirely without grand expectations."

"A pity we had to disappoint him."

"Aye," Sparrow sighed. "The lads had him sighted on their arrow tips every blink of the way."

"They will have him again, when the timing better suits our needs. Right now, Onfroi de la Haye is of more use to us alive than dead."

"Aye, my lord," the little man said, "So you keep telling us."

"So it shall be," the Wolf insisted. "The Sheriff of Lincoln is a fool, a weak incompetent puppet; one whose every move we can predict and anticipate with laughable ease. Put some-one else in his stead—his sweet wife, for example—and we would see her quenching her thirst for blood in ways we have not even thought of yet."

"No shy blanchflower, our Bawd," the gnome agreed.

"And if anyone other than myself makes a target of her brass-tipped breasts"—the tall, copper-haired outlaw stepped quietly forward—"they will have me to answer to."

Sparrow looked up and, although Servanne could not swear to it, she thought the bold little elf edged a cautious inch closer to the protective bulk of the Black Wolf. "I am not forgetting, Gil of the Golden Eyes. Not wanting to feel the sting of your arrows either. She's yours, all yours, and welcome to her. God's teeth, but we are touchy about it, are we not? Not enough Norman blood shed to wet your arrows? Ho! Still most a quiver full, I see. And a string as slack as Lack Jack's back."

Gil Golden smiled slowly, ominously. "Easily enough remedied. A daub of sparrow blood should turn the trick."

"You would have to catch me first, you great lumbering hulk!"

Quick as a wink, the tiny man darted forward, planted a

flying kick on Gil's shin and vanished behind a solid wall of alder bushes. His tinkling laughter, first in the alders, then beside them, then far above in an arching tangle of hawthorns indicated with what unsettling swiftness he could move, and also why he bore the name Sparrow. Moreover, before the cursing outlaw could finish hopping a circle on his uninjured leg, an arrow no longer than a man's palm zipped through the air and carried away Gil's prized green felt hat.

"That cuts it!" Gil swore. "The wretched puck is going to pay dearly for it this time."

"Are ye already forgetting what happened the *last* time?" roared Robert the Welshman. "It were not only yer hat what got a hole in it, but yer breeks and butt as well!"

Gil's eyes narrowed. "My thanks for reminding me. When I catch him, I will pin both his ears back for the leather he owes me."

The other foresters guffawed openly and began fishing in belts and sleeves for copper coins.

"A denier says Gil Golden wins this round," the Welshman wagered, doffing his cap and dropping the coin into the crown. A score or more coins clinked good-naturedly into the pot, some with an "aye" attached, some with a "nay." Even the two captive ladies found smiles wanting to come to their lips as they watched the agile huntsman stalk into the woods in pursuit of his diminutive quarry. Servanne caught hers just in time when she realized the icy-gray eyes of the outlaw leader were observing her.

"It appears, Biddy," she murmured brusquely, "these *children* have no grasp of the seriousness of their crimes."

The Wolf moved closer, his eyes glinting in the afternoon sunlight. "You should be thankful, my lady, we are still able to see some humour in the world around us."

"Humour, sirrah? In murder and kidnapping? Pray, you will forgive me if I do not share your amusement."

"You say the word murder as if we were the only ones guilty of it."

"I saw none of your men lying dead on the road, victims of a cold-blooded ambush."

"Ambushes are rarely warm affairs, nor do they lend themselves to a fanfare of trumpets."

"You mock me, sir," she said coldly.

"I mock your ignorance, madam. I mock your inability to see past the tip of your nose . . . although it is held so high, I should not wonder at the difficulty."

Servanne felt the redness creeping up to her brow. "I am not distressed. Your own nose, wolf's head, has been sniffing up dung heaps so long it cannot distinguish fair from foul."

Intrigued despite himself, the Wolf studied the square set to the young widow's jaw and pondered how the pearly row of small, even teeth had remained intact all these years. His own hands tingled with the urge to curl about her throat and rattle a few loose.

"Methinks I have been away from England too long," he mused, the slanted grin barely moving around the words. "Too long for such haughtiness and greed as I see in some to be the cause of such misery as I see in others . . . or are you blind as well to the starvation, the cruelty, the beatings, cripplings, and degradations to be found in every town and village throughout the kingdom?"

"If a man starves, it is because he is too lazy to work the fields. If he is punished, it is because he has committed some offense against the crown. As for the haughtiness and greed of which you speak, I suggest the worst offender is the cur of the forest who aspires to gain his wealth and recognition through thievery and murder . . . or do your own eyes suffer some difficulty in seeing the irony of your piousness?"

Her quickness of wit and tongue was beginning to make an impression on his men and the Wolf could sense that part of their amusement was a result of his inability to bring her under his thumb. She possessed far more spirit than was healthy or wise. Spirit bred contempt and contempt fostered rebellion—something he had neither the time nor the inclination to tolerate.

Conversely, fear bred caution, and both were qualities he would sorely prefer to see shading the vibrant blue of the widow's eyes.

"Robert . . . take the men on ahead and see that everything has been made ready for our guests."

"Aye. Shall I take this un for ye as well?" A thumb the size of a small anvil crooked in Servanne's direction.

"No," said the Wolf, his grin a misty suggestion about the lips. "I will bring her along myself."

He took up Undine's reins again and murmured a comforting "whoa" to the mare as the foresters and their burdened rouncies filed past. Servanne held Biddy's worried gaze until the last glimpse of her luffing wimple had disappeared behind the wall of green, then she had no choice but to look down at the outlaw . . . which she did with the vaguest stirrings of unease.

The Wolf was bareheaded under the blazing glare of the sun and his hair shone with red and gold threads tangled among the chestnut waves. He looked somehow bigger and broader, more powerful and far more dangerous on his own than he had surrounded by his men. And, as Servanne found herself earning the full brunt of his stare, she could not help but feel the heat of a threat behind it, a promise which coiled down her spine in a fiery ribbon and pooled hotly in her loins.

"I believe I gave you a promise that no harm would befall either you or your waiting-woman," he said in a calm, detached monotone. "But madam, as you are undoubtedly already aware, you present a worthy—nay, almost an impossible test for a man's patience."

Servanne moistened her lips and fought to keep her voice

equally cool and steady. "On the contrary, sirrah. When I am treated with respect and courtesy, most men claim they enjoy my company immensely."

"I am not most men. And you are not here to fulfill my desire for . . . company. You are my hostage, madam. A piece of valuable property to be bartered for and released when and if a suitable price is agreed upon by both parties. If at all possible, I should like to honour my pledge to return the property to its rightful owner in an . . . ah, *undamaged* condition. However, if some damage does occur—through negligence or sheer stupidity, as the case may be—I will hardly be driven to don the horsehair shirt and whip myself raw in repentance of a broken vow. In other words, Lady Servanne, you will behave yourself . . . or I will not."

"I doubt your behaviour could sink to any lower depths, rogue," she fumed unwisely. "And I doubt you could cause me any further discomfort than you have already."

The outlaw sighed and turned his head away for a moment. Before Servanne could react, he reached up and clamped his broad hands around her waist, lifting her unceremoniously out of the saddle. Her legs, long ago gone numb from the hours on horseback, would have crumpled the instant her feet were set to the ground if not for his support. One of his arms snaked around her waist, forcing her to press against the iron-hard length of his body. His free hand cradled her chin and tilted her face upward at an uncomfortable angle that emphasized both his height—which was as immense and imposing as one of the towering pines that surrounded them—and her sudden vulnerability.

At once, a mindless drumming caused the blood to surge through her veins and her heart to trip over several rapid beats. Her lips trembled apart and her fists curled into tight little knots as if the fingers could not bear the even more debilitating sensation of contact with a body that offered no apology for its granite hardness. Straining with virility, he crowded against Servanne so that there was no part of her left unaware of the intimacy of heated male flesh.

"The challenge, I believe, was to cause you . . . discomfort?" he asked.

Servanne had to catch at her breath before answering. "Better than you . . . *worse* than you have tried and failed!"

"Is that so? And I suppose you are hardened and worldly-wise enough to know what a man's best and worst might be?"

Servanne's stare threatened to turn liquid. She knew, without a doubt, the man holding her with the possessiveness of a barbarian king was nothing so trifling as a man or a king.

"Let me go," she gasped, squirming to break out of his embrace. Her fists scraped against his chest, displacing the carelessly open V of his shirt so that her knuckles skidded into the curling mass of crisp, dark hairs. The flesh beneath was all muscle and steamy hot skin. There was no give, no indication she could have won a response with anything less than the business end of a quarterstaff.

"Let . . . *go!*" she cried. "How dare you touch me!"

"How dare I?" he repeated, his breath warm and promisory against her cheek. "You should pray I dare no more, my lady, than just touch you. Although"—the hand at the small of her back shifted lower, caressing the curved roundness of her buttocks—"the notion is fast becoming less of a trial than first imagined."

Servanne's mouth dropped wide with shock. He was pulling her forward, holding her in such a way as to boldly forge the shape and contour of his thewed limbs upon hers. Heat met heat and pressed deep, scorching her through the layers of samite and silk as if the garments were made of air. A moist shudder convulsed deep within her, a reaction to his animal maleness that was beyond her control, and his arms tightened further, as if he had felt it and was offering more.

"No!" she cried, beginning to fight like a wildcat to free herself, her arms flailing, her nails seeking to let loose rivers of blood. With a snarled curse, he merely squeezed her into the wall of his chest, pinioning her there until she discovered she could not breathe. Her struggles weakened, then ceased altogether. The simple act of clawing her fingers into the wolf pelts drained her and she sagged limply in his arms, drooping into the encroaching blackness of a faint.

The Wolf eased his grip slowly, letting the air back into her lungs, and, as the blood flooded back into her limbs, he looked down at her, his face as impassive as marble. She was quiet enough now. Subdued. Drawing her breath in soft, broken gasps. He watched the colour flow back into her cheeks, the sparks of blue fire rekindle in eyes that would soon begin to fight back in silent, guarded hatred. He admired what he saw. The lush, provocative temptation of her lips drew his gaze and for a moment, he felt an arousal so intense, so completely unexpected and unwarranted, he almost drew her forward again to kiss her.

Instead, he pushed her out to arm's length and sprang away as if she had suddenly burst into flame. The rebuke permitted Servanne to stumble haltingly well out of reach. Her fingers flew up to cover the pulsing heat of her lips and while she could swear he had not kissed her, her mouth felt scalded as if he had.

"Do you still have doubts that my behaviour could worsen?" he asked quietly.

Servanne's blood continued to roar through her temples, making it difficult for her to think, let alone speak. Her skin had seemed to shrink everywhere on her body, most urgently so wherever it had been branded with the contact of his own. Her eyes stung with unshed tears of indignation—tears he watched form and swell along the thick, honey-coloured wings of her lashes.

"Well, my lady?"

She looked up, the back of her hand still pressed against her lips, the fingers curled and trembling.

"Will your stay with us be an easy one, or will I be forced to use harsh measures to win your cooperation?"

"How . . . long do you intend to keep me prisoner?" she asked in a shaky whisper.

"The shortest time possible, I promise you." Aware of the tension that had caused his own body to tauten like a bowstring, the Wolf felt it break now, and the fire in his gaze burned down to smoky gray ash. "It will seem shorter still if we have no more need of these verbal jousting matches. Especially ones where the outcome is a foregone conclusion."

Servanne's lashes were still damp, but the brightness sparkled with frost. He was laughing at her; mocking her futile efforts to defy him. Smug, arrogant bastard! He had insulted her, had dared to lay his hands upon her, and now, to make the degradation complete, was addressing her with the flippancy one used to pacify a simpleton!

A hot welter of resentment rushed to fill the void so recently drained by panic and in a moment of sheer and utter desperation, she whirled around and started running toward the same wall of trees that had swallowed Sparrow and Gil Golden so efficiently. She heard an angry curse explode behind her, but ignored it. She heard Undine nicker and whinny loudly, and guessed the outlaw had tried to push her aside to pass, but the horse had taken umbrage and valiantly stood her ground. It was enough. The extra seconds it took the Black Wolf to skirt the rearing hooves, combined with every last scrap of energy Servanne could will into her pumping legs, carried her past the barricade of saplings and well into a dense weaving of juniper and alder.

Running with no thought other than escape, Servanne dashed under broken limbs and plunged through barriers of fern that closed into a solid wall behind her. Her skirts hampered her and the branches snatched at the flying wings of her wimple as she ducked and darted her way deeper into the forest, but she neither stopped nor slowed to remove any hindrances. She was aware of angry, pounding footbeats thrashing through the undergrowth behind her, but they took a wrong turn, then another, and for a time she could not hear them at all over the loud slamming of her own heartbeat.

She stopped to catch her breath and listen, and that was when she learned to move with less haste and more caution, for it became apparent that he too stopped every few paces and listened as well. But she was a good deal lighter, and fear gave her the swiftness of a startled doe. Also, the shadows were dark and cool, kinder to the prey than the hunter, offering pockets of safety that became blacker and more frequent as the sun slipped lower in the sky.

Constantly twisting and turning in the labyrinth of vines and trees, Servanne ran until her sides ached and her legs grew buttery with fatigue. She lost all sense of time and direction. Once she thought she smelled woodsmoke and, fearing she had inadvertently run straight into the outlaw camp, she backed away and fled in the opposite direction. She had no way of knowing how far she had traveled or how much farther she would have to go before a road or village might present itself. What slices of the sky she could see through the latticework of branches overhead were a dull, uniform pewter gray, indicating the sun was fading rapidly. She knew she had to find shelter and a safe place to hide before the darkness settled over the forest. There was already a thin veil of mist swimming about her ankles, soaking the hem of her gown and causing her toes to squeak with the wetness inside her shoes.

A low, hauntingly familiar sound brought her to a dead halt in the midst of a green sea of waist-high ferns.

She heard it again and released a misty puff of startled air.

A bell, by Mother Mary's holy angels! A monastery bell tolling the hour of Vespers!

With the echo still ringing hollowly in her ears, Servanne waded through the ferns and stumbled to the bottom of a steep incline. At the base of the gorge, was a thin sliver of a stream that meandered between two enormous hillocks of rock and gorse. She picked her way carefully along the moss-blanketed bank, following the stream and eventually emerging from behind the hillocks to find herself standing less than two hundred yards from the long, low, lichen-covered walls of an abbey.

Gloom and pine-scented shadows cloaked the clearing in which the abbey stood, but the bell tower was plainly visible rising above and behind the heavy oaken doors that held the inhabitants cloistered from the rest of the world.

Servanne moved toward it as if in a trance, her feet gliding soundlessly through waves of long grass, her skirts trailing fingers of displaced mist. At the gates, she spread her arms in supplication and collapsed against the support of the dew-stained wood for the time it took her to compose herself. Fighting back tears of relief, she pulled the rusted iron chain that hung down the wall, and nearly sobbed aloud when she heard the corresponding tinkle of a small bell inside the courtyard. When she rang it a second time, her attention was drawn to her hand, to the dirt and grass stains that marked not only her skin, but marched up the sleeves and down the skirt of her tunic. Her face would be in no better condition, she surmised, but for once, her appearance did not concern her. Nothing concerned her other than the welcome sound of wooden-soled sandals hurrying toward the gate to investigate the disturbance.

A small square window in the oak portal creaked open a cautious inch. A single brown eyeball peered through the gap, flicking back and forth over the span of the meadow before thinking to angle downward. A second eyeball joined the first as the window opened wider, the two eyes surmounted by a worried frown.

"My child?"

"Father . . . help me please."

"Good heavens—" An eyebrow arched upward in surprise, temporarily unseating the frown. "Are you alone?"

"Yes. Yes, I am alone, but there is a man chasing me—"

The window snapped shut and an instant later, the iron hinges of the gate heaved a mighty protest as one of the double doors was swung open. The cowled monk stepped out and immediately stretched out his hands in gentle concern.

"What is this about a man chasing you?"

"Please, good father," she gasped. "I beg you, please hide me. There are outlaws in the woods. They are chasing me, hunting me; they mean to kidnap me and hold me to ransom. I managed to escape them once, but . . . !"

"My child, my child!" The monk caught her hands in his. They were smooth and warm and not a little callused from long, thankless hours of toiling at God's labours. The face beneath the coarse gray hood was serene and unlined; a scholar's face; a face filled with compassion. "Are you hurt, my child? Did they hurt you in any way?"

Servanne struggled for breath and words. "There was an ambush. They took me hostage . . . killed the guards . . . now they are chasing me. The Wolf. The Black Wolf of Lincoln, he calls himself. He means to kill me, Father, I know he does. Please . . . you must hide me. You must give me sanctuary until a message can be sent to Lord Lucien, Baron de Gournay."

The name seemed to have no effect on the acolyte and she began urging him back through the abbey gates when she heard the ominous beat of horse's hooves cutting through the gorge. She did not have to look back over her shoulder to know it would be *him,* yet she did, and the sight of him riding out from under the canopied froth of trees caused her belly to commence a sickeningly slow slide downward.

"It is him," she managed to whisper, cowering behind the cowled shoulders. "It is him . . . the Black Wolf. Please . . . you must help me. You must not let him take me away."

"Have no fear, child," the monk declared calmly. "He will not be taking you away from this place."

Not entirely convinced by the note of assurance in the monk's voice, Servanne regarded the Black Wolf's approach with only slightly less trepidation than that with which she had welcomed the first time a chirurgeon had attached a row of slimy leeches to her arm to drain the ill humours of a fever. There was anger, cruel and unyielding, etched into every line and crevice of the outlaw's face, bristling from every tautly held muscle in his body. His jaw was clenched, the veins in his throat and temples stood out like throbbing blue snakes.

He reined the enormous black beast he rode to a halt in front of them, his figure blotted darkly against the faltering sunset. Servanne experienced another deep, moist shudder; this one pressing so heavily over her loins that her knees almost buckled from the strain.

She was terribly, physically conscious of the way the ice-gray eyes inspected every smudge and scratch she bore. And when she was summarily dismissed, like some minor annoyance, and his attention focused on the monk, she felt a further clutch of fear stab at her belly. Who was to say he was not above slaying a man of the holy order? Who was to say he would respect the sanctity of the church or obey the unwritten law of sanctuary? This wolf's head was a law unto himself, acknowledging no authority but his own, no rules but those of his own making.

The Black Wolf swung one long leg over the saddle, the leather creaking softly in the misty stillness of the air.

Servanne flinched reflexively as he walked slowly toward them; if not for the monk's stalwart protection shielding her, she was certain she would have fainted from the sheer tension that approached with him.

"Friar," he said quietly.

"My son," was the equally unruffled response.

The Wolf's gaze flicked over to the pale face that was peeping from around the monk's shoulders, and he grinned like a sleepy lion.

"Ringing the bell seems to have been a worthwhile risk after all," he mused. "It saved us the time and bother of scouring the woods for you. You can thank Friar for the idea; he worried your soul might become easy prey for the Devil if you were left on your own throughout the night." A wider grin brought forth the flash of strong white teeth. "Not to mention what wild boar and wolf might make of you."

"Ahh, now," the monk sighed. "Can you not bend a little from your usual tactful and gallant self? The poor child is already half-convinced you mean to kill her and devour her whole."

"The idea has growing appeal," the Wolf replied dryly.

The monk turned then, one of his lean hands reaching up to brush back the hood that had concealed a full, untonsured shock of jet-black hair. "Forgive me, Lady Servanne, but the deception was necessary, if only to ensure you did not spend the night alone and unprotected in the woods."

Servanne was too shocked to respond, too stunned to do more than brace herself against the waves of blackness that threatened to engulf her.

"Are the others inside?" the Wolf was asking, his voice sounding low and distant, as if it was coming from the far end of a tunnel.

"All but the extra sentries Gil and Sparrow dispatched to ensure the bell did not attract any unwanted visitors. Not that I think it will. This mist is thick enough to muffle the sound and direction well."

The Wolf glanced back over his shoulder, noting with a grunt of agreement that the drifting white stuff had already obliterated the exit to the gorge. "You are probably right, but we shall keep a sharp eye out until morning anyway. There is no sense in inviting more trouble than we already have."

This last comment was said with a direct and caustic glare toward Servanne, who did not think it worthy of a rebuke.

"What is this place?" she asked. "What have you done with the real monks?"

Seeing the glint of villainy in the Wolf's eye, Friar was quick to intervene. "The abbey has been abandoned for almost a hundred years. As you will see in a few moments, the buildings are scarcely more than shells, sacked and put to the torch long ago."

"Surely the local villagers would know of its existence and direct the king's men to search here first," Servanne pointed out, somewhat surprised at the oversight.

"Local villagers," the Wolf said succinctly, "if you can find any who will admit to knowing of the existence of Thornfeld Abbey, will also tell you the ruins are haunted. Plagued by pagan Devil-worshippers. Cursed by demons who breathe fire and feed on human flesh. All of which suits our purposes well enough," he added, "if not our intent."

"If it . . . ah, gives you any comfort," Friar interjected hastily, "I once attended a seminary and came within a chasuble's width of being ordained. It appeases the men, who call me Friar, to have me offer daily prayers to ward off any evil spirits who may linger about the woods."

"I am not so easily frightened by tales of witchcraft and deviltry," she said, her words a little too shrill to be entirely convincing.

"Good," the Wolf remarked. "Then you will not question

the source of the blood pudding you find before you on the tables this night."

With a slight, sardonic bow, he took up the stallion's reins and walked past Servanne, his stride fluid and powerful, coldly dismissive. Friar, his brows folded together in a frown, won back her startled gaze with a gentle touch on the arm.

"Come. Your maid is inside, and the chambers we have prepared are really quite warm and comfortable, despite appearances."

Appearances, Servanne thought bitterly. A monk who was not a monk; a man who was a wolf, who claimed to be another man who she was beginning to believe had only ever existed in her mind. The dream had become a nightmare. The nightmare a reality.

With weary, leaden steps, she walked through the abbey gates. Cobbles underfoot were broken and upheaved with tangles of weed and bracken growing wild from every nook and crevice. Pathways, once groomed and even from the daily shuffle of sandaled feet, were choked with brambles, overgrown to the point where only a keenly discerning eye might yet detect their true course.

As her despondent gaze roved farther afield, the shape of the ruined buildings grew out of the shadows and gloom. Roofs, once comprised of great wooden beams and slate tiles, were now grotesque arches of skeletal black ribs, strangled by ivy, jutting up over scorched walls. Two long wings of decayed stone formed the almonry and pilgrim's hall. Flanking the far end of the courtyard were the remains of a priory church and refectory, both scarred and corrupted by wind and weather. The outer wall that had seemed so formidable and protective from the greenslade, was a breached and crumbling facade, long ago conquered by an army of trees reclaiming it for the forest.

The darkness had fallen so swiftly Servanne had not noticed it. But now, being led toward the looming stone hulk of the pilgrim's hall, she could clearly see the pulsating, misty saffron glow rising from the campfires within.

Her footsteps faltered and she pulled back from the smell of roast meat, woodsmoke, and careless camaraderie. She would have preferred the company of wild wolves and boars to what awaited her here. She most desperately would have preferred to have never heard of Lucien Wardieu, Baron de Gournay; to have never suffered the prideful notion of becoming his future wife; and to never, ever have thought her former life as Lady de Briscourt dull and boring and needing a change for the better.

3

Less than twenty miles to the north, beyond the verge of thick, dense forest known as Lincolnwoods, stretched a low-lying moor of bracken and long, slippery grasses. Spring was the only time of year there was any colour on the moor to break the monotony of metallic gray skies, dull granite cliffs, and windswept beaches that were treacherous to man or beast. Tiny crimson anemones stubbornly thrust their heads through the mire in early April and, depending upon how long it took the deluge of icy rains and merciless winds to turn the land into a bog of rotted grass and muck, the moor glowed red from morning till night. Some might have likened the sight to a carpet of scarlet silk thrown down by an apologetic god to alleviate the forbidding hostility of the sea coast. Others, especially those who had lived through wars and crusades and seen firsthand the aftermath of slaughter on a battlefield, compared the landscape to a sea of blood.

The stone keep built at the farthermost tip of the moor had been inhabited by the second kind of man. Draggan Wardieu, from the district of Gournay in Normandy, had crossed the Channel with William the Conqueror in 1066, and for his loyal, enthusiastic efforts in defeating and subjugating the Saxons, he had been awarded, among other parcels of fertile land and estates in Lincoln, this remote, desolate strip of coastline. Flanked by violent seas, fronted by an impassable moor, Draggan's eye for natural defenses bade him construct his castle there, at the very edge of the eagle's eyrie.

Towering sixty feet high, built from huge stone blocks quarried from the cliffs it sat upon, the original Bloodmoor Keep was hardly more than a three-storey square block of rock and mortar. The ground floor was without windows or doors and served as a huge storage area for the grain and livestock taken in tithes from his serfs and tenants. The second floor consisted of the great hall, and was just that: one enormous, vaulted room that served as living quarters for the entire household. Family members were only distinguished from the servants and guards by way of the small, private sleeping chambers hewn into the twelve-foot-thick walls. The rest of the inhabitants of the keep worked and slept in the common hall, which was also the dining hall, the armoury, the judiciary court when necessary, and the core of the keep's defenses. The uppermost floor was roofless, the walls high and crenellated with spaces on the battlements every few feet where archers could stand and launch a hail of arrows down on the unprotected heads of any attackers. There were no windows. Archery slits cut high on the walls of the great hall and reached by means of a narrow catwalk that surrounded the chamber, never allowed in enough light to alleviate either the gloom or the dampness. Cooking and heating fires were built on an iron grate in the centre of the hall, the smoke left to its own initiative to find the exit cut in the ceiling. Smoky, dark, perpetually damp and malodourous, the early keep was not the pleasantest of places to live, an even less accommodating place to visit unexpectedly.

Surrounding the keep was the bailey, an outer courtyard where the stables and pens were located. Protecting this was a high curtain wall, again of solid stone, forty feet high and twenty feet thick, with walkways all around to hold patrolling sentries. The outer wall was connected to the keep by a drawbridge, which could be raised against the keep wall at the first alarm to completely seal off the only entrance to the main tower. The outer wall was, in turn, surrounded by a moat and protected by a second drawbridge, guarded by a barbican tower built to hold a thick iron portcullis gate. The walls were also fitted with overhanging projections through which burning pitch or boiling oil could be poured, and were serrated with *meurtrières*—V-shaped vertical slots that gave the archers inside a wide range of movement to fire upon the enemy, but conversely presented a narrow, almost impossible target for returning fire.

This was the crude but effective fortification Draggan Wardieu built and successfully defended during his long lifetime. His sons, William and Crispin, along with their sons and grandsons, built on additional courtyards, halls, palisades, gatehouses, and towers until the original keep occupied only a small, isolated corner at the northernmost end of the stronghold. Within the sprawling outer bailey, there grew a self-contained village of tradesmen. The castle boasted its own smithy, tannery, armoury, alehouse, and mill, as well as vast stables, barracks, gardens and fruit orchards, all within the barrier of the stone walls. Farmers and outside tradesmen had attempted, over the years, to construct dwellings within hailing distance of the forbidding castle walls. But the terrain proved to be so unforgiving, the moor so wet and bleak, the sea such a thunderous scourge against any fishermen who tried to tame her, that the huts of mud and wattle that cringed in the shadow of the castle walls lasted only a season or two before being abandoned into ruin.

Only the immediate inhabitants of Bloodmoor suffered no lack of luxuries. The walls were thick enough and high enough to buffer the coldest and sharpest of winds. The castle was perched high enough on the cliff's edge to mock the fury of the turbulent seas churning below. No one came to Bloodmoor uninvited. No one stayed unless they were wanted. And no one dared turn back once the huge iron-clad gates were swung closed behind them.

"If you want me to leave, just say so. It is not very often my company bores a man to lethargy and great, vast lapses of silence. Frankly, I could better waste my time elsewhere."

The woman spoke with a low, sultry voice, emphasizing the more pertinent words with a moist, rolling purr of the tongue. Nicolaa de la Haye was a beauty and needed no confirming glances in polished steel mirrors to tell her so. The shocked look in men's eyes was confirmation enough. The forthright rise in the front of their tunics was proof she was as desirable now, in her thirtieth year, as she had been in her thirteenth—the age at which she had left her first lover a gasping, sweating hulk of quivering exhaustion.

There had been many lovers since then, some good, some bad. Some so exceptional she had maintained her affairs with them throughout the years, needing them as urgently and as frequently as some women required possets of henbane and opium to help them endure their dreary lives.

Slightly taller than average, Nicolaa undulated rather than walked, and was proficient in using her breasts, hips, and hands in communicating with a man in ways unknown by the spoken word. Her hair was black as coal, parted in the middle, and streamed in an ebony cascade halfway to the floor. Her eyes were so dark a green as to be almost black, heavy-lidded to suggest she was constantly on the verge of arousal—which she usually was. Her lips were full and sensuous, naturally tinted a deep shade of vermeil that teased a receptive eye into speculating where, other than on another mouth, they could bestow the most pleasure.

At the moment, most of her considerable prowess and charm was indeed being wasted. Her husband, Onfroi de la Haye—a wretched, sullen pustule of a man—was somewhere in Lincolnwoods awaiting the arrival of the widow De Briscourt. Nicolaa had hastened ahead to Bloodmoor Keep, ostensibly to help oversee the preparations for the upcoming nuptials—oh, how her teeth ground together each time she heard that word—but in reality, she had wanted this time alone with the most magnificent of her lovers, the Dragon himself, Lucien Wardieu.

Had there ever been a man created to see so perfectly to a woman's every need? The mere sight of him was enough to take anyone's breath away: a tall blond giant of a man with herculean shoulders and eyes more dangerous than the thrust of a lance. The sound of his voice triggered liquid shivers along her spine. The scent of him encapsulated the sun and the wind and the savage primitiveness of the moor he called home. The touch . . . the lightest touch from the veriest tip of a long, blunted finger set rivers of heat raging through her loins, rivers that swelled and burst into torrents from the instant his flesh plunged into hers, to the moment of blinding madness that welcomed the last hot spurt of his fountaining seed.

Even now, standing as he was in the shadows of the window embrasure, his back turned to the room, Nicolaa had difficulty keeping the tremors out of her voice. Moving, let alone walking, was a trial of balance and control. The slightest friction of her tunic against breast or thigh drenched her in such heady waves of erotic anticipation, she was growing concerned the eager dampness would begin to puddle at her feet.

"Lucien?" she murmured petulantly. "Have you heard a word I have said?"

"I have heard you, Nicolaa, my love. How could I not?"

"Then it must be I am disturbing you, and you would prefer your own company tonight."

The low purr of sarcasm broke his concentration and he turned slowly from the window. The cloud of distraction lingered a moment longer, dulling the incredible azure blue of his eyes, but in the next instant it was gone, brushed away by the thick sweep of lashes.

"Nicolaa," he said with a soft laugh, "any man who admitted such a sight disturbed him"—he paused and lowered his gaze to where the flimsy silk of her tunic was molded around the generous swell of her breasts—"is not much of a man."

The wife of the sheriff of Lincoln returned his smile. "A certain Lionheart might argue the sentiment."

Wardieu shrugged and drank from the goblet of mead he was holding. "Richard has his preferences, I have mine."

"I am relieved to hear it. How the women of Lincoln would flock in droves to hurl themselves off the nearest cliff, should the news reach them that the mighty warlord, the Dragon de Gournay, has taken to heaving himself at the buttocks of young boys."

"Tastefully put," he remarked dryly.

"'Tis a distasteful image one conjurs at the thought," she countered evenly, then sighed. "Especially when one considers the waste of such a splendidly virile specimen as Richard, Coeur de Lion. In truth, I did not believe it for the longest of time."

"And no doubt attempted to disprove the rumours yourself?"

"Well . . ." The tip of her tongue slid along her full lower lip to moisten it. "I did have an opportunity to seek a private audience with the king when Onfroi was vested as sheriff."

"I would have given a thousand crowns to witness the exchange," the baron said, his eyes glinting with humour.

"No doubt you would, you beast. I felt quite sorry for him, myself—and even sorrier now for the innocent little Berengaria, his intended bride."

"You? Feel sympathy for another woman?"

The dark eyes narrowed. "It has been known to happen a time or two."

"Usually only after you have crippled, maimed, or blinded one of them. Come now, Nicolaa, false sentiment does not become you. Turn soft and sincere and there truly would be a mass plummeting of mankind over the cliffs—out of fear."

"Melancholy. It happens whenever I am feeling neglected."

"Neglected? How so?"

Nicolaa sighed with mock frustration. "It has been over a month, my bold lusty lord. Four weeks. Thirty-two days and a good deal too many hours since these poor thighs have held a real man between them."

The azure gaze strayed downward, following the deliberately laid trail of a meandering finger as it flowed from throat to breast to waist to thigh. She wore nothing beneath the pale yellow tunic. Her nipples were clear, dark circles straining against the fabric, and where her thighs met, the nest of down bushed against the cloth like a mossy hillock.

It was rumoured she bathed in blood to keep her skin so supple and startlingly white. For a certainty, she employed the skills of several herb-women who fed her insatiable vanity by supplying creams to prevent wrinkling, powders to keep her teeth white and her lips red, possets to leave her hair smelling always like wild musk on a spring breeze. She had once ordered a clumsy dressmaker boiled in oil for scratching her flesh with a needle. Another waiting-woman had found herself impaled on a stake for daring to whisper, within Nicolaa's hearing, that her mistress made love as often to a mirror as to a man.

As for her to have gone so much as a sennight without something hard and hot between her thighs, it would have had to have been because of a grave, life-threatening illness striking her prone. Even then, she would have found better ways to raise a sweat than with hot poultices.

"How do the plans for the wedding celebration progress?"

she asked sweetly. "I suppose I should ask, since it was my excuse for arriving early."

"The preparations go well. William the Marshal has sent his acknowledgment, as have Salisbury and Tavistoke. Prince John should arrive early in the week, as will Fournier from Normandy, and La Seyne Sur Mer from Mirebeau."

"The queen's champion?" Nicolaa arched a brow. "You should indeed be honoured that Eleanor of Aquitaine would send her favoured knight as envoy. A pity the wrinkled old sheep's bladder is too feeble to make the journey herself, but surely a feather for you that she persuaded La Seyne Sur Mer to journey in her stead. Will he participate in the tourney?"

"It remains to be seen," De Gournay said, the merest trace of pleasure betrayed in his expression. "I suspect he might be eager to establish a reputation outside of Brittany."

"Saints assoil us," Nicolaa murmured. "You would share your own laurel wreath with the Scourge of Mirebeau? How generous of you."

"Wisdom before generosity, my love. The wisdom to see his skill firsthand and judge his mettle by mine own eyes rather than rely solely on the reports of others."

"It is said he has yet to meet his equal in the lists," Nicolaa remarked with a sly lack of subtlety.

"He has yet to venture more than a hundred miles from Mirebeau," Wardieu shot back. "Much less come to England to meet his match."

Nicolaa shivered deliciously, riding the ripples of a series of small inner fluctuations. Wardieu angry, or Wardieu impugned usually set the stage for an incomparable bout of lovemaking and she felt her thighs slicken with anticipation.

"Then you intend to challenge him?"

"The notion has its merit."

"But will your bride be sympathetic to the possibility of

losing her groom before she has had a chance at true wedded bliss?"

Lucien stared a moment, then gave way to a slow grin. "Ahh, the crux of the matter. I thought I detected more green in your eyes tonight than was normal."

"Plague take you, Lucien Wardieu. What, by all the saints, do I have to be jealous of? A timid little widow with knocking knees and a sallow complexion? You forget, I have seen her, my lord; I was present at her wedding to Hubert de Briscourt, and a sorrier sight could not be imagined. Three years of laying fallow beneath an invalid could not have wrought much improvement either, and if the gossip-mongers speak the truth when they say the old viper died of the pox, then she is undoubtedly riddled with the disease herself and will appeal to neither your sense of sight nor smell."

At that, a laugh escaped him. "Sir Hubert died of a sixty-year-old heart."

"Weakened, I am sure, by the sight of a poxy trull waiting in his bed each night."

"Nicolaa . . ." He shook his head slowly, causing sparks of candlelight to glint off the magnificent mane of golden hair. "Is it any wonder poor Onfroi sweats himself into pools when he is near you? Your tongue is sharp enough to flay any man or woman into a cowering shadow of their former self. Now, come. She cannot be as bad as all that."

"Have you seen her?" Nicolaa asked pointedly, knowing full well he had not.

"Once," he admitted. "I think. The room was very crowded, and she was standing very far away."

"There, you see? She was so ugly she was kept well out of the way to avoid giving offense."

Lucien unfolded his thickly muscled arms and moved away from the window. He set his goblet on a nearby table and crossed over to where Nicolaa stood, stopping in front of her. Reaching out, he placed a hand on either trim hip, grasping the slippery silk of her tunic between his fingers and sliding it upward.

"So what would you have me do?" he murmured, casting the flimsy garment aside and watching the fall of black hair drift back down to cover the lusciously nude body. "Let some other lout petition for her hand and win her estates?"

"Is that truly all you want her for? She is very young."

"I can have youth anytime I want it," he said, reaching out again, this time to flick aside a ribbon of hair that had tumbled over her breast. "Along with the whining, and bleating, and tears of inexperience that go hand in hand. No, Nicolaa, I am not marrying her for her youth."

Knowing the dark eyes were intent upon his face, Lucien deliberately avoided meeting them while a lazy thumb and forefinger began to trace a light pattern around one engorged nipple. The rushlights cast a mellow golden glow over the luminous, satiny curves of her body; the fire crackling in the hearth behind them might have been the sound of the sparks leaping from one heated body to the other.

Nicolaa closed her eyes and leaned boldly into the caressing fingertips. "Will you bed her?"

"Would you have me ignore her and rouse questions concerning my . . . preferences?"

"I would have you kill her," came the husky whisper, shivered from between clenched teeth. "Wed her, and kill her as soon as the properties are secured in your name."

Lucien bowed his head, burying his lips in the arched curve of her throat. Her groan sent his arm curling around her waist, and the hand that had been teasing the bloodred aureole of her breast left the bountiful peaks to slide down into the soft, mossy juncture below. Nicolaa clutched at his upper arms for support and parted her quaking limbs wider, moaning feverishly as his fingers stretched deeply and deliciously into flesh that was all too ready to respond.

"You know how I abhor unnecessary violence," he said

sardonically, his words muffled against a mouthful of succulent white flesh.

"I would do it," she gasped. "I would do it gladly. Gladly! *Oh . . . !*"

His fingers left a shiny wet path on her belly as they stroked upward to surround and engulf her breast again. His mouth crushed down over hers, smothering her cry of protest, the kiss as savage and mindless as the tearing fingers that scratched runnels into his skin in their haste to rid him of the short, shapeless tunic he wore. The cloth was shredded in her frenzy, but it mattered not. The hard rasp of red-gold stubble on his jaw burned her cheek and throat, but the flames were indistinguishable from the others that seared her body internally.

Running her hands beneath the torn edges of his tunic, she spread her fingers greedily over the firm planes and muscular ridges of his chest and ribs. She pushed the rent in the garment lower, baring the flat belly, the explosion of coarse blond hairs at his groin. A final tug and the fabric fell away, leaving her hands free to grasp and adore the blooded fullness that rose up between them.

"Mon Dieu," she cried hoarsely. *"Mon Dieu . . . !"*

Her mouth ravaged the taut column of his neck, the firelit expanse of his chest, the bronze discs of his nipples, and she started to slip down onto her knees, eager to worship the bold, virile body. His big hands forestalled her. They grasped her buttocks, lifting her against him, and, as he splayed his own legs wider for balance, plunged her fiercely down over the thickened spear of his flesh.

Nicolaa's head arched back. Her mouth gaped and froze around a jolt of pleasure so intense the sensation hovered somewhere between ecstasy and agony. He eased the pressure briefly, allowing her only as many moments of clarity as were necessary to wrap her arms and legs avariciously around him. Then he brought her weight slamming down again . . . and again . . . and the pleasure verged on pain before erupting in a thousand starbursts of unending rapture.

Her hair enveloped them in a silky black cocoon, the curls jumping to and fro to the rhythm of the damp, heated clash of their bodies. Their silhouettes were cast onto the wall behind them, two huge shadows undulating with wild abandon.

Lucien's great strength survived the first convulsive foray into oblivion, but as he felt the second building within him, he laughingly chastised Nicolaa to interrupt her own recurring climaxes until they could gain the support of the bed beneath them. Her answer was a guttural curse, her response a wave of such protracted gratification that she was drenching both of them in its effects as Lucien lowered her onto the high platform bed.

"By Christ's holy vows," he rasped, furrowing deeply into the sleek and trembling haven once more. "How does a man like Onfroi even begin to satisfy you?"

"He never has," she gasped, quaking through a shiver of aftershocks. "And never will. That is why I need you, my lusty lord. And this—" She arched her head back into the linens, straining into the joy of each thrust as he plunged his flesh repeatedly into hers. "This is why you need me as well. We should have married, you and I. All those years ago . . . we should have married."

"We would have killed each other by now," he grunted. "One way or another."

"Ahh, but what a sweet death it would have been, locked together, bound together in ecstasy forever. Admit it, damn you. Admit you have never found another woman who can satisfy you as I do!"

Lucien admitted nothing, not in so many words. His body, however, spoke eloquently, surging deeper, harder, faster; held in her pulsing grip, driven by the passion raging through every vein, muscle, and tautened sinew.

Nicolaa's nails drew ragged red gouges on his flesh as she raked them from his shoulders to his flanks. She levered her hips higher, and watched his handsome face contort in the firelight. Spasms wracked his body, rendering him as helpless and vulnerable as a babe in arms and she knew she could have stabbed a dagger into his heart at that moment and he would not have been aware of the threat. She could have slashed his throat or signaled to someone concealed in the shadows to attack him from behind, and he would not have suspected the danger until it was too late.

He should not take me for granted, she thought darkly. Nor should he doubt for a moment that I would hesitate to kill—as I have done before—in order to get what I desire most in life. A nubile young bride keening her pleasure beneath him, she most certainly did not desire. She knew full well a steady stream of girls, women, wenches, and whores frequented his sleeping couch, but never, not once had he ever contemplated marriage. Not even when the dower lands of a proposed match could have doubled or trebbled his present wealth. So why this one?

Nicolaa *had* seen the widow De Briscourt. Tiny as a bird, delicate as a blush, as blonde and dewy with youth as the early morning sunlight.

What if Lucien saw her and . . . and . . . ?

The moan that welcomed the panting, drained mass of spent ecstasy back into her arms was not entirely feigned. She held him and combed her fingers through his damp blond locks, savouring every last shiver and shudder that racked the mighty body.

Nicolaa was not going to lose him again. Not this time. She had been patient all these years, tolerant of the need for discretion and caution. But there was no one now who would dare point a finger at the Baron de Gournay and remind him his father had been branded a traitor, his brother slain as a murderer. The last of his line, he had succeeded in overcoming the taint of both tragedies. He was Richard's trusted ally and Prince John's confidant; the time for patience was rapidly drawing to an end. She would have her great golden warlord. She would live at Bloodmoor Keep as its mistress, and she would remove without qualm anything or anyone who stood in her way!

4

It seemed to Servanne that outrage upon outrage was to be heaped upon her for as long as she was expected to endure the outlaw's company. Not only was she being forced to join them in defiling the holy ground of the ruined abbey, but she was also pressed into taking part in further indignities. Scarcely had she been permitted the luxury of scrubbing the grime and dampness of the forest off her face and hands, when she was summoned to join the motley band of renegades while they consumed their evening meal. An adamant refusal was met, moments after it was relayed, by the appearance of the Black Wolf himself in the doorway of the tiny, windowless cubicle that had once been a monk's sleeping chamber. A clear warning was delivered: refuse again and she would be thrown over his shoulder and carried to the dinner table.

Her eyes red-rimmed from weeping, her body aching and bruised in too many places to recount, Servanne accompanied the rogue to the long pilgrims' hall, the only building of the three still boasting a partial roof, and the one that had obviously been taken over as living and sleeping quarters for the band of outlaws. To complete her humiliation, Servanne de Briscourt was seated, as guest of honour, with the Black Wolf and half a dozen of his more important henchmen on the raised stone dais that dominated one end of the vaulted hall.

It was an eerie feeling to be seated at a long trestle table,

its surface covered with a prim white cloth and laid with fine
silver and pewter, and to overlook a hall whose walls were
scorched and blackened by fire, bristling with the nests of
enterprising colonies of swallows. Mouldy rushes and de-
composed leaves littered the floor, rustling and even moving
now and then with small living things. Horses nickered and
scuffed heavily against one another in a crude pen constructed at the far end of the hall. Their smells of offal,
sweat, and leather mingled unpleasantly with musk and decay, which in turn was flavoured pungently with the oily
black smoke that rose from the pine-pitch torches burning in
iron cressets set into the stone walls.

Two longer tables had been erected at either end of the
dais to form an open-ended square, while the fourth side was
taken up by a firepit filled with glowing red coals. Squirrels,
hares, capons, and other small game were turned on spits by
men who defied the heat and flames to snatch at pieces of the
sizzling meat and crackling skin. Larger shanks of venison,
mutton, and boar were overseen by two bustling women—
the only two in the camp so far as Servanne could discern—
who turned their spits and basted their meats with large copper ladlefuls of seasoned oil. Another fire, pitched over an
iron grating, kept cauldrons of water boiling, steaming the
air, and smaller pots of stews and sauces burping sluggishly
at the end of long iron hooks suspended from crossbars.

Even to the casual observer, it would be obvious that these
were not men accustomed to hardship. The life Servanne had
envisioned for outlaws who spent their days poaching and
their nights avoiding capture was definitely not one of fine
linen, rich food, and flagons encrusted with gold and silver.
Moreover, common foresters would hardly move about the
countryside with a large stabling of horses, and most especially not the heavy-shanked, muscular animals that
Servanne saw being fed and well tended in the pens. They
were no ordinary plow-horses, nor were they nags stolen

from merchants who used them to draw carts or carry packs. Sir Hubert had kept a fine stable of warhorses—huge beasts trained to respond to a knight's commands, to kill if provoked, to bear the burden of full armour and heavy weapons.

At least half of the two dozen animals penned under the charred and rotted archways of the pilgrims' hall could have rivaled the best Sir Hubert had kept in his stables. And one of them, a huge black destrier with a silver mane and tail whose slightest grunt or annoyed sidestep sent the rest flinching nervously out of range, would have compared favorably to the white rampagers bred for King Richard's use.

Who were these men if they were not common thieves and outlaws?

Her curiosity roused, Servanne took a new interest in examining the faces around her. To her immediate right was the Black Wolf—an enigma from start to finish, and far too complicated for a cursory perusal. To her left, the mercurial sprite, Sparrow, equally baffling. Sandwiched between the half-man, half-child and the stoically formidable presence of Biddy, was the one they called Friar. He had shed his monk's robes and was dressed more comfortably in lincoln green leggings and linsey-woolsey tunic. As serene and smooth as his countenance might be, there was narry a hint of softness in the breadth of his shoulders or the solid muscle in his arms and legs.

Gil Golden sat on the Wolf's right-hand side, which gave Servanne a clear view of the terrible, ravaging scar that distorted the left side of his face. He too could not boast of an inch of excess flesh, but his was a wiry trimness not thinned by starvation or deprivation. To his right sat a pair of scoundrels so identical in features, clothing, and gestures, Servanne had initially blamed a weakened constitution for causing her to see double. Twins were a rarity in England. The fact that these two—nicknamed Mutter and Stutter by their comrades—should have survived to adulthood with no twisted limbs, missing teeth, or pockmarks to distinguish them apart, was truly a wonder. They lifted their eating knives in unison, chewed in unison, and, after the third goblet of strong ale, turned red as raw meat and belched in unison.

As for the others—a score who sat at tables—there were not a few oddities caught by Servanne's sharp eyes. A hand raised to call for a servant or squire and quickly withdrawn on the recollection that none were there. An easy camaraderie only found among men who had spent a good many years together, not a few furtive months of skulking and thieving.

And the man who sat in their midst like an uncrowned king? Those shoulders and that musculature could not have been developed behind a plow or a serf's thralldom! Those arms had known the weight and fury of sword and lance; those eyes, keen and canny, had seen the world—perhaps too much of it? And that voice, that carefully controlled, precisely articulated manner of speaking belonged to no peasant churl. He chatted amiably with the other outlaws at the table, and most of the time spoke in clear, unaccented French. Occasionally, however, he addressed the handful of retainers who laboured over the fires and tended the pens, in the barbaric Saxon tongue that branded them as locals. Once he even responded to a raucus jibe from the Welshman in the same melodic but totally unpronounceable gibberish native to the bearded mountain of a man.

Much as he sought to conceal it, the Black Wolf of Lincoln was well born, well educated, and well traveled. A knight turned rogue? An outcast who had surrounded himself with other knights who, for some reason or another, had chosen to break with every honour and vow they had once held more sacred than life itself? And what of his claim? Only a crackbrain would give any credence to his claim of being the real Baron de Gournay, so who was he? And why was he thieving his way through the forests of Lincoln, murdering, kidnapping, and wreaking havoc in the name of Lucien Wardieu?

Sinking deeper into a mire of confusion, Servanne tried to recall every scrap of gossip, good or bad, she had heard about the reclusive knight who resided at Bloodmoor Keep. There was some cold business, many years ago: false charges of treason against the father which were later proven beyond doubt to have been contrived by his enemies—but what powerful baron did not have enemies? Lord Lucien had hunted down each and every one of the conspirators and forced their sealed confessions, too late to save his father from a traitor's death, but boldly enough to win back most of the estates confiscated during the trial. There was more, but nothing that would give her a clue as to why two men would be laying claim to the De Gournays' violent, warlike ancestry.

"The broth is delicious tonight."

Startled, Servanne looked up at the Wolf's lopsided grin, then at the two-handled *écuelle* he was politely offering for her consideration. The steaming contents of the bowl gave off a rich, meaty aroma that started the glands beneath her tongue spurting with a vengeance.

It was the custom in all great homes for the diners to sit in pairs when there were ladies present, and for each couple to share the same soup bowl, wine cup, and thick trencher of day-old bread that served as a plate. It was also the gentleman's task to serve the lady, to offer soup or wine to her first, to present the choicest cuts of meat, and to even feed her bite-size morsels of bread or cheese if she desired it. In this court, under these charred beams and torchlit ruins, Servanne regarded such formalities as ludicrous. Intolerable. The linen, the gold plate, the silver and bejewelled eating knives only added insult to indignity and made her want to scratch the mocking grin from his face.

"Perhaps the venison will be more to your liking," said the outlaw lord, undaunted by her cold blue stare and even colder silence. He drained every last drop of soup from the bowl and set it aside to be collected, then smacked his lips with greater relish as a cheerful server replaced the used vessel with platters of still-sizzling meat. Mutton, venison, and hare were offered alongside bowls of leeks, onions, and peas. Eels turned inside out and boiled in wine gave off a sour-sweet aroma; fresh crusty bread, pasties, and quenelles swimming in savoury sauces and gravies prompted a need in Servanne to grip the edge of the table beneath the snow-white linen. Her stomach wept in protest as each dish was offered and refused. Her throat ached for a taste of bread and honey; her eyes drifted in a blur from platter to platter; her belly rumbled and quaked in an attempt to break down her resolve.

"My lady?" A sliver of tender hare's meat wavered in front of her, flourished expertly on a silver blade. Servanne stared at the delicate pink morsel, following the movement of her tormentor's hand until the meat was taken away and deposited between his own lips. A dribble of clear juice ran over his lower lip and trickled down his chin. Servanne's tongue peeped out anxiously from the corner of her mouth, lingering there even after a casual wipe of his hand had removed the trail of sweet grease.

"A bite of lark pasty, perhaps? This way you can judge for yourself our boasting over Goodwife Mab's skills."

"No. Thank you," she whispered.

He shrugged and the tender, delicate shred of meat, wrapped lightly and lovingly in a blanket of egg-glazed pastry, went the way of the declined hare. In the next instant, she swore she could hear the buttery pastry crunching between the strong white teeth; she had her own imaginary tidbit half chewed and swallowed before she caught herself and clenched her jaws tightly together in anger.

He was only being attentive because he knew she must be

starving. It would serve him right if she fainted dead away and—

"Delicious," he murmured, drawing the word out to ten syllables. "Mistress Mab, you have outdone yourself."

A short woman, round as a dumpling and just as soft, giggled and bobbed gratefully after the compliment.

"Indeed, mistress. The fare is by far the best I have tasted in quite some time, and that includes a visit to the royal kitchens at Windsor."

Servanne's eyes opened wide. Hardly believing her ears, she looked to her left and confirmed that it was Biddy who had spoken, her mouth stuffed with the lark pasty. Moreover, all three layers of chin were dobbed with grease, and there was an unmistakable flush of warmth on her cheeks to indicate her wine goblet was not being refilled for the first time.

"Shall we cry 'Judas' and have her flayed for insubordination?" a husky baritone mused in her ear.

"Biddy is . . . older; not as strong. She needs to keep up her health."

The explanation sounded feeble, even to Servanne's ears, but her salvation was quick to come from another source.

"You should eat something as well, sweet lady," Sparrow advised. "The rare air here in the greenwood thins the blood if it is not well fed. Even an apple, or a bit of cheese will help keep the humours balanced. You would not want to fall ill and have to rely upon the services of old Norwood the Leech, now would you? He came to us with Mab and claims to be a fair barber and a drawer of teeth, but as to his leeching talents . . . we have not yet found a survivor to accredit them."

A sad shake of the tousled brown mop of hair sent Servanne's attention to a large, toothless toad of a man who was grinning at her from the lower tier and waving a dripping joint of mutton by way of acknowledging the compliments.

He had a red, leaky nose fully as broad as his face, and wore an apron of leather that had become so stained and encrusted, it was moulded to his body like armour.

"Perhaps . . . a bit of apple," Servanne conceded.

Sparrow jumped up to stand on his stool so that he could reach the far side of the table. Quick as spit, there was a small collection of choice, tasty bits of meat, pastry, and other delicacies heaped on a freshly cut slab of white bread. This he placed in front of her and settled back onto his stool, his feet dangling several inches off the ground. He was aware, as was Servanne, of the smouldering gray eyes that had followed his every move, but if the threat of sudden flame troubled him, it was not reflected in his next piece of sage advice.

"The best way to stop a fly from annoying you is to stop swatting at him," he said with a wink and an elfin grin. "Eventually it gets bored and flies away to pester someone else."

There was wisdom in what he said, and, the fact that it caused the Wolf's brows to furl together like the gathering clouds of a storm, prompted Servanne to breach her resolve to starve to death. She reached for a thin slice of capon and took the tiniest bite into her mouth. It was delicious, which made her stomach groan for a second morsel, then a third . . .

When her trencher was emptied, refilled, then emptied again, she unselfconsciously tore the gravy-soaked plate into bite-sized pieces and removed all evidence of its existence down to the last crumbs. Sparrow's drinking cup had also ended up between them and she found the wine to be surprisingly fresh and full-bodied, of a far better quality than the vinegary possets that often graced the tables of wealthy nobles.

Mutter and Stutter, bowing to howled demands and flung food, took their leave of the table and, kicking aside the dogs who fought happily amid the crunch and snap of discarded bones, placed their stools in the bright glow of the fires and set their fingers to plucking out tunes on the lute and viol.

The food, the wine, the music cast a dreamy sense of unreality over everything. The fire sent gauntlets of orange and yellow flame leaping toward the blackness above. The enclosing stone walls formed a cavern of light and shadow that was almost cozy in its isolation.

Servanne could feel her eyelids growing heavier and heavier, the weight of her wimple beginning to pull her chin lower and lower onto her chest.

"So, my lady." The Wolf's sonorous tone brought her head up with a start. "You have supped on the king's deer and prolonged your stay on earth awhile longer. You have also shown a remarkable restraint in the matter of the ransom I shall demand from your groom. Are you not curious to know the value of your life—or rather, what value your groom will place on your continued good health?"

Servanne sighed wearily, in no mood to take his bait.

"I am certain, whatever you have demanded, he will pay."

"A true adherent to the codes of chivalry, is he? Gold spurs flashing, swords thrusting, damosels rescued from the clutches of evil at any cost? He sounds almost too good to be true."

Servanne glared in silence.

"So, you have no doubt he will pay whatever I demand?"

"Have you?"

"Madam, I doubt everything and everyone—even my own good sense on occasion. It is a credo that has kept me alive while others have perished and turned to dust."

"A pity you were not less insightful," she murmured tartly, putting a deal of frost in her gaze before turning her attention back to the minstrels. "I have no doubt my stay here will be a short one."

"One way or another," he agreed smoothly. "Still, ten thousand marks is a goodly sum of coin."

Servanne stiffened, then whirled to face him. "Ten thousand marks! Are you mad?"

"Are you afraid he will not part with that much silver?"

She released her breath on a gasp of exasperation. "If you are asking if Lord Lucien has the wealth to pay such an . . . an *outrageous* sum, the answer is yes. Ten times over."

A dark brow arched inquisitively. "Then I should have demanded more?"

"*No!* I mean . . . no." She stopped and chewed savagely on her lip. "Ten thousand is . . ."

"A fair test of his devotion?"

"Too much to expect a man to pay for—"

"A bride whose angelic disposition nearly overwhelms her vast inheritances? Tell me honestly—if you can do such a thing without compromising the staunch beliefs of your gender—have you not wondered what his motives were in seeking this union?"

"His *motives?*" Frustrated, Servanne clasped her hands into tight little fists and fought to keep her temper in check. "The purpose behind your aggravating persistence eludes me, sirrah. What is it *exactly* that you wish to know? Lord Lucien is a fine, noble gentleman—"

"Who loves you to the point of distraction and cannot bear to think of a prolonged separation."

"*A noble gentleman,*" she reiterated furiously, "who—"

"Who wants something you have, and is willing to sacrifice his much prized freedom to get it."

She flushed hotly. "There may have been some consideration given to the dowry, but—"

"My lady," the rogue laughed outright. "You are far too modest. With what you bring into the marriage, you will turn Lincoln into his small, private domain. A kingdom, if you will, with a dragon on the throne and a nest of serpents writhing at his feet, eager to do his bidding. Mind, it does you some credit to understand from the outset what he wants from you. Most women would be inclined to look no farther than the closest mirror to explain a sudden, pressing need for wedded bliss."

"He will not suffer for his bargain," she said archly.

"Spoken with true humility," he grinned. "And for the sins of vanity and ignorance, you shall recite ten *pater nosters* to the good Friar."

"You should be the one begging repentance," she countered angrily. "For surely you traded your soul to the Devil long ago. As a Christian, I shall pray for your redemption."

"Save your prayers for yourself, my lady. You will need them far more than I, whether the ransom is paid or not."

Servanne gritted her teeth. "If you are threatening me, or endeavouring to frighten me—"

"My dear lady, I am not endeavouring to frighten you any more than you should be already. In truth, I would rather open your eyes to a few unpleasant facts."

"By first demanding an outlandish ransom, then suggesting it will not be paid? How truly thoughtful of you, messire. Are you this considerate to all your hostages?"

"One or two have screamed quicker for mercy, but the methods improve with each outing." He paused and his eyes were lured down to the moist pink arch of her lips. "Unless I am misinformed, you are Sir Hubert's only surviving heir?"

"I do not see where that is a concern of yours."

"There was a nephew," he said, ignoring the sarcasm. "But I was told he had a fatal accident a few weeks back and fell on his own sword. Three times. Clumsy fellow, would you not say?"

This was the first she had heard of it and her silence caused the slate-gray eyes to fasten on to hers again.

"Moreover, you are an orphan yourself, are you not? As such, should you perish before another husband has been procured, all dower rights of inheritance revert by law to the crown, to be kept, sold, or dispersed as the king sees fit."

"King Richard would never—"

"King Richard is away on his crusades," the Wolf interrupted bluntly. "It would therefore fall to Prince John's discretion, in his role as regent, to dispose of Sir Hubert's properties and chattal. Of the two brothers, which one would you say had the greasier palms?"

"Prince John," she whispered, intrigued despite herself, to see where this was leading.

"And of the two royal scions, who would have the most to gain by parceling out the late baron's properties quickly and quietly, with as little fuss as possible?"

Prince John, she thought, temporarily chilled out of her anger and weariness. Acting on the king's behalf and using the excuse that the funds raised would be going to finance the Lionheart's crusades in the Holy Land, Sir Hubert's estates could be divided and sold to interested bidders, with a portion of each sale discreetly ending up in the prince's own coffers.

The Black Wolf was watching her reactions closely. "In the same vein, if I had a choice between paying out ten thousand marks ransom for a bride I had no desire to take in the first place . . . or to bide my time and pay a good deal less to buy only those estates I wanted . . ." He paused and shrugged his massive fur-clad shoulders. "I might be sorely tempted to let someone else do what my vaunted code of chivalry prevented me from doing myself."

Servanne blanched, then sprang to her feet.

"Enough!" she cried, incensed beyond reason. "I will not sit here and endure such insults! Your logic is very sound, coming from a man who is both a traitor and a thief. I have no doubt you *would* choose the easier path to obtaining your goal, which only *proves* you are not who you claim to be. You are *not* Lucien Wardieu. You are not even a *man*! You are a

corrupt and twisted shadow of a creature who has obviously
decided that stealing a man's identity and committing heinous crimes in his good name somehow satiates a petty need
inside you to become more than what you are. You have no
honour. You have no shame. I hope, nay, I pray for the *real*
Lord Lucien to come into these woods and hunt you down! I
pray he catches you and stakes you down on the ground, and
leaves you there for the dogs and boars to chew away strip
by bloody strip! Moreover, I pray . . . oh, how I do pray to
be present when he does so, to have the privilege and immense pleasure of watching you die inch by gored inch!"

She stood there, her face flushed, her chest heaving with
anger. Not only the outlaw leader, but every man within
earshot of her outburst—which included nearly all present in
the pilgrims' hall—had stopped what they were doing to
turn and stare.

The Wolf, in particular, was staring at the gleaming, jewelled eating knife she had snatched off the table and was
holding in a clenched fist only inches from his nose. Half an
eternity passed before he spoke, his tone silky, the words said
with a quiet intensity that set off a roaring in her ears.

"I met Sir Hubert de Briscourt some years ago in France.
A fearsome warrior on the battlefield, he brooked no insult
from any quarter, servant or noble. It is a true wonder then,
that in three years of marriage, he was not once driven to
strangle you to death."

Servanne's lips were parted, the cool air giving ghostly
substance to her rapid breaths. She stared down into eyes
that were like banked fires, glowing and dangerous, apt to
erupt at the merest provocation.

"Put the knife down," he instructed calmly. "Or use it."

For a moment, her fingers tightened, and the knuckles
glowed pinkish white. Then her senses cleared and her hand
flexed reluctantly open, dropping the knife as if the hilt had
suddenly become red hot. The sound shattered the absolute

silence, releasing the tension everywhere but in the immediate area of the two principals. They continued to stare at one another over the resumed buzz of movement and conversation.

"Never, ever lift a knife to me again, madam, unless it is done with firm intent"—his voice was so low she could barely hear it—"for you will not be so lucky twice."

Servanne believed him. Only a blind fool would doubt the savagery that lurked just behind the hooded, soulless eyes.

"You are despicable," she said, the words tight in her throat. "I pray to God I do not live long enough to hate another human being as much as I hate you."

"Sit down," he commanded brusquely, "before the strain of all that prayer drains your strength and accomplishes your desire prematurely."

"I have no wish to *sit down,* sirrah. Not now. Not ever."

His jaw clamped ominously. "None at all?"

"None."

"Very well, if that is your *wish*—" He stood abruptly, his patience snapped like a taut thread. "Sparrow!"

A meek corner of the pale, elfin face peeped around Servanne's skirts. "Aye, my lord?"

"Have the table and stools cleared away. Lady Servanne will be remaining exactly where she is, by her own request. The night ahead promises to be a cool one, so by all means fetch a mantle and rug for the lady's comfort, but under no circumstances is she to sit or lie down at any time without first seeking my express permission to do so. If she dares to attempt either, through stubbornness or feint, have her bound hand and foot and chained upright to the wall. Is that understood?"

"Scoundrel!" Biddy gasped. "Cad! Inhuman monster!"

The Black Wolf turned from the defiant sparkle in Servanne's gaze to launch a particularly venomous glance at the spluttering matron.

"You may share your mistress's dicipline if you see fit. If not, you would be wise to remain in your chamber for the duration of the night lest you be mistaken for an intruder and shot out of hand. Gil! Friar! We have plans to discuss for the morrow. Ladies . . . I bid you a pleasant and comfortable evening."

Servanne watched him skirt the table and stride across the firelit floor. Her body was trembling with anger; pride and obstinacy gave her the added strength to stand her ground and glare contemptuously at the sheepish ring of onlookers. She would stand there till hell froze, if she had to. Ask his permission? She would cut off her tongue and choke on it before groveling to him or anyone else for favours. Ask his permission, indeed!

"Lady?"

A gentle tug on her surcoat drew Servanne's blurred gaze down.

"Lady . . . he bears a heavy burden on his mind, does my lord. Aye, and at the best of times he has a temper that rankles most foul when pricked. It cools just as quickly, however, and I warrant he would be happy to reconsider if I went after him and—"

"The man who causes injury to a woman only shames himself," she quoted stoically. "And, if he so injures her, she breaks his will more by refusing to bow to that shame."

Sparrow's eyebrows flew upward, losing themselves beneath the tumbled locks of his hair. Did she think the Wolf was a normal man?

"My lady," he cautioned earnestly, "it is neither wise nor necessary to prove your will to be as strong as his. Many have tried; none have succeeded."

"I have no wish to prove myself stronger, only to prove I am not easily broken."

"Methinks he is well aware of that already," Sparrow muttered, scratching furiously at a prickling sensation at the nape of his neck. "No one in my memory has had a voice left after raising it to him. As for the knife . . . dear oh dear, that *was* a sight to behold."

"My lady . . ." Biddy began. "Perhaps young Woodcock is right. Perhaps you should—"

Servanne lifted a hand to silence her. "There is no point in two of us enduring the cold and damp, Biddy. My bones are a good deal younger than yours, and I am quite resigned to wait out this ruffian for as long as it takes. Go to your bed with a clear conscience, I would prefer to have you well rested for whatever new trials await us in the morning."

Biddy clamped her hands together on her lap and swelled her bosom to prodigious proportions before pushing herself to her feet. "If you want me moved from this spot, you will have to have me dragged away by the heels! These decrepit old bones, as you think them, have a dole of life left in them yet, and shame to you for thinking so poorly of them and me in this time of tribulation! You! Woodcock!" She glared icicles at Sparrow. "Fetch those furs and mantle, and be quick about it. Bring the thickest pelts you can lay a hand to for my lamb to stand on, and a length of wool to wrap about her feet for warmth. Well? What are you waiting for: All Hallows Eve?"

The newly christened Woodcock planted his hands on his hips and looked as if he might balk at the chain of command. But a glance up into the sad and lovely eyes of the young demoiselle, who was fighting so bravely to choke back her tears, made him swallow his indignation and collect an assortment of blankets, furs, even a warm pair of mittens he had been hoarding in his own pack.

This done, he scampered off to his perch high on one of the undamaged wooden arches. From there he could look down over the entire cavernous refectory, seeing more than he was perhaps intended to see.

The Wolf was there, standing well back where the shadows

were thickest and his presence not likely to be betrayed by the firelight. He stood as still as the stone wall he leaned against, and while Sparrow could not see his expression, he was mildly troubled by the suspicion that the wide brow would be frowning with perplexity.

In all the years they had been together—ten now since the Wolf had rescued him from a nightmare world of freak shows and fairgrounds—Sparrow had rarely seen him display anything but bored deference to the women who, more often than not, chased after him with their skirts raised and their eyes wanting. He was no fool to refuse what was so readily and eagerly offered; some he had even liked well enough to remember their names in the morning.

But this was strange. Very strange indeed. Prior to the widow's appearance at the supper table, the plan had not changed from its original conception. She was a hostage and hostages were fair game, especially when there were old scores to be settled. Rape, forced marriage, even mutilation was not unexpected in most cases of rivalry and revenge, and the Wolf had given serious contemplation to each of the three options at one point or another.

At the very least he should have boxed her ears a dozen times throughout the afternoon and evening. The fact he had not even *touched* her . . . ! Well, it was too much for Sparrow's tired head to support.

Yawning against the lull of heat and smoke that remained trapped under the dome of the roof, Sparrow settled more snuggly into his nest of furs and let the hypnotic effects of the dying fires spare him the burden of further puzzles to solve.

5

Servanne's young body ached from top to toe. She had
fought off bouts of faintness and nausea all through the long,
seemingly endless night of torment. There had been no bells
tolled to mark the passing hours. The fires inside the shell of
the pilgrims' hall had been banked, fading from insipid red
to frilled white ash. All but two of the torches that sat in
black iron cressets had been doused early in the evening. The
remaining two had been allowed to burn down to stubs, and
then left to smoke listlessly in their rusted cradles. Only the
waning brightness of the stars overhead marked the slow
passage of the hours, and they, for the better part of the
night, had been cloaked behind drifting banks of opaque
mist.

Dampness and cold were Servanne's only companions.
Biddy had fallen fast asleep within an hour of her declared
tenacity. Apart from the odd restless nicker from the horses
and the contented snores of the men who had made their
beds on piles of old rushes, there was only the occasional hiss
and crackle from the dying fires to break the leaden silence.

Slowly, however, the gloom and shadow that had enveloped the abandoned abbey distilled to a murky, half-lit
dawn. The mist began to receed into the forest. Figures and
objects, smothered by darkness, slowly took shape and substance again and, responding to some inner timepiece, the
huddled figures began to stretch and yawn, and push knuck-
led fists into crusted, bleary eyes. A round of coughing and

spitting bestirred the dogs, who took up where they had left off the night before rooting in the rushes in search of food scraps. The men greeted one another, some groaning over swollen heads and sour tongues, some exchanging ribald complaints over other stiffened, ill-exercised joints. Somewhere a goat bleated and an ax bit into wood. Beyond the stone walls, a flock of birds were startled out of their rookery and rose above the gaping, scorched beams in a screaming black cloud.

Sparrow came swooping down out of nowhere, landing with a whoop and cry that nearly sent Biddy tumbling sideways off her log stool.

"You said you did not want to sit," he chirruped good-naturedly to Servanne. "Did you also mean you did not care to wash or clear away the night vapours?"

Servanne was too weary to take offense at his humour. "I would like very much to refresh myself."

"Follow me, then. Follow me."

Biddy's stiffened joints creaked and cracked as she tried to heave herself to her feet, and with Servanne's help, she finally managed. Moving was another matter entirely and she scooted her mistress on ahead while she followed at a slower, more cautious gait.

Sparrow led them out into the courtyard and around to the rear of the stone buildings. Here, the thick outer wall had once boasted a low postern gate through which the monks could enter or leave the grounds without disturbing the main gates. The entryway was all but overgrown by weeds and thick ropes of ivy, but a space had recently been hacked through the bramble and it was there Sparrow paused, grinning back at Servanne as he beckoned her through the gap.

For a brief, lack-of-sleep-induced moment, she thought the little man was helping her escape.

The spurt of newfound energy the thought triggered lasted only until she was on the other side of the wall and saw the path that led into the greenwood. Returning to the abbey along the path were the two women she had seen the previous night, both of them carrying full buckets of water.

"The cistern inside the abbey has gone dry," Sparrow explained, ignoring Biddy's muffled oaths as she fought off a web of vines that had fallen on her. "But there is a sweet stream just ahead. Follow me. Follow me."

He danced cheerfully into the deeper woods, his stubby hands fluttering as he pushed aside the saplings and pale green fronds that overgrew the pathway. He kept chattering to himself, or singing—Servanne cared less which. Nor did she care that the air was fresh and cool, tinged with the pungent smell of evergreen, or that their footsteps made very little sound on the rich, loamy earth they walked on. So absorbed was she in her own misery, she did not see Sparrow halt. A sharp cry and quick hands saved them both from tumbling headlong over a ten-foot drop of rock that marked the abrupt end of the path.

To the left was a steep, rounded escarpment which rose to a high, bare promontory of jagged rock. Silhouetted against the metallic blue of the morning sky was the outline of a man, undoubtedly a sentry, who, from his elevated position, would be able to see a fair distance in all directions. Halfway down the rocky escarpment, a wide smooth sheet of water flowed out of a fissure in the wall, streaming over a series of moss-covered ledges, cut like steps into the curve of the cliff. It collected in a deep blue basin below, part of the pool darkened by the shadow of the overhanging promontory, the rest sparkling warm and inviting in the early sunlight.

Obeying Sparrow's pointed finger, Servanne carefully picked her way down the narrow trail that edged the embankment. At the bottom, it leveled out and she was able to walk onto a flat table of rock that leaned out over the water's shallow end.

"You can have a bit of privacy here, if you want it," Sparrow said. "I will go back and see where Old Shrew-Tongue has gotten herself. T'would be a pity to see her spill arse over heel into the pool." He thought about the image a moment and added with a chuckle. "Aye, a dreadful pity."

He was gone in a wink, vanished back into the undergrowth that swarmed the edge of the embankment. Servanne stared at the fronds until they had finished rustling, then gazed instinctively up at the sentry, who made no effort to pretend he was not staring directly back down at her.

Escape was the farthest thing from her mind as Servanne gingerly lowered herself onto her knees. She bowed her head and leaned forward to stretch the aching muscles in her neck. With a weary sigh, she unfastened the heavy samite surcoat and peeled it off her shoulders, then, on an afterthought, removed the jewelled broach that held the linen bands of her wimple pinned closed at her throat. Slowly, moving with the stiffness of a ninety-year-old woman, she unwound the starched collar bands and set the headpiece with its flowing caplet of cloth neatly on the blue crush of samite. She uncoiled the two thick braids of her hair and, using her fingers as combs, unplaited each glossy braid and shook the long, rippled mass free. When it was completely unfettered, she ran her splayed fingers across her scalp to massage it, nearly weeping with the pleasurable sensation of freedom.

As she was bending to dip her hands in the glassy surface of the pool, a loud splash farther along the shore caused her to jump and stare across the pond. A pale shape streaked below the water, erupting from the silver-black surface again several yards ahead of the spreading rings he had generated. Servanne recognized the chestnut mane of hair even as the Black Wolf shook it vigorously to scatter the clinging droplets of water. It was apparent he had not yet seen her, however, for as he began to walk into the shallower water, he was intent upon scrubbing his chest and arms with the handfuls of fine sand he had scooped from the bottom. A second dive brought him out of the shade and into the sunlight, and this time, when he stood, the water streamed in glistening sheets from his head to the tops of his powerful thighs.

A man's naked body held no surprises for Servanne. Her husband had slept nude beside her for three years. Visiting knights and nobles had thought nothing of stripping naked and either being bathed by her or in front of her as was the custom in welcoming a guest to one's castle. Some had been as virile and solidly thewed as this forest outlaw, although she could not, upon the instant, recall a chest quite so broad, or a belly so tautly ridged with bands of muscle. The hair on his chest glittered like a copper breastplate; a sleek line of it funneled down to a smaller thatch that swirled around his navel. Lower still and it grew into a tight, dark forest at his groin. What lay like a restless beast within that forest would have been more than enough to cause Servanne's heart to leap over several erratic beats if it were not already stumbling headlong over another disturbing sight.

Furrowing down his right side was a swath of misshapen scar tissue fully as wide as her hand, as long as her arm, distorting the surface of his flesh from his armpit to his buttock. Circling the same shoulder was a shiny patch of skin, resistant to the sun's tanning effects, and marking clearly where a chirurgeon's crude efforts had attempted to compensate for skin and muscle pared away from the upper arm. The shoulder itself was as gnarled as bark. His left thigh bore similar evidence of horrendous wounding—injuries one sustained from a battlefield, not a cornfield.

Under different circumstances Servanne would have been amused by the look of complete surprised that jolted the stern, stoic features when he realized he was not alone in the small glade. His hands froze halfway to reaching for a weapon that was not there. His eyes widened and flared with something akin to panic—though she could not imagine there could be anything on this earth able to rouse a fright in his soulless heart. As it was, she could hardly find cause to laugh at his reaction when her own sorry predicament was just as unsettling. Her head was bare—an unthinkable breach of propriety, even here in this pagan's forest. She was *alone.* (Where the Devil had Biddy taken herself to?) She was certain there must be smudges of dirt and dried tears streaking her face, and her hands shook like those of a palsied invalid.

The Wolf blinked more water from his eyes, cursing whatever misguided part of his brain had convinced him he was seeing a golden-haired sea nymph rising out of a pool of sunlight. She was golden-haired, all right, but far from being an enchantress. Just a flesh-and-blood nuisance who had no business being there.

Even after the initial start of shock had passed, the Wolf continued to experience some difficulty in regaining control over his composure. He did not like being caught unawares, did not relish the sensation of baring his scarred body to a woman in broad daylight, nuisance or not. It was not that he was ashamed of his appearance, for he cared little for what anyone thought; it was more a defensive reaction to the pity, and sometimes the recoiling horror he saw reflected in eyes unused to such sights.

As discomforting as it was to feel the clear blue eyes upon him, it was similarly distracting to know they were having a distinct effect on the way his blood was flowing through his veins. Because of the strict modesty of the wimple she had worn, he'd had no idea until that moment, of the colour, length, or incredible sheen of the blonde hair hidden beneath. Now, where it spilled over her shoulders, it resembled liquid gold, emphasizing the porcelain whiteness of her skin, the large almond-shaped eyes, the fine lines of her nose, chin, and mouth. While each feature on its own could claim no great or rare beauty, when flattered by the luminous cloud of her hair it lured a man to speculate over what other misinterpretations he might have made regarding her form and figure.

Seeing no reason why he should deny his curiosity—since she was so openly humouring her own—he followed the slender arch of her swan's throat down to where the clinging fabric of her gown afforded little modesty for the impertinent thrust of her breasts. Not so large as to cause a man difficulty in breathing, they were nonetheless of a proud shape and bearing, the nipples jutting like little round buttons against the cloth. He guessed he could span her waist neatly with his two hands, and her limbs, folded so gracefully beneath the shimmering pool of her hair, would be long and lithe, and would feel like warmed silk against his palms.

Servanne, silent throughout his inspection, endured the probing heat of his eyes until a flush of light-headedness threatened to topple her. It was difficult not to stare at the steaming dampness that rose from the surface of his skin; nearly impossible to ignore the power and strength sculpted so boldly into every inch of bulging muscle. Worse, she suffered a vivid recollection of having been held in those arms, crushed against that chest, threatened by those lips that were even now moving without sound . . .

". . . a long way from camp, my lady?" he was saying. "You found your way here alone?"

"S-Sparrow brought me," she replied, quickly lowering her gaze and focusing on where her hands were clasped together on her lap. "He . . . he thought it would be permitted for me to wash and refresh myself. I . . . am sorry if my presence has interrupted your bath, but Sparrow assured me I would have the pool to myself."

"He did, did he?" The Wolf arched a brow. "And yet he knows my habits almost as well as he knows his own."

Servanne hated the flush she could feel blooming darker in

her cheeks, and she hated the diminutive forester for indulging in what had obviously been another of his pranks.

The Wolf looked down at the golden crown of her head and for no good reason that he could think of, reassured her with a dry laugh. "He needs to have his nose tied at least twice each day to keep it from poking where it does not belong. But, since I am finished here anyway, you may have your privacy." He turned, retreated half a stride, and hesitated again. "You might want to heed a warning and stay well clear of the waterfall. It may look harmless enough, but the bottom is tangled with weeds as thick around as a man's arm."

She shook her head without looking up. "I do not know how to swim. I would not venture deeper than my ankles, but . . . I thank you for the warning."

The Wolf's mask of determined indifference slipped yet again and he raked his hands through his hair with an impatient gesture. "I make no excuses for my behaviour, but it has been a long time since my men or I have been in the company of gentlewomen, and, tempers being what they are . . ."

Servanne clasped her hands tighter. Was he attempting to apologize? Was he suffering pangs of guilt over the abominal way he had treated her last night—*as well he should!* If she thought it was worth the effort, she would have spat in his face and told him how much she cared to hear his lame excuses and apologies.

"It is not my wish to cause you any further discomfort, Lady Servanne. My quarrel is not with you."

"It is with the man who is soon to be my husband," she said tersely. "Therefore, sir, your quarrel is indeed with me."

The faintest hint of a bemused smile passed across the Wolf's mouth. Spirited . . . and loyal too; qualities that would do her good stead in the days ahead. Whether they would be enough to see her through, he had no idea, but for the moment, they earned her more respect than would have been won through weeping, wailing, and swooning off her feet at each turn of a phrase.

He accepted her rebuke with uncharacteristic silence. His slate-gray eyes lifted to the burnished blue vault of the sky above and moved slowly, speculatively around the ring of trees until they settled finally on the source of the waterfall high on the escarpment.

"This place is called the Silent Pool," he murmured absently. "According to legend, it was filled by the tears of a maiden who had fallen hopelessly in love with one of the monks from the abbey. Unfortunately, the bishop lusted after her too, and one night, on his way from the monastery to the village, the young monk met with an "accident" and fell from the promontory. The maiden knelt by his body and wept until the basin was filled with her tears, ensuring that she and her lover could remain here undisturbed for all of eternity. To show their sympathy and approval for the sacrifice she made, the druids cast a spell over the pool . . . a spell of absolute silence," he added cynically "that can only be broken by a love fulfilled."

Servanne found herself swaying to the melodic drone of his voice. "You believe in curses and spells?"

"I believe what my eyes see and my ears hear. Look around you. Listen. The forest is teeming with birds and animals, but not one is ever seen or heard near the pool. The waterfall makes no sound where it runs into the basin; the leaves move on the branches, but say nothing to the wind."

Servanne raised her head with an effort. Surely this was another form of torment, for she heard sounds, a great many of them rushing and hissing in her ears. She tried to obey his command to look up at the trees, but the sun was a hot, hazy blur and its glare off the surface of the water made her feel dizzy and disoriented. Cleaving that glare into a mass of sparkling pinpoints of light, was the tall, shadowy figure who moved suddenly toward her.

The Black Wolf reached the lip of the rock an instant before Servanne's head would have struck it. The act of catching her jolted her eyes open briefly, but they fluttered closed again, the lashes falling like stilled butterfly wings against the ashen skin.

"Little fool," he murmured. "It is a wonder you have held your head up this long."

Cradling her against his chest, he lifted her carefully into his arms and waded with her to a point on the bank where he could more easily step out of the knee-deep water. He carried her back up the slope and returned along the path to the monastery, where, once inside the crumbling, vine-covered gate, a scowl warned away the curious stares that followed his naked buttocks through the pilgrims' hall.

In the chamber set aside for Servanne and Biddy, he gently deposited her on a sleeping couch made of fresh rushes and fur pelts. Somewhere along the way, she had roused enough to drape her arms around his neck, and she held fast to it now, reluctant in sleep to exchange the luxurient heat of his body for the cooler bed of pelts.

The Wolf gently pried her hands from around his neck, and, with only the silent walls of the cloistered chamber to bear witness to the crime, he ran his fingers down the shiny wavelets of her hair, tenderly brushing aside the curls that had clouded over her face. The chamber was windowless and the candle unlit. Even so, in the sparse light that flared through the open door, her hair glowed like the phosphorescent waves on a moonlit sea, her skin was pale and radiant, almost blue-white against the darker furs.

A frown pleated his brow as he looked down and saw that the hem of her gown was wet from having been dragged through the water. A hesitant glance at the door was shrugged aside and without further thought, he unfastened the belt of fine gold links she wore girded about her waist and eased it out from beneath her. Not the least doubtful of what her reaction would be if she could see what he was doing, his smile was wry as he slid the skirt of her gown up to her hips, collecting the lower edge of her thin linen undergarment—also wet—and manipulating both above her waist, breasts, shoulders, and finally tossing them free of the tousled mass of her hair.

It was when he lowered Servanne back onto the bed of furs that his smile faded and the gray of his eyes took on a new, smouldering intensity. He became suddenly aware of the feel of her naked flesh where it pressed against his, and acutely aware of his own nudity for the first time since leaving the Silent Pool. His hand was a paltry few inches from the round fullness of a breast, and of its own accord, the fingers traced a light path to the dark pink blossom of the velvety nipple. An intrigued palm measured and marveled over the firmness of the flesh that seemed specially moulded and shaped for just that purpose.

A low, almost inaudible moan drew his gaze up to her face. Her lips were parted and invitingly moist. Her body trembled slightly at the intimate contact—so slightly he might have thought he imagined it if not for the berry-hard nub that formed beneath his cupped hand. His fingers moved again and a second soft, breathy sigh set the nerves down his spine tingling.

The tingle burned all the way into his belly and groin, and the heated curiosity of his gaze roved from her breasts to the fine golden thatch of silk at the juncture of her thighs. It was soft to the touch, the curls parting and luring him deeper into the enticingly shadowed cleft. This time, there was no mistaking the tremor that welcomed his explorations, no denying the response that deepened the stain of colour in her warming flesh.

The Wolf withdrew his hand and clenched the treacherously inquisitive fingers into a tight fist. He knew there was nothing to stop him from taking her; indeed, had that not been an integral part of the plan from the moment he had heard the Dragon had chosen himself a bride? She was no virgin, untried, untouched, but she belonged to the Dragon and that made her an important gamepiece in his pursuit of revenge. An eye for an eye, was it not written?

The Wolf sank back on his haunches, not wanting to remember, but unable to prevent the memories from crowding into his anger.

Nicolaa.

Young and vibrant, lithe as a whip and just as deadly efficient in stripping away the innocence and guile of youth. Nicolaa had been the one who had introduced his adolescent body to worldly pleasures other than fighting, jousting, and training for war. She had taken his raw, aggressive lust in hand and had spent weeks of steamy days and nights instructing him exhaustively on the art of making love.

Nicolaa.

During that time he had imagined himself wildly, passionately in love with her. He had gone so far as to have a petition of marriage drawn, knowing the match was as sound politically as it was personally. Her eager and immediate acceptance had sent him thundering to her father's castle, where, in a burst of love-smitten irreverence, he had not waited for her to be summoned, but had sought her out in her private solar.

The sight of her, all white skin, raven-black hair, and flashing eyes, naked and grappling blindly to the churning hips of another lover had stopped him cold in the doorway. Seeing the man fling his golden head back to keen his ecstasy, and recognizing who was drawing the guttural screams of rapture from Nicolaa's arched throat, nearly caused him to unsheath his sword then and there and slay the pair at the height of their betrayal.

Instead, the Wolf had waited, his heart building a wall of ice around it while he watched their rutting acrobatics grind to a sweating, shivering halt. Nicolaa had seen him first, and had screamed. Her lover had turned toward the door and . . . smiled his triumph.

Without a word, he had torn the marriage contract asunder and left the room, left the castle. A week later, he had sailed away from England, his gypon emblazoned with the red cross of the Crusader.

An eye for an eye, the Wolf reminded himself as he flexed his hands open and slowly lowered them to the pale, sleeping form of Servanne de Briscourt. It was a cruel, callous world —crueler by far to a woman than a man, but there too it was Fate who ultimately decided which gender should spring from the seeds sown. It was his fate to have been born a man of destiny; hers to have been born the pawn whose life or death meant very little in the scheme of things. He could not afford to think of her as anything else, despite the innocence and vulnerability she tried so hard to conceal behind the snapping blue eyes. If he did, if he dared feel any compassion or regret, all of their lives, including hers, would be forfeit.

The messenger thundered up to the castle gates on a horse lathered nose to rump in the sour white foam of haste. The man himself was so winded he could barely communicate his demands to the guard who angled a bleary eye through the portcullis gates to identify him. Once admitted, he was escorted through the outer bailey, across a wooden drawbridge to an inner courtyard, through more gates and more annoying questions, until finally he was admitted to the innermost court. The horse's hooves clacked loudly on both wood and cobbled surfaces, echoing the urgency of the message he carried, scattering the throngs of servants and pages who were going about their morning duties. Dismounting at last, he forced his cramped legs to run up the enclosed stairway to the entrance of the main keep, where he reiterated, with no small amount of irritation, his breathless demand to see Lord Lucien Wardieu.

The seneschal, a dour and grim-faced stub of a man, warned with equal acidity that the lord was still abed and would not humour an interruption. The guard, against all sane advice and protocol, shoved the seneschal aside and bolted the length of the corridor to enter the narrow stone spiral of stairs that led up into the lord's private tower.

At the top, he was delayed by the poniards and drawn swords of the two alerted squires who slept in the anteroom adjoining their master's sleeping chamber. The ruckus they caused in challenging the intrusion was sufficient to bring the naked and enraged Baron de Gournay slamming out of the chamber, his own sword unsheathed and gleaming in readiness.

"What the devil goes on here?" he demanded. "Rolf! Eduard! Who in blazes is this man and what does he want?"

"Please, my lord," the guard gasped, his one arm bent to the breaking point by the elder of the two squires, Rolf. The younger one, his face earnest with intent, jabbed the point of his knife deeper into the intruder's straining throat, causing a fine thread of blood to leak from the cut.

"Please, my lord! Hear me out! I bring urgent news from the sheriff! News I was commanded to relay to your ears only, my lord. Your ears only!"

Some of the tension eased from Wardieu's arms as he lowered the huge steel blade. After another taut moment, he nodded curtly to his squires, who relaxed their grips only enough to allow the man breath and speech.

"Well? Deliver your news."

"It . . . it comes from the Lord High Sheriff, my liege. F-from Onfroi de la Haye."

"We know full well who the sheriff is," came a belligerent voice from the inner chamber. Nicolaa de la Haye appeared a moment later in glorious dishevelment, the sheet she had snatched up off the bed held haphazardly around her waist and looped over one shoulder.

The sight was so startling, the guard was struck dumb. He gaped first at the mottled pink splendour of a nearly bared breast, then at the telltale scratches and bitemarks that scored the baron's virile body.

"*Well?*"

"Th-there was an ambush, my lord. In Lincolnwood. More than a score of brave men slain, the rest robbed and forced to leave the forest on foot."

For several tense moments, Wardieu continued to stare expectantly at the guard, his brain slowed by a night of wine and sexual excess. It cleared, however, on an oath so violent and graphic, the squires looked over, startled.

"The Lady Servanne!" he exploded. "Where is she?"

His eyes bulging with fear, the guard stammered what he had been told to report of the ambush. "The cavalcade was set upon by outlaws, my lord. Their leader . . . called the Black Wolf by his victims . . . took the Lady Servanne hostage and advised the remainder of the guard to remove themselves from the woods ere they drown in their own blood along with their fallen comrades. H-he also insisted a message be delivered to"—the guard's eyelids shivered closed and he swallowed hard—"to the Dragon of Bloodmoor Keep, advising him that a ransom of ten thousand marks is necessary for the safe return of the hostage."

Wardieu's icy blue eyes narrowed to slits. "Ten thousand marks! Who is this madman, this . . . *Black Wolf*? Why have I not heard of him before now? And where, by Christ's holy rood, was our vainglorious high sheriff while this travesty was being committed?"

The golden knight advanced upon the cowering guard as he spoke, his hand once again clenched around the hilt of his sword. So terrifying a visage did he present, a naked and unyielding wall of solid muscle, that the guard could not have answered had he wanted to.

"The Black Wolf of Lincoln," mused Nicolaa de la Haye. "Onfroi has mentioned him on occasion."

Wardieu spun around to confront her. "*What?* Why have *I* not heard of him before today?"

"Good my lord, as you well know, my husband never boasts of his failures. This wolf's head has been playing at skittles with Onfroi's bold guardsmen for . . . oh, a goodly month or more, at least. I am sure he would have had to tell you eventually, since the rogue seems to be encamped within hailing distance of your own borders. In his defense, however

—though God knows why I should bother—his mind has been strenuously *taxed* with other matters of late."

Wardieu deliberately ignored the veiled reference to the sheriff's current round of revenue collecting—taxes supposedly levied to help finance the king's army, but in reality, going to finance Prince John's feral ambitions.

"If your husband required help ridding the forest of a nest of thieves," Lucien growled, "why the devil did he not come limping to me as usual?"

"Perhaps he was trying to stand on his own at long last?" Nicolaa suggested, her voice so heavy with sarcasm, the words dripped. "Perhaps he feels his manhood has been threatened enough by your superiority in other matters?"

Wardieu clamped his jaw into a steely ridge. "Rolf—fetch my clothes and armour. Eduard—call out my personal guard and tell them to be prepared to ride within the hour."

As the squires moved hastily to comply, the frosted blue gaze flicked back to the guard, who was endeavouring to restore circulation to his twisted elbow. "Where is the sheriff now, and where are the men who were escorting the cavalcade? I want to question them personally."

"My lord sheriff anticipated you might. He has set up temporary camp on the green above Alford Abbey to await your pleasure. Meanwhile, he has sent patrols back to the point of ambush and expects, what with the rain and damp we had earlier in the week, the tracks will not be too difficult to cipher."

"Onfroi has difficulty tracking his way to an over-full latrine," Nicolaa drawled, stifling a yawn. "I expect I should dress and accompany you, Lucien. The men are so much more eager to prove their worth to *me* in fulfilling their duties."

"Please yourself. I'll not be stopping or humouring any delays between here and the abbey."

"Provide me with a worthy mount," she said, her eyes

raking boldly down the powerful length of his body, "And you will not hear me balking at the thought of a hard day's ride."

Lucien turned to the gaping guard. "Go below and have my seneschal find you some hot food and drink, then be ready to lead us back to the green."

"Yes, my lord. My lord . . . there was one other thing."

Wardieu had already started back into his chamber to dress. "Yes, what is it?"

Sweat popped out across the man's brow in tiny, oily beads. "It comes from the Black Wolf, my liege. He said it should be delivered with a further message so that you would know his intentions were true."

A shaking, gloved hand reached into a leather pouch strapped to his belt. A small canvas sack was withdrawn and held out to the frowning baron. The thong binding the mouth of the sack had become loosened through the long journey and, before Wardieu could unthread it fully, the sack gaped open and the contents fell onto the floor by his bare feet.

It was a finger; a woman's severed finger, judging by the size and shape of it.

Wardieu drew a deep breath. "What was the message?"

The guard's chin quivered and he looked from Nicolaa to the baron. "Only . . . only that if you did not pay the ransom, you would not see your bride again . . . leastwise not in pieces large enough for anyone to recognize."

Nicolaa, sidling closer for a better view, was the first one to break the ensuing silence.

"Well," she murmured, "if nothing else, this Black Wolf knows how to make his meaning perfectly clear."

7

Onfroi de la Haye was a spike-thin, ferret-faced man cursed with a propensity for breaking into clammy, prolonged sweats when subjected to any kind of stress. He suffered nervous ticks in his high, gaunt cheekbones which set his brows and eyelids twitching in alternating spasms. Perpetually dry lips—even though the rest of his body might be drowning—continually brought his tongue flicking forth like a snake to chase the dried flakes to a crusted scum at both corners. His eyes were set too close together to allow for normal vision, with the result that when he was not twitching, he was squinting myopically to see objects only a few paces away. His nose was long and hooked, his chin pointed, his skin—beneath the few scrawny hairs he was able to cultivate into a beard—was a pitted and pocked testament to a sickly childhood.

Sweating torrents, twitching spasmodically, and picking morosely at a favorite weal on his cheek, Onfroi paced before the smoking ashes of the campfire, tracing and retracing a worn path in the flattened grass. By his calculations it had been nearly eighteen hours since he had bolstered his courage enough to dispatch his messenger to Bloodmoor Keep. Given the time required to ride from Alford to the castle and back . . .

The sheriff came to the end of his measured track: halted, swiveled abruptly on his heel, and paced back.

. . . it would be well nigh onto midnight before a missive could return along the same route.

Onfroi paused long enough to squint out across the common on which his men had pitched camp. The abbey was nestled in a shallow valley, the monastery and its surrounding fruit orchards separated from the wide meadow by a sparkling ribbon of water. An orderly compound of buildings made of quarried stone and pitched slate roofs, the abbey was tranquil and rose-tinted in the dusk light, the air singing occasionally with the lowing of a lamb or a tinkling of a goat's bell. The small bronze bell in the priory had rung at dawn to call the holy brothers to mass, then had vibrated the stillness again at three-hour intervals until the last—Vespers—nearly an hour ago. It had allowed for plenty of time to go over every detail of the ambush again, to anticipate every question and demand that would come his way.

Onfroi swabbed his brow with the fold of his velvet sleeve. He could not even begin to imagine what form Wardieu's anger would take. Having witnessed all extremes in his ten years as sheriff of Lincoln, he was not certain which to dread the most: the cold, icy calm that caused an offender's bowels to turn to jelly; or the hot, rampaging fury that resulted in flesh and tissue being splattered in all directions. The man was a spawn of the Devil, no doubt about it. Unreadable. Unpredictable. Unfriendly. And unflinchingly possessive of his property. How should he be expected to react to the kidnapping of his bride?

Halt. Swivel. Pace.

There had to be a reasonable explanation of how thirty armed guards could allow themselves to be taken by surprise, stripped of everything of value, and herded out of the woods like guinea fowls, dressed only in shirts and chausses . . . but what was it? By what possible *reasonable* logic could he, Onfroi de la Haye, hope to explain how an outlaw had managed to dig himself a forest lair that had defied discovery for nigh on two months now? How could he begin to explain the existence of a spectre in black wolf pelts who struck and vanished, struck and vanished and never left so much as a turd behind to show he had ever been there? Men could not track him. Hounds could not track him. Armour —no matter how thickly forged—could not deflect his bowmen's arrows, nor could the swiftest of horses outmaneuver the silent death that stalked them from the greenwood.

Halt. Swivel. Pace.

Reasonable? The very word mocked him. Why, by the Devil's loins, could he—Onfroi de la Haye—have not contented himself with the two small estates his father had bequeathed him? Why, by the fruit of those same viperous loins, had he allowed Nicolaa to push and prod and manipulate him into seeking the appointment as reeve of Lincoln?

Nicolaa! Bah! A beauty to look at, but long ago corrupted by greed, ambition, and a lust for immortality. She was a clever bitch. Cold and conniving. And so in love with herself it was no surprise she had little room for anything else in that frigid heart of hearts. Onfroi knew he was a laughingstock because of Nicolaa's excesses. Truth be known, it was just as well she sought her perverted pleasures in every other bed but his own; truth be told, he was more than a little afraid of where those perversions might lead someday. Blood and pain delighted her; torture was viewed as an evening's entertainment; a victim's disembowelment was a prelude to a hearty feast.

A bitch, a reclusive warmonger, and a vengeful wolf's head. Was it any wonder his blood had turned sour and his belly ran liquid from morning till night?

Halt. Swivel . . .

Freeze!

Onfroi stood stock-still, his eyes briefly startled wide enough to show the red-veined whites. A low and distant rumble was drifting toward them from the east, carried on a breeze that smelled of sweat and anger.

Christ Almighty! Could it be Wardieu already? If so, he must have ridden out of Bloodmoor in the dust of the messenger, and by the sound of it, brought his entire castle guard!

A panicked glance around the campsite caused the veins in Onfroi's neck to swell and pulsate. Half of his guards were lounging about in blank-eyed boredom, the others were gathered about a tapped keg of ale.

"Insolent oafs!" he screamed, kicking viciously at two men who were stretched out, fast asleep. "Up! Get up, damn you!"

He ran across the grass, boots and fists launching out at anyone foolish enough to remain in his path. "Lazy, insolent oafs! I'll see how easily you sleep with hot irons poking out of your skulls! Arrest those men!" he shouted, pointing at the two unfortunates. "Get them out of my sight before I take a knife to them here and now!"

"God curse me for a fool," he continued, ranting to himself, searching for more flesh to abuse in the scattering troops. "It is no wonder that damned wolf's head has no fear of the forest. He could be a dozen paces away . . . *pissing into the soup pot!* . . . and not one of these oafs would notice!"

Onfroi ran out of obscenities just as the thunder of hooves rounded the sweeping mouth of the valley. Wardieu's destrier commanded the lead; a huge white beast, a trained rampager hewn from solid muscle, with the blazing red eyes and flared nostrils of a demon bred in hell. His master was hardly less fearsome. Riding tall in the saddle, his blue mantle rippling out from broad, armour-clad shoulders, Lucien Wardieu wore an expression of cold, grim fury. Directly behind were his squires, their mounts less formidable but still throwing back clods of torn earth on every galloped pace. In their ominous wake, two score of armoured knights appeared, each wearing surcoats embroidered with the Wardieu dragon, but carrying kite-shaped shields emblazoned with their own distinctive crests and arms.

"God in heaven," Onfroi muttered, and fought to suppress the urge to cross himself. It was worse than he thought: Among the warlike faces of Wardieu's vaunted army of mercenaries, was the one countenance in particular that caused his sphincter muscle to lose control.

D'Aeth. A huge, brooding bulk of a man whose face was so hideously scarred it went beyond the normal bounds of ugly. As bald as an egg, as broad as a beast, he was Wardieu's subjugator, and there, dangling from his saddle like a tinker's wares were the dreaded tools of his profession —iron pincers for the crushing of bones and testicles, leather straps and studded whips, a long thin prod with a wickedly barbed five-pointed tip (the purpose of which did not bear thinking). Who was Wardieu planning to have tortured?

De la Haye willed away a wave of nausea as the baron's warhorse pounded to a halt in a swirl of grass and flayed earth. Wardieu sat a long moment, glaring around the makeshift camp, then swung a leg over the saddle and vaulted to the ground.

"M-my lord Lucien," Onfroi stammered, rushing over at once. "I did not anticipate your arrival so soon."

The piercing blue eyes came to rest on the sheriff's sweating face. "Obviously there were a great many things you did not anticipate these past two days, De la Haye."

Onfroi repressed a shudder. The baron's voice was calm enough, but then so was the wind in the eye of a hurricane.

"You have prisoners?"

"P-prisoners? No, my lord. Unfortunately no, the outlaws moved too swiftly. By the time the survivors had reached us at the fens, the men who had perpetrated the ambush were scattered in a hundred different directions. That is their habit. To strike with the speed of vipers and vanish in the undergrowth as if they had never been."

Wardieu's face was as blank as a stone. "You know them well enough to have established their habits? Then this is not the first time this particular band of vermin has appeared in these woods?"

A violent tic in Onfroi's cheek closed his left eye completely. "Th-there have been rumours, my lord, nothing more. Rumours of a man who dresses in wolf's pelts and plagues the merchant caravans traveling to and from Lincoln Town. But they are only rumours. You yourself are aware of how these local peasants exaggerate the smallest incident into an adventure of epic proportions, especially when the outlaws perpetrate their crimes in the name of Saxon justice."

"The Bishop of Sleaford will be pleased to hear you refer to his mishap last month as a 'small incident,'" Lucien remarked coldly. "As will the Lady Servanne."

Onfroi's tongue slid across his lips. "There is no proof the two crimes can be attributed to the same villains, my lord."

"Oh? Then you would have me believe there are two packs of wolves hiding out in these woods? Two separate packs who have managed to elude your patrols for . . . how long? A month? Two months?"

"We have searched, Lord Lucien," Onfroi whined. "The patrols have been doubled and their frequency increased. Hounds have been put to the scent every day. Foresters have been brought from the villages to aid the search. No one sees anything. No one hears anything. Spies do not return, and, if their bodies are found, they have had their throats slit and their tongues pulled through the gap. The Saxon rabble do nothing to help. Why, only last week we burned an entire village to the ground and hung the peasants one by one, but none would betray the outlaws. Not a single man, woman, or child would speak to save his own life."

Wardieu's lips compressed around a grimace. "Your methods are as crude as your abilities, De la Haye. Did it not occur to you that slaughtering an entire village would only provoke this Black Wolf—if he is one of them—to retaliate twofold? Did it never occur to you to warn me that guests traveling to my demesne might have some reason to fear for their safety?"

"The men ambushed this time were your own!" Onfroi blurted unthinkingly. "Christ above! Who would have thought *for an instant* that Bayard of Northumbria could not outwit a band of half-starved woodcutters and thieves! *He* was well aware of the threat, if you were not. *He* at least ventured out of the castle now and then to listen to tavern gossip!"

Wardieu halted in the act of removing his leather gauntlets. The look he gave De la Haye brought forth an immediate, gasped apology.

"God spare me, what I meant to say . . . I mean, what I did *not* mean to imply, er, to say . . . that is, what I meant was . . ."

Wardieu turned his back and signaled to one of his mercenaries. "Cull a dozen of your best men and go to where the ambush occurred. Search the area thoroughly. A man on his own can seem to disappear easily enough, but not a score or more, and not if they took women and packhorses. I want to know *exactly* how many are in this wolf's pack, and in which likely direction they headed. And I want results, Aubrey de Vere, not excuses."

"You shall have them, my lord," declared De Vere and wheeled his big horse around.

While the selections were being made, one of the knights who had gathered with the other silent onlookers from the sheriff's camp, limped forward, his gait favouring a wounded, bandaged thigh. He was neither tall nor especially pleasant-featured, but he was obviously a seasoned veteran of many battles, and when he spoke, it was with a voice that sounded like two slabs of rock grinding together.

"Sir Roger de Chesnai," he said in answer to the question in Wardieu's eyes. "I am captain of Sir Hubert de Briscourt's guard, and was part of the escort sent to protect Lady Servanne."

"I should not brag about a job ill done," Wardieu said, removing his steel helm and pushing his mail hood back off the sweat-dampened locks of tawny gold hair.

De Chesnai blinked, whether to clear his eyes of the fever-induced moisture that slicked his brow, or to absorb the insult to his honour, it was not revealed by his expression.

"Command fell to me when Northumbria was slain," he said, staring intently at the Dragon's face. "I would ask for the opportunity to return to the site of the ambuscade with your men, if you will permit it."

Wardieu glanced down at the blood-soaked bandaging. "Bayard was a good man. Before I would consider your request, I would know what happened."

De Chesnai flushed and balled his fists. "They dropped on us out of nowhere, my lord. Northumbria had taken the precaution of sending men on ahead to ensure the way was clear, but they must have died between one blink and the next, with nary a cry or shout to mark their passing. We found the bodies later, all four of them pierced clean through the heart; a dozen more were lost the same way when the main party was ambushed. They just came upon us out of nowhere. No sound. No sight of them, not even after they had made good their first kills."

Lucien waited until the wounded knight paused to grit his teeth through another fevered chill before he queried part of the story. "You said . . . their arrows pierced through armour?"

"Aye, lord. Some of the rogues use longbows, with arrows tipped in steel, not iron."

"Steel?" Wardieu repeated, his brow folding with skepticism. "Woodcutters and thieves"—he spared a particularly venomous glance toward Onfroi de la Haye—"using steel-tipped arrows?"

De Chesnai met the blue eyes unwaveringly. "Yes, my lord. And while none were wasted, none were retrieved either, as if they were in plentiful supply."

Wardieu recognized the importance of such flamboyance and rubbed a thoughtful finger along the squared line of his jaw. That the weapon of choice was the bow and arrow was not as much of a surprise as the fact that these outlaws used precious—and vastly expensive—steel in place of the softer, more readily available iron arrowheads. Iron had difficulty penetrating the bullhide jerkins worn as armour by common men-at-arms; they deflected harmlessly off chain mail worn by knights. Steel, on the other hand, tempered and hardened a hundredfold over crude bog iron, could slice through bullhide like a knife paring cheeze, and sever the links of chain mail with hardly more effort.

"Go on. What happened then?"

"The leader revealed himself, exchanged a few words with Northumbria, then slew him. Not without provocation, to be sure, for it was Bayard who loosed the first arrow, but I have it in my mind the outlaw would have slain him anyway. Something"—he looked steadily into Wardieu's face—"in the eyes spelled death."

"You said they exchanged a few words . . . what was said?"

"I was not close enough to hear, nor did they speak as if they desired an audience. But again, something in the outlaw's manner made me believe he knew the captain, and that Northumbria was startled into a similar recognition."

De Chesnai turned away for a moment, as if some part of his recollections had left a more disturbing impression.

"What is it? What are you remembering?"

Bayard of Northumbria had possessed the courage and fighting experience of ten men; who was he, Roger de Chesnai, to even suggest . . .

"He looked more than surprised, my lord. He looked shaken. As if he was seeing something that should not be there. In any case, he was certainly angered beyond reason, for he took up his crossbow and attempted to shoot the outlaw where he stood."

"And the outlaw?"

"He managed to aim and strike dead centre of the eye before the captain had even released the trigger."

"A fair bowman, then, you would say?" Wardieu questioned dryly.

"The best I have ever seen, my lord."

Wardieu studied the knight's haggard face a moment then stared out across the gold and pink avalanche of clouds rolling toward the setting sun. "Describe him to me. As clearly as you remember."

"I did not have a clear view, my lord, and the shadows were thick, but I could see he was very tall. Equal unto yourself, I should say."

"Hair? Beard?"

"Brown hair, my lord. Very dark. And uncut as the Saxons prefer it, although I would give pause to say the rogue was of that breed."

"Why say you that?" Wardieu broke in quickly.

De Chesnai answered with a shrug and a frown. "A feeling, my lord. A sense that all was not as it was meant to appear to be. Also, he wore a sword, and had the stance of a man who knew well how to use it."

Wardieu nodded, absorbing yet another bit of information. Common woodcutters and thieves would scarce be able to afford the steel to own a sword, much less possess the knowledge of how to use one to any effect.

"His face was coarsely shaven and well weathered. His

eyes were of no special colour. Gray, perhaps . . . or dull blue."

"Devil's eyes, they was," muttered one of the servants who had survived the ambush. "Not natural, they wasn't. Gave a man a chill just ter look into them—as if Satan hisself were inside the body gawpin' out."

"How would ye be knowin' that, Thomas Crab?" demanded a second voice, owned by a man who had the sense to keep his head lowered and his eyes downcast to avoid notice. "Ye had yer head tucked 'atween yer legs the minute ye saw that great bluidy bow o' his."

"Aye, an rightly so," the first man countered. "Cursed be the fool who watches the flight of a left-thrown arrow! Satan's own hand pulls the string, so it does."

Wardieu had only been half attentive to the outburst, but at this last righteous declaration, he again held up a hand to interrupt De Chesnai and stared at the servant.

"What was that about a left-thrown arrow?"

Before Thomas Crab could persuade his trembling legs to carry him forward to reply to the question, the pain pounding in De Chesnai's temples relented enough to smooth the frown from his forehead.

"By God, the fool is right, my lord," the captain growled. "The outlaw did favour the left hand. Why . . . there could not be five archers in all of England with his skill. Discover the name of the one who shoots with the Devil at his elbow and we will have the true identity of the rogue who dares to commit his crimes in your name!"

It was Lucien Wardieu's turn to feel his composure shaken. "He . . . *used my name*?"

De Chesnai stiffened slightly, his dark eyes flicking to the sheriff, but Onfroi was still too engrossed questioning his own sanity at offering insult to the Baron de Gournay to worry that he had neglected to include this rather astounding claim on the outlaw's part. Foremost in his mind, even as he sweated and twitched, oblivious to the conversation between the two men, was the expectant grin on D'Aeth's face. The watery piglet eyes were glazed with thoughts of bloodletting, and De la Haye treasured every drop that flowed through his veins.

"Was there . . . anything else in his appearance that you recall?" Wardieu asked, his voice sounding forced and ragged. "Anything unusual? Any . . . scarring, or . . . obvious disfigurements?"

"No, my lord. He was in full possession of all his limbs and appendages. There were no scars or brands that I could see. He was a big brute, to be sure, but it was possible he was made to look more so by the vest of wolf pelts he wore."

Wardieu forced himself to take a slow, steadying breath. For a moment there, he had almost thought the impossible. He had almost thought . . . but no. Despite the nightmares and the premonitions, the dead remained dead.

To cover his brief lapse he asked, almost as an afterthought: "The Lady Servanne . . . she endured the ordeal well?"

"As well as could be expected, my lord," De Chesnai answered, his loyalty for his mistress fairly bristling across his skin. "She was frightened, to be sure, but very brave and courageous. I thought she was wont to scratch the outlaw's face to ribbands when he dared use your name, but she was taken away unharmed, by God's grace."

Wardieu accepted this avowal of his betrothed's courage with a pang of guilt. If his life was dependent upon an answer, he could not have described in detail any given feature belonging to Servanne de Briscourt. The best of his recollections, as he had admitted to Nicolaa, presented her only as a pale shadow he had once glimpsed standing alongside the frail old warhorse, Hubert de Briscourt. It was the land he wanted, not the thrall of a bride. Prince John had already demanded and received an outlandish price for arranging his brother's seal on the marriage petition, and now, ten thousand marks was a great deal to pay for something he did not want. Unfortunately, there were too many equally rich and powerful men who knew of his hunger for the De Briscourt estates, and he could not afford to trust either Prince John's greed or an outlaw's promise to gain control of the lands.

"Unharmed," he murmured. "Then this"—he held up the blood-stained canvas sack—"does not belong to the Lady Servanne?"

"No, my lord. The wolf's head took it from one of the dead guards. All he added—and then only after a lengthy debate—was the ring."

"The ring?" Wardieu loosened the thong and emptied the contents of the sack onto his hand. The finger tumbled out freely enough and was tossed aside into the grass with no further thought. But an object caught up on some of the unraveled threads of jute, needed to be forcibly pulled away from the cloth.

It was a gold ring, and, even before Wardieu had wiped away the clinging bits of dried flesh and blood, he could feel an iron fist close around his heart and begin to squeeze.

The face of the ring was carved in the image of a dragon rampant, the band moulded to resemble scaled claws. A single bloodred ruby marked the eye, and, as it trapped the fading rays of the sun, it seemed to catch fire and reflect shafts of burning flame.

Wardieu's fingers curled slowly inward. His hand began to tremble and a fine white rim of fury etched itself deeply into the bitter set of his mouth.

"My lord—?"

The stark blue eyes seared through De Chesnai without seeing him. The grizzled knight took an involuntary step back, shocked by the depth of the rage and hatred that was transforming Lord Lucien's face into a terrible and terrifying mask.

"My lord . . . your hand!"

Lucien looked down. Forcing his fingers to open, he saw
that he had squeezed the carved fangs of the golden dragon
into the hollow of his palm, cutting the flesh and causing
blood to flow between the clenched fingers. Blood slicked the
dragon's body and shone wetly off the faceted surface of the
ruby eye. The sight brought another image crushing into
Wardieu's brain, stretching and swelling the bounds of reason until it verged on madness itself.

The image was of death. Death on the hot desert sands of
Palestine. The face of death had dark chestnut hair and
piercing gray eyes; it spoke with a curse and a vow to return
one day and avenge himself upon the world.

That day was finally here.

Death had come back to England.

8

Servanne slept twelve hours without so much as rolling from one hip to the other. She would have slept even longer if not for the loud blowing of a ram's horn from somewhere beyond the refectory walls, calling the outlaws to their evening meal. She awoke with a groggy, thick sensation stalling her eyelids, and would have gladly lowered her head to the furs again had she not caught a fleeting glimpse of the nerve-shattering glare Biddy launched at her from across the room.

"Biddy? What is the time? How long have I been sleeping?"

"I am not familiar with the hours these wolverines keep," Biddy replied archly, her back as stiff as a swaddling board. "There are no bells to toll Vespers; thus I have been praying quite fervently on my own for some time now."

"Praying? For what?" Servanne yawned.

"For salvation," Biddy declared. "For redemption in the eyes of God and man—assuming it is not too late to plead for forgiveness before either!"

"Oh Biddy—" Servanne frowned and stretched cozily within the warm cocoon of furs. "What are you talking about? What has happened now that requires forgiveness?"

"What has happened?" she demanded shrilly. "You can lie there and ask me what has happened? Better it is I who should be asking you—as if mine own eyes have not already given me the answers. Sweet Mary Mother in Heaven, I should have known it would come to this. I should have

known it was his intent from the outset. And *you*! I blame
only myself for what has become of you. Too innocent, you
were. Too much talk, too great the temptation. Oh yes, I
could see the temptation; who could not? Who could not?"

The older woman blew her nose savagely into a sodden
scrap of linen and cursed as she was forced to wipe her fingers on the hem of her tunic. In the next wailing breath, she
resumed her self-condemnation before an utterly confused
and bewildered Servanne de Briscourt.

"In all of my eighteen years as your nurse and companion,
I never dreamed I would bear witness to such wanton behaviour. From other women—plain women, common women,
trulls and whores, oh yes, I should have expected it and
known how to deal with their urges. For women such as
those, taking a lusty man to their beds is as commonplace as
lifting a leg to piss."

"Biddy!" Servanne gasped, jolted wide awake.

"But you! I thank the Lord your sweet, saintly mother did
not live to see such a thing. And with such a one as *him*!
Sweet *Jesu,* had I but suspected such a need in you, I would
rather have seen you serviced by one of the guardsmen along
the way—"

"Biddy!"

"—than by that great, lustful brute! At least it could have
been arranged with some discretion! Not like this! Not . . .
not *brazenly* walking through the hall, with him naked as a
bull and you"—Biddy waved a hand in unfathomable distress—"*you* hanging off his neck, looking as if you could
scarce wait to have a bed beneath you!"

Servanne made a strangled sound in her throat and sat
bolt upright. "Biddy! What are you saying? What are you
accusing me of doing?"

"Do you deny you were hanging off his neck when he
carried you in here?" Biddy demanded with narrowed eyes.

"I was not *hanging off his neck*! I was in a faint!"

"So would any normal woman be to see the size of him," came the scandalized retort. "Curse me if I did not think he had grown a third arm to support you!"

Servanne flushed. "Biddy! He was naked because he was bathing in the pond. I fainted because I was . . . I was exhausted—you, of all people should know why! And he must have carried me back here because I could not walk the distance on my own."

Biddy stopped fussing with the bit of linen long enough to arch a brow sardonically. "And I suppose he helped you out of your clothing because he was concerned they might choke you in your sleep? I suppose he remained with you in here for nigh unto an hour because he was worried you might not be able to fall asleep on your own?"

Servanne clutched the layer of furs to her naked breasts. "He . . . unclothed me?"

"He did indeed. *And* he enjoyed the view for considerably longer than it should have taken to fold the garments and lay them neatly aside—had he troubled himself to do so, that is."

Servanne followed an accusing finger and felt her mouth go dry at the sight of her gown and under-garments strewn across the earthen floor. She swallowed hard and pressed a trembling hand to her temple.

"I do not remember," she whispered. "I do not remember anything after I fainted."

Yet that was not exactly the truth either and she did not have to hear Biddy's snort of disdain to feel the heat creeping upward in her cheeks. She did remember something—a feeling, or a sensation of intense warmth and pleasure. But . . . it was not possible for him to have lain with her and not left something of his presence behind.

Servanne flung the pelts aside and examined herself critically, searching for bruises or faded blotches that would either condemn or vindicate her in Biddy's eyes. There was nothing, however. No marks on the ivory smoothness of her body, no scent of human contact, no telltale tenderness between her thighs. Surely a man of his size, his weight, his temperament would have left a mark of some kind, either branded onto her body or seared into her mind.

Lacking proof one way or the other, she drew upon her anger. "Where were you all this time? How do you know he was alone with me for an hour? Why were you not here by my side to defend and protect me?"

A new flood of tears sprang from the matron's hazel eyes. "I tried, my lady! Oh how I tried to run to your side! It was that wretched Woodcock who held me back. Firstly, he led me on a merry chase around the forest. Then, when he finally returned to the abbey—just in time to see the outlaw leader bringing you in here—the rogue drew his knife and bade me sit in company with several other ruffian misfits while his lord 'attended his private affairs privately.' To have moved or cried out would have earned a blade thrust into my breast, and I did not see how I, dead upon the ground of a pierced breast, could have been of any further use to you."

"What use are you to me now," Servanne snapped, trembling with anger, "when you refuse to believe me when I say I have no memory of what happened, and no cause to feel shame or guilt over my behaviour!"

A second anguished wail from Biddy's throat sent Servanne's eyes rolling skyward and her hands crushing against her temples. A further distraction—the swirl of her uncombed, unfettered hair around her shoulders—sent her anger boiling in another direction.

"Where is he? Where is the rogue: I shall have the truth from him myself!"

"Oh! Oh, my lady, no. No!"

"My clothes," Servanne commanded. "My combs, my wimple—where are they?"

"Not within my grasp, my lady," Biddy replied, sniffling

wetly. "What trunks were fetched with us in the ambuscade have not appeared since. Where they are or what has become of the contents, I cannot say."

"Never mind, then. Just help me dress."

Biddy hastened to collect up the scattered garments. The gown was slightly more crumpled and stained from its stay on the floor, as were the knee garters and short silken hose. The samite surcoat was nowhere to be seen, but Biddy removed her own plain gray mantle and wrapped it securely about her charge's shoulders for warmth. She was about to part and plait the tousled skeins of hair into more modest and manageable braids, but Servanne pushed the fussing hands away and swept out into the corridor.

After a moment's pause to gain her bearings, she followed the dank stone hall to the right. It emerged at the top of a shallow flight of steps overlooking the pilgrims' hall at a point midway between two of the roofless stone arches. The scene before her appeared much as it had the previous evening, with fires crackling in the roasting pit, and torches burning smokily from their wall sconces. Cauldrons bubbled steamy clouds of aromatic mist into the cooler air, adding to the dull sheen of moisture that clung to the charred walls and broken ribs of the abbey.

Trestle tables had once again been set in an open-sided square under the sheltered portion of the roof. *He* was sitting there on the dais, the vest of black wolf pelts reflecting glints of fire and torchlight. He was engrossed in a conversation with Gil Golden, but when the latter's eyes flicked to the far wall, the Black Wolf stopped and followed his stare.

Servanne had no notion of the image she presented, nor would she have cared a potter's damn if she had. The dark woolen cloak she wore completely encased her slender body from shoulders to toes, leaving only the wild, voluminous cascade of silver-blonde hair to outline an ethereal image against the shadows. The ghostlike apparition startled sev-

eral of the outlaws, even those who were open in their scorn
for the legends and superstitions surrounding Thornfeld Abbey. Many went so far as to reach instinctively for their
weapons before recognizing the figure as being of this mortal
earth.

The Wolf rose and walked slowly around the end of the
table and down the hall. If not for the fickle light that kept
his features veiled in shadow, she might have noticed the
strange gleam that mellowed the gray of his eyes, softened
them, even, to a shade verging on pale blue.

"I trust you are feeling better for your rest?" he asked.

Servanne said nothing until he had come to a full halt
before her. When she did speak, it was in a voice so low he
almost had to bend forward to hear.

"I trust you enjoyed the liberties you took *while* I was
resting?"

"Liberties, my lady?"

"How dare you *touch* me," she snapped, "let alone remove
so much as a slipper from my foot!"

"Ahh," he said, and straightened. "*Those* liberties. You
would have preferred to sleep in cold, wet clothes?"

"My clothing was not wet," she objected. "I was no nearer
the edge of the water than I am to you now."

His grin broadened. "You were very nearly headfirst into
the mud and weeds had I not caught you in time. Furthermore . . ." His gaze raked appreciatively down the shapeless form of the cloak and left no doubt as to what he recalled seeing beneath. "I did what any chivalrous fellow
would do to save his lady the possible discomfort of fever or
flux."

Servanne clenched her small hands into fists. "I am *not*
your lady. And if you were so concerned over my health,
why did you not call my waiting-woman to attend me?"

"I could have," he agreed blithely, "but I thought it a
convenient opportunity to assess the precise value of the

goods I am holding to ransom. Had I done so earlier, I heartily believe I would have put a much higher price on returning them undamaged."

"Then . . . you did not—" Servanne bit her lip, resenting the flow of ruddy colour that made his smile widen further.

"I am crushed, indeed, my lady, that you should have to ask."

"Biddy believes you did more than see to my comfort. She does not believe I have no recollection of what happened after I fainted beside the pool."

"My reputation as a lecher will be in shreds," he murmured.

"Did you or did you not take ill advantage, sirrah?" she demanded, giving her foot a little stamp of annoyance.

"If I did?"

"If you did"—she searched his face in vain for a trace of humanity—"then you are a lower, viler creature than ever I could have imagined."

The Wolf laughed. "I was under the impression your estimation of my character could sink no lower than it was already."

"I have erred before in crediting a man with too much character," she retorted. "For that matter, most men in general tend to show a glaring lack of consistency when their true faces come into the light."

"Spoken like a woman who is tired of being sold into marriages with one stranger after another."

"Nay, wolf's head. I am simply tired of men who continually deign to know what is best for me and who then proceed to rearrange *my* life to suit *their* needs."

"And what needs, might I inquire, would you prefer to have tended?"

Servanne flushed again. "*Mon Dieu,* but you are an exasperating cur! Will you or will you not answer my question truthfully?"

"Truthfully—" He said the word in such a way as to raise a spray of gooseflesh along her arms. "Had I seen to my own comforts as well as yours, you would not now have the shield of a blank memory to hide behind. Nor would there be a need to ask what manner of liberties I had taken, for your body would still be singing their effects loudly and clearly."

Servanne's jaw dropped inelegantly. She took a small, stumbling step back, and then another, but before she could turn and run from the mocking gray glint of his eyes, a sharp *fff-bungg*! split the air and left an ashwood arrow quivering in the wooden arch beside her. A shriek sent her jumping forward and the Wolf suddenly found himself standing with an armful of trembling, soft femininity.

"Runner coming in, my lord!" someone called.

"Who?" the Wolf asked, not troubling himself to turn around.

"Sigurd's handiwork," said Gil Golden, noting the arrow's fletching with a wry grimace. "No one else wastes so much quill."

None of the other outlaws contributed comments. None even appeared to have heard Gil's, or so it seemed to Servanne. Everyone—the men at the tables, the men not yet in their seats, even the two women who bent over the cooking fires—all of them stood frozen in place, like statues turned to stone. Apart from the hiss and crackle of the fires, there was only silence. A silence so acute that when a second arrow streaked through the darkness to strike the same archway, one could almost swear to have heard the resonant twang of the bowstring.

Like magic, the tableau dissolved. The men and women resumed their conversations and their tasks at hand. Servanne, having once again buried her face in the protective thickness of the wolf pelts, felt a pair of gentle hands pry her loose.

"We use the double signal to ensure the men coming in are

our own," the Wolf explained. "Even those who possess lim-
itless courage have been known to give away the deepest of
secrets under expert torture, and, since it is not inconceivable
to assume the sheriff has sent his pack of hounds out after us,
we have arranged different signals for each day."

"Bah! Old Noddypeak should have chased his tail into a
fine tangle by now," Sparrow chuckled, materializing out of
nowhere. "Especially since he was sent chasing it in ten different directions."

"I should think Sigurd will be bringing news of a new
hound in the forest," the Wolf mused thoughtfully. "One
whose nose is tuned to a sweeter scent."

Wardieu, Servanne realized, the excitement flaring within
her like a sudden flame. Lord Lucien Wardieu was in the
forest, come to rescue her from this . . . this . . .

With a start, she became aware of how close she was
standing to her tormentor. Her fingers were curled around
shanks of gleaming black fur; his hands were still resting on
her shoulders, the intimacy of the contact hidden from view
by the flowing mass of her hair, but one that was felt most
disconcertingly throughout every inch of her trembling flesh.

His potent maleness was unsettling; more so when a vivid
picture of him flashed into her mind and remained there—a
picture of him standing naked in the knee-deep water of the
Silent Pool, his flesh steaming, his muscles rippling beneath
the sheath of taut skin.

Conscious of the fact that he seemed to have little difficulty in reading her thoughts, Servanne quickly lowered her
lashes and extricated herself from his embrace. As before,
she missed the flicker of colour that came and went in his
eyes, nor did she see the way his fingers curled and hoarded
the distinct, tingling memory of her warmth.

"I would like to return to my chamber now," she said.

"Whereas I would enjoy your company beside me at the
table again."

"I am not hungry."

"I am. And unless you would care to see my appetite roused for more than food, you would be wise not to attempt to defy me in this."

Servanne looked up. The promise was there for a blind man to see, as was the disturbing realization it had only been by the slenderest thread of chance she had awakened alone in her bed.

"I . . . should at least like to make myself more presentable," she said tremulously, reaching up with an unsteady hand to smooth the flown wisps of her hair.

"You are more than presentable just the way you are," he insisted, extending an arm in a mockingly gallant gesture.

Servanne doubted she could touch him again and come away unscathed. She gathered the folds of her skirt and cloak in her hands to lift them clear of the fouled rushes on the floor, and, with as much indifference as she could put into the tilt of her chin, preceded him to the raised dais.

The meal progressed as it had the previous evening, the exception being that Servanne shared her settings with the outlaw leader rather than with Sparrow. The latter, happily taking on a joint of mutton almost as large as he was, kept the conversation light and easy, but though he tried his valiant best, failed to win a smile from their silvery-haired hostage. He assumed it was because she had overheard Sigurd's report, delivered halfway through the meal, that there was indeed a new player in the game of hide and seek. While he was not far wrong in his guess, he was not exactly right, either. For every one thought Servanne had concerning the whereabouts of the Baron de Gournay, she had three for the man who sat on her right-hand side—the man who met her gaze each time without a hint of shame, or guilt, or regret; just the infuriatingly smug self-assurance of someone who believes his way is the only way.

"Who are you?" she asked quietly. "Why have you come to Lincoln?"

"I have already told you who I am."

"You have not told me why I should believe you."

He seemed to want to smile at that. "Have I ever lied to you?"

He was looking at her, into her, through her, and Servanne felt the flesh across her breasts and belly tighten, as if left on a tanner's rack too long. "As far as I know, you have lied to me about everything."

"Everything?" he asked, his thigh brushing not-so-accidently against hers.

Servanne shifted on her stool and laced her fingers tightly together on her lap. "You have lied about who you are, and what you are," she insisted softly. "You hide behind the lincoln-green badge of an outlaw, yet your motives for being here in these woods have nothing to do with bettering the conditions of the poor, or righting injustices committed in the king's name, or fighting against oppression—real or imagined. You have gathered about you a few local villagers to give some credence to the charade, but you are not from these parts. I doubt you have been in England as long as it took to grow the hair past your collar—or long enough to know there have been no black wolves in Britain since King Henry laid a high bounty on their pelts. Certainly not enough to fashion so fine a mantle, or be willing to throw so casually on a bed."

The Wolf was mildly taken aback; moderately impressed. After some consideration for the surprised silence that had fallen over the other outlaws seated on the dais, he carefully wiped the blade of his eating knife clean, sheathed it, and stood up, indicating the door with a tilt of his head. "Come. Walk with me. There is but a half moon tonight, perhaps enough to hint at what the gardens may once have held."

"Absolutely not!" she gasped, horrified at the suggestion.

The Wolf gave her a moment to reconsider of her own accord, then leaned over close enough that his words went no further than her pink-tipped ears. "You can either walk with me now, or lie with me later; the choice is yours where we take a few words of private conversation."

The mist was more pervasive out-of-doors. Thick, opalescent sheets of it swirled at knee level over the slick cobbles, masking the weed and rot, the neglect, and the decay. There were no torches lit outside the hall, but as Servanne's eyes adjusted to the faint light of the crescent moon, she could see the vague outlines of the other ruined buildings, the stone cistern in the centre of the court, the vine-covered arches that formed a narrow walkway leading toward the chapel. She was thankful for Biddy's warm woolen cloak, and drew it close about her shoulders. Tiny droplets of mist clung to her face and throat, and coated her hair like a fine-spun silver web.

"The gardens are this way," said the Black Wolf, walking toward the arches. "If you look closely enough, you can still find the odd wild rosebush growing amongst the bracken."

How vitally important to know, Servanne thought angrily, stepping around a jagged gap in the stone cobbles. She stretched her arm out for balance, startled slightly when she felt his huge, warm hand take hold of hers. Rather than jerk it away and appear twice the fool, she permitted the infringement until the footing was once again solid beneath her. A short distance into the steeped silence of the ancient gardens, she balked completely, refusing to go another step in the company of a man whom she had every reason to believe would kill her without hesitation if the situation arose.

"Who are you?" she asked again. "And why have you come to Lincoln?"

He stopped on the path just ahead of her and slowly

turned around. "My name is Lucien Wardieu," he said quietly. "And I have come home."

"You *say* you are Lucien Wardieu, but if you are, why do you hide here in the forest like a common outlaw? Who is the man who is now residing in Bloodmoor Keep? Why has he taken your name if it does not belong to him? And how has he managed to keep it all these years without anyone challenging his identity before now?"

The Wolf crossed his arms over his massive chest and leaned back against one of the arches.

"A great many questions, my lady. Are you sincere in wanting to know the answers?"

"I want to know the truth," she said evenly.

"The truth should not require proof, and a man should not have to prove who he is if he swears to that truth upon his honour. I know who I am. So does the impostor residing at Bloodmoor Keep."

"That . . . impostor, as you call him . . . has ridden to war with Richard the Lionheart."

"I do not doubt he has."

"Prince John trusts and confides in him."

"You would use such a recommendation to vouchsafe a man's character?" he scoffed.

"It has even been whispered that if John ascends to the throne, he will be sufficiently indebted to the Baron de Gournay to appoint him chancellor, or marshal!"

"John Lackland does not bear up well under debts; he prefers to hire assassins to repay them. As for his ascending the throne—how do these whisperers of yours say he will overcome the annoying matter of Prince Arthur of Brittany?"

Servanne bit her lips, sensing yet another verbal trap looming before her like a snake pit. Of King Henry's five sons, only Richard—the eldest—and John, the youngest, were still alive. Geoffrey, next to youngest, had died several yéars ago, but had left as his heirs, a son and a daughter. Since he would have been in line to the throne after Richard, the right of succession would naturally pass to his son Arthur upon the king's death, and after him, his sister, Princess Eleanor.

The snakes in the pit writhed a little closer as Servanne offered lamely, "But Arthur is only a child. Prince John would never—" She stopped again, catching the treasonous thought before it took on substance.

The Wolf held no such reservations.

"John would never kill his own nephew? My dear deluded lady: Prince John of the Soft Sword would kill his mother, his wife, his own children if he thought their removal would win him the crown of England. How long do you suppose Richard would have survived poison in his cup if he were not already hell-bent on killing himself on the end of some infidel's sword?"

"I do not believe you," she said without much conviction. "Not about Prince Arthur, at any rate. And besides, he is quite safe with his grandmother, Eleanor of Aquitaine, in Brittany. *She* would never allow any harm to befall him, most decidedly not at the hand of her own son!"

The Wolf looked away, looked up at the slivered moon for a long moment, then looked back at Servanne. "What if I were to tell you an attempt has already been made on the prince's life? What if I told you he and his sister were kidnapped from the dowager queen's castle at Mirebeau four months ago?"

"Kidnapped?"

"Stolen away in the middle of the night under the eyes and ears of a thousand of Eleanor's most trusted guards. It took a full week just to discover how the kidnapping was done—a rather cleverly executed gambit, I might add. Two men shinnied up the small tower that carries the castle wastes down into the moat. Someone should have smelled the pair about their task if nothing else, but alas, no one did, and the children were smuggled out the same way.

"Luckily," he continued with a sigh, "their escape from Brittany was not so well planned or executed, and Arthur was safely retrieved before he could be put on board a ship for England. One of the men involved in the kidnapping was taken alive and revealed quite an interesting tale to his, ah, inquisitor. The more questions that were asked, the more answers were received, and in the end, most of the pieces of the puzzle made sense once they were fit into place."

"No! It makes no sense at all!" she cried. "Why would anyone want to kidnap the prince? He is but a child."

"A child first in line to the throne," the Wolf reminded her. "Keeping him prisoner, or better yet, bending his mind enough to eventually have him judged insane, or incompetent to rule . . . John would be the natural choice to assume the throne in his stead."

"You are forgetting the Princess Eleanor."

"The sister of a mad prince? Hardly a likely candidate."

"So you think John was behind it?"

"No one else would have half so much to gain."

Thrust and counterthrust. Talking to him was like taking a lesson in swordplay.

"Has the queen challenged John with the accusation?" she asked.

"Challenge a ferret to explain the feathers stuck to his mouth? What good would come of it, especially when the chick came to no harm?"

Servanne's brows drew together in a frown. "You speak with a great deal of liberty and familiarity. I hope . . . I *trust* you are not daring to imply that you hold the queen's confidence?"

"Me, my lady? By your own words a rogue and wolf's head?"

"A rogue most certainly," she said carefully. "But as I

said before, no more born to the forest than I was. I may not know *who* you are, sirrah, but I do know *what* you are, and have known from the instant you stood your challenge to us on the road."

"Have you now," he mused, his eyes catching an eerie reflection from the moon. "Suppose you tell me what you know . . . or think you know."

"Will you tell me if I am right?"

"That depends on how right you are."

Parry, and thrust. Servanne accepted the challenge, however, knowing this was as close as she was likely to come to a confession, or an admission.

Mimicking his arrogant stance, she crossed her arms over her chest and slowly walked a half-circle around him, inspecting the powerful body with a detachment better suited to choosing livestock at a fair.

"Throughout most of my life I have watched knights training and fighting," she began. "I know the musculature of a well-practiced sword arm, and the look of limbs that are more accustomed to feeling horseflesh between them than soft deerhide. Your arms and shoulders have been thickened against the constant chafing of heavy chain-mail armour, and the scars I saw on your body this morning were not earned in a forest or on a farm, but on a battlefield, and in the tournament lists."

He said nothing to either confirm or deny her observations, and Servanne continued even more boldly.

"You carry your years well," she said, glancing speculatively up at the shadowed face. "But there are more behind you, methinks, than ahead. Five and thirty, I should guess."

"Too close by three to the grave," he chided dryly, "But commendable."

"Take away at least twenty of those years for the time it took you to earn your spurs, and that leaves . . . mmm . . . twelve full of mysteries to solve. Too many, I think, for one quick judgment, but shall I pick one or two for consideration?"

"I confess, I am intrigued, madam. Pray go on."

"Will you acknowledge your knighthood?"

"Will it change your opinion of me if I do?"

"Not one wit."

"Then I acknowledge it," he grinned, bowing to her cleverness.

"And yet," she murmured, almost to herself, "You are well schooled in the use of a bow—not a common weapon for a knight. In fact, I rather thought nobles disdained any knowledge of archery beyond the value of entertainment."

"The result of a physic's wisdom," he conceded, shrugging his broad shoulders. "He had some idea the drawing of a bowstring would quicker restore the strength to my arms while I recovered from my wounds."

Servanne spared a thought for the incredible corded tautness of his muscles and applauded the physician's judgment.

"And your men? Were they all recovering from wounds as well?"

"Wounded vanity, perhaps. They are a competitive lot and would not see their captain with a skill better than they possessed."

"Captain?" she asked, pouncing on the slip. "Past rank, or present?"

The Wolf took too long to answer, which was all the answer Servanne required to feel a surge of triumph.

"That you have been on Crusade is scarcely worth the breath to debate, but I would hesitate to put forth the suggestion that any infidel could have wrought such damage as in the scars I saw today."

"You question their skill as worthy opponents?"

"Oh, I have no doubt they are most worthy; both savage and dangerous, as well as fearsomely skilled fighters, else King Richard would have laid their army to dust years ago.

But to fight *you,* my lord wolf's head, they would have to have the added skill and knowledge of how to attack a man who favours the left hand. Most soldiers never encounter a left-handed opponent in a lifetime of battle and thus are rarely able to defend an attack, let alone overcome an enemy with your skill and strength. No. Whoever left his mark upon you knew exactly what he was doing. He knew where your weakest, most vulnerable points lay, and he struck at them with relentless accuracy. Moreover, he would have had to have been almost your equal in size and skill to have done as much damage as he did and live to walk away."

The Wolf frowned with genuine curiosity. "What the devil leads you to suppose he lived?"

"When you were bathing, you were very meticulous about touching upon each scar—a ritual of some sort, I imagine. Men do not continually refresh the memory of wounds delivered by dead men, only those delivered by enemies upon whom they might still seek revenge."

The Wolf fell silent. And waited.

"Therefore," she concluded, "we now have a man who was—or is—of the order; a man who makes vague claims to be engaged in the honourable service of Eleanor of Aquitaine, yet who definitely took a *dis*honourable foray into kidnapping so that he might . . . what? Revenge himself upon an old enemy? An enemy he claims has stolen his name and birthright?" Servanne stopped and glanced up in the darkness. "You call this supposed usurper by the none-too-amiable appelation of Dragon. What was he once called . . . friend?"

The Wolf shook his head slowly, too far into the battle to sound a retreat.

"Worse than that, my lady," he said with frightening intensity. "He was once called brother."

9

"*Brother?*"

"Bastard born, but nonetheless of the same blood."

Servanne stared. She had expected almost anything but this, and yet . . . the fact that they were brothers would explain a great deal. It would also present looming gaps in reason and understanding.

"Why?" she whispered. "How . . . ?"

"I told you one of the kidnappers was very cooperative? When pressed into revealing where they were to take the children in England, he indicated a castle in Lincolnshire—a castle on a cliff with a golden-haired dragon as master."

"Bloodmoor," she gasped.

"Until that moment, I had no idea Etienne was still alive." The Wolf paused and plucked a leaf from a nearby vine, then started to tear it into tiny shreds as he continued. "I have not set foot in England for nearly half a lifetime because so far as I knew, the De Gournay titles and estates had been stripped away years ago and dispersed against a charge of high treason."

"Treason!"

"A charge as false as my brother's heart," he said savagely. "But one that went uncontested while my father was deliberately starved to death in a traitor's cell. I had heard Etienne had died as well, a result of his conniving and greed, and had no reason to question his demise. I welcomed it, in fact, for it freed me to forget who I was and make a new life elsewhere. As it was, I was laid up some twenty months at a stinking desert oasis while these wounds you so expertly assessed healed. Another three years and more were spent gaining back memories the sun and fever had scorched from my brain. By the time I rejoined the living, Normandy had become my home and I was quite content to keep it that way. I sold my services to the kings and queens of Europe. I fought their wars, led their armies into battle, and won a reputation for myself as"—he stopped, seeming to reshape the words in midair before they tripped off his tongue—"as a rogue knight who would sell his sword to anyone with enough gold to pay."

A mercenary, Servanne thought. Yes. It fit. That much of it, at any rate, for there was no doubt he was a dangerous man, adept at living on cunning and nerve. He was clever, daring, unprincipled. And far too close.

She took what she hoped was an unobtrusive step back. "You called him Etienne?"

"It is his God-given name: Etienne FitzRobert, born to my father's mistress some three months after my own appearance in the world. It was said we were so alike in size, colouring, and temperament in those early years, we might well have sprung from the same womb. Even later, there could be no mistake we were of the same mould; his hair was lighter, his eyes darker, but all small things. Nothing that could not be altered or overlooked temporarily if one wanted to substitute for the other for a time. Moreover, we were both away five years under the desert sun. So much time spent in the heat, squalor, and stench of blood will alter any man's appearance, as well as dull the perceptions of those who welcome him home."

Servanne strained the limits of her powers of recall, trying in vain to conjure a clear picture of the golden-haired knight to whom she had been betrothed. Whether it was a trick of the mind, or simply the influence of the brooding figure in front of her, she could manage to do no more than replace the Wolf's darker locks with those of honey-gold, his coarsely stubbled, blue-black jaw with that of a clean-shaven mirror image.

Impossible! The whole story was impossible and implausible. How could one man take the place of another for nigh on twelve years without someone uncovering the ruse? What about friends and family? What about the servant who used to carry ale to the table and serve it to Lucien Wardieu? Surely *someone* would have noticed a change in his appearance?

The Wolf laughed softly, reading her thoughts as clearly as if they had been spelled out letter by letter across her face.

"My mother died within a few hours of my birth. Etienne's dam went mad and threw herself from a castle tower, screaming—so they say—that the Devil had cursed her. As to the rest—aunts, uncles, cousins—there were none. Or at least none who were close enough or cared enough to visit overlong at Bloodmoor Keep. Surely, as its intended chatelaine, you must have been forewarned of the horrors and spectres who roam the corridors and passageways? The walls that sweat blood? The footsteps in empty rooms? Stories all very carefully nurtured to keep the curious away."

Servanne studied him for another full minute without so much as a hair moving against the mist. "Why did he want to kill you?"

"Greed, among other things. Had I died a natural death, Etienne would have inherited some of the estates, to be sure, but not Bloodmoor, and never the title of Baron de Gournay. Those would have gone to a distant cousin—another clumsy fellow whose 'accidental' death occurred within a few months of the baron's heroic return from the Crusades."

"He could not have managed such an elaborate scheme alone," she said slowly.

"No," he agreed quietly. "He could not. He would have

needed someone's help to arrange the warrants for Robert Wardieu's arrest; he would have needed guarantees those charges could be rescinded again at the appropriate time."

"Prince John?" she gasped. "Are you suggesting Prince John was involved?"

"He shares a similar hunger for power and wealth, not to mention an ambitious jealousy for his brother's possessions. No doubt he demanded and received a huge payment for his services and seal, but I imagine Etienne thought the loss of a few properties a small price to pay. Especially since he has managed, by one means or another, to gain most of them back." The Wolf's eyes narrowed. "The acreage around Lincolnwoods is the last demesne of any importance to be reclaimed."

Servanne stiffened at this. The Lincolnwoods acreage was part of her dower lands, to be deeded to her new husband upon their marriage.

"Are you . . . do you *dare* to imply that Sir Hubert was a part of it?"

The Wolf regarded her with a calmness that did not reveal whether or not he had noticed she had moved a healthy pace away from him. "Sir Hubert acquired the estates innocently enough, in lieu of a debt owed him by the regent."

Servanne released her pent-up breath, but her head was spinning. It was too much to absorb, and there were too many twists and turns to try to unravel.

"Why should I believe you?" she asked, her fingers trembling visibly where they clutched the folds of her cloak. "Why, indeed, should I believe anything you tell me?"

"It is your prerogative, madam, to believe me or not. You wanted answers to your questions: I gave them."

"I wanted the truth."

"You wanted proof of the truth," he corrected her gently. "And that I cannot give you until I am inside the walls of Bloodmoor Keep."

Servanne's teeth bit sharply into the flesh of her lower lip. "If . . . *if* what you say is true, why do you not just step forward and declare yourself to be the real Lucien Wardieu? For that matter, who do you declare yourself to be? Surely Queen Eleanor would not employ among her retainers a rogue known only as the Black Wolf!"

A grim smile touched the saturnine features. "Actually, the queen did have a hand in coining the name."

"She believes your claim?"

The Wolf plucked another leaf and began destroying it in a similar fashion to the first. "In *truth,* I . . . thought it best not to burden her with all the sordid details of my past. Not just yet. She needed someone who knew the area—"

"She *sanctioned* a troop of her own men to sneak about the forests, thieving and murdering in the name of justice?"

The Wolf stared long and hard. He was not a man to tolerate continued skepticism, especially from a woman who was obviously accustomed to wielding her disdain like a sword to cut lesser beings to their knees before her. Moreover, he had already revealed far too much. Any further "truths" would be far too dangerous for her to know in the harsher light of day.

"The queen's methods and justifications are her own," he said coldly. "Suffice it to say she could not very well send an army into England."

"So she sent you? A man with blood on his hands and death in his eyes? A man who kills without thought or remorse; who takes women as hostages to act out his petty games of revenge! Truth?" She spat the word at him in a blaze of fury. "You would not recognize the word if it lay prostrate on the ground in front of you!"

He had had enough. Despite the two broad paces that now separated them, he was by her side before she could react to avoid him. A brutal and crushing grip on her wrists forced her even closer as he twisted both arms around to the small of her back.

"I gave you fair warning, madam," he snarled. "Yet still you seem bent on testing just how long it will be before *you* are the one prostrate on the ground."

"Was that not to be part of your revenge all along," she said bitterly, the anger crowding the fear in her eyes. "Was that not what you *intended* all along?"

"Madam," he said carefully, "had it been my intention *all along,* I would have had you on your back this morning, or last night, or, by *Christ,* in the glade when you first defied me to behave at my worst!"

"Should I feel gratitude then, that you have spared me this long?" she cried, her body beginning to tremble so badly, she would have crumpled to her knees if not for the support of his arms . . . arms that tightened further, forcing her to rise up on tiptoes and bring her face within a scant few inches of his.

"You should feel gratitude that I am not my brother," he said thickly. "Were our positions reversed, I have no doubt he would have had you chafed raw by now, merely for the pleasure of knowing he had been there before me."

Tears that had been collecting in shiny crescents along her lower lashes, splashed free on a horrified gasp and streaked wetly down her cheeks. Her chin quivered and her limbs shook like young saplings. The shock of contact was sending her senses reeling farther and farther from the bounds of reason and logic. She no longer cared who he was by name, she only knew . . .

"You are the Devil! Let me go!"

"The Devil?" he rasped, taken aback enough to grin sardonically. "So now you think I am the Devil?"

"Yes!" she cried. "Yes! Yes!"

For the longest moment, the ardent desire to shake her into oblivion was foremost in his mind, but then he saw the wide, wet path of her tears, and felt the fear, as vibrant within her as the trembling of a lamb being led to slaughter. The anger began to drain out of his hands, and the vengeance to fade out of his eyes, and he recalled the look on her face when she had seen his scarred body that morning.

"The Devil," he mused. "Deformed and maimed, capable of conjuring ghouls and grotesques . . . even *elfin demons* at the snap of a finger. Yes . . . I suppose the comparison is a fair one."

Servanne could not answer. She could not *think* for the scalding ribbons of fear, apprehension, and . . . anticipation that began to twist through her belly, circling, swirling, rushing to tauten the skin everywhere on her body until her flesh was so rigid, she feared the slightest movement would shatter her like glass.

"Look at me," he commanded softly.

Servanne opened her eyes, unaware she had sealed them tight against unwanted intrusion. The vast, dark breastplate of his chest filled her view; the heat of intimacy was like a flame, scorching and searing her through the layers of her clothing.

"*Look* at me, damn you."

She shook her head, and kept shaking it until he caught her face between his hands and forced it to tilt upward. Her eyes were slower to obey, climbing by halting fractions from the broad, strong column of his neck, to the angular savagery of the uncompromising jaw. Driven by dread from the blatantly sensual mouth, she found herself drawn into the deep, merciless centres of his eyes, and a smothered gasp sent her fingers clawing into the thick fur pelt of his vest. A surge of wildness rose within her—a wildness that changed, between one heartbeat and the next, from an all-consuming terror, to a sudden, terrifying desire.

"I am only a man," he insisted quietly, his words passing over her skin like velvet gloves. "I feel pain and I bleed like

any other mortal man. I have scars, yes, and deformities
hideous enough to be an offense to eyes as . . . innocent,
and . . . as lovely . . . as yours. Yet you have seen them
and survived. If you touched them, you would not burst into
flame or see the bones turned to ash on a devil's curse. Here.
You say you seek the truth—"

He released one cloudy fistful of her hair and pushed aside
the shoulder of his vest and shirt. He took her hand and
pressed the ice-cold fingers over the healed ridges of scar
tissue that serrated his flesh, and, while he would not have
admitted it, nor expected it, the shock of contact was no
longer hers alone.

Servanne stared at her hand where it lay against his flesh,
then at the strong, lean fingers that remained curled around
her wrist. She *was* melting. She *was* on fire. But the heat
came from within, not without, and the flames were spilling
down, pooling heavily in her loins, causing her to suffer
stark, bold images of two naked bodies fused together,
gleaming as they writhed under the mist and moonlight.

His hand moved again, traveling the miles from her wrist
to her chin, drawing her so close her neck was arched and
her hair dragged almost to her knees. His mouth was but a
breath away, then it too conquered the seemingly interminable
distance, claiming hers with a gentle pressure, shaping
her lips to his, challenging her to seek what further proof she
needed.

Proof? It was there—as she should have known it would
be—in the unholy thrills that assailed her with the deliberateness
of the caress. It was there when his tongue probed for
resistance, found none, and effortlessly breached her lips to
demand and win full possession of her mouth. And it was
there, flaring hotter and brighter, when she heard herself
moaning softly, helplessly in wondrous submission.

His assault became bolder and she could feel herself dissolving,
liquefying everywhere—breasts, belly, thighs. Un-

thinkable urges and desires began to flood her senses, defying her not to respond as her mouth was plundered, held captive with a ruthless tenderness her young body was not prepared to defend against, nor any too eager to repel.

She was powerless beneath that mouth, surrendering everything he asked—and more. When his hand dared to skim under the woolen edge of her cloak, it was all she could do to curl her arms more desperately around his shoulders, all she could ask for to cling to the drugging surety of his embrace. His hand moulded purposefully around the aching tautness of her breast, and she could have screamed from the pleasure. Yet it was the Wolf who made an indistinguishable sound deep in his throat.

He found the nipple a proud, hard bead, surrounded by flesh that was warm, supple, and lush with promise . . . and for the first time in too long to remember, he wanted to know where that promise led.

The questing fingers, not surprisingly, took her ragged little cries to mean she shared his awakening appreciation, and they traced a route of quivering invitations downward to the silky V at the juncture of her thighs. For all of two . . . three disbelieving gasps, Servanne welcomed the exquisite pressure of his hand, even shivering her limbs apart so that he might find some way to ease the incredible throbbing ache that was blinding her.

But somewhere in the growing shame of her need and his impatience, the spell was broken. Their mouths were pulled apart by feverish necessity and she saw him reaching for the clasp that held her cloak fastened around her shoulders. The ingrained response to such a liberty was to strike out . . . and she did. Her hand flew up and the palm caught him fully on the bronzed plane of his cheek, the crack of flesh on flesh sounding like the breaking of a quarterstaff.

The slap had no less a devastating effect on the tension strung between them. The Wolf jerked back, too stunned to do more than repress the trained response to return the blow. Servanne stumbled back as well, still shaken by the emotions he had unleashed within her, still burning, trembling, aching with the need for assurances she knew were beyond his ability—or desire—to offer. Her lips felt bruised, her body violated. She wiped the back of her hand across her mouth as if she could remove the taste and feel he had left branded upon them, but her hands were themselves victims of his overpowering maleness and could not be trusted.

"I should kill you for that," he said hoarsely, his face still turned away, his fists still clenched against the need for violence. "I may not be the demon you would take me to be, but in all good sense, madam, I would tell you to go. Now. Run back to the warmth and the light before I forget who I am and become what you would make me."

Servanne's eyes were two shimmering discs of moonlit tears as she whirled and ran along the broken path, her cloak belling out behind her, her haste startling small corkscrews of mist to whorl together in her wake.

Sparrow, stopped on the path by the sound of voices ahead, was nearly bowled top over toe by the sobbing figure who ran past. He had barely finished setting himself aright when an explosive curse, followed instantly by the fractious meeting of a fist against a hapless tangle of ancient grape vines, sent the wary fellow inching cautiously forward again.

"Is it a man or a wild boar loose in these gardens?" he queried hesitantly.

The Black Wolf wheeled around, the expression on his face rivaling the blackness of the night. His one hand was clasped about the wrist of the other, and, as he recognized Sparrow's diminutive form, he released the wrist with a savage oath and shook the spasms of pain out of the scraped fingers.

"I trust it is not a sudden dislike of grapes that makes you want to deny them further longevity," Sparrow remarked, wafting out of the fog like a faerie gnome.

"It is not the grapes I would deny longevity," snapped his glowering companion after a moment.

"Ahh." Sparrow puckered his lips thoughtfully. "Such pretty pieces usually do end up being more troublesome than appearances would imply."

"Troublesome?" The word was raked past gritted teeth. "You do the word an injustice. Vipers are troublesome. She-cats are troublesome. *That* one . . . !"

"Tut tut. You like vipers and she-cats well enough when your thoughts are not occupied elsewhere."

"Well then, thank the good Christ they *are* occupied. Saints assoil us—!"

"Here, give it to me, you great heaving lummox," Sparrow said, reaching up to catch the flexing hand. His stubby fingers prodded and probed the thicker, more heavily calloused ones and decided nothing was crushed or bent out of shape. "You might at least have put a foot to a rock instead of a hand through a wall of vines. Better still, a fist to the jaw that caused such an outbreak of distemper. A fair beating would have tamed her to your purposes soon enough, I warrant."

The Wolf reclaimed his hand with a scowl and sucked on a bleeding knuckle. "It would take more than a beating to tame that one, and a bigger fool than me to want to try."

Sparrow sighed expansively. "You have been lurching about the forest like a pissed newt since she first crossed your path. If the wench is proving to be so resistant to your overwhelming charm, why not just toss her on her backside and have done with it? It will not be the first time you have persuaded a reluctant pair of thighs to spread, nor the first time you have won a reluctant pair of lips over to singing sweet and long after a night in your bed."

"I doubt if rape would win her as a friend to our cause," came the dry response.

"You do not have to win her. Only unbalance her so that

there is room for doubt. She could prove a useful ally, not to mention a useful pair of eyes and ears to have inside the Dragon's lair."

"You place too much store in my abilities between the bed sheets."

"Not so much so as I have not seen you send a filly from your thighs as bright-eyed and addled as a drunken maybug. What is more: A woman who fights the hardest also falls the farthest. To my mind, our quivering little peahen appears more than ripe and ready for a steep tumble . . . and if not by you, then surely by her lusty bridegroom. I warrant he'll have no reservations about taming her."

Sparrow saw, by the Wolf's grimace, that his bolt had struck home, and did not know whether to be pleased or worried. Their leader bore heavy burdens on his shoulders, that much was indisputable, but would a dalliance with Servanne de Briscourt remove some of the pressure, or add to it? As it was, it had taken the strength and sheer brute force of a dozen stout men to keep the Wolf from going berserk when he had first learned his brother was alive and well and living in secluded luxury at Bloodmoor Keep.

Hearing of the impending wedding might have been the final straw—indeed, everyone in camp had braced themselves for an eruption of monumental proportions, for it did not take a scholar's wit to trace the blame for the Wolf's indifference to women (other than whores) to an event in his mysterious past. But to their surprise, he had taken the news calmly and coolly. He had even devised this clever plan to unsettle the Dragon and possibly open a breach in the impenetrable defenses surrounding Bloodmoor Keep.

Who would have thought a chick-pea with yellow hair and frosty blue eyes could have turned the tables and penetrated the armour around the Wolf's heart instead?

"Bed her," Sparrow advised sagely. "By rape or by charm,

it makes no matter, for 'tis a certainty the Dragon will expect
it. Would he do otherwise in your place?"

"I am not my brother," the Wolf growled, pricked by the
need to defend himself a second time that night.

"No, but you have aspired to put his bowels in a pinch.
What better way than to molest, ravage, or even marry his
bride from under him if it should suit your mood or purpose?"

"What if choking her suits my mood and my purpose?"

"Then I would hold her ankles for you while you did so,"
the little man said with a shrug. "Bedding her would bring
more pleasure to you, however."

"I am not come in search of pleasure."

"Revenge, then."

"I have it already, whether she leaves here bruised or
not."

"You mean . . . he will not believe her to be untouched,
whether she is or not?"

"Would you?"

Sparrow pondered it a moment. "No. But would you condemn her to all the pain and none of the enjoyment?"

"She takes the greater enjoyment in her own chastity and
purity. If anything, I should endeavour to give her a deal
more over the next few days. As much as she can bear in
maintaining those lofty heights of unblemished virtue. Yes,"
he said slowly. "Yes, I should send her away from here believing she is a far better person for having frustrated me at
my lusts and perversions."

"And when the Dragon affixes hot irons to her toes to
crimp the truth from her?"

"A few heartfelt screams should convince him of her righ-
teousness," he said evenly. "It will also convince her of *my*
purity and *my* selfless sacrifice for her honour. Furthermore,
he will not be alive long enough to crimp anyone's toes. Nor
would he attempt such a thing until the nuptials have been

witnessed and blessed, and the deeds to the dower estates locked in his strongbox. She should be safe enough behind her protestations until then."

Sparrow sighed. "It would be easier just to rape her. And far less of a strain on your own state of health."

"My health is fine," said the Wolf gruffly. "I would hasten to say yours might be in some jeopardy, but my own is fine, thank you very much. And now, if you have no more dilemmas to solve, or wisdoms to dole out, I suggest you fly on up to your nest and put your nose to sleep for the night to save it being wedged beneath someone's boot."

Sparrow scrambled prudently aside as the Wolf strode past him on his way back to the pilgrims' hall. His feathers ruffled, he muttered to himself as he followed a discreet distance behind, wondering why there was so little appreciation in the world for people who saw other people's problems so clearly, and could have resolved them so easily if allowed.

"Fine," he grumbled to the darkness. "Your shoulders are overburdened? Fine. Let her go to the Dragon with her fear of you still wet on her lashes. Let *him* warm her thighs with sympathy and compassion and see how long it takes her to decide that *he* is the real Lucien Wardieu, and *you* are the impostor! *Paugh!* Great heaving lummox," he finished querulously.

He emerged from the arbor of tangled weed and clinging vines and stopped dead in his tracks. Only his head and shoulders rose above the thickest layer of mist, making him look like just another of the stumps dotting the edge of the garden.

For a full minute . . . three . . . five . . . he remained utterly motionless, and was on the verge of cursing the fog for having raised the hackles on his neck, when he saw another flicker of movement out of the corner of his eye.

Someone else had been waiting, frozen against the shadows, questioning his instincts. It was not the Wolf, who, despite his size could slip about with enough stealth to cause bulk in a man's drawers over the suddenness of his appearance. It *was* someone who did not want to be observed, however, but because his patience had run out a split second before Sparrow's, was seen clearly as he melted from tree to tree and eventually ducked furtively through the gap in the outer stone wall.

"Hello?" Sparrow murmured under his breath. "Who are you and where might you be sneaking off to this time of the night?"

Nowhere necessary, he decided, since the privies and the stream were both on the other side of the grounds.

Sparrow debated sounding the alarm, but dismissed the idea as swiftly as it had formed. An alarm would send the men out into the woods, but he had seen nothing more than a blurred outline, thus the quarry could easily blend in with the searchers and return to Thornfeld, his secret intact.

What secret?

The sentries were not due to be changed for several hours yet. There were no villages close by, no whores with open thighs to lure a man and his coin into breaking trust with the camp—certainly not this way. Besides, the men had, for the most part, been together for several years; their needs and appetites were well known and always taken care of. Only Gil Golden and Robert the Welshman were recent recruits, but both had proven themselves above reproach.

Or had they?

Heedless of the Wolf's warning to guard his nose, Sparrow checked to see his bow was slung securely over his shoulder, and his quiver was full of arrows. He wasted no more time on his conscience, but moved quickly toward the same dark opening through which his quarry had disappeared.

Whoever he was following was very good; there was no telltale crackling of twigs, or crunching of leaves to betray the path he had taken. Then again, he was not as good as

Sparrow, who climbed hand over foot into the nearest tree and took his first marker from the disgruntled hoot of an unsettled owl.

It did not take him long to identify the prey he stalked, nor, after two hours of carefully trailing the Judas, was there any doubt the path they were taking led directly to the Dragon's camp at Alford.

10

The Dragon was not a man. He was not human, decided
Onfroi de la Haye as he fidgeted nervously on his stool, his
eyelids squinting alternately between the belligerent countenance of his wife Nicolaa, and the distracted, self-absorbed
features of the Baron de Gournay. Nicolaa had arrived in
camp several hours after the others, her palfrey lathered and
blowing hard to suggest she had striven valiantly to keep
apace with Wardieu and his mercenaries. But a palfrey was
no match for a warhorse, and true to his warning, Wardieu
had neither stopped nor given in to her outlandish demands
to be provided with a stronger steed. Venting her temper in
the wake of such a humiliating failure, had cost one of her
personal servants a severe whipping, and her groomsman a
broken arm.

Onfroi, knowing better than to interfere or to stay her
hand, had kept well away from the shrieking Fury until sheer
exhaustion had rendered his wife more amenable to human
companionship. Even then, he kept a prudent distance from
the small, wickedly knotted leather lash she used to emphasize her words and gestures.

A wooden trestle table had been erected in one of the
larger tents. A late supper had consisted of cold mutton and
hard cheese purchased from the dour monks at Alford. Conversation had been limited to a few perfunctory words exchanged between Onfroi and his wife; Wardieu had remained
gloweringly silent throughout the long evening. Onfroi knew

the look well enough, and did not like what it forebode. No, he did not like it at all.

"For pity's sake, Onfroi, stop squirming like a blistered worm," Nicolaa said, snapping the handle of the lash against the tabletop. She had regained most of the energy she had expended on the long, hard ride, and felt as tense in the unnatural silence as a bubble about to burst.

"Forgive me, my dearest. I was not aware I was . . . ah, squirming."

"Squirming, twitching, sweating—*Mon Dieu,* but you reek of a cesspool. Can you not go out and . . . and see if those lazy wastrels have groomed my poor Arabella properly? If not, if they have ruined her, I swear I shall whip the lot of them until the flesh is shredded from their miserable hides. I shall hang them by their entrails and—" She stopped and glanced up as Wardieu stood. "My lord?" Her voice was instant sweetness. "You have hardly touched a morsel of food. Will you not have more ale? Some grapes, or an apple perhaps?"

In lieu of answering, the golden-haired knight ducked through the opening of the tent and strode out into the darkness. He walked the length of the camp and came to a halt on the knoll that overlooked the slope of the valley. The lowlands were muffled under a pale blanket of mist, but high above the blackened crust of trees were thousands of pinpricks of starlight, and behind him, hung against the velvet sky like a gleaming sickle, was the thin, silvery rim of the moon. There were no lights showing from the windows of Alford. It was past midnight, and the monks, being frugal as well as bone-weary after toiling long hours in their daily duties, wasted no candlewax past the hour of Compline.

"What the devil can be keeping De Vere?" he muttered aloud. "He has been in that accursed forest for hours."

"You set him a difficult task, my lord," said Nicolaa, coming quietly up to stand beside him. She touched the sleeve of

his chain-mail shirt and ran her fingers possessively onto the
quilted thickness of his surcoat, sighing as if she found herself having to explain the very obvious to a petulant child.
"It was already dusk when you sent him into the forest; he
could hardly be expected to search in the dark."

"De Vere could track an ant through a meadow on a
moonless night. A two-legged wolf should present no great
problem."

Nicolaa lifted a brow delicately. It was not unlike Wardieu
to be cross and impatient in the face of inefficiency, nor to
become tense and intractable with too many hours of physical inactivity. Some of their more memorable trysts, in fact,
had taken place between bouts of a tourney, with him still
splashed with the blood of one opponent, and waiting feverishly to split the bones of another. The challenge of rooting
out this Black Wolf of Lincoln should have had a similar
effect on his carnal urges, and was one of the more prurient
reasons why Nicolaa had insisted on accompanying him to
Alford.

Yet this was no ordinary tension she could sense thrumming through the finely honed body. Something was distracting De Gournay, tempering the voracious appetite of
her prize stallion to the point where he had not glanced in
her direction once all evening—an affront to her vanity she
could not be expected to entertain in good humour.

"Lucien?" Her hand drifted downward, skipping over the
wide leather belt strapped around his waist, and cupped sug-
gestively around the slashed V where his chausses met beneath the hem of his surcoat. There was no response at all.
Not even a flicker on the angular planes of his face to show
he was aware of the invitation.

"Lucien! For the love of God—" She lowered her voice to
a throaty rumble. "You are acting like a man possessed. One
would think you would be grateful to this Black Wolf for
providing you with a solution to your problem. The marriage

contracts have been signed; you are as good as wed to the little bitch now. No court in the land would deny you your right to her estates simply because of the interference of a blood-lusting outlaw."

Wardieu turned and stared wordlessly.

"It is *perfect,* do you not see? Let him have her. Let him keep her. Send him your blessings as well as a sharpened blade to do the carving!"

He continued to stare, his gaze so cold and hard Nicolaa felt a corresponding rush of anger surge through her veins.

"First you claim she means nothing to you," she hissed between clenched teeth. "Now, suddenly, you are acting as if she means everything! I warn you, I will not be played the fool, Lucien. Not again. Not by you, or any man!"

"Was it you?" he asked in a disbelieving whisper. "Was this your poor idea of a jest, Nicolaa?"

"Was *what* my idea of a jest? Kidnapping the girl? Good my lord, were it my idea to take her and hold her to ransom, it would not have been her finger I had carved from her!"

"Then tell me . . . how did he get the ring?"

"What are you talking about?" she demanded archly. "What ring?"

"The ring he gave you as a pledge of his troth."

Nicolaa caught sharply at her breath. *"Onfroi?* That miserable circlet of gold he gave me—?"

"The *ring,* Nicolaa," Wardieu interrupted ominously. "The one worn by the rightful heir of the Wardieu estates."

"Lucien," she gasped. "Are you mad? What are you talking about?"

Wardieu held his rage in check with an effort, but even as he had voiced the accusation, he had known he was grasping at the wind. Such subtleties were not in keeping with Nicolaa's methods. If she had kept something as damaging as the ring all these years, she would have produced it and used it long before now to bend him to her will.

"I am talking about this," he said quietly and uncurled the fingers of his fist.

Wary of the threat of violence in his every look and gesture, Nicolaa slowly tore her gaze from his and focused on the ring that lay cradled in his broad palm. The gold sparkled dully and the ruby eye winked in the moonlight, but at first glance, she could see nothing unusual in the design. Dragons, serpents, lions, and other menacing grotesques were commonly worked into rings, crests, and armourial bearings. The craftsmanship in this particular ring was exceptionally good; the beast appeared to be on the verge of a strike, with the scaled jaws gaping and the forked tongue poised to spit flame.

Nicolaa's heart missed a beat.

She snatched the ring out of Wardieu's hand and held it up so that the light from the campfires would augment the glow from the moon and stars.

"God spare me," she whispered.

"God spare us both if you had no hand in this," he said tautly.

"Me?" She looked up, shocked. "You think I . . . !"

"If not you, Nicolaa, then who else?"

Her eyes grew rounder, wilder. "No! No, it could not be! There must be some mistake!"

"Look at the ring, Nicolaa. There is no mistake."

"A duplicate! It must be a duplicate!"

"Look at the ring, Nicolaa. There is no mistake."

She did not have to obey the command in the ice-blue eyes to know there would be a jagged point of gold marking where the tip of one of the dragon's ears had been broken off.

"But"—she gripped his arm and her voice became shrill with panic—"it cannot be. How can you believe he survived? *Mon Dieu*—all these years. He has been dead . . . forgotten! All these years!"

Wardieu's fingers pinched her arm cruelly as he led her

farther away from the curious eyes and ears of the camp. "Lower your voice, damn you. We have enough problems as it is without drawing a host of others down upon our heads."

She halted, dragging back on his arm. "A jest," she cried. "As you suggested, it must be someone's foul, bloodless idea of a jest!"

"Who else knows enough of the truth to make such a jest?" Wardieu took the ring out of her hand and thrust it up beneath her nose. "Bayard was the only other one—apart from Lackland—who knew more than he should . . . and Bayard is dead! Killed by someone he recognized; someone who, according to De Chesnai, *caused Northumbria to act as if he had seen a ghost!*"

Nicolaa's heart suffered another choking setback. "But you brought him down yourself! *You said you saw him die!*"

"I said there was no man on earth who could survive such wounds. I did *not* say I stood there and watched him die. He was my *brother*! I struck him down, I left him broken and bleeding on that hell of a desert. I could not stand over him and wait for him to die!"

"And for your compassion," she spat, "he has now come back to take his revenge. God's blood, he must be insane with hatred. But why has he waited so long? Why has he not come forward before now? And why this elaborate ruse as the Black Wolf of Lincoln?"

Wardieu's fist closed around the ring again. "He wants me to know he is there, waiting. Watching. He wants me to jump at every shadow, sweat over every morsel of food, challenge every new face I see. The Black Wolf: how appropriate. I should have guessed it right away. The wolf hunting the dragon hunting the wolf."

"What will you do?" she asked, hugging her arms through a sudden chill.

"Do, Nicolaa? Why, I will do what I must do, of course.

Come morning, I will dispatch a party back to the keep to collect the ransom."

"You intend to pay his outrageous demands?"

"I cannot see where I have any other choice," he mused, smiling tightly. "If I refuse to pay the ransom, he will take the greatest delight in sending the pieces of De Briscourt's widow to me in a series of tiny bloody sacks. When he does, whether it is the widow he slices or not, the news will travel the length and breadth of England like wildfire. Lackland will hear of it and panic. He will think at once that his own stupid schemes are at risk, and there will be bodies thrown from the parapet walls before he can be calmed enough to see reason."

"Calmed? Lackland? I was told he frothed for a week when he found out you were planning the wedding so soon. He should turn into a ravening madman when he hears about this. Can you not find this . . . this Black Wolf"— she hissed, unable to admit the spectre had another name— "and kill him before the threat goes any farther?"

"Find him? In these woods?" Wardieu scanned the dense fringe of tall pines and sweeping oaks that blackened the horizon. "You forget, he knows every footpath and deer track in this forest as if he were indeed a wolf and this his natural domain. My men could search for months and never come within bowshot. It was a game with him, almost since he was old enough to drag the weight of a sword behind him, to hide in the forest and defy Father's best gamekeepers and woodsmen to find him. Few ever did."

"A pity you did not indulge in his games," Nicolaa said dryly. "Then you might have known one or two of his favourite lairs and spoiled whatever his gambit might be."

"There is more than one way to trap a wolf," Wardieu said evenly. "And more than one kind of bait to use against a man's emotions."

The second chill that trickled down Nicolaa's spine caused

her to turn slowly and follow the direction of Wardieu's stony gaze. Silhouetted against the leaping orange flame of the main campfire were De Gournay's two squires, their heads bent forward as they dexterously cleaned and polished weapons that were already burnished to a mirror brightness. Rolf, the eldest by three years, had been fostered into Wardieu's care at the behest of a neighbouring baron who hoped his son could learn his skills at the feet of a master. Eduard, taller than his thirteen years would suggest and quicker to accept the increased responsibilities of his promotion from page to squire a year earlier, had also been a part of Wardieu's household since the tender age of six. Both young men were trustworthy, courageous, and loyal. Both burned for the opportunity to earn their own spurs of gold through deed or battle, and until then, to serve their powerful and mighty liege lord in whatever capacity demanded of them.

Nicolaa had never paid one more heed than the other, treating both with the same indifference she allotted any menial who sat below the salt. Only in moments of great weakness—or drunkenness—did she allow herself to remember the pain of giving birth, of pushing the screaming infant away from her breast, of banishing it into the north country so that no one should know or suspect its origins.

"Eduard has grown into a fine young man," Wardieu murmured in her ear. "A son any man would be proud of. A year or two more and he will no longer be content just to split Rolf out of a saddle, but will be turning his eye to me."

"When he was born," she said bitterly, "I wanted to take him out-of-doors and dash his brains out on the nearest rock."

"Ah, compassion," he retorted blithely, echoing her scorn of only moments ago. "It comes back to haunt us all, at one time or another. It will be interesting to see whose back Eduard will protect when he discovers the truth."

"He need never know the truth. He believes he is yours, bastard-born, as does every other pair of eyes in the shire. There is no living soul who could gainsay him differently. Not even I could swear by my blood or yours whose seed it was took root and swelled within me."

"Could you not? *Can* you not, Nicolaa? Look closer at the living flesh and tell me with all honesty—if you can—that you know not for certain where you have seen those eyes before, or warmed to that smile. Watch his hands, Nicolaa. Your servants did well in breaking him of the habit to favour the left, and I am sure he does not even remember a time when he did not grip a sword or a lance by the right. But the small things betray him. In the end, the small things betray us all."

Nicolaa was watching Eduard, but in her mind's eye, she saw only *him.* She saw him as clearly as if he stood before her now, his gray eyes almost colourless with resentment and disbelief. It was true, she had gone to him to beg forgiveness for her earthly sins and rampant appetite, but he could see nothing through those noble eyes but betrayal and impurity. In disgust she had torn the ring from her thumb and hurled it at him, and he had simply turned away and walked out of her life without so much as a glance back.

"Does it not rankle to see him every day?" Nicolaa asked, flinching from the robust sound of Eduard's laughter as it drifted past her on the cool night air. "How could you even take him in if you suspected he was sprung from your brother's seed?"

"The suspicion did not trouble me as much as it troubled you to know I had found him, despite all of your cunning attempts to keep him hidden."

"I sought only to spare you pain," she insisted darkly.

"What is pain if not too-perfect pleasure?"

"Was it your pleasure, then, to keep him by your side, flaunting him before my eyes at every turn?"

"It was my pleasure . . . and my wisdom . . . that bade me keep a small hold over you, my love."

"He means nothing to me—nor to you if your treatment of him is any judge."

"Nothing dead," Wardieu agreed. "Alive, he serves as a reminder."

"Reminder of *what*? That your brother was in my bed first?"

Wardieu laughed suddenly. "Why do you think I pursued you at all, if not because my brother was there first? The fact you betrayed him so eagerly and so . . . wholeheartedly, even knowing you carried his seed, well, it serves to remind me that things oft repeat themselves in life."

"I would never betray you!" she insisted. "I . . ."

Nicolaa caught herself, a breath away from an admission. She could see the incandescent heat was gone from his eyes, replaced once again by the almost insufferable indifference that would have turned any kind of an admission into another weapon he would think nothing of using against her. And, even as she fought to regain her composure, another insufferable intrusion appeared on the crest of the knoll, running toward them with the beetling self-importance of a noisome gnat.

"Good my lord!" Onfroi de la Haye hailed them, an arm raised and flailing the air for attention. "A message from Sir Aubrey de Vere . . ."

Wardieu's annoyed gaze flicked to the sheriff . . . then flicked again as he caught a brief glint of light where no light should have been. It took his superb reflexes only a split second to identify the metallic flash of an arrowhead streaking out of the woods, and he was able to shove Nicolaa out of its path as it hissed toward them, flying straight and true to the point where Nicolaa's heart would have been.

Wardieu spun around, his sword already halfway out of

his scabbard, his eyes searching the blackness for an enemy he could not see.

Behind him, Onfroi de la Haye felt something hot and sharp punch through the quilted velvet of his surcoat. Meeting with very little fleshy resistance, the arrow had enough force behind it to pierce through muscle, gizzard, and tissue, and to exit out the other side a full six inches before the stiff feather fletching snagged on cloth and torn sinew. Onfroi stared down at the protruding feathers and screamed. He gaped uncomprehendingly at his wife, at Lord Lucien, at the shaft of the arrow that had found him by sheer mischance, and he opened his mouth again, screaming until Nicolaa's bunched fists struck him to the ground.

Less than fifty paces away, concealed by heavy shadow, Gil Golden cursed and swiftly drew another arrow out of his quiver. He nocked it and realigned his quarry, but before he could shoot, he was trammeled to one side by a pair of booted feet. The bow and arrow were startled out of his grip as a solid weight crushed into his shoulders. An instinctive grab for the hilt of his sword was cut short by the familiarity of a high-pitched voice cursing at him from the clump of thicket.

"What do you think you are doing, Addle-Brain!" Sparrow shrieked in a strident whisper. "Christ's blood, are you mad? Has the whole world gone mad this night!"

Gil's fury gave him no chance to vent an intelligible answer. Beyond the fringe of trees, Onfroi de la Haye's screams were causing a minor eruption of chaos in the Wardieu encampment. Torches were blazing to life. A flurry of shouted orders was bringing a small army of armoured feet running down the slope toward the hem of trees. In seconds, the woods would be swarming with knights and men-at-arms.

Sparrow extricated himself from the thickets and gave Gil a resounding thump in the ribs even as the taller outlaw was bending over to search for his fallen bow.

"Move, you ape! Run to deeper cover before they fetch the hounds and loose them on us!"

"I almost had her!" Gil spat, crashing through the tangle of saplings and gorse behind the fleeing Sparrow. "I would have had her too, by Christ, if you had not swooped down on me like the wrath of hell! Where did you come from? What the devil are you doing so far from camp?"

"What am *I* doing so far from camp? What are *you* doing so far from camp! And what do you mean you almost had her . . . had who?"

"Nicolaa de la Haye," Gil snarled. "The sheriff's godless wife."

"Nicolaa de la Haye!" Sparrow exclaimed, tumbling to an abrupt halt. "But I thought—"

"You thought I was aiming elswhere? You thought I would set out on this miserably dank night to risk the ire of the Black Wolf by piercing the one breast in all Christendom he chooses to reserve for himself? You think me that much of a fool?"

"Would that I thought so highly of you, you hulking bandysnatch!" Sparrow retorted. One ear was tuned to the camp and he heard the sudden howl of dogs, a sound that raised a cool prickle of sweat across his brow. He hated dogs. Loathed the mangy, fang-toothed demons as much as he had the capacity to loathe any of God's creations. An early attraction in one of the fairs he had been sold into had been the pitting of a manacled dwarf against a salivating, red-eyed demon hound from Hades. Both his body and his mind were scarred from those horrific bouts, and he could barely tolerate the gentle, tamed beasts that had attached themselves to the Wolf's camp.

"Do you realize the trouble you have caused me?" he demanded, running again. "Do you have half a head's worth of notion how many different treasons I have condemned you of over the past few hours? Skewering the Dragon would

have at least made the trip worthwhile, but you, you poxy
snipe, you tell me now you had not even that much ambition!
You tell me all you wanted was the skewered bosom of the
Lincoln Bawd!"

"I almost had her too, damn my luck. A beat sooner . . .
a *blink* sooner and she would have been as neatly spitted as a
suckling pig."

"A more deserving fate I could not envision for you, Gil of
the Golden Eyes!"

"I did not ask you to follow me," Gil countered. "Nor will
I thank you for interfering, if that is what you expect."

"Save your gratitude and your sweat for the hounds,"
Sparrow snorted. "Perhaps your luck will fare better and
they will tear you apart before the Dragon's men have a
chance to mould a copper mask to your face. *And* before
milord hears of this folly and pins your ears to your heels!"

"He will only hear of it if you tell him."

"Aha! Now the knave begs favours!"

They weaved and bobbed from one shadowy stand of trees
to another, moving as swiftly as they dared in the darkness.
The sound of their braying pursuers had veered to the west
of them, but both knew it would not take long for the
pointed noses to relocate their scent.

Gil, seeing how hard Sparrow was churning his legs to
keep apace with his own longer, lither ones, felt as vulnerable
as a newborn babe without the comforting weight of his
longbow slung over his shoulder. Halting again, he grabbed
Sparrow around the waist and, without delaying to ask,
hoisted the squawking bundle onto a nearby branch.

"Up into the treetops you go," he commanded. "You can
move twice as fast through the branches, especially if you do
not have me to hold you back."

"What will you do?" Sparrow gasped.

"My legs are long enough to cover the same ground, only
in a more earthbound fashion. Do not worry about me."

"But the dogs—"

Gil wiped a hand across his brow and glanced back over his shoulder. "There is a wide stream up ahead. I will cut it down the middle until I have gone a ways to dilute the scent."

"And you expect me to just leave you!" Sparrow sounded shocked—and hurt.

Because the little man was now on eye level with the taller forester, the latter could feel the clutch of fear in the gnarled, stubby hands as they grasped his shoulders.

"I will be all right, Puck," he assured him. "We will meet up again at the fens in . . . an hour. In fact, a sovereign says I arrive there first, in plenty of time to cut and pare myself a new bow frame. Are you game?"

" 'Tis not a game, Gil," Sparrow objected morosely.

"I know." Golden reached out and ruffled Sparrow's curly locks. "But I will best you just the same, so you had better put in a good effort, else have your coin waiting at the other end."

With that and an extra tweak on Sparrow's rump, Gil set off at an agile, loping gait that quickly carried him out of sight in the misty gloom. Sparrow sent an oath after him, and would have given chase except for a sudden, bowel-clenching burst of braying and howling that was far too close for lengthy debate.

Scrambling nimbly up to the highest branches, he swung from tree to tree, his heart pounding loudly and steadily within his chest. He kept his eyes trained on the ground as it rushed below, hoping against hope to catch a glimpse of Gil running safely through the forest. Not even his keen eyes could see anything, and once or twice, the hot sting of tears almost caused him to misjudge the distance and angle between branches.

"God give you speed, my friend," he whispered to the night air. "God give you speed."

11

"God give me strength," the Wolf snarled. "You did what?"

Gil and Sparrow, looking as if they had both been dredged through a thorn patch, fidgeted guiltily, shifting their weight from one foot to the other while the Wolf showered accolades upon their intelligence.

"You left the abbey without consulting anyone; you crept within a few hundred paces of the enemy camp, then, without a thought or consideration for the consequences, proceeded to singlehandedly jeopardize all of our safety by throwing arrows at Nicolaa de la Haye?"

"She does not figure to be of any significance in your mission for the queen," Gil said sullenly, then added in a hushed voice. "In truth . . . I only wanted to see her. When I heard Sigurd mention she had joined the Dragon's camp, I . . ."

"Only wanted to see her," the Wolf repeated belligerently. "And?"

"And . . ." The gleaming amber eyes lifted to meet his. "And I saw her. She was standing fifty yards away, a clear shot, bold as evil under the moonlight. I did not even realize I had fit an arrow to my bow, or raised the bow to my shoulder until the string was drawn and the arrow in flight."

"You *shot* her."

The crown of unruly red curls bowed again. "I shot *at* her. I missed."

The Friar, perched quietly nearby as a casual witness to

the proceedings, crooked an eyebrow. "You missed? A clear shot from fifty yards . . . and you *missed*?"

Gil reddened, for it was something that did not occur with any great frequency.

"She was not alone. Whoever was with her must have seen something and pushed her out of the way just as I loosed my arrow and . . . well . . . before I could notch and fire another, Sparrow flew down on me out of nowhere and—"

"Saved your crusty hide, no doubt," the Wolf cut in bluntly. "Did they not give chase?"

"They tried, but we lost them. There was no harm done."

"No harm," Friar snorted.

"Except to the sheriff," Sparrow chirped brightly, his smile fading almost instantly on a slanting glare from Gil.

"What about the sheriff?" the Wolf asked guardedly.

Gil chewed a lip and looked as if he regretted not staking Sparrow out as a tidbit for the wolfhounds. "The sheriff just happened out of nowhere—"

"He was behind the Bawd when Gil's arrow went sniffing," Sparrow provided helpfully.

". . . and when she was pushed out of the way—"

"The shaft found him a ready target!" the elf concluded happily.

Friar and the Wolf both stared.

"You shot Onfroi de la Haye?" Friar asked at length. "Is he dead?"

"He took the arrow in the belly," Gil shrugged, indicating the worst could be assumed.

The Wolf continued to maintain an unbroken silence for a full minute before he released a short, sharp gust of air from his lungs and turned away.

The four were standing near the main gates. There, the early pastels of dawn and an alert sentry had conspired against the two culprits' attempt to regain entry to the abbey grounds unnoticed. Sparrow's face and hands were smudged with sap, his clothes torn from his journey through the tree-tops. Gil was not so leafy, nor so sticky, but a seam of his deerhide jerkin had parted at the shoulder and the flap hung down like a limp pennant on a windless day. Both recalcitrants were wary of their leader's temper. Both squinted upward from time to time, curious to know how the sun could continue to shine so brightly up above while the gathering storm clouds bristled so ominously below.

Friar, debating whether or not he had ever seen a blacker expression on the Wolf's face, shook his head sadly and looked down at his hands.

"The Dragon will not be pleased with this turn of events," the Wolf said, almost to himself. "To have his puppet sheriff slain in the midst of a kidnapping, with an unholy wedding pending and a conflict with a brother he thought long dead . . . all at a time when the secrecy and stealth of his actions should have commanded the utmost priority? Nay, the sheriff's untimely death will not please him. *Not* that it pleases me—" he added with a pointed glance at the two penitents. "But knowing it will please *him* less and prick Prince John's ears to attention sooner, takes away some of the sting that should have been applied to both your hides. You, Gil Golden, are still guilty of disobeying direct orders; and you" —the piercing gaze launched a dagger in Sparrow's direction —"should have had better sense than to go chasing after Gil on your own."

"There was no time—"

"There was no mischief to be made, you mean, in sharing the hunt with someone else. Suppose Gil *had* been a traitor seeking to sell information to the Dragon's camp? Suppose the pair of you had been caught and plied with milord D'Aeth's special talents for prying secrets? Or suppose you had spilled headfirst out of a tree and lain somewhere broken and bleeding the night long with no one the wiser for your absence?"

"No one would have mourned the loss," Sparrow said petulantly and kicked a pebble with the toe of his boot.

"To be sure," the Wolf agreed, narrowing his gaze to suggest a cataclysm had not been entirely avoided, "no one will mourn either one of you if your recklessness brings the hounds too near Thornfeld. The abbey is not so darkly steeped in legends of druids and pining ghosts as to have completely escaped the memory of local foresters—some of whom might be only too willing to lead the Dragon's men here in exchange for a coin or two. We will have to double the guards for insurance."

"I will see to it," Friar nodded.

"Aye, and while you are about it, see to fetching these two a pair of stout shovels. My nose has been telling me it is long past time to fill in the old privy trenches and dig new ones. That should quench their sense of adventure for the time being."

Friar grinned. "Their 'scents' of all else too, I warrant."

Gil looked dismayed, Sparrow was plainly indignant. Neither was foolhardy enough to protest the punishment, knowing it could have gone much worse for them. Still, Sparrow would not have been Sparrow if he had not delivered the final, parting comment. Luckily the breeze was kind enough to delay the words "like a pissed newt" from reaching the Wolf's ears until he and Gil were safely around the corner of the pilgrims' hall.

The Wolf was still scowling—perhaps not in exact accordance to Sparrow's description, but near enough to deserve fair comparison—when his morning solitude was interrupted a second time. He was seated on the cracked stone lip of the cistern, his head bent over in concentration, his fingers working dexterously with knife and whetstone. The small, thin blade of his poniard glittered on each stroke; the sound of the steel scraping slowly along the stone could have been likened to a whispered warning.

The cistern and its extended stone trough had at one time brimmed with water from an underground well, but now held only the stains and decay of mouldy leaves. The circular portion was in the full sunlight, the trough in the shade of an old drooping yew. The Wolf was seated midway along the trough, his vest set aside in deference to the warm day, his linsey-woolsey shirt gaping open to the waist. It was apparent he had recently come from the Silent Pool; the dark chestnut hanks of his hair curled damply over his shoulders, and his feet were bare, stretched out at the end of his long legs to bask in the heat of the sun. His tall deerhide boots were folded on the ground beside him, and within an arm's reach away, his longbow and quiver of arrows; beside that, a brace of neatly skinned, gutted rabbits.

The sight of him caused Servanne to stop so suddenly, the hem of her skirt fluttered forward several inches before creaming back around her ankles.

The ruined monastery boasted few chambers where either privacy or comfort from the damp and decay could be found. Servanne and Biddy had been taking their time strolling to the stream and back, not the least bit anxious to relinquish the warm sunshine for rancid gloom. Biddy had harangued an ill-tempered Sparrow until he had relinquished the missing trunks, and the plain velvet gown Servanne wore, if a little wrinkled from mishandling, was at least clean and cut in a prim enough style to discourage more than a cursory inspection. The neckline came close up to her collarbone, the bodice was tight to extreme and embroidered stiff enough to obscure all but the slightest hint of shapely breasts beneath. The sleeves were long and full from the elbows, the waist rode low on the hips and was encircled by a girdle of hammered gold links.

Plain, had been her critical opinion, and with the addition

of a starched white wimple: prudish. Unworthy of attracting the notice of a flea . . . or a wolf.

Servanne released the breath she had been holding and gauged the distance from the trough to the door of the pilgrims' hall. Twenty paces, no more, and most of it dappled in soft, musty shadow. Unfortunately they would have to walk past the cistern to reach the hall, but since it could not be avoided, it would be best accomplished with haste.

Servanne lifted a slippered foot and inched it forward. The gray eyes came slowly up from the whetstone, tracing an impudently bold line from the toe of her shoe to the pink stain on her cheeks.

"God's day to you, ladies," he said, his tone so sweet it left crystals on his tongue. "I trust you slept well last night?"

Biddy harrumped and swelled her bosom for battle. Servanne sniffed the air as if the leaves were not all that smelled rotten in the heat of the sun.

"The accommodations are deplorable," said Lady de Briscourt icily. "The company is crude, unbearable, and utterly without conscience. I did not sleep a wink last night, and therefore see nothing to give God thanks for."

The Wolf responded with a lazy grin. "You might want to give thanks your virtue is intact. Conversely, your lack of sleep may be due to regrets that it is not. If you wish to reconsider, I would be only too happy to oblige."

The audacity of the remark was as unexpected as the tingle that skittered down Servanne's spine. She had indeed lain awake most of the night, turning and tossing restlessly upon her wretched little sleeping couch, cursing each errant needle of straw that thrust its way through the ticking. Most of all, she had cursed the man who had caused her body to suffer through one shivered memory after another, all unbidden, unwanted, unconscionable. He might well have been physically in the bed beside her, for his face and body had never been more than a despairing groan away. She had not been able to will him, force him, or dream him away. Her lips had lost none of their bruised tenderness, and her breasts had ruched with treacherous insistence each time they had brushed a pelt or blanket. As for the relentless aches elsewhere in her body . . . they did not bear thinking about. Most certainly not now, not when her tormentor was but a few paces away, grinning like the predator whose name he bore, making her acutely aware of each flicker and stroke of the tanned, tapered fingers.

"How long do you plan to keep us prisoner?" she demanded.

"Ah, rebuffed again," he murmured. "Perhaps in a week or two, you will have a change of heart."

"A week!" she gasped. "Two! Have you not delivered your outrageous ransom demands to Lord Lucien?"

"I have delivered my demands to the man who *calls* himself Lord Lucien," he countered smoothly. "I have also offered to relieve him of the task of disposing of you should he be entertaining second thoughts on the marriage. It is a great deal to contemplate in the short time since we plucked you from the road; the choices too tempting to deliberate in haste."

The tint in Servanne's cheeks burned darker. "There is no choice, m'sieur. You will hear from my lord within the week."

"Really?" He folded his arms across his chest. "May I ask why you sound so confident?"

Servanne lifted her eyes from the forest of dark hairs that covered the hard, banded muscles bulging through the opened shirt . . . and almost forgot the question.

"Th-the wedding," she said lamely. "The preparations have all been made."

"Have they, indeed. What an inconvenience not to have the bride present for the service. Perhaps I could offer yet another compromise: a marriage by proxy. I could take the place of the groom here, in the forest, while some equally affable damosel stands your place at the castle. In this way, he could carry on with the feasts and entertainments he has undoubtedly already paid for in good coin, while we"—the wolfish smile stole across the insolently handsome face again —"we could find some way to celebrate the union in our own fashion. As I mentioned before, the Dragon and I are much alike in countenance and bearing. Not so much so as Mutter and Stutter, but near enough to give you a healthy idea of what to expect when you draw back the sheets in the bridal bed."

Servanne's belly turned a slow, sluggish somersault. Beside her, Biddy's mouth gaped open in shock and she sucked in enough air to have stirred the leaves overhead.

"On the other hand," he continued blithely, bending over to pull on his boots. "There are some things we do quite differently, and I should hate to think your pending days of wedded bliss might suffer from an unfavourable contrast."

Servanne's face, throat, and breasts were now burning. The Wolf, seeing her discomfort, stood up and walked slowly toward her, stopping close enough for her to detect the scent of leather and greenwood that was a part of his overwhelming maleness. He had shaved earlier in the morning, and the reason for sharpening the edge of his knife was evidenced by the two clotted cuts beneath his chin.

At that precise moment, Servanne would have rejoiced in seeing ribbons of blood flowing from ear to ear; a greater ecstasy would be to carve them there herself.

At the same time, she felt a sudden shifting in the weight of her emotions. If this verbal jousting was the best he could do—and would he not have done his worst last night if it *had* been his intent?—surely she had little to fear for all his arrogant boasting. A man who had kissed a woman the way he had kissed her, yet had done nothing to carry the threat further, was likely to be no threat at all! If any of a dozen

knights of her past aquaintance had found her in their arms
and won half the liberties this rogue had stolen, neither pleas
nor beating fists, nor gouging knives would have deterred
them from taking what they wanted then and there. And not
one in a score of knights of her aquaintance had a tenth of
the motive for revenge this Black Wolf declared himself to
have.

Perhaps he should have raped her. She might have begun
to believe his claim to be Lucien Wardieu.

Expressing her newfound indifference to his petty vulgari-
ties, Servanne sighed and turned to Biddy. "Now I understand what you mean when you say all men judge all things
in life by the size of the brain they carry between their
thighs. The smaller the brain, the dimmer their judgment,
the larger the voice they use to convince the world they are
giants among men. How true. And how sad."

She tucked her arm through Biddy's and, without a further acknowledgment of the Wolf's presence in the sunlit
courtyard, strolled sedately past him and entered the shadowy sanctuary of the pilgrims' hall.

Biddy, light-headed from the amount of gasping and spluttering she had done to maintain her silence out-of-doors,
barely managed to keep from swooning until they were in the
privacy of their chamber.

"Lost, I tell you!" she wailed. "We are lost! He plans to
ravish you and kill me, and leave our bones to rot upon the
road for some unlucky traveler to stumble over."

"Oh, Biddy—" Servanne was feeling none too steady herself. "Not now. I can hardly keep my head up."

"From shame, I should not wonder!" came the instantly
revitalized retort. "What did the rogue mean: rebuffed
again? Did something happen last night you did not tell me
about?"

Servanne was grateful for the need to touch the flame of
one candle to the wick of another before there was enough

light to see clearly through the gloom. To buy another few moments, she tipped the second candle and dripped the hot wax onto the stone, making a secure seat for the base.

"Nothing happened. We walked. We talked. He tried to convince me he was in England on an honourable mission for Queen Eleanor—no doubt to gain my support for whatever other heinous crimes they intend to commit before they are all caught and hung. Aside from that . . ."

Biddy's eyes were as bright as polished steel and twice as keen when it came to parting half-truths from outright lies. Servanne was hiding something and she had a fairly good idea what it might be. The girl had not blushed so much since her wedding to Sir Hubert, and then only for as long as it took her to realize a bride's bed was not made of rose petals, nor a man's attentions necessarily as rewarding as all their grunting and sweating might promise.

"Curiosity is a curious thing in itself," Biddy said, deflated by the knowledge her lamb might somehow be suffering a malaise not able to be leeched out or cured. "It tempts us all to do the things we know can only harm us the most. Rarely does anything good come of knowing what lies beyond the bend in the road. Rarely do we like what we find when we dare to take it, but by then, it is already too late to turn around and retrace our steps."

"Must it always be so, Biddy?" Servanne asked softly. "Is there no risk worth the taking?"

Biddy came quietly up behind her. "I would be the first to agree he is a handsome beast, my lady, but a beast nonetheless. He will have no use for you once the deed is done—the challenge for his kind is in the pursuit, not the surrender."

Servanne stared at the heart of the candle flame, her eyes stinging, her breath dry in her throat. Biddy was right. No good would come of knowing . . . well . . . of *knowing*. It was odd and unfair that a man who was a beast should be so

much more of a man than she had ever encountered before
. . . but there again, what good would come of knowing?

What good would come of knowing, Friar wondered as he
stood near the edge of the embankment and waited for Gil to
belt the last of his washed, sodden garments into place. Dusk
was well on its way to becoming night and there was little to
distinguish between shadow and tree. Gil had finished the
filthy task he and Sparrow had been set to and nearly ran all
the way to the Silent Pool to strip and scour away the stench
and slime of the privies. Judging by the haste with which he
dressed, Friar suspected Gil had marked the glowing approach of the horn lantern as it shifted and throbbed through
the trees. Friar had brought it as a precaution, not against a
twisted ankle or misjudged footfall, but out of deference to
Gil's sharp eyes and quick bowhand. It was not wise to be a
shadow moving among shadows, not in these woods, and
more particularly not when Gil Golden was out of sorts with
all mankind.

Friar stepped out into plain view and raised the lantern
above his head. "I thought I might find you here. Sparrow . . . ?"

Gil shrugged. "He will probably stew in his own juices a
day or two longer to punish us all."

Friar spared half a smile and set the smoking lantern down
on the rock. The light it emitted was minimal, and not so
dramatic out in the open as it had been in the heart of the
forest darkness. The thin sheets of pressed horn that guarded
the weak flame from draft produced a glow the colour and
pattern of cobwebs where it was flung across the stone. Everything it touched took on the pale colour of ash—everything save the bright, coppery sheen of Gil's hair.

"You will catch your death of a cold in those wet clothes,"
Friar remarked, noting how the linsey-woolsey and the deerhide shed fat droplets with each move Gil made.

"I have survived worse."

"So you have. Moreover, I can see this newest escapade will only bolster your already considerable estimation of your abilities."

The golden eyes flickered up angrily. "I am not a child needing a lecture from you, good Friar."

"Your behavior last night would argue the point."

"My behavior," Gil spat, starting to push past the other man, "is none of your concern."

"It is when you take unnecessary risks to threaten not only your own life, but the lives of every man in camp. Gil!" He reached out and grasped an arm as the master archer strode past, but the leaner and lither Golden whipped around with a curse and yanked his arm free.

"Would you be here having this motherly conversation were it anyone else but me?"

Friar absorbed the curse and the anger without batting an eye. "You are not any other man, *Gillian.* And if you were, I would hasten to suggest our vaunted leader would not have been so lenient on you as he was. It was a damned stupid thing you did to go off on your own, and you know it!"

"I can take care of myself," Gil seethed, cinching the belt so tightly around her waist that Friar could not help himself from glancing down at the small, firm breasts where they jumped into prominence. "Do you not forget: I joined this troop and lived as one of you—fought as one of you . . . *killed* as one of you when it was necessary, for several weeks before any of you were the wiser."

How could Friar forget? Gillian had concealed her secret well, coming among them as a man, sharing the rugged duties in camp as well as on raids, her skill with the longbow winning unreserved respect and admiration from the rest of the men. It was Sparrow who had uncovered the ruse, and Sparrow who, oddly enough, had been her staunchest defender when the vote was placed before the others whether to allow her to stay or to send her away. The daughter of a local bowmaker, her knowledge of the area had been a strong point in her favour. Her unabashed and single-minded hatred for Nicolaa de la Haye had not hurt her cause either.

Friar had simply been relieved to know he had not been affected by his early years cloistered with monks who slipped back and forth between each other's chambers in the dead of night. He had been fighting an attraction for "Gil" since the outset; discovering she was a woman made it a good deal easier to accept, although at times, relief aside, Gillian's bold bravado made him want to take hold of her and shake her until her teeth rattled.

"I am well aware of your abilities to protect yourself," he said, taking a firm grip on his patience. "But because you prefer to dress like a man and can wield a bow and arrow better than any soul alive—it does not make you any less inviolate to the cut of a swordblade. For Christ's sake, woman, you could have been caught by Wardieu's men. You and Sparrow both could have been dragged before the Dragon and used as fodder for his rage. Think you he would have spared you D'Aeth's skill with iron tongs and hot coals? Think you Nicolaa de la Haye would not have recognized her own handiwork?"

Gil lifted a hand self-consciously to the scar that ran the length of her left cheek.

"It has been more than five years," she said in a hushed voice. "The Bawd cannot possibly remember every face she has had plied with brands . . . there have been too many."

For several long moments Gil wrestled with the spectre of her memories while Friar wrestled with the desire to take her in his arms and demand to know what had caused so much hatred to build inside her. It was not just the branding—a hideous enough reason in itself, for with her flame-coloured hair and her smile (when she dared show it) as wide and bright as a summer day, she would have been a rare, exqui-

site beauty. To Friar, all the physical perfection in the world
could not have rivaled her courage, her pride, her strength of
spirit. If he could just convince her of this, draw her out of
her anger long enough to see she need not be alone in her
suffering . . .

What then, he wondered. What good would come of it?
What manner of promises could they make to one another
when the probability of surviving another sennight was not
even guaranteed?

"We all walk about with ghosts and demons on our shoulders," he said finally, breaking the silence with a sigh. "At
times I confess to a pressing need myself to throw back my
head and bay at the moon. But then I think: What good
would it do to turn as savage and bloodless as those who
would only rejoice to see the work they have done in bringing us so low?"

"It would feel good," Gil said flatly, coldly. "It would feel
as good for me to see my arrow pierce the iron tankard of De
la Haye's heart, as it must have felt for you when you
plunged your knife into the breast of the Bishop Mercier."

"The situation was different," Friar said slowly.

"Why? Because it was done in the heat of the moment
while the girl he was raping and mutilating was still bleeding
on the altar before him? Or because you, Alaric FitzAthelstan, were born of noble blood and it was the *noble* thing to
do, to avenge the girl's death?"

"I did not feel noble doing it," he said quietly.

"But would you have felt human *not* doing it? Could you
have lived with yourself? Could you have lived with the guilt
of doing nothing to avenge her death?"

Alaric knew the answer even as he saw the hard glitter of
satisfaction in Gil's eyes. He reached out and grasped her by
the shoulders, squeezing hard enough to cause the water
trapped in her shirt to seep through his fingers.

"At least I did not keep the burden of pain to myself. I

shared the guilt and the horror, and by doing so, was able to find peace within myself again."

"There will be no peace for me until Nicolaa de la Haye is dead," Gil insisted. "Just as there will be no peace for the Wolf until he sees the Dragon lying dead at his feet. Yet I do not see you cautioning him to make peace with himself. Nay! I see you doing everything in your power, risking everything you say you so solemnly hold to value . . . to help him in his quest!"

His grip tightened further. "I would help you too, if you would but let me."

"I . . . do . . . not . . . want . . . your . . . help!" she fumed. "I do not want anyone's help, only God's—and then only to keep the aim of my arrow straight and true."

Friar held the resolute stare for another full minute before he thrust her away with an explosive "Bah!" of frustration. It was no use. She was as stubborn as a mule and twice as thick-headed.

"Sparrow is not the only one who spites himself by thinking to punish the rest of the world. The stench of your self-pity would rival his any day, and I leave it to you gladly!"

Gil watched him stride out of the dull halo of light. He was almost to the edge of the fern-covered slope before she cried out and took a step after him.

"Alaric . . . please! You do not understand."

"No," he said, halting, his back still to the lantern light. "I do not understand. I have tried, Gil. God knows. But a man can only slam his head against a stone wall so many times before he realizes the one will give long before the other, and he should waste his efforts elsewhere."

"I have never encouraged your . . . efforts," she stammered.

"No. But they have always been yours for the asking."

He climbed up the slope and was swallowed in the darkness, leaving Gil Golden a black silhouette by the inky waters of the Silent Pool. He did not hear the tortured gasp that was his name, nor did he see the shining wetness of the tears that began to flow down her cheeks.

12

Servanne spent the next two days diligently avoiding all unnecessary contact with the Black Wolf. It was not a difficult
goal to achieve since he had elected to stand guard throughout most of the first day, and had led a small party of men
out to determine where the sheriff's men were searching the
forest. On the second day, he took Gil and two others out
hunting and returned with a large buck, which was more
than enough to replenish their food supplies. In the evenings
she was forced to sit through the repeated mockery of a
formal meal, but there again, she found him so preoccupied
with other matters as to be generally uninterested in sparring
with her.

Mutter and Stutter, the twin minstrels, were assigned as
her personal guards and she went nowhere without the pair
of them bickering good-naturedly a discreet few paces in her
shadow. Not that there was anywhere to go outside of the
ruined gardens and the Silent Pool—neither of which held
any appeal for Servanne with their associated memories.
And not that there was any pressing need to visit either
place, for the weather had turned sullen and miserable, the
sky an oppressive mass of unbroken cloud, which periodi-
cally spit torrents of water down upon the mouldy buildings
in an earnest effort to make the unpleasantness of their surroundings even worse.

The walls dripped constantly. The birds who had made
the refectory arches their homes for generations, screamed

and quarreled incessantly, and made walking from one end of the hall to the other a hazardous roulette of bird droppings. The fires smoked blackly and could not hold a proper flame long enough to generate any real heat or relief from the damp. The chambers were cold and musty, and stank of animal excrement and decay.

On the fifth day of Servanne's captivity, the sky was once again blue, albeit seen through the hazy, misty vapours of the forest steaming dry. She ventured gladly out into the courtyard after her morning prayers, thankful to feel the heat of the sun again on flesh that had grown wrinkled and clammy from dampness. The other members of the Wolf's camp greeted the sunlight with the same enthusiasm and immediately went about setting up targets to practice their archery, quintains to sharpen the aim of lance and sword, and cordoned squares where men stripped to the waist and wrestled one another to stretch the lethargy out of cramped muscles. Even the huge war-horses were taken through their paces. The constant thunder of hooves and the trembling of the ground underfoot made one wonder if the crumbling masonry could withstand the abuse. But it held, apart from the odd startled stone, which was more than could be said for the field outside the main gates. It was left churned and pitted and trampled as if there had been a great battle fought on the common.

"It is just like being part of a tourney or a fair," Biddy remarked with grudging admiration. "These scoundrels certainly do know what they are about."

She was making a specific reference to Gil Golden, who had taken up a position at the far side of the courtyard, her back straight as a rod, her long legs braced apart, her bow prepared with such loving precision it could have been an extension of her own limbs.

"Now, my lady, you will see . . ." Mutter began.

". . . a fine entertainment," Stutter finished.

"For Gil Golden has no equal with a bow . . ."

". . . although Sparrow tries daily to prove the claim false."

"Think you, brother, one day he might succeed?" Mutter asked, his frown suggesting the question was of the utmost importance.

Stutter's brows mirrored the concern. "Oh, nay, brother. As clever as our Sparrow might be in some ways, his faerie powers hold no sway on Gil's bow arm. Watch."

In the courtyard, Gil nocked an arrow and let it fly, sending it straight to the heart of the target—a small canvas sack filled with kernels of corn. The sack hung from a branch that grew over the wall at the opposite end of the monastery grounds, a distance of perhaps two hundred yards.

"Paugh! Where's the challenge?" Sparrow demanded, sighting the skewered target from under the visor of his hand. "I could hit it myself, blindfolded."

Gil lowered the bow and glared at the little man. "Your best is not my worst, and well you know it, Puck."

"We will see about that," Sparrow snorted and scampered across the courtyard to chase down the target. He loosened the string at the neck of the sack, spilling all but a spoonful of dry corn out onto the grass. Reduced in size to a boll no bigger than a child's fist, Sparrow rehung it and, for an added test of skill, gave it a heave so that it careened back and forth like a drunken pendulum.

"Now, Master Boaster," he shouted through cupped hands. "Earn your keep the hard way."

Gil tracked the erratic pattern of the swinging sack for as long as it took to draw an arrow from her quiver and notch it to the bowstring—all of two seconds. She drew and snapped her fingers to release the arrow, then without waiting to see if it struck home, drew, nocked, and fired another.

Sparrow, standing alongside the swinging target, let off a startled squawk when the arrow struck at the widest point of

the arc, impaling the sack to the wall a mere two inches from
his pugged nose. The second arrow, *hissssing* so close upon
the fletching of the first as to make the sound of their flights
unbroken, was a stomach-lurching inch closer and carried
away a lock of tightly curled brown hair in passing.

Gil's grin was shared by every member of the band but
one. With his eyes as round as his gaping mouth, Sparrow
hastily retrieved his bow and quiver and scurried off into the
tangle of the gardens, leaving gales of laughter following in
his wake.

"Serves him right," Biddy chuckled. She had not forgiven
him his many sins of mischief-making—sins which had
grown increasingly inventive in the close confines caused by
the poor weather—and seeing Sparrow run in a circle, his
ear tingling with wood-burn did her bosom a good turn.

Servanne was only partly attentive to Biddy's gloating.
Two new combatants were taking their place in the courtyard, drawing eyes and ears away from other activities as if
the world had suddenly shrunken to a circle twelve feet
round.

Friar and the Wolf were testing the weight and balance of
their swords, the naked steel glinting in the sunlight as both
men shrugged aside the precaution of using leather guards
for the blades.

"Now, this should be worthy of a stopped heart or two,"
Mutter confided to Biddy.

"Indeed," Stutter added earnestly, "they have come close
on occasion to stopping their own."

"In the beginning, of course . . ."

". . . Friar was no match for milord, not in strength or
skill. But now . . ."

". . . they are so evenly matched, the blades must cut
close to the veriest edge of peril in order to declare the winner."

"Peril in a pig's bladder," Biddy declared, glaring at the twins. "Surely the blades are dulled and the intents feigned."

"Oh no," Mutter assured her. "They draw blood quite regularly."

"'Tis how the men exchange their money back and forth, wagering on who has the meanest look in the eye that particular morning."

"Today, methinks it is Friar," Stutter added confidently. "He looks better rested."

"He does look sleepy," Mutter agreed, fishing in his tunic for a copper coin. "Too sleepy to oust milord."

Stutter produced a copper of his own and the two sat happily clutching their wagers as the opening feints of the match began.

Servanne was compelled to glance up from the bits of straw she was absently plaiting in her hands. She had not formed any preferences, one way or the other, for any of these so-called outlaws, but of the lot of them, the Friar seemed the most considerate, the most genteel and level-headed. If not for the way he flaunted his disdain for the church, and for the lingering humiliation of having believed him to be a real monk, Servanne might almost have admitted a fondness for his wit, his charm, and most notably, his ability to hold his own against the Wolf's arrogance and broodiness.

So it was, she watched and cheered secretly to see the Friar's blade draw some of that blood from the Wolf's bravado.

At first, he looked to be entirely outmatched against the Wolf's brutish power and prowess, but with the opening cuts and slashes, it became quickly evident that what Friar lacked in muscle, he made up for in speed. The two men struck and lunged, thrust and feinted. Steel clanged and shrilled, the metallic clash of swords echoed within the walled confines of the courtyard. Beside her, Mutter clutched at Stutter's arm

when the Wolf's blade came streaking down in a silvery arc,
the light flaring along the polished surface as it met the Friar's blade in a jarring impact. They both gasped and added
their cheers to the others as the Friar pivoted on the heels of
his feet, avoiding a slicing sweep across his flanks with barely
the width of a prayer to spare.

Cords of muscle bulged and rippled in the Wolf's arms.
Beads of moisture slicked his brow and temples, darkening
the unruly locks of chestnut hair where they whipped and
lashed against cheek and throat. He wore only a loose-fitting
shirt of lincoln green over his deerhide leggings; heat and
concentration had already caused the cloth to cling in damp
patches to the vast slabs of granite that bunched across his
shoulders and chest. His hands gripped the sword as if they
were born to it, wielding its power smoothly, effortlessly,
never once breaking tension in the wrist or upper arm.

Servanne's hands fell motionless on her lap, her throat was
suddenly as dry as parchment—an oddly disturbing contrast
to the rest of her body, which seemed to be drowning under a
deluge of liquid warmth.

She had indeed tried hiding away in her chamber, pleading
illness and fatigue to avoid his company, but not seeing him
at all was somehow worse than having only the company of
her memories to contend with. Memories could not be re-
futed, only embellished. His hands, his lips, the tempered
hardness of his body . . . If he was there, in the flesh, she
could always find things about him that annoyed her and
thus enabled her to use her anger and contempt to defend
against the frequent lapses in vigilance.

Mon Dieu, how she burned with shame each and every
time she found the Wolf's smouldering gaze upon her. How
she ached with the knowledge of where his hands had been
and what they had done. What did he think? What did he
remember? Could it be one tenth . . . one hundredth part

as devastating as what she agonized over each time she drew a breath or released it?

A resounding shriek of metal slicing along metal startled Servanne's thoughts back to the sun-drenched courtyard. The two antagonists were crouched and stalking in a slow circle, their swords gripped double fisted, their faces tensed into murderous grins. There was blood dotting the Wolf's sleeve and a row of cleanly severed thongs hanging where the front seam of his shirt had once been bound together. Sweat sleeked his hair; it streamed down his face and neck, and glistened from the breastplate of dark hair that clouded his chest. His flesh was undoubtedly hot. Steaming. Salty.

Servanne cleared her throat and sat a little straighter on the wooden stool. She was aware—acutely aware—of a heart that beat too fast, of blood racing too quickly and too warmly through veins that ran alternately hot as fever, cold as ice. A knot of tension sat in her belly like a fist, growing and twisting upon itself until it seemed to be sapping the strength from her limbs as well as draining it from her chest.

Out in the courtyard, the two men rose up like rampant lions, their bodies clashing together, their blades crossing one over the other, locked in a tremendous outpouring of raw energy. The Wolf snarled an oath questioning Friar's ancestry, and lunged mightily to throw his adversary off balance. Friar feinted to the left, his sword arcing off the Wolf's with enough force to create a shower of sparks. Two clean, blunt strikes later and the blades crossed again, grinding in a screaming weal of flashing silver to lock again at the hilt guards.

"A draw?" Friar suggested through his clamped teeth.

"The third this month?"

"Fourth. But one I fear may be too violent for the more faint-hearted in the bower."

The gray eyes flicked to the shade of the ancient yew. Servanne's pale face registered first as a blur, then as a glaring, fundamental mistake any bowed-legged page should have been able to see through. But before he could correct the error, Friar had already taken advantage of the distraction to hook a foot around the Wolf's ankle and thrust forward with his full weight. The two crashed heavily onto the ground in a churning cloud of dust and cartwheeling swords, and, when the curse-laden air cleared, the Wolf was flat on his back, his neck forced to an impossible arch by the biting tip of Friar's dagger.

"Declare it, my lord!" he gasped triumphantly.

"An unfair win," protested the Wolf.

"A win nonetheless. And by the same tack you used to best me but a month ago. Declare it, by God, or forfeit the need to shave for a week."

The Wolf laughed. "A fair win, you black-robed bastard! Now heave off me, and give a shout for ale, else we both die of thirst before we have a chance to celebrate properly."

Coughing with laughter and the effects of their strenuous bout, Friar collapsed beside him on the scuffed earth. The Wolf was grinning with genuine pleasure, for he was not one to grudge a man his due, and Friar had indeed come a long way from being the soft-eyed, soft-voiced acolyte he had rescued from a death cell seven years ago.

He was still grinning when he stood up and started smacking the dust from his shirt and leggings. A round of good-natured bickering between Mutter and Stutter drew his gaze to the old yew again and, after a brief moment of debate, he walked over, noting the care Servanne took to studiously ignore his approach.

"I trust you regained the coppers you lost last week," he said to Mutter, surprising and pleasing the twin into squirming himself into a state of deep crimson. The Wolf was one of the few who could tell the twins apart at a glance, although how he did so was anyone's guess. This unfathomable ability was what had once saved the brothers from being impaled and burned as demons—which had, in turn, made them loyal to their mentor to their last breath.

The Wolf looked at Servanne. "And you, my lady: I trust you were not overly bored by our practicing."

"I . . . was . . . much impressed by Friar's skill," she said hesitantly, unable to quite lift her eyes above the heady view of his bared torso.

The Wolf glanced down and casually thumbed the severed thongs.

"A hair less skill," he agreed with a crooked grin, "and I warrant I would be sporting a fine new red stripe."

Servanne's flush darkened to the point of discomfort, for now his scent had surrounded her and threatened to engulf her. The rich, pungent musk of well-spent sweat swamped her senses, prompting every movement, every gesture he made to result in a shower of hot, silvery sparks slithering down her spine.

"I . . . fail to understand why either of you would risk life and limb in such a . . . a meaningless display of male rivalry. Especially if, as you would have me believe, there are far weightier matters to be decided by blood and by sword."

The Wolf lowered his hands slowly, ignoring the salty moisture that continued to roll down his temples and cheeks. Her eyes commanded all of his attention . . . and his interest. He was as conscious of her delicate state of arousal as if he were inside her body sharing it, and its discovery intrigued him.

"In truth," he murmured, "Alaric and I have practiced some moves that are deliberately intended to look more dangerous than they are. It . . . inspires confidence in the men."

Her gaze inched a tiny measure higher, stalled again by the broad column of his neck. "Alaric?"

"*Friar* . . . Alaric," he said by way of an explanation. "He of the horsehair robes and wood-soled sandals."

Servanne's eyes fled downward to where her hands were clasped tightly in her lap, surrounded by a shredded bed of straw. It felt like the fine hairs at the nape of her neck were being similarly shredded; his nearness was playing havoc with her determination not to succumb to any more curiosities about the man—an impossible resolution, as well she knew it. She could look neither right nor left, not up nor down without feeling the seductive pull of his virility.

"I should think it would be a sacrilege to assume the guise of a priest of the Holy Order."

A dark brow arched. "We all of us commit small sacrileges at one time or another. Alaric's is no lesser and no greater than most."

"Why did he not complete his vows?"

"He lost his love for the church."

"It could not have been a very strong love to begin with."

"It was a good deal stronger than mine."

"You can say that, having nearly lost your life on Crusade?"

"My reasons for taking up the cross were far from holy. Nor was it God's wrath that challenged me on the deserts of Palestine."

"Still," she sighed, "I have seen you join your men in prayer each Matin."

A small grin betrayed more than his amusement. "It also inspires confidence in the men."

The Wolf was finding it difficult to keep his eyes from wandering down to the pouting softness of her lips. Equally alluring was the telltale prominence of the two hard buds of flesh straining against the sea-green velvet of her gown. A corresponding hardness in his own body was giving him some reason for distraction, and for the briefest of moments he allowed himself to recall the taste and feel of her, and the sound of the ragged little gasps that had almost been his undoing the other night in the garden.

He drew a deep, cleansing breath to fill his lungs, then flexed his arms. "Friar's skill seems to have taken a heavier toll on my old wounds than I had supposed. I have in my mind a hot soak would ease them."

"A hot soak? As with every other basic convenience you have so thoughtfully provided, both tub and hot water are but dim memories."

"If I could provide you with both? Would you then play hostess to my aching muscles?"

Servanne was instantly on guard and this time her gaze climbed as high as the sardonic grin tugging at his lips. Playing hostess by way of assisting a man to bathe was a duty often performed by the chatelaine of a castle, paying honour to a visiting guest of importance. But this was no castle, she was not the chatelaine of the forest, and this pagan renegade was of no importance to anyone but himself! Furthermore, there was no bath anywhere on or near the abbey grounds. Biddy had already conducted a most thorough search and there had been no receptacle large enough to escape her keen nose.

He was still grinning—a grin that was widening over her perplexed expression.

"Would you not even condescend to scrub my back?" he murmured. "Tsk tsk. Poor Sir Hubert. Was he made to groan and grovel to you each time he sought to beg a favour?"

Servanne's eyes flicked up to his, driven by a reckless sparkle of disdain. "Sir Hubert never had to beg for anything. All I did for him, I did gladly and willingly, and . . . with the greatest of pleasure."

It was the Wolf's turn to stare, for she had melted her tongue around the words *greatest* and *pleasure,* and had done so with enough relish to win snickers of delight from Mutter and Stutter.

"An obliging wife and hostess, were you?"

"Obliging . . . and *eager.*"

"I would see some of this saintly domesticity firsthand," he mused, the silkiness of his voice as deceiving as the stillness of his body. "Come. The thought of a bath grows in appeal."

Servanne flinched as if it were a hot coal being extended toward her instead of a hand. "Certainly not!"

"No? Do I still frighten you, my lady?" he asked with mocking indulgence.

"Not by half so much as your incredible arrogance would lead you to believe, wolf's head," she retorted.

"*My* arrogance?" he laughed softly. He turned away, leading Servanne to believe she had emerged from the fray unscathed, but in the next gasped breath, she felt her hand firmly grasped in his, her arm stretched nearly out of its socket, and her wimple flung end over end to blind her as she was lifted like a sack of grain and slung over his shoulder.

Shrieking with indignation, she was carried across the courtyard, her hands beating against his back, her feet kicking and her limbs wriggling in outraged mortification. Biddy's screams echoed her own for a moment or two, along with her rushing footsteps, but both were silenced under a round of hearty laughter.

Upended in this inglorious manner, Servanne was bounced, jostled, and manhandled perfunctorily through the garden and out the breach in the wall. She knew they were walking through the forest by the crunching underfoot and the saplings that snagged the folds of her wimple. She surmised they were skirting the bank of the Silent Pool when she rode out the sickening descent along the crumbled embankment.

He did not stop there as she expected, but kept walking, entering deep thick brush again and lurching down yet another, steeper incline. The bright sunlight they passed through at the pool disappeared, smothered under a dark,

damp blanket of shadow. The muscles across his shoulder
and back tensed as he used his falchion to hack a path
through the underbrush, but by then, so much blood had
rushed to fill her head, there was no room for questions,
fears, or recriminations. Servanne's body went limp. Her
hands lost their frenzied grip on his shirttails and started to
slip down, hanging as forlornly as the folds of the linen wimple.

The lapse was temporary, ending abruptly with the jolt
that set her upright on her feet again. Someone—not her—
resettled the flowing ends of her wimple, smoothing it back
over her shoulders so that she could see, but since she had no
idea where she was, she needed several astonished seconds to
realize what she was looking at.

He had brought her into a grotto of sorts, a low-ceilinged,
elongated cavern hewn out of the solid rock. The mist of
fright and anger she had supposed was blurring her vision
proved to be clouds of steam rising off the surface of a small
pool. It was fed from beneath the ground rather than above,
and was obviously heated by nature's grace, from some unknown source far below the surface of the rock. The basin of
the pool was no wider than two tall men stretched head to
heel, and was as clear as glass, with a bottom of fine white
sand. At the very centre, at a depth of perhaps three feet, the
sand was molded in the shape of a small volcano with occasional featherings around the rim of the crater to suggest
erupting jets of hot water.

Overhead the rock glistened wetly. Drops of water fell like
dew from the short, pointed stalactites hanging from the ceiling. The domed shape of the cavern trapped the heat and the
steam, while the open end was curtained by a thick wall of
ivy and ropes of fragrant honeysuckle. What hint there was
of the dazzling sunlight beyond the wall was muted and
filtered by the leaves, only to be refracted in the million tiny
fragments of phosphorescent sand embedded in the rock.

"What is this place?" she asked in a tremulous voice. "Where have you brought me?"

"You questioned the existence of a hot bath," the Wolf replied matter-of-factly. "And since you claim to have no apprehensions about myths or superstitions, it should not trouble you to know the druids who were said to inhabit this forest long ago, used the waters of this particular well to purify their sacrificial offerings."

Servanne looked at him aghast. She had never said she was not superstitious, and jesting about druids and sacrificial offerings was a sure call for doom.

She swallowed hard. "Very well, I have seen your bath. I would like to go back to the abbey now."

"Without taking advantage of the hot water and obliging hands? You said yourself you craved the pleasure of a scrub —here is your opportunity, and here am I to assist."

"Assist! I would sooner trust the assistance of a whoremaster!"

He looked wounded. "Why, you act as if I want more from you than to exchange a simple courtesy. In truth, I ask only for a bath. A request for anything else must needs come from you."

Her mouth dropped open in shock.

"Take me back," she insisted shrilly. "Take me back at once, do you hear?"

He ignored her and pulled the sweat-soaked tails of his shirt over his shoulders and flung it aside. Servanne pressed as far back into the shadows as she could go, her feet slipping on the lush carpet of thick green moss, her hands finding nothing to support her on the smooth, wet walls.

Under her horrified stare, the Wolf casually unfastened the leather points that held his leggings taut about his hips. The deerhide was peeled down the solidly thewed thighs and discarded along with his boots, shirt, and stockings in a crumpled heap beside the pool.

Naked as a gladiator he stepped into the steaming water and waded to the centre of the basin.

"Ahh—" he sighed and sank down in a cloud of swirling mist. He stretched his arms out and let his head fall back, submerging himself below the surface of the water. He reappeared a few moments later, his long chestnut mane plastered sleekly to his head and shoulders, his bronzed torso streaming crystalline sheets.

Almost as an afterthought, the gray eyes returned to the shadows and he grinned.

"I await your convenience, my lady," he said, spreading his arms.

"You may wait until hell freezes, milord! How dare you think . . . *presume* you can treat me this way!"

"What way is that?"

"Like a . . . like a common tavern wench, or a . . . a . . ."

"Yes?"

Servanne saw the arrogant smile and squared her slender shoulders in defiance. "You treat me as though I were someone who should fawn at your knees, or at the very least faint with awe over this . . . this paltry dividend of flesh you seem to hold in such vaunted esteem!"

Since she was pointing so disdainfully at his groin, he followed her gaze and noted, with wry alacrity, that he was indeed somewhat lacking in substance. But, having been addressed so personally, not to mention slandered, the object in question began to slowly, steadily rouse itself for a rebuttal.

Servanne's eyes widened in horror. Her throat worked to dislodge the lump that was steadfastly threatening to smother her, but to no effect. Disbelief, incredulity . . . *fear* . . . whatever kept her gaze fixed on the naked satyr also drew her hands upward to attempt to confine the wild beating within her breast.

The Wolf's smile faded. The jest was suddenly no longer a

jest and he could feel the heat in his blood rising to match the heat of the water.

"Come into the pool, Servanne," he ordered quietly. "You know you want to."

Her eyes flicked up to his, filled with shame and anger. "No," she gasped. "No . . . I want no such thing!"

With a muffled sob of desperation she ran for the wall of ivy, but having been upside down and backwards when she was carried in, as well as dazed by too much blood pounding in her temples, Servanne could not immediately find the break in the vines that led to fresh air and freedom. She pushed and plucked and tore at the tangled greenery, all the while aware of splashing movement behind her.

The steamy air thickened perceptibly with the scent of his closeness and she knew without turning around that he was standing behind her.

"What will it take for you to learn that you cannot defy me?" he asked calmly, quietly. "And when will you realize that the source of your defiance is your own desire?"

"Let me go back," she gasped. "Please . . . let me go back."

She heard him take a deep breath and release it slowly. "I think not, my lady. I think I would know what it was you did for Sir Hubert so gladly . . . so willingly . . . and with such great pleasure. And I think you have some curiosity to know if what he did in return was worth such a valiant defense of his memory."

"No," her voice was barely a whisper. "No, I have no such curiosity."

"You have no skill in telling lies either," he murmured.

The long, tanned fingers worked without seeking assent of any kind to unfasten the bands of her wimple and uncover the golden skeins of her hair. The fat, gleaming braids were uncoiled and the strands separated, combed into a rich spill of silk-soft curls by hands that worked reverently at their pleasure. Servanne stood motionless, frozen with shock. Her skin flamed outwardly, while inwardly her body pulsated with a sensation not unlike a million shards of icicles melting downward into the ground.

Once her hair was freed and tumbling below her waist, the Wolf's hands sought the clasp that bound the wide girdle of intricate gold links around her slender hips. Servanne's hands fell, out of some last desperate attempt at salvation, and for a moment they did win the attention of the hard, lean fingers, but then they moved again and the girdle slipped to the ground, and Servanne's fingers were left trembling over empty air.

The laces binding the gown of sea-green velvet were unthreaded with deliberate care; the shoulders and sleeves peeled away and the skirt encouraged to crumple into the swirling eddies of mist. All that remained was the long, shapeless white silk sheath she wore as an undergarment, and the dextrous fingers indulged in a lengthy hesitation before riding lightly down the slippery outline of her hips and thighs.

Servanne's hands clutched at the vines of ivy as she felt him take up the hem of her sheath and raise it above her knees. Each stocking was painstakingly rolled from knee to ankle, then removed along with her dainty pointed slippers. By now, the liquid heat that had warmed her in the courtyard was all but paralyzing her. Her body was alive with coiling, shifting sensations. Her thighs trembled, the flesh bridging them grew achingly hot and throbbed with expectations that both mortified and thrilled her.

"When you are ready, my lady," he murmured. "Our bath awaits."

Servanne squeezed her eyes tightly shut, willing away the waves of sinful pleasure his voice evoked. It was not right. It was not possible. It was *unthinkable* that she should turn around, turn away from the opening in the ivy she could see so clearly only a pace away . . .

The Wolf stretched out his hand. She stared at it, knowing that to touch him of her own accord would be to admit defeat, to *be* defeated by the heat and flame, the passion of desire that raged through her with such incomprehensible urgency.

Servanne's hand shook where it was buried in the ivy. Her fingers released their grip and moved haltingly to where the thicker, stronger ones awaited with such infinite patience. She saw his hand close around hers and she could not stop the small sigh that escaped her lips.

It *was* unthinkable to surrender to him, and yet Servanne did so, moving without the strength, the energy to resist any longer the lure of his male potency. She followed him into the clear, steaming water, and it was warm. So warm. And the sand was soft, enveloping her foot like a feather pillow. He drew her another step and the water was only slightly deeper, rising just above her ankle. Another brought the warm caress rippling around her calves, and with the next, the hem of her sheath floated out in a wide white circle midway up her thighs. The incredible wall of boldly sculpted muscle was in front of her, still as a statue, tall and terrifyingly virile in his nudity. The mist and shadow and eerie blue-green glitter of the cavern surrounded them like an unearthly spell.

Without speaking and with a carefully blank expression, absent of any hint of triumph, the Black Wolf turned and sank slowly to his knees in the water, presenting her with an agonizingly stark view of the scarred shoulders.

Deformed and maimed, capable of conjuring ghouls and grotesques, even elfin demons at the snap of a finger.

His words, mocking her.

Touch them, you would not burst into flame or see the bones turned to ash on a devil's curse.

Her fingertips barely creased the surface of the water and she raised them with a curious detachment, watching the droplets fall brightly back onto the glassy surface. She dipped and raised them again, this time lifting a cupped handful of the steaming stuff and observing the glistening path it left on the hard-surfaced flesh. With the scantest tip of a finger, she traced a wet curl of chestnut hair from the base of his neck to the solid ridge of his shoulder. She lifted more water, smoothing it in with long, circular motions that tempted her hands down the plated knuckles of his spine, then up and over the wide, hard slabs of muscle that armoured his shoulder blades.

Despite the moistness in the air, her throat was dry and her mouth felt stuffed with raw, unspun fleece. The skin across her breasts was stretched so taut it felt brittle; the slightest abrasion from the silk sheath sent shivers of icy pleasure into her nipples until they were puckered tight, straining with impatience.

The Wolf had not moved; he did not move now as she waded from the side to the front and stood before him, the black centres of her eyes dilated, the surrounding rim of blue shimmering with the weakness that throbbed and vibrated through every vein and nerve in her body. The broad expanse of his chest filled her gaze; it lured her hands like the sin of untold riches, and she did not even use the feint of bathwater as an excuse to lay her palms against the bulge of muscles, or to drag her fingers through the crisp, lush pelt of curls. They climbed slowly to his shoulders, then to the broad base of his neck. Of their own accord, her fingers buried themselves in the thicker, lusher waves of his hair.

Servanne's lips trembled apart. She did not know what to say, or how to ask. She did not even know what she was asking for, but the Wolf knew, and his hands rose up from the water, caressing her skin, moulding to the narrow indent of her waist. He drew her forward against the incredible heat

of his chest and his mouth was there to smother her gasp.
His lips moved forcefully, possessively over hers, his tongue
barely waiting to reacquaint itself with the supple outer contours of her mouth before it was delving boldly, deeply, hungrily for sweeter rewards within.

Servanne's cry went unheeded when, with brutal disregard
for her sanity, her mouth was left gaping and abandoned
while his lips plundered the swanlike arch of her throat. He
sent her senses reeling on waves of carnal promises as he
blazed a fiery path from the tender underside of her chin to
the silk-encased tautness of her breast. She gasped without
sound as the moist, suckling heat closed around her nipple.
A curse and the sigh of tearing silk brought the heat closer,
gave bolder texture to the rolling, kneading thrust of his
tongue. She shook her head as if to deny the shock and the
pleasure, but her own voice betrayed her. Pleas and clawing
fingers guided him with shallow, urgent cries of assent when
he lifted his mouth from one trembling peak and gallantly
went in search of the other.

He also seemed to know the exact moment when her legs
could no longer support her. With the ghostly vapours of
steam cushioning her descent, the Wolf drew her down beside him, to where the water was a thin, warm sheet over the
fine sand, and the sweet green moss was the perfect pillow
for her head. Half in, half out of the water, he lowered his
mouth to her body again, his hands raking into the golden
mass of her hair, spreading it beneath them with a reverence
that caused his arms to tremble.

A gust of hoarse incredulity acknowledged the lusty imprint of his flesh where it intruded, swollen and impatient
between her thighs. Her limbs were coaxed wide by a body
that had difficulty disguising its eagerness, and she gasped
again, clutching frantically at the muscles that tensed across
his back as his weight bore down over hers.

There was none of the gentle, apologetic hesitation which

had marked Sir Hubert's couplings. The prideful thrust of the Wolf's flesh was like the man himself—wild, savage, primitive, unyielding. It breached her hard and fast, stretching, swelling, filling her to the bounds of reason, then surging even deeper, deeper, until she could feel him touch upon the very depths of her soul. And when he moved within her . . . dear God, when he moved within her, she had no more thoughts to waste on pride or shame, only the desire, the need to clasp her arms, her limbs tighter around him so that she might know the glory of total possession.

The Wolf heard her cries of awe and was conscious of his own astonishment as he felt her lithe young body strain and arch to accommodate him. The velvety fist of her womanhood closed around him without guile or avarice, and for the first time since he had vowed to close his heart and mind to any soft intrusions, he felt the formidable barriers of ice and steel threatened. The loner, the renegade, the black knight within him fought the encroachment with as valiant an effort as any he had put forth in the lists, knowing the dangers of falling blindly into the chasms of emotion. The man in him, the ardent lover of so many years ago, succumbed to the heat and the drenching oblivion, he stumbled and fell headlong into the misty well of imploring cries and passion-haunted eyes.

He slid trembling hands beneath her hips to raise her, brace her as he felt the tide of pleasure begin to swell and burst in scalding founts of ecstasy. Servanne's head thrashed against the moss, her eyes wide and staring as she soared through peak after peak of rapture, each one higher, sharper, brighter, hotter than the one before. She thought she heard someone screaming, the sound as shivered and splintered as the shafts of fiery consummation that ravaged her body with unending spirals of flame.

The Wolf groaned and rolled onto his back, carrying her wet and streaming body with him, seeking to hold her steady

until he could collect his wits and will about him again. But
she was already far beyond the authority of his hands and,
challenging his efforts to hold her still, she curled her hips
forward and slid them back, forward and back, shamelessly
triumphant to discover she was not dependent upon his permission to exploit the deep, throbbing friction within her.
The rough, calloused hands were clamped rigidly around her
waist, but they could no more resist the succulent temptation
of her breasts, than her hips, once free to obey her instincts,
could fail to quicken to a blur as their ecstasy reached another shuddering crescendo . . . and another.

It had been his intention to brand himself on her mind and
body forever, but in the end, clinging to her as desperately as
she clung to him, he feared she would be the one seared into
every nerve and fibre of his being until he drew his last
breath.

13

Servanne opened her eyes slowly, the lids heavy beyond belief. Her head was still pillowed on the bank of fragrant green moss, her body as yet suspended on several inches of warm, lapping water. The sand beneath her had been hollowed and contoured to fit the shape of her body, and enfolded her more snugly than the heated ticking of a feather-filled mattress.

She uttered a tiny gasp of dismay and allowed her lashes to flutter closed again. She knew she dared not look down to where the dark crown of his head was moving slowly, languidly between her thighs. She could feel the hungry insistence of his mouth and tongue and that was bad enough. To acknowledge she had regained the full use of her senses, or that she might have found enough strength to deter or dissuade him, would only make matters worse.

Worse? What could possibly be worse than lying helpless and vulnerable to a passion she had not known she was capable of feeling? What could be worse than permitting his hands and his lips free access to her body, or to respond to each deliberately provocative thrust of his tongue with soft cries and indelicate shudders that only invited and encouraged more unthinkable wickedness?

Her teeth tore at her lower lip to keep her from groaning aloud as she felt his hands skim up the gleaming litheness of her body. She halfheartedly cursed the knowledge in his dancing fingertips as he curled them around the straining flesh of her breasts, and, finding the nipples flushed with anticipation, he pulled them gently, abrading them with the calloused pads of his thumbs.

She stretched her own hands wide on either side of her, searching for something solid to grasp hold of. There was only water and sand on the one side, moss and slippery lichen on the other, and with a groan of resignation, she reached down and threaded her fingers tightly into his chestnut mane. She dug her heels deeper into the fine silt, aware of the water beginning to splash more violently over her hips and belly. Her arms tautened and her head pressed back into the moss. The heat leaped and flickered within her like a candle flame, the blue-white core burning in her loins, the orange and red sparks flaring and bursting behind her tightly squeezed eyelids.

Her gasped sobs of pleasure echoed wetly off the damp walls and ceiling of the cavern. Her shivers and shudders vibrated the steamy fingers of mist, causing them to thicken, she was certain, where the heat was becoming almost unbearable.

The Wolf's mouth relented and his hands clasped her waist, drawing her down to where he knelt in deeper water. Servanne felt the urgency in his grip as he lifted her, held her against the incredible splendour of his chest, then slowly lowered her down over his turgid flesh. His dark eyes locked mercilessly to hers and there was nothing to be gained or lost by trying to deny the instant and violent spasms of pleasure that welcomed the solid, sliding penetration. There was nothing she could do but curl her arms more frantically around his neck and weather the same storm of pulsating contractions that forced him to pause and press a muffled groan into the curve of her neck.

He gathered her close, crushing her against the hard breadth of his chest, his powerful muscles bunching under the deluge of moist shivers that urged him deeper into her silken body. He was loathe to move too soon. The pleasure of holding her, of feeling the heat of her pour over and around him almost pain—indeed, it was an agony demanding to be assuaged with each breath torn from his chest.

The Wolf rose off his haunches, carrying her with him, the wet skeins of her hair dragging through the water like spilled honey. He laid her back against the shifting mattress of sand and swallowed her cries as his thrusting body brought them both to a swift, savage release. Once, twice, Servanne's hands tore at the bulging muscles across his back. Thrice she gasped and sent the feverishly gouging fingers to his flanks to ride the plunging motion of his hips.

Flung through one shattering wave of ecstasy after another, Servanne strained and writhed to a stunning climax beneath him. Even after their bodies ground to a dazed, reeling halt, the pleasure of his heat and presence within her continued to send tiny little spirals of sensation whorling outward from her loins to the farthest tips of her toes and fingers.

Worse, and worse again.

She should have heeded Biddy's warning and stayed well clear of this creature of the forest. She never should have given way to her curiosity, never touched a hand to the hard, virile promise in his body, and never, never opened herself so greedily, so wantonly to the desires he roused in her. She should, by all rules of sanity and logic, be longing to see the last of him. Instead, she longed only to feel his hands roving hungrily over her body. She longed only to lie here in the steaming, mystic peace of the grotto, his hard body joined to hers, the texture of belly, hips, and thighs imprinted vividly on her flesh.

Moreover, she longed never to have to move from this place, never to have to discover any truths other than what she knew and felt to be irrefutable now and to her mind, forever.

But of course the dark head moved, as she knew it must, and the Wolf's somber gaze sought hers through the glowing phosphorescence. He said nothing. In truth, he had said nothing—neither of them had—since she had taken her first tentative steps into the heated pool.

She suffered another mildly disconcerting shock as he bent his lips to hers and kissed her with tender thoroughness. When he released her, he did so on a sigh of feigned consternation.

"What am I to do with you now?" he asked quietly.

"Do?" she whispered, her eyes growing rounder and darker with alarm. "What more could you possibly do that you have not done already?"

The Wolf would have laughed if not for the suffocating pressure her words placed around his heart. He raised himself on his elbows and stared down at the bruised lushness of her mouth. Swollen and pink from his attentions, the sight was not kind on his composure. Nor was the damning residue of tears on her lashes, or the softly mottled flush that warmed the delectable plumpness of her breasts. And the mere thought of the fine golden hairs meshed with the coarser, blacker ones at his groin made it painfully clear there was little hope of regaining the cool indifference that had served him in their dealings thus far.

"Why is it I am left with the distinct impression you were a virgin in all but the strictest sense of the word?"

Servanne reddened, as much from the directness of the query as from the shivered response his voice triggered in her body.

"I . . . was *not* a virgin," she insisted lamely.

"You were no longer in possession of your maidenhead," he agreed, "But you were a virgin nonetheless."

Servanne attempted to avert her head so she would not be forced to endure his mocking humour, but a resolute thumb tilted her chin back with ridiculous ease.

"Sir Hubert never bedded you?"

It was not so much a question as it was an expression of puzzled disbelief, and she could feel fresh tears welling along her lashes.

"He . . . never bedded me . . . like this," she admitted haltingly.

Her words, and the ravaged emotions behind them, prompted the gray eyes to narrow and the Wolf to regard her in a new and disturbing light. Their bodies were so motionless, the surface of the water calmed to molten silver and the mist dared to venture close again, enveloping them in a creamy white veil.

"I did not miss the attention," she explained in a rush, thinking his silence a request for such. "He was very kind and very good to me. A gentle, loving, and considerate husband in every other way. But . . . he was old, and . . . tired very easily. And . . . since I had no way of knowing . . . I mean, no way of judging . . . well, I did not know enough *not* to be content."

"A woman's logic," he mused. "And you will have to forgive my ill-mannered curiosity for asking, but why did he not make other private arrangements for you?"

"Arrangements?" she asked, the warmth of only moments ago fading under an uncomfortable chill. "I was not aware my ignorance was such an offence."

"No, little fool," he said, smothering any hint of rebellion under the power of his lips. "I meant arrangements to insure you delivered him an heir."

"A stud?" she gasped, shocked anew. "For breeding purposes!"

The Wolf shifted his weight forward to confine her outrage to a few half-hearted squirmings. "A *man,*" he said firmly. "For the purpose of protecting you against being sold or traded away in another marriage of someone else's convenience. Surely Sir Hubert was aware of his shortcomings. He

should have contrived to keep you from falling victim to a
king's greed again—especially if he was as gentle, considerate, and loving as you say he was. Had it been me," he added
intently, "I would have gone to whatever lengths necessary
to protect you, even to finding a stud to breed you . . . even
to binding you hand and foot to the bed and overseeing the
deed myself."

Servanne had no rebuttal, for indeed there was none. She
would not have been in this predicament if she had given Sir
Hubert an heir. Both she and the child would have become
wards of the king until the heir came of age, but she would
have been well within her rights to refuse any proposed
unions which she did not favour.

What the rogue's theory failed to consider, however, was
that up until a few short hours ago, she had been more than
content with the future arrangements made for her. She had
been looking forward to her marriage to Lucien Wardieu
with a naïve eagerness that bordered on childish glee. There
again, content in her ignorance, she had not been aware of
any other choice available to her.

But was there any other choice? She had only his word he
was come to England on a secretive, honourable mission for
Eleanor of Aquitaine. She had only his word the golden-
haired knight known throughout England as the Baron de
Gournay was a cheat and an impostor. This man had bedded
her, had introduced her to the wonders of her woman's
body, but was passion and pleasure any way to measure the
truth from the lie?

The chill within her deepened and spread. Despite claiming revenge had played no part in this, would he not, when
clearer, calmer reasoning prevailed, consider it a minor triumph to have bedded his brother's intended bride beforehand? Men were all vainglorious creatures when it came to
testing and proving their prowess; why should the Wolf's
motives prove to be any purer?

Fear, conscience, uncertainty . . . and a sudden aware-
ness of where she was—sprawled naked and wildly dishev-
eled in a cave hissing with the ghostly voices of pagan rituals
—caused Servanne to tense noticeably. She lowered her
hands from where they rested on his shoulders and placed
them like a subtle barrier between his flesh and hers.

"Please, I . . ."

"What is it? What is wrong? Surely you still do not fear
me as a demon with horns and a forked tail?"

"Devilish," she admitted softly, her fingers curling involuntarily into the crisp pelt of hair on his chest. "But no devil,
although it does confuse me profoundly to try to find a difference."

He smiled crookedly. "Confusion is a woman's normal
state of mind, so I neither take nor lay blame for causing it in
you."

Servanne watched as he bowed his head and caught one of
her slim, delicate fingers between his lips.

"You have done what your brother will have expected you
to do," she said matter-of-factly, and reclaimed her hand.

His gaze lifted slowly to hers. "That was not why I did it."

"Nevertheless"—she spoke slowly, searching his eyes for
the truth before she continued—"the deed is done and he
will know."

A long pause—long enough for a future of loneliness, regret, and despair to flash before Servanne's eyes—ended on a
faintly snarled oath. "You will be safe enough. The Dragon
will not take his anger out on you."

"But . . . he *will* be angry."

"He will be angry," the Wolf conceded.

"And . . . knowing this . . . you are still determined to
sell me back to him as planned?"

"Your choice of terms leaves much to be desired," he answered with a frown. "I am not selling you back to him. I am
sending you on ahead to Bloodmoor Keep because, for the

time being anyway, it is the safest place for you to be until the matter is resolved."

"Safe?" she gasped. "How can you expect me to feel safe when you have said and done everything in your power to warn me *away* from Bloodmoor Keep?"

"I have only endeavoured to warn you away from the man who resides there as its master. Bloodmoor itself cannot be held to account for the taint he has brought to it. You will be safe," he repeated. "The castle is full of wedding guests—important guests—and the Dragon will do nothing to rouse anyone's suspicions until the halls and chambers are empty again. If anything, he will be only too eager to act as if nothing has happened beyond paying an enterprising outlaw for the release of his bride. He will not willingly admit to anyone his brother has come back from the dead, or that there might be some reason for the nuptials to be delayed or postponed. Moreover, there are other reasons for secrecy and silence; reasons which forbid both Etienne and myself from settling our conflict openly and speedily, and those I dare not tell you, for it would most definitely place you in certain danger."

"But . . . would it not be better for me to know of this danger?"

The Wolf brushed his fingertips over the tight, damp coils of hair clinging to her temples. "I told you he and I were much alike. Just as I can see so clearly what you feel and think at times, one look, one glance into these wide blue eyes of yours and he would know you were hiding something behind them."

"Knowing this, you would still send me to face him alone?"

"I think you are more than a match for whatever tests the Dragon may put you through. Furthermore, you will not be completely alone," the Wolf promised, twining his hands into the wet tangle of her hair. "Nor will you be without recourse if something . . . *anything* happens to frighten you. The queen's official representative at the wedding is Lord Randwulf de la Seyne Sur Mer. You can trust him. He or any of his men will provide help or sanctuary if you need it."

His frown cleared and he smiled in an attempt to soften the bluntness of his words. "La Seyne is another black-hearted bastard you will undoubtedly take to task for his boorish manners, but he is loyal to the queen, and none too fond of anyone who shares the humour of Prince John. You *can* trust him. I do . . . with my life."

Servanne's eyes brimmed slowly with fat, shiny tears. Seeing them, seeing the uncertainty behind them, the Wolf tightened his hands and drew her forward. She tried to avoid his mouth as it came down over hers, but his hands were firm and his lips forceful. His tongue was quick and efficient at reminding her how futile any show of resistance might be, and Servanne moaned softly, helplessly. She went so far as to push against the lowering wall of muscle before her hands betrayed their true desire and crept up and around the bronzed width of his shoulders.

At almost the same moment as Servanne de Briscourt was experiencing the greatest joy in her young life, the Dragon de Gournay was flushing with excitement.

"We believe we have found their lair, my lord," Sir Aubrey de Vere reported. "We did not dare take the risk of creeping too close lest we betray our presence, but all signs indicate the Black Wolf has made camp in the ruins of an abbey once known as Thornfeld."

"Thornfeld?" Wardieu's blue eyes narrowed sharply. "Why am I not familiar with the name?"

"It is . . . *was* a cloister inhabited by monks who shunned all contact with the outside world. It is but a half-day's ride from here, no more, and not five leagues from where we lost the scent of the two foresters the other night."

"By God, right under our noses," muttered Wardieu. "And no one thought to search this ruined abbey before now?"

De Vere frowned uncomfortably. "It was believed the brothers who lived there were followers of the Antichrist. At any rate, the abbey was put to the torch and the monks slaughtered, and for nigh on eighty years, no one has set eyes upon the ruins or dared to venture anywhere near that part of the forest."

"No one? Not even the hounds of our fearsome Lord High Sheriff who professes to have scoured every square inch of the forest in search of the outlaw and his band?"

"It is not an easy place to find," De Vere said. "The trees are thicker than flies on rotted meat, and the hills are pocked with caves and gorges to easily lead a man astray."

"Surely the local villagers know of its location, especially those who poach the king's deer with impunity."

"Indeed, my lord, and to them this Black Wolf would be a rogue hero; they would not betray his whereabouts even if they knew it. We could only find one toothless old crone who would even admit to knowing of the place, and then only because she was an imbecile and has kept to her own foul company in the woods these past twenty years."

"Perhaps we should make this imbecile sheriff then," Wardieu said angrily. "Who else would think to look first on cursed grounds for a man who would like the world to think of him as a spectre who can appear and disappear at will? By God, it is just as well Onfroi de la Haye lies so near death; I would strangle him myself for all the worth he is to me."

Nicolaa de la Haye emerged from Wardieu's pavilion and scowled up at the sun. Light filtering through the overhanging flap gave her milk-white complexion a faintly bluish caste. Her eyes were puffed and her stance unsteady, for she had needed strong decoctions of crushed willow bark to help her sleep without dreaming too vividly.

"What is all this about strangling Onfroi?" she grumbled. "I have been entreating you to let me do so for years, but you have always stayed my hand."

"Thornfeld Abbey," Wardieu asked brusquely. "Do you know of it?"

"Thornfeld? Thornfeld . . . the name tastes familiar somehow . . ."

Wardieu allowed a flicker of disgust to cross his face as he regarded her unkempt, dissolute condition. Was it just the sickly blue glow from the pavilion overhang giving Nicolaa's raven beauty a brittle edge, or was it the stirring of memories that vaguely repulsed him? She had clung to him like a leech the past two nights, and while her body had afforded its usual erotic release for his tensions, there had been no real pleasure derived from her frantic manipulations.

Wardieu turned back to De Vere. "Have the men in full armour and ready to ride in twenty minutes. Are you certain you can find the place again?"

De Vere smiled wanly. "We still have the hag and she still has possession of half her fingers and toes. Milord D'Aeth has been most persuasive in winning her cooperation thus far; I have no doubt he can continue to do so."

"Tell him he can have more than her fingers and toes to chew on so long as she lives long enough to guide us to Thornfeld Abbey."

It might have been an hour, a week, or a month later when Servanne wakened from her passion-induced drowse. The air was markedly cooler where they lay twined together on the moss, although there was more than enough heat emanating from the Wolf's body to maintain hers at a rosy flush. The edge of the pool was a few inches from where her fingers rested limply on the moss, but the slight disturbance caused by uncurling them and dipping them into the water produced a distinct change in the tempo of the heart beating beneath her ear.

Servanne sighed and raised her head with an effort. He was awake, but not much longer before her, judging by the heaviness around his eyes.

"The hour must be dreadfully late," she said, warming self-consciously when she saw how intimately their bodies were positioned, one cradled atop the other in contrasting lengths of palest white and weathered bronze.

"You were sleeping like a kitten. I had not the heart to waken you."

The Black Wolf of Lincoln—admitting to a heart?

Servanne smiled at the thought and looked around her in the gloom. Their clothes would undoubtedly be damp and wrinkled beyond any possible logical explanation. Biddy would know—the whole camp would know where they had been and what they had been doing for most of the afternoon. Her hair would take hours to dry and tame into a semblance of order. Her knees, back, and buttocks felt chafed raw from the sand, and she was certain, in any but the dimmest light, the whiteness of her skin would be marred by visually explicit bruises.

The gray eyes were observing her every change of expression and it was not too difficult to interpret her thoughts. An unexpected surge of protectiveness gripped him and he had to keep his hands flat by his sides to stop them from reaching out and gathering her back into his embrace.

He had not wanted this to happen, had not intended this to happen and for the very reasons that sickened and appalled him as he saw her trying very hard to shield her thoughts and emotions. The Dragon would see her guilt as if it were a beacon on a stormy night. Arrogant bastard that he was, it might not occur to him that she had allowed herself to be despoiled willingly. Hopefully his rage would remain focused where it should: on the man who had kidnapped and ravished his bride. But if the Dragon suspected for a moment there had been no force, no rape involved in Servanne de Briscourt's submission, or if she betrayed by the slightest word or gesture that she preferred the touch of one man over the other . . .

Cursing inwardly, he turned away and started rummaging beneath the mist for his discarded clothing. He was shrugging his heavy shoulders into the green linsey-woolsey shirt when the touch of her hand on his scarred flesh stopped him again. It was only the tips of her fingers that gently traced the hideously misshapen weals, but it could have been a red-hot iron searing his flesh for the same impact it left on his body.

"These must have caused you a great deal of pain for a very long time," she whispered.

"Wounds of betrayal hurt far more than any wounds of the flesh," he said flatly and pulled the shirt down to cover the scars.

Servanne sat motionless a moment longer, chastened by his sudden anger, yet ignorant of the cause. She began sorting through the tumbled ruin of her own clothes, each small movement emphasizing the empty ache inside her. Even her hair, brushing over her bare skin, produced shivers that would never again foster innocent thoughts.

Had he been left unaffected by the passions they had unleashed together? Could a man do all that he had done to her, share all they had shared, and not be changed, altered in some way? She did not expect declarations of undying love and devotion but neither did she expect to have her clothes tossed casually across the moss as if, for him, it had been but a pleasant afternoon's diversion.

"Might I ask another question without fear of having my head snapped off?"

"Ask it," he said sharply. "And we shall see."

"This black-hearted knight you would foist me upon to ease your conscience . . . does he know who you are and why you are here?"

"La Seyne?" Something akin to a smile glimmered in the dark eyes. "He knows."

"Does he also know of this other . . . *danger,* to which you referred?"

"He knows more than he would care to have as a burden."

"You said you could not provide proof of who you are until you are inside the castle. Is La Seyne here to back your claim when and if it becomes necessary?"

The Wolf looked at her with a grudging respect. A claim made against one of Prince John's allies was useless and suicidal without the support of equally formidable and influential witnesses. La Seyne Sur Mer was the dowager queen's champion; a knight regarded as being above reproach, who would be no easy man to fool or slough off with half-truths.

"You had best not show yourself to be too clever around the Dragon," he warned softly. "He does not take kindly to minxes with sharp noses and sly tongues."

"Another similarity with his brother. I confess I am becoming more intrigued by the moment to meet and compare qualities myself."

The Wolf was leaning over to retrieve his deerskin leggings when the unexpected sarcasm of her words halted him. With their faces only inches apart, and the light from the mouth of the cavern at its most generous angle, Servanne again thought she saw something flicker in the guarded depths of his eyes. If she did, it was quickly hidden and her humour as effectively quashed.

"As I told you before, there are some things we do quite differently. If you doubt me, ask any one of his scores of former mistresses . . . or his current one: Nicolaa de la Haye."

Hurt and confused by his unwarranted bitterness,

Servanne stared down at the crumpled folds of velvet she
held in her lap and wondered why it seemed to be his prime
task to perplex and confound her to the verge of tears. Reso-
lutely, she gathered her courage to ask one more important
question of him, but when she looked up, her emotions as
exposed as an open wound, he was not even paying her any
heed. Something had drawn all of his attention to the wall of
ivy, and that something was causing him to turn as still as
stone.

"What—?"

His hand lashed out to cover her mouth and stifle the
question against her lips. Another moment passed before she
heard it too: the squeak of leather, the faint chink of metal
on metal, the snap and rustle of carefully bent saplings.

There was someone in the woods nearby. Someone moving
with the deadly stealth of a hunter closing in on a wolf's lair.

14

The Wolf's first thought was for the sentry up on the promontory; he should have seen the intruders in plenty of time to have passed an alarm to the abbey. His second thought exploded inwardly on a curse, for he had waved the sentry away when he had carried Servanne past the Silent Pool. In an even more shocking breach of his own rules, he realized he had left his bow in the courtyard, along with his sword. He had his falchion and a dull eating knife—neither of which would do much good unless he could creep unseen to within a few feet of an enemy.

Pressing a finger to his lips, he cautioned Servanne needlessly to silence and crossed to the mouth of the cavern. He was just a shadow hunched against the mist, but she saw him sink into a low crouch and melt back against the stone as a particularly loud crunch of twigs occurred within a pace or two of where the entrance lay hidden behind the ivy.

Servanne held her breath. She suffered a fleeting glimpse of men-at-arms and knights locked in mortal combat with the Wolf's men, screaming, charging through the woods, their swords gleaming red and wet. And in the midst of it all, she would be running and screaming as well, but to which camp? To whose arms?

Servanne screamed the answer just as the Wolf sprang forward and crashed through the gap in the ivy. There were muffled sounds of grunts and scraping feet, the paunchy *thud* of a well-met fist . . . then silence.

She rose up onto her knees, her gown clutched over her bare breasts, her heart in her throat, her eyes stinging with fear. Another ripe scream was bubbling up from her toes just as she recognized the Wolf's broad shoulders dragging something or someone back into the gloom of the cavern.

"Sparrow! Goddammit!" he shouted.

Servanne's gasp relieved the pressure building in her lungs the same instant the Wolf's hand lifted away from the elf's mouth, releasing a string of shrilled oaths and invectives. They were choked back sharply as the Wolf thrust him hard against the wall and held him by the scruff of the neck, leaving the stubby arms and legs to flail the empty air in panic.

"Sparrow, by Christ, I warned you—!"

"We have all been out searching this past half hour for you, my lord," Sparrow squeaked. "The Dragon's men . . . they are in the woods. They are heading this way!"

The Wolf's hand flexed open and the little man dropped into an abrupt heap on the moss

" 'Tis true, my lord," he gasped, rubbing his throat for circulation. "The Dragon's men . . . two hours away, no more. With armour on their backs and blood in their eyes. They must know we are here—a loose tongue, or a careless footstep."

"*Two* sets of careless footsteps, I warrant," the Wolf snarled. "How many men are there?"

"H-he had two score with him in camp, plus the sheriff's men, p-plus those left from the cavalcade. Not all would have come, but enough to send Sigurd hurrying back with the alarm."

"It was to be expected. We could not have remained here much longer without someone stumbling over us. Are we ready for them?"

Sparrow nodded hard enough to set his curls bouncing. "The men are all dispatched and await your orders. You

were the only one we could not find. You and . . .
and . . ."

The round cherub eyes blinked wider as he caught sight of
a nervous movement through the clouds of rising steam. He
blinked again and swallowed whatever he might have been
tempted to say, in favour of ignoring the plenitude of naked
limbs and awkward tempers.

"Well, then," he said instead. "I have found you both."

"And nearly won a blade in your gullet for the effort,"
said the Wolf, stalking back to the far side of the pool to
snatch up the rest of his clothes. A glare in Servanne's direction was sufficient to unlock her fingers from the folds of
velvet and hurry them in pulling the rumpled gown over her
head. The fabric was damp and chilled her skin, but she
scarcely felt it for the more foreboding chill in the air.

"Why did you not sound the horn?" the Wolf asked,
threading the points of his leggings swiftly through the corresponding loops on his belt.

"We did," Sparrow replied. "Twice. Friar began to worry
you might have pushed each other over the gorge and broken
your heads on the rocks below, but the sentry said you came
this way, where there are no rocks or cliffs"—he glanced
sidelong at Servanne—"only pitfalls."

The Wolf stamped into his boots, straightened, and raked
his hands through his hair to push it off his face. "What
direction are they coming from?"

"West and north."

"Have they sent out any advance patrols?"

"Robert and Gil have their eyes on a brace of them, half a
league from here, but they were told to wait and see what
you wanted done before they did it."

"I want one of them brought to me. Alive."

"So he shall be," Sparrow nodded. He stole another peep
at Servanne and his brow puckered into a frown. "Old Blister was frothing so loudly at the mouth, we had to borrow a

stocking from Norwood the Leech to stuff in her throat. Even so, she managed to make enough noise to bring the birds squirting down on us. She wants mischief done to her if a way cannot be found to keep her silent."

"I will calm Biddy," Servanne said. "She will cause you no trouble."

"Neither one of you had best cause any trouble," the Wolf warned. "Hold your tongues and do exactly as you are told, and with luck, my lady, you will see your fondest wish realized and depart our company by nightfall. Sparrow"—he turned away from Servanne's shocked expression—"Bring her back to the abbey when she is dressed and give her back to Mutter and Stutter for safekeeping."

He paused at the mouth of the cavern, his hand on the webbing of ivy. He turned, at an admitted cost to his soldier's sense of priorities, and met Servanne's gaze through the wisping drifts of steam. Whatever he wanted to say—if he had wanted to say anything more—was gone with the next footstep that carried him out of the cavern and into the forest.

Servanne stared at the ivy until the leaves rustled to a standstill. Sparrow made an impatient sound in his throat, and she finished dressing, hardly aware of what her fingers did or how they managed to don stockings and slippers without feeling. Shame began to course hotly through veins that had so recently sung with pleasure. It was plain to see he had already dismissed their lovemaking as being of little consequence; plainer yet to see she had once again become the pawn, the expendable stakes in a game of rivalry and revenge.

Sir Aubrey de Vere prided himself on his hunter's instincts. It was not far from the truth to say he could have tracked an ant through a cornfield on a moonless night—he had stalked fleet-footed paynims through the desert in wind-

storms while on Crusade; no mean feat for a Norman born
and bred of noble blood.

So it was he could not believe his ears when he heard the
sigh of an arrow streaking past his mount. His companion, a
knight afoot who was bending over, sniffing at the imprint of
a boot freshly set into the forest floor, heeled sideways, his
steel helm unseated by the thrust of the arrow punching
through his skull.

De Vere whipped around, but too late. His horse jerked
forward as a tremendous weight dropped onto his rump, and
by the time De Vere identified the bulk of a man, his own
helm had been torn off, his head twisted savagely to the side,
and stretched back at an angle near the breaking point. A
gap in the chain-mail armour where the hood met the hauberk was laid bare beneath his chin, wide enough for the
edge of a knife to tender a threat.

"Not a sound," a voice rasped in his ear, but De Vere's
instincts, being what they were, had already launched his
two elbows back, digging into what felt like a solid wall of
stone.

Robert the Welshman absorbed the paltry affront to his
ribs with a grunt of disdain, but the movement caused his
hand to slice inward and down with the knife. The steel
carved into the strained layers of flesh, parting the sinew and
muscle like a blade springing the seams of an overfull gourd.
Blood spurted out and over his hand, splattering the front of
De Vere's sky-blue gypon.

"Now look what ye've gone and done," Robert muttered
distastefully.

De Vere raised his hands, appalled to feel the heated wetness of his own blood soaking down beneath the padding of
his surcoat. "I am dead," he gasped. "God love me, I am
dead!"

"Bah! Naught but a wee cut. Ye'll hang on a while longer
to plague the world, Sir Knight, at least until my lord of

Lincolnwoods has a word with ye. For now, ye can drop yer sword an' yer bow, an' spur this nag off the path a ways."

De Vere unbuckled his sword belt and dropped it, along with the starburst and chains that hung from holders on his saddle. Out of the corner of his eye he saw a second outlaw step out of the greenwood and bend over to retrieve the discarded weapons. This second man was tall and lean, and bore a noticeable scar down the left side of his face.

De Vere felt some of the pressure lifted from his throat and did not need Robert's gruff advice to clamp a gloved hand over the bleeding wound. The burly giant seated behind him slid nimbly off the horse's rump and together, he and the red-haired archer led the captured knight deeper into the musty stillness of the forest.

Nicolaa de la Haye was growing impatient. Wardieu had halted his men less than a league from where the abandoned abbey was purported to be, although what he was waiting for was anyone's guess.

The small army of mercenaries had been halted an hour ago by the sight of a blood-smeared shield identified as belonging to Sir Aubrey de Vere. It had been propped deliberately in their path, alongside the body of the knight who had accompanied De Vere into the woods.

Clearly they had lost the advantage of surprise, so it seemed doubly foolish to simply stand in an open clearing and wait for a hail of arrows to descend upon them.

"Lucien, for God's sake, either order the men forward or take them back to Alford."

"Nicolaa, my dearest patient one: Are you not the smallest part curious to hear what my brother has to say?"

"He has already said it," Nicolaa declared, pointing at the bloody shield. "He has said he intends to kill us all."

Wardieu sucked a tiny burst of air through his teeth and looked up, scanning the broken ceiling of greenery in an effort to determine the hour of the day. "If it was his intention to see us all dead, we would be by now. These eyes I feel on the back of my neck would be arrowheads. The voices I hear would belong to saints and angels, although"—he glanced over at Nicolaa and laughed—"in our case, perhaps not so angelic."

"Eyes? Voices?" Nicolaa's slanted black brow arched upward as she followed Wardieu's gaze back into the surrounding forest. A flare of splintered light glittered over the suit of Damascan chain mail she had had fashioned expressly to mold to the contours of her body. Plates of steel had been sewn together front and back, worn over a quilted surcoat of bloodred samite. Her hair was plaited and wound into a single gleaming coil at the nape of her neck, confined within a woven circlet of gold and readily able to be concealed beneath a bascinet of steel links extending up from the mail hauberk.

She was well aware of the stares that charted her every move. Some of the knights blatantly disapproved of a woman in armour; others were wary of the cruelty and bloodlust lurking beneath her astonishing beauty, fearing her sultry orders more than those of any ten men. It had come as no surprise that she had ridden out this day at the side of the Dragon Wardieu, the jewelled collar of the Sheriff of Lincoln displayed proudly and boldly around her neck. She had acted the part of sheriff in all but name until now, and with Onfroi de la Haye clinging to life by the merest thread, it required only Wardieu's nomination and Prince John's approval to make the appointment official.

"There," Wardieu said suddenly, breaking into Nicolaa's thoughts with a start. "Something is moving."

Immediately, from behind, came the sound of conversations cut short and swords rasped out of scabbards. Nicolaa saw nothing through the shifting shades of green and brown, but a flush of macabre excitement tightened the muscles across her belly and thighs, producing an indescribable surge of pleasure as she drew her own shortsword.

"It appears to be . . . Sir Aubrey, my lord!" cried Eduard. "He is in difficulty!"

Several other squires joined Eduard in rushing forward, and, moments later returned to the small clearing bearing the limp, gasping body of Sir Aubrey de Vere. They laid him gently on a cushion of half-rotted leaves, his own squire—a lad by the name of Timkin—supporting his head and shoulders.

"Sweet God in Heaven," Nicolaa murmured dryly, peering down over Wardieu's shoulder. "Can he have any blood left in his body?"

De Vere was breathing badly, with great difficulty. A cloth had been wrapped around his neck to staunch the flow of blood, but the effort of moving him had started the wound leaking again. His tunic looked as if it had been used to mop the floor of a charnal house. His skin was completely colourless and glistened with a sheen of cold, clammy sweat.

Wardieu lowered himself on one knee and gripped the knight's arm. "De Vere, what happened?"

Glazed brown eyes opened tremulously. "My own fault, sire," he gasped. "I did not see them. They were on us before we felt the wind shift . . . like ghosts . . . or devils. This—" He wavered a sodden glove toward his bandaged throat, but the explanation was shivered away on a wave of pain.

"Eduard—some wine, quickly," Wardieu commanded.

De Vere rolled his eyes open again and gritted his teeth against the necessity to speak. "A message, my lord. He . . . wants to meet with you. Alone. At the abbey. He says . . . if you are too cowardly to meet him, or . . . if he sees a single man behind you . . . he will make use of the altar in the abbey and . . . and leave the Lady Servanne's heart as a blood offering to Satan."

A few of the knights gathered around recoiled in horror and crossed themselves at the thought of such a profanity. The more hardened veterans raised glowering eyes to the surrounding greensward, their faces grim, their hands touching the symbol of the holy cross they had earned on Crusade.

Eduard ran up with a wineskin and a ram's horn cup. A goodly portion of the strong red wine dribbled over De Vere's chin, but enough found its way down his throat to ease the way for a few more gasped words.

"He . . . also sends his pledge that you . . . you will leave the abbey alive." The gloved hand reached out and clutched a fistful of Wardieu's gypon. "I do not trust him, my lord. I believe it is a trap! He would lure you to the abbey alone, and . . . and—!"

Sir Aubrey arched against Timkin's arms and a deep, ragged groan rattled from his chest to his throat. Wine and blood formed a pink froth at the corners of his mouth, and his eyes bulged with the vision of some unknown agony. The spasm passed and his body slumped back. A final hiss of escaping air signaled the end and brought his head lolling forward onto his chest.

Wardieu studied the face of the dead knight for several long moments before reaching down and gently prying the clawed fingers away from his tunic.

"Eduard . . . bring my horse."

Nicolaa, absently musing over a memory of the virile Aubrey de Vere groaning in much the same way during a recent visit to her bed, was startled enough by Wardieu's command to grasp his arm as he stood up.

"No! You cannot mean to go to the abbey as he asks! You heard Sir Aubrey say it was a trap!"

The icy blue eyes looked from Nicolaa's face to the hand she had clasped possessively around his forearm. "And I say again, if he meant to kill us, we would all be dead by now."

"What if he has determined just to take you hostage?" she

demanded. "Will you feel so confident of your suppositions when he takes a blade to you and begins to peel the flesh from your body strip by strip?"

"Then we will have discovered his plans, and you will know to be leery of any future invitations."

He pulled his arm away and brushed past her. Eduard was waiting beside the huge white destrier, his eyes burning as if he was battling twelve kinds of fear before daring to speak.

"M-my lord?"

Wardieu did not spare him a glance.

"My lord, I would beg leave to accompany you to the abbey. I am no threat to this Black Wolf, and 'tis sure he would not countenance it a breach of faith for you to bring your squire."

Wardieu stared hard at the boy. Thirteen years of age and he was only a hand's width shorter than the master he served. His shoulders and chest promised great strength and breadth; his legs were already long and well-formed with none of the awkward gangliness of too much growth in too short a span. Other signs of encroaching manhood had been brought to his attention by the castle seneschal; one of the kitchen maids—older by some ten years—was regularly seen hobbling out of the stables after energetic trysts with the young squire.

A son any man would be proud of: his own words.

"Please . . . Father," Eduard whispered tautly, at great cost to his pride. "I would ride to guard your back."

"By all means," Nicolaa drawled, coming up behind them. "Take the bastard with you. Perhaps you can offer him in lieu of the unpaid ransom for your sweet bride."

Wardieu's expression did not change. It did not so much as flicker a warning as he brought his gauntleted hand swinging up and around. The slap would have ripped away half of Nicolaa's cheek had he not checked his fury at the last possible instant. Nicolaa flinched all the same, the blow delivered as sharply and brutally through the stunning rage in his eyes.

"You had best watch where you spit your venom, woman," he said harshly. "I am about at the end of my humour over your petty jealousies."

"Petty, my lord?" she snapped, her cheeks flaming and her lips thinned to an ugly slash of red. "My jealousies are indeed petty compared to yours . . . and your brother's."

A vein pulsed noticeably to life in the Dragon's temple. The skin across his cheekbones seemed to stretch so taut, the surface became more like wax than living flesh.

He raised his hand slowly and cupped it beneath Nicolaa's chin. The fine metal links of the gauntlet depressed the whiteness of her skin, digging deeper and deeper as he increased the pressure to excruciating limits.

"D'Aeth has often expressed an unrequited interest in you, dear Nicolaa," he said quietly. "Perhaps an evening or two in his genteel company would cut a few barbs from your clever wit and remind you by whose generosity you continue to enjoy the use of your tongue. Eduard—arrange an escort for Lady De la Haye. She will be returning immediately to Alford Abbey to be by her husband's bedside."

"Aye, my lord," the squire said quietly, his face still stinging with humiliation. "My lord—?"

"See to your duties, Eduard; trouble me with no more favours."

"Yes . . . my lord."

"And Eduard—?"

The boy turned, his eyes brightening with a spark of hope.

"Never, *ever* address me as 'father' again. Is that understood?"

The boy looked from one coldly dispassionate face to the other and knotted his hands into fists. "Yes, my lord. Perfectly understood."

15

The Wolf had seen the signal several minutes earlier: a single horseman approaching; all clear behind.

"Well, well," he murmured. "So you are still a curious bastard, after all these years."

From the shadowy mouth of the gorge, hazed with late afternoon mist where it spilled open onto the common, came distinct, echoing sounds of a horse's hooves striking the rocks that lined the banks of the narrow creek. The sky was low and sullen, threatening rain, and dusk was a chilly breath away. The scent of wood and pine, of loamy soil and heavy dew accompanied the hour and moodiness of the day, but the Wolf did not notice. His gaze was fixed on the far side of the gently sloping meadow. His fingers were as tight as they could be around the shaft of his longbow without crushing it.

Flanking him, perched at scattered intervals along the stone wall of the abbey were the silent silhouettes of six of his best archers, including Gil Golden. Friar and Sparrow had led groups of the other men into the forest to guard all approaches against a surprise attack.

Cold, steely-nerved, the tension in the Wolf's body was mirrored in the hardness of his eyes. He was so well prepared to see the lone horseman emerge from the shadowy trees, that when he did, the sensation was anticlimactic.

The destrier was reined to an abrupt halt the instant the abbey came into view. Even at a distance, and with the failing light, there could be no mistaking the Dragon of Blood-moor Keep. He sat tall and imposing in the saddle of his fully caparisoned warhorse, man and beast dominating the meadow, reducing it to a small patch of deergrass. He wore a long-skirted hauberk of polished chain mail, as well as chausses of closely fitted iron scales to protect his long, muscular legs. His surcoat was a splash of bright blue against the sombre backdrop of trees; the crest emblazoned on his chestpiece was just a blur so far away, but the Wolf knew every line and filigreed coil of thread as if they were tattooed on his eyes. Nothing of the Dragon's features could be seen beneath the conical steel helm and trunk-shaped nasal, but a hint of wheat-coloured hair wisped out from beneath the mail bascinet and lay against a ruggedly tanned jaw.

"I could skewer him like a cherry pip from here," Gil offered and ran a loving hand along the arch of her longbow.

"Keep your arrows in your quiver unless I say otherwise," the Wolf countered evenly. "Any man who disobeys will die by mine own hand."

Gil scowled and pulled her felt cap lower over her coppery curls.

The Black Wolf of Lincoln took a step away from the wall of the abbey—a step matched on the opposite side of the field as the Dragon nudged his horse forward again. The Wolf's long stride cleaved through the waves of knee-deep grass, his passage leaving a line of downtrodden green in his wake. The Dragon's destrier waded into the same sea of green, his hooves crushing a much wider path, his sawtoothed body cloth hissing like a thousand snakes as it swept over the grass.

The two converged on the centre of the field, halting close enough for conversation, far enough to emphasize their mutual wariness.

The Wolf's gaze had remained steady on the face of his adversary through most of the short trek, but as the chiseled features became clearer, more defined, he could not resist the impulse to assess his enemy down to the toes of the pointed, iron-ribbed boots he wore.

The same reflex caused the piercing azure eyes to stray from their intent focus and the Dragon gauged the remarkable breadth of the chest beneath the gleaming black wolf pelts, the impressive power in the bold, fluid stride, and the total absence of any sign of injury or aftereffects from wounds that should have left the man dead and turned to dust on the sands of Palestine.

Eyes glowering with a quiet look of speculation rose once again to a gaze as frigid and emotionless as Arctic ice.

"It has been a long time," the Wolf said. "The years have served you well."

There was no reaction in the brittle hardness of Wardieu's countenance, no tremor of response in the stern ridge of his jaw.

"What?" The Wolf smiled faintly. "Is there not even charity enough in you to offer similar praise for my own humble appearance? Admittedly, it is not as grand as it might have been under different circumstances, but—"

"What is it you want?" Wardieu interrupted bluntly. "Why have you come back to Lincoln after all these years?"

"I do grow weary of answering that question," the Wolf sighed. "Why should I not come back? Lincoln is my home."

A fine, chalk-white rim of tension compressed the taut lips. "Bloodmoor belongs to me. You will not find a man in all of England willing to challenge my possession."

"One stands before you now," said the Wolf.

The blue eyes flicked past the broad shoulders and returned almost immediately, laden with scorn. "A wolf's head and his band of thieves and cutthroats? Is it your intention to walk up to the gates of Bloodmoor and announce yourself, or shall you and your men place the castle under siege?"

"It is my intention to reclaim what is mine."

"And I say again, there are none who would believe your claim. *I* am Lucien Wardieu. *I* have played host to Richard, King of England. *I* have fought by his side and won the acclaim of my peers."

"And the brother? The coward bred of a Wardieu whore and weaned on greed and corruption? Dare I ask what became of him?"

The Dragon's smile was slower to form, appearing in deference to the rage throbbing at his temples. "Etienne Wardieu died some fourteen years ago, mourned by few, remembered fondly by none. It seems there was some taint of treachery associated with his name—to do with an attempt to implicate his father on charges of treason. Part of my unflagging efforts over the years has been to exonerate the name of Robert Wardieu, and to restore the De Gournay name to its former prominence. In that respect, the name of Lucien Wardieu ranks high in royal esteem and you would have greater success declaring yourself to be Richard the Lionheart."

"I come to claim only what is mine to claim."

"Attempt to do so and there is not a man in Lincoln who would waste a second thought before striking you dead on my command."

"Assuming you were alive to give the command," the Wolf pointed out.

Wardieu glanced away, letting the silence drag for a long moment, and when he looked back, there was a wry, sardonic smile on his lips. "Why am I not surprised to learn your word still means nothing? Nothing then . . . nothing now."

The Wolf crooked an eyebrow. "I gave my word you would leave the abbey alive. I said nothing about the meadow, or the forest, or the Lincoln road."

The Dragon's smile lingered, the smug satisfaction in it

rankling the Wolf more than if he had drawn his sword and challenged the affront. It struck him then that his brother had expected the archers on the wall. He had come onto this field fully accepting that death might come from one source or another—further, that he would be judged to have met it boldly and bravely, with his honour as a knight unimpeached.

The Wolf relaxed his grip on his bow. "Did you really think I would make it this easy for you? An arrow through the heart, an honourable exchange of swordplay? Quick . . . painless . . ."

The blue eyes narrowed, but the Dragon said nothing.

"No. No, you seem too eager to see an end to it. Methinks I should let you live a while longer. Live . . . knowing I am here—" The Wolf spread his hands congenially to encompass the trees, the sky, the meadow. "Knowing I am watching you, biding the perfect moment to strike—a week from now, perhaps. Or a month. Perhaps in a year, when you have grown short of temper and twitch with sweat each time a shadow creaks at your back."

"We will end it now, damn you," the Dragon vowed, his hand reaching for the hilt of his sword.

Before he could draw it from its sheath, the Wolf had raised his bow and nocked a slender arrow to the string.

"I have determined not to kill you this day," he warned. "But I would gladly give my arrow a taste of maiming you in any limb you choose. An elbow . . . or a knee? You were sorely disappointed not to see a cripple walk onto this field— perhaps we can arrange to have a cripple leave it?"

The Dragon slowly, furiously lowered his sword back into its leather seat.

"A wise decision. A comforting one as well for your bride, who seems not to have the stomach for violence."

"The Lady Servanne." The words were grated through the Dragon's bloodless lips. "Where is she?"

"Awaiting your pleasure. And since she has already provided me mine, you may take her away with my fondest wishes for wedded bliss."

If it was possible, the Dragon blanched whiter. "If you have dared to touch her—"

"Be assured," the Wolf broke in bluntly. "I have indeed *touched* her; would you have expected less? Frankly, I expected a good deal more. Oh, she is a pretty enough piece to look at, but between her weepings and swoonings she would sooner shrivel a man's best intentions as slake them. I found her hardly worth the trouble. Then again, I assume it is not a zealous craving for her body that hastens you to the altar. As I understand it, the lady comes to you dowered heavily enough to more than compensate for any shortcomings between the sheets."

The Dragon's steed bolted an agitated step sideways in response to the sudden tension communicated through his master's body. He was brought quickly and savagely under control again, but his flanks quivered and his nostrils flared with the scent of possible violence.

"You will release her to me at once," Wardieu seethed.

"Gladly. We will even waive the ransom—consider it my wedding gift for you and your lovely bride."

He turned and passed a signal to Gil, who nodded down to someone behind the closed gates of the abbey. The oaken doors creaked open on their wooden hinges and Mutter appeared first, leaning forward to urge a reluctant white palfrey through the narrow archway.

Servanne de Briscourt, cloaked against the chill and mist of the evening vapours, sat astride Undine, her small hands gripped to the leather pommel, her face a pale, wan oval beneath the draped folds of the scarf she wore around her head and shoulders. A second horse, led by Stutter, clopped out of the courtyard and through the gates with Biddy sitting as straight as Fury, her expression bleaker than an ax blade.

Soft yellow whispers of hair were dragged forward across Servanne's cheeks by the breeze. She had not been permitted an opportunity to comb or plait it, nor to remove the dulling tarnish of moss and dried sand. Waiting by the heat of a fire had scorched the dampness out of the green velvet gown, but it was crushed and wrinkled beyond any hope of repair, the cloth scuffed and stiffened, the seams so weakened in places her bare flesh gaped through. She looked and felt bedraggled. Her hands trembled and her heart beat like a wild, caged thing within her breast, and she knew if she looked up, if she dared search out the Wolf's face, she would die then and there of shattered pride.

As it was, when she heard his voice and realized he was addressing his remarks to her, she grew so faint, she needed Biddy's quick hands to steady her upright in the saddle.

"I have been telling your betrothed what a pleasure it has been to have your company these past few days. I explained I was only trying to give you a truer idea of what might be expected of you by way of marital obligations. Hopefully your husband will not find you so difficult to thaw."

Servanne was shocked, horrified. How could he say such things? How could he humiliate and shame her so heartlessly?

With her eyes flooding with resentment and her heart still pounding to burst, she lashed out with the only weapon available. The wide leather strap of Undine's reins cut him sharply across the face and neck, hard enough to break the skin and raise a bright, stinging red weal on his flesh. She would have struck again, but for Undine's confused response to a misread command. The mare caracoled sideways a step, then leaped forward in a startled attempt to avoid tangling legs with Biddy's horse.

Wardieu reached out in a reflexive action as the mare danced close to his own snorting warhorse. For a moment their eyes met; Wardieu's incensed and burning beneath the

steel nasal of his helm, Servanne's as bright as glass behind a
thick film of outrage and defiance. They each looked away
again, focusing their pain and hatred on the man who
watched the exchange with grim indifference.

"A deserving bride and groom," he murmured wryly, lowering his hand from his cheek, frowning at the spidery
threads of blood on his fingers. "I bid you both a pleasant
hereafter . . . for as long as you may live to enjoy it."

The heat of Servanne's anger, as well as a scalding sense of
betrayal, kept her well warmed on the winding journey back
through the forest. Her last sighting of the Wolf—his face
turned away as he strode back to the abbey—was seared on
her brain like a smouldering brand. He had not looked over
his shoulder. He had not shown a trace of remorse or guilt
over the cruel, callous way he had used and dismissed her.

Her eyes ached with the fullness of tears but she refused to
give way, fearing if she once started to weep, she would not
be able to stop again. It was her own fault; she had brought
this travesty upon herself by succumbing to the very curiosity Biddy had tried to warn her against. She had wanted to
know the feel of his arms around her, the press of his hot
flesh against hers. She had not once tried to stop him, or stay
his hands or lips from whatever wicked, depraved pleasures
he sought to bestow. Her body had been his body to do with
what he would, and she had shamelessly, shamefully begged
him *not* to stop. Even now, when she should have been using
all her strength to concentrate her hatred on the man, she
burned with the memory of his hands, his mouth, his flesh
moving over her, in her . . .

Servanne bowed her head to muffle the sound of her
sobbed breaths in the folds of her cloak. If Wardieu heard
them, or questioned their cause, he made no attempt to offer
solace by word or gesture. He rode in the lead of the small,
miserable procession—a sullen, brooding figure whose flow-

ing blue mantle belled from his shoulders to his horse's rump, giving him neither shape nor substance below the conical steel helmet.

Biddy rode in the rear, berating her own inadequacies as matron and guardian, intoning prayer upon prayer until Servanne's nerves were stretched almost to the breaking point.

They rode through the dark mist, and, as if there was not enough grief to contend with, the skies cracked open on a jagged fork of blue-white lightning and after a few moments of thundrous sound without fury, the deluge soaked its way through the overhead branches and began pelting the earth with icy lancets of rain.

The Black Wolf of Lincoln tilted his chin upward and let the rain beat down on his face. The welt from Servanne's slashing reins stung vividly where the flesh was torn, and where the blood had not yet congealed it was washed down his neck in a reddish smear.

He leaned his weight briefly on the top of his longbow and pressed his brow against the comforting tension of the resined string.

"It had to be done," Friar said quietly. "You could not have kept her with us. Nor could you have sent her away with stars in her eyes and a keening lament for lost love in her heart; the Dragon would have seen it in a minute and either killed her outright for the insult, or kept her alive long enough to use her against you. God knows, if a man's heart is his weakness, a woman's anger is her strength."

"I know," the Wolf said wearily. "I know. But will she be strong enough?"

Friar pursed his lips thoughtfully. "How angry did you make her?"

"Angry."

"Enough to make her want to strike out with more than

just a leather strap? Enough to spill everything to the Dragon in a rampage against you, including your recommendation of La Seyne's trustworthiness?"

The Wolf glanced over, his questioning frown confirming Friar's supposition.

"I did not think you would just throw her to the lions without giving her some avenue of escape," he remarked dryly. "I only hope she does nothing foolish with the confidence."

"For that, I will rely on my brother's own arrogance. Instinct tells me by tomorrow he will have convinced himself he has come away from here the victor. Since he is incapable of feeling compassion, he will not show any to Lady Servanne, and it is *my* hope she will then see enough of the real Etienne Wardieu to be on her guard."

"You are risking a great deal on instinct."

"It has kept me alive longer than my enemies care to believe."

With the gloom and the rain there was not much he could see of the Wolf's expression, but what he could see gave Friar an uncomfortable feeling of walking too near the edge of a cliff.

"You . . . did not tell her about the Princess Eleanor, did you?" he asked slowly.

The Wolf straightened and glared at his companion. "I may have been behaving like a fool these past few days, but I have not completely forsaken my senses." He saw the look in Friar's eye and sighed. "Perhaps I did mention the attempt to steal Prince Arthur from Mirebeau, but"—he held up a hand to forstall Friar's aghast interruption—"like everyone else, she assumes both children were returned to the queen's protection unharmed. She has no reason to suspect the Princess Eleanor is anywhere but in Brittany with her grandmother."

Friar continued to stare, prompting the Wolf to vent his

temper on a hiss of air. "You act as if this was all my doing! As if I had a hand in kidnapping the children; as if I knew beforehand of Lackland's plans to use a threat of death against Arthur in order to force the queen to throw her support behind John being declared Richard's successor." He paused and wiped angrily at the rain coursing down his brow. "Moreover, when John realized his plans were foiled and the best he could hope to gain was a ransom for the return of the Princess of Brittany, you would think I personally volunteered the services of La Seyne Sur Mer to oversee the exchange!"

"No. You only volunteered to come to England beforehand under the guise of having once been familiar with Lincoln and its surrounds."

"The queen approved the idea."

"Only because she thought you might be able to find some way to rescue the princess without her having to pay a ransom she can ill afford. She was not aware nor advised that her captain of the guard boasted intimate knowledge of Lucien Wardieu and Bloodmoor Keep."

"Prince John chose Bloodmoor to make the exchange because he thought a wedding of such prominence would afford the perfect camouflage for his political intrigues. La Seyne was chosen by Queen Eleanor to deliver the ransom and collect the princess because she knows Lackland would not dare any of his tricks or double crosses against the Scourge of Mirebeau. All of this was decided long before I was even told the identity of the master of Bloodmoor Keep!"

"Aye, and when you found out, you could not resist planting a thorn in the Dragon's side."

"I have done nothing to jeopardize La Seyne's mission in England."

"You call it nothing to steal the Dragon's bride and have him empty his castle of mercenaries to overturn the country-

side in search of you? You call it nothing to fall in love with
the girl yourself and thereby give us all two reasons to risk
our lives instead of just the one?"

"I have asked no one else to risk their life for Servanne de
Briscourt," the Wolf retorted. "And who the devil says I am
in love with her?"

"Well if you are not in love, you are giving a good imitation of a boiled fowl. And what is wrong with being in love?
What is wrong with admitting you are human?"

The Wolf glared for a long moment. "I do not have time to
be human."

"Aye. That much has been obvious for the past ten years.
It is a malady that appears to be contagious."

Friar walked away, brushing past the approaching Gil
Golden, making her the innocent recipient of a meaningful
scowl.

The Wolf watched him go, his expression grim, his nerves
drawn so taut, Gil had only to look at the whiteness of his
knuckles to know she was better off seeking conversation
elsewhere.

16

Servanne was thoroughly soaked and iced to the bone by the time they arrived at the encampment at Alford. Wardieu had not stopped when he met up with his men again in the forest. Despite the rain and the condition of the two women, he had wordlessly ridden through the huddle of dripping, frowning mercenaries and left them scrambling for their mounts in his wake.

Aching, exhausted, numbed in body and spirit, Servanne was scarcely aware of being deposited at the gates of the abbey, or of the helpful, concerned hands of the monks who fussed about her like vexed peahens. Two of her waiting-women, Giselle and Helvise, had been sequestered at the abbey since the ambush, and greeted their returning mistress with weeping and prayers of thanksgiving. Servanne's clothes were quickly removed and a fire stoked beneath the huge oaken barrel that served as a laundry tub for the monks.

Biddy, as exhausted and stiff of limb as she was, took personal command of the maids while they tended her lamb, ordering a gentler touch here, and more care in scrubbing there. She frowned and clucked her tongue through waves of despair and self-recrimination when Servanne made little or no response to the helping hands. Her eyes filled and her nose leaked each time she noted a bruise or chafed patch of redness on the perfect whiteness of her lady's skin.

The sleeping chambers at the abbey were hardly more accommodating than the chambers at Thornfeld. Bare stone walls, bare earthen floor, a single candle, and a narrow wooden cot were the essentials provided by the monks. Clean linens, armloads of thick quilts and feather cushions arrived from the encampment on the hillside, along with trenchers of soup, cheese, and meat sufficient to cause the monks' eyes to water as they carried the repast to the lady's chamber.

Servanne's belly turned over at the thought of food. She did consume a healthy portion of strong, warmed mead in the hour it took Giselle and Helvise to comb her hair into a sleek golden cascade. By then her eyelids were so heavy and her thoughts so dulled, she could barely see the feet at the end of her legs as she was led from the chair to the sleeping couch.

She was asleep before the quilts were drawn over her shoulders.

Come morning, it was still raining. The sky was an oppressive mantle of cloud, with low, metallic-green underbellies rumbling constantly with thunder. Servanne opened her eyes briefly around midmorning, but since there was nothing to greet her aside from blank stone walls and Biddy's open-mouthed snoring, she closed them again and slept until well past noon. A summons was conveyed from the abbot's refectory shortly thereafter: The Baron de Gournay was there, awaiting a private audience with Lady Servanne de Briscourt.

"What shall I do, Biddy?" Servanne whispered. "What shall I say to him?"

"Do? Why, you shall do nothing, my lady. He cannot possibly hold you to blame for any of this. If anything, he should bear the greater burden of guilt for having permitted such a travesty to occur on his lands. He should prostrate himself on the ground at your feet and beg forgiveness. You should have been better safeguarded. He must have known the forests were unsafe. He must have known they were populated by murderers, thieves, and rogues. He should have had them burned out and their hiding places razed to the ground rather than endure the risk of having our cavalcade ambushed! No, no, my lady. You must not meet him with guilt in your breast and a plea for penance in your eyes. This was none of your doing. None at all!"

Servanne sighed wearily as the diatribe continued on behind her. Obviously Biddy had exonerated them in her own mind. For women to be kidnapped and held to ransom was almost an accepted method for two enemies to exchange hostilities. The resultant outrage and sympathy, if any, was usually directed toward the man whose pride and honour had been blemished. Rarely did anyone consider the poor woman's feelings or even acknowledge the fact that she had been the one to suffer the most throughout the ordeal.

Servanne's plight would be regarded no differently. After all, she had been neither a virgin nor bound to Christ by vows of chastity and purity. She had been fair game to anyone who sought to tickle Wardieu's nose for revenge or profit, and her own anguish would be forgotten in a day or so, dismissed by men whose ire would be roused in defense of Wardieu's tarnished honour. That was how the world would see it, how Biddy had worked to convince herself to see it, and how Servanne would be expected to accept it now that she was back, safe and sound, under Lord Wardieu's protection.

The trouble was, she did not accept it. She felt angry at being used and betrayed, but she was also hurt and confused, and the last thing she wanted to have to do now was face the knight who called himself Lucien Wardieu, especially when her mind and body were filled with the essence of the rogue who sought to challenge that claim.

Arriving at the threshold of the small antechamber set aside as Abbot Hugo's sanctum, Servanne was halted by a rush of torn emotions. The Baron de Gournay was standing in front of the miserly fire that had been built in the corner alcove. The light from the solitary window was dim at best, the air murky with smoke and dampness, the crack and hiss of the weak flames adding nothing to the sinister atmosphere but a sour smell.

As she stared at his broad back, she realized he was easily as tall as the Black Wolf, disturbingly as long-limbed and muscular. He had abandoned the glittering ominousness of chain mail for a rich velvet surcoat and a long-sleeved doublet. Well-fitting hose shaped the powerful thickness of his thighs and calves, while low deerhide boots moulded his feet like slippers. His head was bare; the gleaming gold waves of his hair curled to the top of his collar, lying like fine silk against the dark blue velvet.

A second movement, deeper in the shadows, startled Servanne's gaze to the opposite side of the chamber. Her surprise was not diminished in finding the dark green gaze of a woman had been studying her with the same silent intensity she had been studying Wardieu. The look in Nicolaa de la Haye's eyes did not invite any attempt at speech. Rather, it commanded Servanne to stand and endure a slow, increasingly disapproving inspection that climbed from the hem of her subdued, modest gown to the embroidered linen headpiece that capped her wimple.

"Lucien, darling." The full scarlet lips curved into a semblance of a smile. "The moment of truth has arrived at long last."

A frown of annoyance was cast sidelong at Nicolaa, then, realizing they were no longer alone in the airless chamber, Wardieu turned fully around.

Regardless of the Wolf's forewarning of a resemblance between the two, seeing Wardieu's face without the impediments of the steel helm or the gloom of the forest, was enough to send Servanne's hand digging into Biddy's for much-needed support. The stern line of the jaw was the same, as was the width and authority of the brow. The straightness of the nose, the resolute firmness of the mouth bespoke a long and shared ancestry of noble Norman blood. Moreover, Servanne found herself drawn deeply and helplessly into eyes that were dangerously familiar in raw, sensual magnetism. Instead of being pewter gray, steeped in quiet secrets, these were a stunning cerulean blue, hard as gemstones and equally rich in self-esteem.

"Good God," Nicolaa murmured, drifting closer to where Servanne stood. The contrast of the young widow's plain woolen gown with her own richly woven and embroidered silks seemed to please the beauteous Lady de la Haye, as did the comparative lack of shapeliness beneath the dull homespun. "Ten thousand marks does not buy much these days, does it? Just as well you were saved the expense, my lord."

"Leave the girl alone, Nicolaa," he commanded softly. "She has been through enough already without having to contend with your cat's claws."

Nicolaa smirked faintly as she looked down and busied one red-stained talon with scraping some hint of dirt out from beneath the crescent of another.

Wardieu moved away from the fire, his eyes narrowing against the gloom as Servanne's features grew more distinct. What little he had previously recalled about his betrothed had not inspired him to regard her too closely upon her release to him. Nor had it prepared him for the smooth, translucent complexion he saw now, or the delicate oval of her face with its sweetly arched mouth. Her eyes were a darker hue than his own, the blue flecked with tiny triangles of gold and green, but he had already seen them sparked to deepest sapphire with anger and could not help but wonder if passion would have the same effect.

This last speculation took him by surprise and was re-

flected in the timbre of his voice as he bowed low over her
hand and pressed his lips to her cool fingers.

"My lady, I praise God you have been returned to us
unharmed."

Servanne dared not look up into his spellbinding stare. It
was all she could do to hold her wits together to face the
questions she knew he would ask her. He would ask. There
was no question but that he would ask, the only question was
whether she could answer without betraying herself.

"Unharmed?" It was Biddy's voice, coming her rescue.
"Indeed there was not a sense or sensibility *left* unharmed!
The food was spoiled and malodourous, crawling with vermin. The wine was as rancid as vinegar, the rushes we slept
on so mouldy and slimy with rat droppings, it will take a vat
of steamed rose petals to cleanse the stench from our nostrils. Why, another day in the hands of those . . . those
rogues and villains and 'tis a certainty my lady would not
have had the strength to draw another breath. See how pale
my poor lamb has become? See how frail and ill she has
fallen? Oh, I cannot even bring myself to recount the horrors
she was subjected to in the company of that beast! That
brute! That . . . that *wolf*! Black-hearted and cruel he was;
cunning as the pox and as likely to come upon you unawares
despite his size, by the bloody rood."

She paused to trumpet her nose into the hem of her apron,
and the knight regarded her puffed countenance with a smile
that did not quite touch his eyes.

"This . . . Black Wolf, as he called himself," Wardieu
asked, "Did you ever hear another name used? A Christian
name, perhaps?"

"He called himself Lucien Wardieu," Biddy recalled with
a sniff of outrage. "But only the once, and only at the beginning, to shock us, methinks. Why, any soul with half an eye
could see he was no more noble born than a farm mule, and
the fact he chose you, my lord, to support his charade,

proves he is no smarter than the selfsame ass. Who, in all of England, does not know the Baron de Gournay by sight? Who does not know of your courage, your honour, your strength? Why—"

"Yes, yes. I thank you for your commendations, good-wife," Wardieu interrupted, then looked from the maid to Servanne. "My lady? Surely he used some other name in your presence?"

Servanne's heart jumped upward to lodge at the base of her throat. "In truth, my lord, he only called himself Lucien Wardieu, as Biddy has said."

"Did you not question his usage?" Nicolaa asked with a sneer. "A man committing crimes in the name of your be-trothed should at least have roused some curiosity."

Servanne looked at her calmly. "I spoke to the outlaw as seldom as possible."

"What about when you were beneath him? Did you not ask what name he would prefer you cry out?"

Servanne flushed a deep red but held her tongue, fully expecting Wardieu to rise to her defense. After a long mo-ment, when nothing was forthcoming over and above Bid-dy's renewed sobs of despair, she looked at De Gournay, only to find him returning her gaze as calmly as if they were discussing a recent repast.

The Wolf had said he and Nicolaa were lovers. If it was true, it would explain Nicolaa de la Haye's open hostility. It also made Servanne wonder what kind of man would bring his mistress to a meeting with his future bride.

"Bastard," she said evenly. "I called him bastard. What would you call a man who used you and flung you aside like a scrap of soiled linen?"

Nicolaa arched a raven brow. "I might call him *lover,* if he was any good."

Servanne's cheeks were flushed, her hands were balled into fists. There was the bitter, coppery taste of blood in her

mouth from where she had bitten down on the fleshy pulp of
her lip, but instead of tearing Nicolaa de la Haye's throat
out, shred by shred, as she longed to do, she startled everyone present in the chamber by sinking slowly down onto her
knees in front of De Gournay.

"Good my lord, I am most deeply grateful for everything
you have done on my behalf."

"My lady—?"

"Even so, I would beg one more small favour of you."

Wardieu looked down upon the bowed head, a puzzled
frown gathering across his brow. "What is this . . . favour?"

Servanne tilted her face upward, the shine of unshed tears
bright in her eyes. "If you could but spare me the necessary
escort to see me safely back to Wymondham, I would gladly
compensate both you and your men for any inconvenience
you have been caused."

"You would prefer to return to Sir Hubert's estates?" he
asked in amazement.

"I cannot, in faith, remain here, my lord. Not when I am
no longer worthy of your . . . respect, or . . . consideration."

"You would wish to reconsider the terms of the betrothal
agreement?"

"I would wish to release you from all promises, my lord,"
she corrected him quietly. "Your good name must not be
besmirched by the stain my own now bears."

Behind them, Nicolaa de la Haye smiled with satisfaction.
Her smug good humour lasted only until she saw Wardieu
lean forward with studious care and bring Servanne de Briscourt up off her knees.

"I appreciate your concerns for my good name, Lady
Servanne, but be assured I am well able to defend it myself.
As far as I am concerned, nothing has happened to make me
any less determined to share it with you in holy wedlock."

"I . . . do not want your pity, monseigneur."

"I reserve my pity for fools and cripples. In my opinion, you are neither. Nor should you be held accountable for the actions of a depraved outlaw. I am satisfied the terms of the marriage contract have been met. It is my wish that we put this unpleasantness behind us as quickly as possible and look only at what lies ahead." He paused and tucked a finger beneath her chin. "Unless of course, it was never your wish to marry me, in which case, I would not force you to do so now against your will."

Servanne's senses were reeling. "You would allow me to return to Wymondham?"

"My lady, if, in the few short days remaining before our wedding is to take place, you cannot reconcile yourself with the idea of becoming my wife, I will escort you back to Wymondham myself."

Servanne searched the depths of his eyes for signs of duplicity, for any hint he was someone other than the man he claimed to be . . . but if there was something there, it eluded her. It gave her little comfort, however, for evidence of him possessing any other shreds of emotion eluded her as well and she was left with the chilling impression he knew only hate and anger.

"I . . . will accept your hospitality, of course," she whispered. "Until then."

"Good. Then it is settled. My men are making preparations, even as we speak, to break camp and return to Bloodmoor with all haste."

"Bloodmoor?" Biddy gasped. "In this weather? I absolutely forbid it!"

The blue eyes turned crystalline as they moved slowly from Servanne's face to focus on Biddy.

"I cannot allow it," she said, displaying an unusual disregard for self-preservation. "I cannot conceive of such a heartless notion. Why, we have just escaped a wolf's lair where our lives and safety were in constant peril! Can you not see my poor lamb is exhausted? Would you ask her—even though her legs wobble with the effort required to simply stand before you—to clamber up upon a horse's back and endure what additional torments such a heinous journey would surely extoll?"

"You . . . forbid it, you say?"

Biddy thrust out her prodigious bosoms stubbornly. "My lady requires rest and solitude, peace and undisturbed sleep if it is to be hoped she may begin to recover from her ordeal."

Wardieu clearly looked as if he might like to knock one or both fists against the side of Biddy's head, but he nodded, barely perceptibly at first, then with somewhat more conviction as a precipitous crash of thunder shook the abbey to its foundations.

"The weather shows no sign of improving, as I had hoped," he conceded. "And even with Lucifer at our heel we would not reach Bloodmoor before midnight. Very well, we will take advantage of Abbot Hugo's kindness one more night."

A second nod to someone who had arrive unseen in the doorway, brought Sir Roger de Chesnai hastening into the chamber and dropping instantly onto one knee to greet the Lady Servanne.

"Sir Roger!" She smiled with genuine affection for the first time in a week. "You are recovered from your wound?"

" 'Twas nothing, milady. A pinprick scarce worth a leech's fees."

"You will remain with Lady Servanne and see to any comforts she may require," said Wardieu. "Deliver my warm regards to Abbot Hugo and tell him we will be vacating his field at dawn; have him also prepare either a coffin or a litter for the sheriff at that time."

"Aye, my lord. It shall be as you ask."

"Lady Servanne," De Gournay bowed to her again. "Your own guard will remain with you for the night. I trust their presence will ease your mind of some burden."

"Thank you, my lord," she whispered. "I did not mean to imply—"

But he was gone, swept out of the chamber with a swirl of his blue silk mantle. Nicolaa de la Haye was a pace behind, taking two steps to each one of his, her voice reduced to a low growl by anger.

"Are you not going to ask her about the Wolf? You were bristling with questions the whole morning long, and now you mean to just walk away?"

"The old witch was right," he said thoughtfully. "She was in no condition to be badgered."

"Badgered?" The disbelief in Nicolaa's expression caused her to slow her steps. "Every hour we delay gives him an hour more to plot against us. Why, in heaven's name, did you not send your men back to Thornfeld immediately upon your return with the chit? Why did you not attack and burn them out when you had the chance?"

"Because there was no chance, Nicolaa. He would undoubtedly have moved his camp the instant we rode away. What is more, he and his men have had eight weeks to familiarize themselves with the forest. They could have picked my men off one at a time and laughed out of the sides of their mouths while doing it."

"But the girl—maybe she knows something. Maybe she knows where they would have moved. And if she does, we must have the information from her now."

Wardieu stopped and glared. "And if she knows nothing more? Will not your incessant questions and jealous ravings only rouse her to wonder if there was more to it than a simple kidnapping?"

"You speak to me as if I were a child!"

"You are acting childish, you leave me little choice." He

stared down at her glowering countenance a moment longer, then walked back the few paces to where she stood. "There will be no more games, Nicolaa. No sly remarks. No taunting, no teasing. No gossip. The girl is here and I intend to marry her as planned. I intend to legally assume title and deed to Sir Hubert's fiefdom and, by God, if I choose to bed her before, during, or after the wedding ceremony, there is absolutely nothing you can say or do to stop me. In fact"— he cupped her chin in one of his hands and forced her to raise her blazing green eyes to his—"if these jealous rages of yours persist, I will not only make a point of bedding her every hour upon the hour but I will do so with you bound and gagged and lying alongside us. Do I make myself perfectly clear?"

Nicolaa's thick black lashes lowered slightly. "Perfectly, my lord."

"What?" Wardieu ground his teeth at the sweetness of her voice. "What did you say?"

"I said . . . if you want the chit that badly, by all means have her."

Wardieu was instantly on his guard. It was not like Nicolaa to give in so easily, and certainly not with regard to another woman. Glancing over his shoulder, he saw a low, iron-bound oak door leading off the corridor and, after thrusting it open and ensuring the small room was empty, he grabbed Nicolaa by the arm and ushered her inside. It was a storeroom of some kind, with shelves lining the walls holding an assortment of crockery jars and twine-bound stacks of parchment. Light from a low, arch-shaped window covered in panes of pressed horn, reduced everything to the texture and colour of pond scum with the exception of the two angry faces, livid and occasionally blue-white through flashes of lightning.

"Admit it, my love," Nicolaa seethed. "You find the chit interesting."

"She has a comely enough face," he agreed.

"Comely?" Nicolaa backed up closer to the window. "You find pale and insipid . . . *comely*? I vow she will prove to be a frigid little cullion—did you not see the way she shrank from your touch? The first time she sees you naked, I warrant there will be a stinking puddle around her feet, especially if your brother was less than feather-gentle with her."

Wardieu grasped her shoulders between his hands. "You will be civil to her, Nicolaa. You will be sweet as honey and do everything within your power to see she feels welcome."

"And if she does not? If she decides she would rather run away back to Wymondham?"

"She will not," he said evenly. "We will both endeavour to ensure she will not."

"I do not like her!"

"You do not have to like her. You *do* have to accept her."

"Never."

Wardieu's hands squeezed harder. "She is to be my wife."

"A temporary inconvenience."

"Perhaps."

The green eyes glanced up sharply. "What do you mean . . . *perhaps*?"

Wardieu smiled thinly and released her shoulders. "She has good blood. Sir Hubert had strong ties with William of Pembroke and, in fact, it was the old marshal himself who gave final approval for the marriage in Richard's stead."

"So?"

"So . . ." He arched a tawny brow. "One simply does not toss her from the ramparts at the earliest convenience. One might even consider it prudent to breed a child or two on her first. Bloodmoor needs an heir. The future of the De Gournay name and title must be secured."

Nicolaa gaped at the golden-haired warrior openmouthed. On more occasions than she cared to remember over the past fourteen years, she had been obliged to seek the skills of

herb-women versed in the ways and means of scouring unwanted seeds from the womb. Wardieu had made it abundantly clear he wanted no part of fatherhood. One of the
carefully guarded secrets she had paid heavily to learn was
that he habitually made gifts to D'Aeth of the women foolish
enough to boast of carrying his seed. Now, suddenly, he
wanted heirs? Now, when her own womb had been scoured
so many times she was barren?

Controlling her fury, she turned her face into a lightning-
bright flash of illumination from the window. Rain was beating as savagely on the horn panes as her heart was beating
within her breast, and she was thankful for the diversion.

"You made certain promises to me," she reminded him
tersely.

"They have been honoured. You have more wealth, more
power, more influence than any other woman in the reeve.
And you know full well as soon as your devoted husband
relinquishes his soul to the Devil—what in God's name is
keeping him alive, I would ask?—you shall have a good deal
more."

Nicolaa angled her face enough to slant her eyes up at
him. "Sheriff?"

"I can think of no man better suited to the task. Even
Prince John agreed, on his last visit, there is good reason for
the people of Lincoln to fear and respect your wrath. Methinks he fears you a little himself."

Nicolaa knew she was being placated, thrown tidbits to
sooth her vanity and win her cooperation. Then again, it was
good to know he felt a need to placate her.

"I will have full claim to the title? Full power? Full authority?"

"You will be able to order the flesh stripped from any
deserving lout between here and London if the mood suits
you. Even an undeserving lout, for that matter, if it pleases
you."

Nicolaa experienced a flush of giddiness at the thought of the power lying within her grasp. Onfroi had been a weak and indecisive agent of the king. He actually grew pale and belched vomit while witnessing the putting out of eyes or the paring of flesh with hot knives. Once, when she had ordered the chest of a murderer split open so that she might hold the warm, beating heart in her hands, Onfroi had swooned away like a virgin.

"Money?" she asked, looking up again.

"As much as you can levy in taxes without cheating John of his due."

Seeing the faint smile on his lips, Nicolaa's temper prickled to the surface again. "It will hardly compensate me for all these years of loyalty and compliance."

Wardieu laughed outright. "You are loyal only unto yourself, Nicolaa. As for being compliant"—his gaze roved down to the voluptuous outline of her breasts—"I do not recall ever having to force you into my bed, nor ever demanding a pledge of faithfulness from you."

"I was as faithful as I could be under the circumstances," she said, taking exception to his sarcasm.

"Circumstances that included a groomsman hung like one of his stallions, and a seneschal who makes D'Aeth look like a gamecock?"

Nicolaa moistened her lips. "I was not going to pine away my life waiting upon you to send for me. Furthermore, I do not recall you ever going too long without a maidservant or two clawing at your shoulders."

"You always had Onfroi."

"Onfroi? Saints assoil me, a pity the arrow could not have struck lower—at least he would have died with something hard sticking out from between his thighs."

"Such loving concern," Wardieu mused. "And him lying so near death the monks have twice annointed him in preparation for the shrouds. Have you no sympathy for his suffering at all?"

"Because the fool lies there spitted like a capon, am I supposed to hover about him wiping away the snot and breathing air befouled by fever and pus? Is it any fault of mine he was shot in your stead? Indeed, perhaps it is you who should be hovering and chanting mea culpas."

"Perhaps. Although we cannot be certain the arrow was intended for me."

"Not for you? Then who—me?"

"It is likely, is it not, for my brother to have recruited a few local malefactors to help familiarize him with the forests again? There was a face yesterday . . . one of the archers he had placed on the abbey walls . . . it bore a scar on the cheek."

"A thousand men bear scars," she retorted dryly.

"Shaped to the initial *N* by a loving hand?"

Nicolaa turned fully around. The significance of the *N* was directly related to a quirk of her own vanity; it was the brand normally reserved for women whose beauty was deemed to be a threat in some way.

"Are you implying he numbers women among his archers?"

"Only one that I saw, and then only if mine eyes were not too blinded by the passions of the moment. Is it so entirely outside the bounds of reason to believe a woman could learn to hold a bow as well as a man, or that a woman could have just as much reason to hate as a man? On the other hand, the culprit was using a longbow to keep my ballocks properly shriveled to the saddle; not an easy weapon for a man to master at the best of times."

"A longbow?" Nicolaa asked, visibly shaken. "You are certain it was a longbow?"

"It is a difficult weapon to mistake for any other," he commented wryly. "Besides being identical to the one we found in the woods after Onfroi's tragic mishap—the same one that made you pensive enough to consume two full flagons of wine."

Nicolaa stared out the window, her eyes clouding with a memory. "There was a master bowyer in Lincoln several years back, the only one skilled in the making and firing of the Welsh weapon. He had a daughter . . . a daughter whose skill equaled his own . . ."

Wardieu waited, intrigued to see something that might have been construed as fear flicker across Nicolaa's face.

"But no—" She snapped out of it and faced him again. "As I recall, they were all arrested—the father, mother, and two other daughters, not so sharp-tongued, but equally guilty of . . . of plotting insurrection against the crown. They died, the lot of them. It could not be her."

"Just like it could not be my brother out there in the woods?"

A particularly loud and close crash of thunder sent Nicolaa flinching away from the window.

"All the more reason why you should have ordered your men into the woods," she said angrily. "The chance to rout them would have been well worth the risk of a few losses."

"Does my brother's presence in Lincoln trouble you so much?" Wardieu asked. "Does his presence bring back such fond memories?"

"I never complained of him as a lover," she countered archly, well aware of the effect her words would have. "Does it not trouble *you* to know there is someone else now who will doubtless compare with your skills, both as a lover and a fighter?"

The finely chiseled nostrils flared and he gathered her roughly against his chest. "You made the same comparison and ended up in my bed, not his."

"I may have had different grounds on which to base my choice."

Wardieu's grip tightened and Nicolaa was not surprised to feel his arousal surging up between them, nor to hear his breath come harsher and faster in his throat.

"Will you tell John of your brother's return?"

"I may be left with little choice in the matter."

"He will not be pleased," she predicted, her own breath forced to rasp through rapidly drying lips. "No doubt he will throw one of his wretched, foaming fits and threaten to burn all of Lincolnwoods to the ground in order to rid the forest of any threat."

"I think I can convince him otherwise," Wardieu murmured tersely, aware of the greedy haste in Nicolaa's fingers as she tore at the fastenings of his codpiece. "Especially once I point out to him the value of having a band of dangerous outlaws on the loose in Lincoln."

"Value?" she gasped. "What possible value could there be?"

"What value in a band of traitorous malcontents? If nothing else, I would have just cause to conduct a very thorough search of the entire demesne . . . thorough enough to rid my lands of any sympathizers, and costly enough to justify an increase in tithes."

Nicolaa moistened her lips. "And . . . as sheriff of Lincoln—?"

"It would only be natural for you to assist me in routing these cutthroats and thieves."

Nicolaa groaned and arched her head back as Wardieu's knee insinuated itself between her thighs. His mouth savaged the curve of her throat; his hands tugged at the pins holding her hair plaited in a thick coil at the nape of her neck. Thunder crashed and reverberated outside the thin-paned window and lightning slashed across the sky. Nicolaa rode the hard muscles of his thigh with the same tempestuous urgency, her breath hissing from between clenched teeth, her body vibrating with sound and fury.

Wardieu ripped the seam of her bodice, exposing the blue-white flesh beneath. A nipple, hard as an arrow tip, dark as desire itself was barely suckled into a brutal mouth before she was sobbing his name and sinking weakly to her knees in orgasmic delirium.

Wardieu followed her down, amused as well as revolted to see that the more forceful he was, the more pain he inflicted, the louder her cries and moans of ecstasy. Despite her ability to drain him to the bone with her carnal skills, Nicolaa was beginning to grow tiresome in her demands. Making her sheriff would appease her appetites in some ways, but there was still the problem of her insatiable jealousy to deal with. Unfortunately she knew too many secrets and was too cunning to have them safeguarded only in her head, otherwise the problem could have been solved long ago with a simple slash of a knife.

The shocking reappearance of the dragon ring after so many years made it abundantly clear he could not take the chance of any more incriminating evidence being uncovered. While Nicolaa may not have kept the ring to hold against him, he had no doubt she would have kept evidence of another kind linking him to Robert Wardieu's imprisonment and his brother's attempted murder. She would not have forgotten, nor would she ever let him forget their treacherous collaboration all those years ago.

Proof of his suspicions, if he needed any further, came each time her body shuddered and her lips trembled around the name, "Etienne . . . Etienne . . . !"

17

As the menacing, fully armed troop of mercenaries rode across the narrow strip of raised land—the only dry approach to Bloodmoor Keep—Servanne's senses were flooded with an array of disquieting emotions. Fear, most certainly, was taking its toll. The sheer size and sinister foreboding of the tall castle ramparts would have started a far stouter heart than hers quaking. The castle was a huge, sprawling monstrosity perched on the edge of a sea cliff, its many tourelles and spires etched against the low ceiling of sullen clouds like hands upraised in desperation. Seagulls screamed into the bite of cold sea air, their cries shrill and echoing over the incessant rumble of the surf beyond.

Servanne had spent the night in the abbey at Alford, shamelessly indulging in another long, hot bath before curling into her bed of furs and cushions. It took Biddy three attempts and a halfhearted lecture on slothfulness to finally rouse her, whereupon she bathed again, to the horror of the monks who were permitted the luxury only four times during the year.

Undine was saddled and waiting for her when she emerged from the abbey chapel. A final, solemn benediction from Abbot Hugo sent her on her way, the promise of a warm morning quickly giving way to the return of bitter winds and a bleak, mottled sky. A spate of stinging rain drove the women beneath the awning of a huge oak barely ten minutes into the journey, but the delay was brief; Wardieu was adamant and the cavalcade was under way in earnest before midmorning. Onfroi de la Haye seemed just as adamant about clinging to life, and he rode, swathed in a bundle of furs, in a small jouncing cart at the rear of the procession.

Rolling hills gave way to fertile valleys, stands of dense game-rich forest were broached and left behind. The few travelers they met on the main road took one furtive look at the De Gournay crest and scrambled off to the side, careful to keep their heads lowered and their eyes anywhere but on the tawny-haired knight who rode in the lead. Once, when Servanne happened to glance back, she saw a peasant woman spit contemptuously into the settling dust. Apparently she had not been alone in her observation, for a moment later a thundering of hooves signaled where a rider had turned back and was pursuing the horror-struck woman into the deeper woods.

Servanne at first thought nothing of the incident. Peasants and serfs were more often than not terrified of their lord. He owned their lives, owned everything they possessed. They could be killed at his whim, broken, maimed, or crippled at his pleasure; their daughters and wives could be raped, sold, or given away as the lord saw fit if tithes were not paid on time, or any one of a thousand private laws were broken. There was no recourse for any but the rich and titled gentry, no means of appealing a sentence regardless of its harshness in relation to the pettiness of the crime.

Sir Hubert, a kind and just lord, had nonetheless always given his full support to his seneschals and provosts when they ordered thieves hung, traitors blinded, and petty offenders mutilated, beaten, or starved to death by way of an example to others. A lord's livelihood depended upon the unquestioning obedience, respect, and servitude of his vassals and serfs, and to show leniency to one was to invite rebellion in another. Servanne had never questioned the functioning or fairness of the system that put so much power into the hands

of the rich and privileged. Conversely, she had rarely seen
such powers abused to the extent of trampling a woman underfoot for the act of spitting. Nor had she ever been betrothed to a man who accepted the report with a faint nod of
disinterest before resuming his conversation with his mistress.

As a result, Servanne was increasingly wary of keeping
company with anyone other than Biddy or Sir Roger de
Chesnai. Not that she would have been eager to strike up
conversation with any of the glowering, brute-faced knights
who rode escort to the cavalcade. To a man they ran their
eyes like dirty hands over her body at every opportunity,
lingering over breasts and thighs.

The moor flanking either side of the steeply banked road
that led to Bloodmoor throbbed and glowed with wildflowers
in every shade of red, from palest pink to the bloodiest crimson. Long grasses rippled like waves on the ocean; here and
there, gaps in the density of weed and wildflower showed the
icy glitter of water and treacherous mud slicks hidden beneath. The closer they rode to the castle, the taller the outer
walls seemed to grow. High and crenellated with jagged
square teeth, their harsh lines were dotted with the heads of
alert, well-armed sentries who patroled the walls. Their steel
helmets caught whatever light was available, dotting the
ramparts with pinprick flashes as heads drew together to
speculate over the arrival of the lord's new bride.

A tremendous groaning and creaking could be heard halfway across the moor as the foot-long rusted iron links of
chain winched the outer drawbridge open. Horses' hooves
sounded like the clatter of drums as the party trooped three
abreast beneath the raised portcullis gate, their heads barely
clearing the spiked points of the thick bars. The inner gate
was opened, the huge beams of oak requiring the strength of
ten men to push open beneath the overhang of the studded
barbican tower. Stone walls slit with *meurtrières* welcomed

visitors at eye level; funnel-shaped spouts of iron were cemented into the stone arch above which one could imagine huge copper ladles filled with bubbling oil waiting to add their warm greetings.

The outer bailey, little more than a wide, defensive strip of field, sloped upward toward the mortared fieldstones of the curtain wall. Here there were deep trenches running in staggered stripes, a casual glance noted them filled with hay, a closer inspection revealed the pointed tips of stakes jutting through. A second wall, a second drawbridge admitted the cavalcade to the village of workshops and stables clustered around the castle grounds. The tradesmen broke work for a few moments to stare at the colourful procession of knights and men-at-arms who rode through their midst. Theirs was a small, bustling town of skinners, vintners, tailors, salters, bakers, brewers, fletchers, armourers—all of whom contributed in some way to sustain the castle and its inhabitants.

By way of showing respect, the men doffed their scruffy felt caps to Lucien Wardieu as he rode past. The women, smudge-faced and brawny with muscles gained by toiling day after day at heavy labour, stopped and used their coarse woolen skirts to wipe ineffectually at the grime coating their hands and faces. They gazed with dull eyes upon the slender figure who rode in the midst of so much masculine power. Servanne attempted to smile at a face or two belonging to those who stared the hardest, but the gesture was met with either blank looks, or overt suspicion.

"Not a very friendly flock, are they?" Biddy observed beneath her breath. "And not a very friendly place to get into or out of with any ease."

Servanne suppressed a shiver and concentrated on what lay ahead. The cavalcade was approaching a smaller drawbridge slung over a dry moat, where a much less threatening portcullis gate was already raised. The bridge and gates admitted a steady stream of pedestrian traffic passing to and from the outer and inner bailey, and here again, conversations ceased abruptly and people scrambled hastily to clear a path for the mounted knights.

Once inside, the men-at-arms and half the mercenaries broke out of the strict formation and veered toward the massive jumble of stone and wood buildings that comprised the castle barracks. The other half remained as escort to Wardieu and the women, who followed a wide cobbled path between buildings and under stone arches until they reached the innermost private courtyard.

Perhaps fifty feet square, the paved space was surrounded by high-walled towers, most covered more than halfway up with a thick, furry blanket of lichen and ivy. Above this, the cold stone facings were gray and weathered, with long ranges of rooms and apartments buttressed to the walls so the square of open sky was reduced by yet another half. Standing in the centre, staring straight up at the small patch of gray sky, Servanne and Biddy felt suitably humbled. Sir Hubert's castle at Wymondham would have fit unobtrusively into a corner niche of one of the outer baileys of Bloodmoor and made very little difference to the imposing silhouette. Neither could even begin to estimate the numbers of servants, maids, and workmen required to keep the castle running smoothly. Provisioning and maintaining accounts would surely require more than one able mind.

Twin arched doors swung open as the horses were reined to a weary halt. Servants poured out into the courtyard, one of whom stopped by Undine and set an elaborately carved set of wooden steps against the single stirrup. A young page of eight or ten years clambered importantly up the steps to assist Servanne out of the saddle. She accepted his hand with an apologetic smile for the stiffness of her limbs, and was grateful to feel solid land beneath her feet once again, regardless of the doubts and fears that had grown with each step taken inside the massive outer gates.

Wardieu finished issuing his orders to the servants and groomsmen, then took Servanne's small, gloved hand into the crook of his arm.

"I do not doubt you will feel overwhelmed at first by the size of Bloodmoor. It is rather overlarge and gaudy for a simple man's taste. I grew up exploring the alleyways and alcoves, yet there are still times I stumble across a corridor or an apartment I have never seen before. Over the years there have been many renovations and additions as well, so I prefer to remain in the main keep; by far the most hospitable area of the castle."

Said with a smile, Servanne was left wondering if she was being given advice . . . or a warning.

"I was never one to enjoy exploring, my lord," she assured him quietly. "A few rooms and a garden will satisfy my curiosity more than adequately."

"There are gardens aplenty within the main bailey. I would most happily take you on a tour myself when you have rested sufficiently from your travails."

Servanne smiled with what she hoped was demure acquiescence and touched a hand to her skirts to lift the hem as he led her toward the stairs.

The great hall, in every castle the centre of all activity, was usually built a storey above ground level, entered by means of an enclosed stone stairway. Constructed with defense in mind—although it seemed ludicrous to suppose any attacking force could ever penetrate this deeply into the stronghold—the stairs were steep and narrowed immediately upon passing through the arched doors. The walls were slanted sharply to the right to hamper a swordsman's arm if he was attempting to fight his way into the keep. Servanne was forced to walk close to the stone in order to keep abreast of Wardieu, who showed neither reluctance nor discomfort in finding his hip and thigh brushing frequently against hers.

At the top, a wide landing opened into a windowless gallery with a high, vaulted ceiling. The only sources of light were large multi-branched candelabrum, some wheel-shaped and suspended from the ceiling on chains that could be raised or lowered, some on tall wrought iron stands fit into niches in the walls. Iron cressets were bolted to the stone to provide racks for extra torches, but they stood empty for the moment. Only the lazily smoking candles yellowed the air with their acrid perfume of animal tallow.

"My dear," said Wardieu, holding a hand toward an open doorway on the right. Servanne's skirts rustled softly over the bare stone floor as she walked to where he indicated. Later, she would think it odd to have heard such a faint, delicate sound when the chamber they were approaching echoed with voices, laughter, and the squall of daily living.

De Gournay halted on the threshold of the great hall, his blue eyes moving slowly around the cavernous interior. Suitably named, the room stretched up nearly as high as it sprawled out. Several dozen men and women bustled about at one task or another, their voices drifting shrilly upward to where Wardieu and Servanne stood at the top of a short flight of steps. An enormous raised dais commanded one end of the hall, and below it long trestle tables flanked the length, the farthest stool looking no bigger than a speck through the haze of smoke and murky light. A relatively modern innovation—a fireplace—was hewn out of one wall, its cavity filled with seven-foot lengths of blazing tree trunks. Ornamenting the empty spaces were the pennants and captured banners, crests and shields of past enemies. Crossed swords, iron starbursts, full suits of heavy armour, crossbows, lances, and scimitars captured on Crusade were mounted prominently on the walls; here and there, stretched out on display, were the skins of exotic animals killed in faraway lands: tiger, leopard, and panther. The floor was covered in rushes, none too fresh by the look and smell. Dogs fought and fornicated in snarling abandonment, and in one corner of the hall, a man and woman had obviously caught a similar enthusiasm and were panting and heaving to the cheers of several rowdy onlookers.

"My men fight hard," Wardieu murmured in Servanne's ear. "It is only reasonable to expect them to play hard as well."

"I would not deny them their right to relaxation, m'sieur," she replied stiffly. "I would only gainsay them the need to do it before an audience."

Wardieu studied her expression a moment then left her in the care of his squire while he descended the steps alone. He walked toward the frenetic group of men and, without warning, drew his sword and slapped the flat of the blade across the man's bare buttocks. The mercenary jerked upright with a bark of surprise, the curse dying instantly in his throat when he recognized who had wielded the sword.

"My lord," he roared with good-natured drunkenness. "Care to 'ave a wee slap at her yerself, do ye?"

"Sunrick, you hoary old boar. Can you not conduct your affairs in private?"

"Eh?" The knight was older, his skin as leathery as bull-hide armour, his hair a shock of snow white scattered over his shoulders.

"My betrothed"—Wardieu cast a meaningful glance to the top of the stairs—"finds such open displays of affection in poor taste."

The knight and his group of merrymakers squinted up through the smoke and sifting dust and gaped at the pale figure standing in the gloom. One of them muttered something ribald enough to win a broken-toothed smile from Sunrick, who spat a rejoinder carelessly out of the corner of his mouth and ran a loving hand over the whore's bare thigh. With a grunt, he bent forward and pulled the wench upright, causing her to give a shriek of laughter as he slung her over his shoulder and carried her into one of the adjoining antechambers. The other men hefted their tankards of ale and followed, some still grinning over their shoulders at Servanne de Briscourt.

"My lady?"

Servanne looked beside her and was surprised to see Eduard's perplexed expression mirroring her own. Apart from Biddy and Sir Roger, the young squire had been the only friendly face in the long journey from Alford—clearly smitten, Biddy would have said, by her ladyship's youth and fragile loveliness.

"The running of the castle has been left in the hands of men too long, methinks," he said, offering one of his rare smiles. " 'Tis certain your presence here will work a change or two for the betterment of us all."

Servanne started to smile back, but a burst of laughter from farther down the hall caused the boy to look away, and something in his profile caused her breath to stall in her throat. For a brief, dizzying moment, another profile as angular and rugged superimposed itself over Eduard's. The similarity was made even more pronounced by the darkness of his hair, thick and swirling softly against the nape of his neck, and, when he turned back to face her, by eyes that were the same smoky gray that placed a hint of wolfish cynicism on every glance.

Servanne stared, and Eduard stared back.

"Eduard!" Wardieu called. "Bring Lady Servanne forward that she might be properly introduced to some of our more loyal retainers."

Eduard's smile shifted again, becoming tauter and grimmer than the situation warranted. He offered Servanne his arm and escorted her down the steep flight of steps, whereupon, at the bottom, she could have sworn she heard a murmured: "Courage, my lady."

The Baron de Gournay strode forward and relieved Eduard of his delicate burden. Like a king leading his queen

to the throne, he held his arm outstretched so that Servanne
had to reach up and out to keep the tips of her fingers in
contact with his wrist. She was led along the length of the
hall toward the dais, her skirt dragging gently over the grimy
rushes, her dainty slippered feet snapping the occasional thin
bone overlooked by scavenging dogs.

Long before they reached the end of their promenade, the
silence had become as pronounced and oppressive as the
windowless gloom. Wardieu extended greetings to a familiar
face here and there, some of them wedding guests who had
arrived early to take advantage of their host's good food and
strong wine. A goodly number of knights and ladies stopped
their eating and drinking to stare curiously at the prospective
bride. They were not of the same ilk as the villeins who
owned tenancy on Sir Hubert's estates. These knights were
bleary-eyed and coarsely dressed; their women were blowsy
and vulgar, their gowns spotted with grease, their fingers and
chins slick with sweet fat.

"Wardieu, ye old Dragon!" One of the knights came forward, a goblet in one hand, a partially gnawed joint of mutton in the other. "I see ye've resolved yer difficulties with the
outlaw rabble. Have her back safe and sound, do ye? Not
tupped, were she?"

"Godfrey, Lord Tydfil," Wardieu murmured by way of an
introduction. "A brazen old warrior, but a stout ally and
keeper of the peace on my marcher estates. The Lady
Servanne de Briscourt."

"Ahh." The mutton was levered to one side for a closer
inspection of the new bride. "God grant ye health, honour,
and joy, milady."

"God grant you peace and health, milord," she replied by
rote.

Lord Godfrey peered up at Wardieu through eyebrows
that resembled nesting squirrels. "Not tupped, were she?"

"My lady finds herself in perfect good health, praise God," Wardieu responded dryly.

"Mmmm." The knight looked disappointed, but he nodded. "Good. Good."

"And your own fair Drucilla?"

A woman with painted cheeks and a rack of teeth broken off to their blackened gums squealed with laughter and tipped a goblet to acknowledge the compliment.

"Bah!" Sir Godfrey spat a wad of yellow phlegm into the rushes and scowled. "A sour old trull she is. Tupp her now and then just to keep my gear well greased, but for pleasure's sake, I'd ruther swive a sweet wee bit like yours."

A broad, leering wink sent Servanne shrinking back against Wardieu's arm, a gesture that was seen and remarked upon by a smiling Nicolaa de la Haye.

"I warrant she might find you a little hard to take, dear Godfrey," she purred, advancing with the sinewy grace of a cat. Her head was bare and her black hair flowed sleek and loose over her shoulders. More than one appreciative pair of eyes widened as she unfastened her mantle and shrugged the garment into the waiting hands of a page.

"Hard to take? Why, 'tis my normal state," Sir Godfrey bellowed, grabbing his crotch for emphasis. "I should hope she'd find me so!"

Wardieu was watching Servanne's face, aware of the tightness growing around her lips and the distinct pallor of aversion draining her complexion as she looked from one guest to another.

"You seem tired, my lady," he murmured. "It would serve you well to rest and refresh yourself before we sup."

"I would beg leave of you to rest the night, my lord," she said. "I . . . fear I would not make happy company tonight."

"Of course she must rest," Nicolaa insisted. "After such an ordeal as she has endured, what can you be thinking,

Lucien, to expect her to sup as if it were any ordinary day? Have you chambers prepared?"

The cool blue eyes narrowed as if he might object to being overruled, but the annoyance passed and he signaled to Eduard.

"I would trust you to see Lady Servanne to her chambers. As well, you may remain to see to any necessity she requires."

"Aye, my lord," Eduard said, bowing and offering his arm almost eagerly. Equally relieved to be able to escape the smell of stale bodies and sour food, Servanne touched her fingers to his wrist and nodded formally to Lucien Wardieu.

"My lord," she whispered.

"God's night to you, my lady," he replied.

Nicolaa moved at once to place herself between Wardieu and Servanne before the latter had even turned away. The sound of her husky laughter and Lord Godfrey's garrulous barking followed the two until they had ascended the steps and removed themselves to the relative quiet of the vaulted gallery.

"This way, my lady," Eduard said, gently covering the lengthy pause she took to fill her lungs with a breath of clean air. He led her to the far end of the gallery and made two wide turns down converging stone hallways before climbing the corkscrew staircase to a private tower. He leaped ahead to open the oak door, then stood aside as Servanne entered a plainly furnished, but comfortably expansive suite of chambers.

The outer room, where the maids would sleep, was fully ten paces square with curtained slumber niches built right into the walls. A second door led into a large wardrobe with whitewashed walls and small painted flowers decorating the stone arched stone ceiling above. A wooden tulip-shaped tub sat on a raised platform at one end of the room; lining the walls on either side were rows of pegs set into the mortar for

hanging clothes. There was space for dressmakers to sit and
sew, a cabinet where a lady's most treasured collections of
scents and spices could be safeguarded. A small table and
chair for the dressing of hair, and a tall, prettily painted
cupboard that concealed the bench for the privy completed
the furnishings.

Servanne absorbed most of it in a single glance before following Eduard through yet another set of doors, these
double-slung and banded in filigreed wrought iron. She
found herself standing in a huge solar, half of it squared to fit
the shape of the main keep, half of it circular and jutting out
over the central courtyard below. There were three enormous windows stretching from waist height to the top of the
domed ceiling. Each was recessed to hold wide window seats,
each rose to a pointed arch and was divided into smaller
lights by decorative stone casings. On a bright day the chamber would be drenched in sunlight, the beams playing across
the dazzling white walls. Lines had been painted in red to
outline each masonry block, and in each block, a depiction of
a rose, a tulip, or a honeysuckle blossom. The high French
bed had red velvet curtains which rose above the top of the
frame, climbing in a thick, twisting spiral to the ceiling.
There were rows of wood and leather chests along one wall
to house valuables, a low table and stools for doing needle-
work, and, the rarest luxury of all: a mirror of polished steel,
the surface so flat and smooth it was like looking into glass.

There was more: a fireplace as tall as a man and deep
enough to hold the big kettles used to heat water for bathing;
there were panels of coloured silk hung on either side of each
window embrasure, used to diffuse the light when the shutters were open, or camouflage the wood when the shutters
were closed.

The floor was stone, covered with wooden planks to blunt
the cold in winter and the damp in summer. There was an
ornate *couvre-feu* made of stained glass to place in front of

the hearth at night to reduce the hazard of jumping sparks. The bed boasted a thick feather mattress covered with snow-white linens, quilts, a fur coverlet, and more pillows than Servanne could count on two hands.

As stark and masculine a war room as the great hall purported to be, Servanne's chambers offered an elegant contrast, but it was all too overwhelming to grasp at once and she could feel the burning pressure of tears building behind her eyes. Her gloves slipped unheeded from her numbed fingers and the sobs that could neither be contained nor muffled behind her splayed hands began to shake her slender shoulders.

Eduard, seeing the beautiful damsel burst into tears before him, was at a complete loss to know what to do and fidgeted from one foot to the other, jumping a full inch off the ground when Biddy burst into the room behind them.

"There, there, my lamb! There, there! What have you said to her, you scurrilous snipe? What have you done?"

"N-nothing, goodwife. I have done nothing. I—I swear it!"

Biddy cradled her sobbing charge against the pendulous cushions of her breasts and glared at the hapless squire. "Out! Out, I say, and terrorize someone else who might be strong enough to endure your ill humour! Out!"

Eduard, swallowing and gulping wordlessly, backed out of the solar and through the wardrobe where the accusing stares from Helvise and Giselle sent him running for the stairs.

"Now then," Biddy said soothingly. "The brute is gone, tell me what is wrong."

"Oh, Biddy," Servanne wailed softly. "I am so unhappy!"

"Unhappy?"

"I know. It makes no sense. I should be anything *but* unhappy. I am rescued, I am safe again, I am here—" She raised a tear-streaked face from Biddy's shoulder and glanced meaningfully around the incredible lushness of the solar. "I should feel angry over what happened to me, relieved it is over, and thrilled to be exactly where I have dreamed of being all these long months . . . but instead . . . I feel lost. Lost and frightened and so unhappy I could just die."

"Frightened?" The fine hairs in Biddy's ears prickled to attention. "Has something happened? Has someone said something to frighten you?"

A soft, wavering sigh sent Servanne back into the smothering comfort of Biddy's bosom. "He was so cruel, so heartless."

"Cruel?" the matron gasped. "Heartless? Why, what has he done that is so cruel?"

"He sent me away. He could have refused to let me go, I know he could have. I—I even think a small part of him wanted to ask me to stay, but the other part . . . the beastly, proud, arrogant part of him did not want it to appear as if he had become weakened or . . . or affected in any way by what happened, and so . . . so he sent me away."

Biddy, her head spinning, wondered if it would be a timely moment to collapse into one of her swoons. "You are not talking about Lord Lucien are you?"

Servanne lifted her head and turned huge, glistening blue eyes to focus on the boldly depicted De Gournay crest and shield carved on the bedboards.

"Yes," she whispered. "I think I am."

18

Servanne spent a restless night rolling and tossing from one side of the big bed to the other. The sense of foreboding she had felt with her first glimpse of the sinister towers and spires of Bloodmoor Keep, had grown in intensity with every passing minute. The Dragon had neither said nor done anything outright to persuade her he was living a lie. To be sure, standing the two brothers side by side, one would have to choose the Dragon over the Wolf as being better suited to bear the De Gournay crest and shield, and yet . . . something told her it was not so. Something told her the Wolf was the legitimate son of Robert Wardieu, the legitimate heir to Bloodmoor Keep.

But if that was true, it meant the man under whose protection she now resided was a murderer. It meant he was a cheat and an impostor, and had schemed to bring about his own father's death.

"This Lincoln Wolf has you bewitched, child," Biddy had said in the small hours of the morning, aghast at the story she had finally coaxed from Servanne's tongue. "Just because he bedded you and put a hunger in your loins, do not be convinced he speaks only the truth! I warned you. By the heart of St. Agnes, I warned you where your curiosity would lead, but did you listen? Did you heed me? Did you even give half a care for this poor heart who loves you so well?"

Biddy had dissolved into a wailing flood of tears, and Servanne had offered what comfort she could, but both had

known it was to no avail, and after a few moments of inco-
herent snifflings, Biddy had resorted to more worldly logic.

"Look around you, my lady: Are these the trappings of a
dishonest man? The baron is the king's champion, and a
friend to Prince John. He is as prominent a figure as William
the Marshal, or Salisbury, and could undoubtedly be vouch-
safed by both as being who he says he is! As for the other
. . . he is nought but an outlaw and rogue knight who kid-
naps helpless women and takes his amusement in filling their
heads with notions of grand intrigues. If he truly *was* Lucien
Wardieu, why has he waited all this time to make his claim?
Why does he wait, even now? And why, by all the mercy
that flows from heaven above, would he have given you to a
man *he claims* has defiled the family name with acts of murder and treason?"

"I do not know," Servanne had answered truthfully. "He
mentioned some other danger—"

"Some other danger?" Biddy shrilled. "Some other excuse,
more's the truth. I may not approve wholeheartedly of some
of the goings-on we have witnessed since our arrival—the
great hall is a nest of pestilence and shall require tending to
at once!—but I have also seen nothing to implicate the baron
in anything more devious than buying himself a bride of
some means. And if you would condemn him for that, you
would have to condemn every other lord, baron, and earl in
the kingdom . . . yea, even the king himself, who has no
more love or affection for the Princess Berengaria than he
would a common pine knot. But he will marry her because of
the political union she represents, and because Queen Eleanor has said he must marry for the sake of peace in the
kingdom."

"There is no kingdom at stake in my marriage," Servanne
had argued quietly, and Biddy, who had expended most of
her breath and logic on her last speech, recognized the stub-

born set to her ward's jaw and clasped her hands over her bosom in a gesture of despair.

"Surely . . . you do not intend to reject the baron's suit? You do not intend to refuse the marriage?"

Servanne had not answered then, nor, after a night of sleepless agony, could she have answered the question now. She had relived, in her mind, every word, every gesture, every memory made by the Black Wolf of Lincoln. His hands had been there to taunt her body through flushes of heat and cold; his lips had been almost real enough to cause shivered recollections from her throat, to her toes, to the very core of her womanhood. He *had* bewitched her, there was no use denying it, but was his ability to render her senseless with ecstasy the only reason she wanted to believe his claim?

Servanne sighed and rolled onto her stomach, refusing to acknowledge the daylight slivering through the cracks of the window shutters.

"Why?" she whispered. "Why did you send me here?"

Your temper is more than a match for whatever tests the Dragon may put you through.

"Such a compliment is laughable," she muttered forlornly, dragging a pillow beneath her and hugging it to her breasts. "Especially since it appears not to have had any lasting effect on you, my lord wolf's head."

She pictured him as she had last seen him, his dark, brooding magnificence muted by the falling shadows; the forest all around him, green and hazed with dampness; the sky a roiling mass of gray cloud, rumbling with distant thunder. Across his cheek, the livid bleeding result of her temper. On his mouth, the arrogant smirk of self-satisfaction. In his eyes there was . . . there was . . .

In his eyes, where there should have been anger or triumph . . . there was only . . .

Only . . . what?

Servanne's heartbeat had quickened noticeably in the past

minute or so, but before she could determine the cause of
this new distress, another was knocking brusquely on the
outer door and bustling into the chamber like a fomenting
hurricane.

"His lordship sends word he is desirous of your company
in the great hall," Biddy proclaimed, sweeping aside the bed
curtains and hastening Giselle and Helvise into the chamber
with an impatient wave of her hand. "I returned the message
you were still abed, and had not even been to chapel yet for
morning prayers, and *he* sent back that you should pray
quickly, for his mood is none too holy this morning. *Then* I
am told Prince John's cortege is expected any hour now, so I
suppose we must forgive the host his poor manners, although
if it were up to me I should not fawn and simper over that
sly fox, regardless if he were regent or king." She stopped
and drew a deep breath for refueling, then swept aside the
coverlets in a grand gesture of annoyance. "Maledictions,
what are you staring at, child? Get up. Get up. Brother Mi-
chael awaits you in the chapel—such a nice young man but if
you wait overlong, he'll have no nails left to chew—and
young Eduard has come whimpering back to offer you escort. Quickly, now. Quickly. Stockings, garters, tunic . . .
Helvise, saints seize my heart, I am lost of a shoe! Fetch it
quickly from the wardrobe while Giselle bathes my lady's
hands and face."

In a flurry of activity, dainty white feet were thrust into
stockings and garters fastened below the knees. A sheer
white chemise replaced the thicker linen sleeping gown, over
which a tunic of fine gold silk was fussed and fretted into
place. The gown Biddy had selected was a rich blue velvet,
elaborately embroidered with the same gold thread as in the
hints of silk that peeped at throat and wrists. A girdle sparkling with jewels encircled her waist; a golden armband, several rings, and a long, looping strand of pearls completed the
toilette.

Servanne watched the progress of her maids through the reflection in the polished steel mirror. When it came time to comb and plait her hair, she showed the first signs of impatience, and remarked to Biddy that at least half of the ladies present in the hall the previous night had not respected the modesty of a wimple.

"Harlots, whores, and trulls wear their heads bare," Biddy declared with an ominous squint in one eye. "And you are on the way to chapel, not the fair."

It was a short journey, down the corkscrew stairs of her own tower and up the twisting flight of an adjacent tower. The chapel was small and dusty, the priest oppressively sincere in droning the litany. At the end of the mass, Servanne and her tiny flock were again herded down into the bowels of the castle, taken to the great hall to break their fast with the lord and his guests. The numbers of knights present at the tables had increased noticeably overnight, and the huge platters of bread, cheese, and ale were disappearing from the linen tablecloths as fast as the servants could bring them out from behind the screened walkway to the kitchens.

The Baron de Gournay stood to greet his prospective bride, his genial smile almost able to counter the effect of seeing Nicolaa de la Haye already seated on his left side on the dais. The sheriff's wife had spared no effort in making herself visible in this place of honour. Her gown was rendered from a bolt of crimson damask—a very small bolt judging by the tightness of the fit and the amount of flesh left exposed to the hungry stares of the male guests. Her hair had been left uncovered and the raven black tresses tamed beneath a meshlike webbing of fine gold wire.

"I trust you are feeling better today?" Wardieu inquired politely, leading Servanne to her place at the table. He noted the whispering silence that had marked his bride's descent into the hall, and cast his own approving gaze along her modestly elegant attire.

He smiled and Servanne's feet nearly tripped over her plummeting heart. He was indecently handsome. Tall and bronzed in complexion, she could well imagine the difficulty in choosing between De Gournay and King Richard for sheer golden splendour. Clad in various shades of blue, his shirt and chausses were dark as midnight, surmounted by a tunic of paler damask, quilted and beaded with hundreds of winking sapphires. The Wardieu crest was emblazoned on his massive chest in silver thread and glittering gemstones, the tangled grotesques seeming to come to life with each gesture or movement. His hand, as he held it up to call for total silence, was broad and calloused, its implied power hardly softened by the smother of gold rings he wore on the long, tapered fingers.

"My lords and ladies," he said, his voice as rich and bold as his appearance. "I give you my bride, the Lady Servanne de Briscourt."

The dais was raised a scant three feet higher than the rest of the hall, but it was enough to catch the last of the early morning rays of sun that streamed down from the slotted windows carved high on the east wall. De Gournay's tawny hair glowed with a golden halo, resembling a spill of pure sunlight, and Servanne could almost hear the sounds of the women's heartbeats pounding hotter and faster in their breasts.

His fingers closed slowly, possessively around hers and he raised her hand to his lips, lingering long enough over the caress for a sigh to ripple through the audience.

"Your chambers are satisfactory?" Wardieu asked, waving away the young page in favour of assisting Servanne into her seat himself.

"Oh yes, my lord. They are very much so."

"You must want for nothing while you are here; you have only to ask and whatever you desire will be laid before you."

At the sound of the solicitous offer, Nicolaa stabbed her

eating knife into a convenient pear with somewhat more violence than the act required. If Wardieu noticed, he paid no
heed. He seemed quite engrossed in studying the newest
points of interest revealed by the morning light, namely, how
truly blue the centres of Servanne's eyes were, and how white
the surrounding orbs. Her lashes were thick and honey-coloured, which led him to speculate and then to search the
edge of her wimple until he confirmed his suspicions that her
hair would be as blonde as his own. Blonder, he surmised, if
the shiny thread of escaped yellow was any indication, and
thinking back, had he not seen a long, gleaming curl of
something silvery-pale flown from beneath her hood the
night he brought her away from the abbey?

He had always preferred his women dark-haired and
white-skinned, finding the contrast more stimulating than
fair hair and ill-defined contours, but now he caught himself
warming to the notion of a golden-haired beauty in his bed.

"Two days," he mused. "It seems an interminable wait,
my lady."

Servanne read exactly the same thing in his eyes as Nicolaa saw, and for once, was thankful when the sheriff's wife
interrupted bluntly.

"You can hardly proceed without Prince John since he is
standing for the bride. And doubtless the old whore herself,
Eleanor of Aquitaine would nail your eyelids to your knees if
you snubbed her precious La Seyne Sur Mer."

Servanne's heart missed a beat. Her gaze focused on the
table linen and she gripped her eating knife so tightly, both
blade and hand trembled. Luckily Wardieu had turned to
reply to Nicolaa and neither saw her reaction to the name.

"It was a figure of speech, Nicolaa," he sighed. "Not a
proclamation of intent. However, with John's cavalcade
nearing the moor as we speak, and La Seyne reported to be
but a day's journey away, it may well suit my purpose to

speed the entire affair along . . . with the good bishop's permission, of course."

Servanne's heart had barely calmed from the first shock when it was sent slamming into her rib cage by a second one. A deep, melodic baritone gave response to Wardieu's question, the all-too familiar voice coming from one of the guests seated at the far end of the dais. Servanne inched her head around by degrees, leaning forward when she found her view blocked by Wardieu's broad shoulder. A painfully constricted breath later and she was able to follow the flow of a capacious black wool sleeve to the ermine collar and gold link chain of office that ornamented the otherwise plain, voluminous robes. A plaited sallet tamed the riot of jet-black hair, and the soft brown eyes that turned to meet hers were as guileless and solemn as they were the day the sandal-footed Friar had greeted her at the gates of Thornfeld. Only this time the sacrilege was not in feigning the posture of a humble monk. This time, Alaric FitzAthelstan had aspired to the robes and rubies of a bishop!

"I bring you God's greetings and the blessings of the church, my child," he murmured piously. "If I am not mistaken, however, we have met once before . . . perhaps in the company of your late husband, Sir Hubert de Briscourt? A brave and gallant crusader, to be sure. And his yearly alms to the church were most generous. Most generous indeed."

A wave of faintness passed through Servanne. What was he doing here? How had he come through the guards, the sentries, the numerous sullen challenges at each tower and gate? And how was it that he was sitting at the Dragon's table, eating the Dragon's fare, chatting with the Dragon and his guests as if they were fond acquaintances?

"Bishop Gautier comes to us all the way from Canterbury," Wardieu said. "Our own Bishop of Sleaford was taken ill last week, and since Canterbury was visiting the area, he agreed to preside at the services."

Servanne met Friar's eyes again. "I . . . thank you for your blessings, my lord bishop," she managed to stammer. "And yes, I do believe we have met before."

For the briefest moment she thought she saw something—relief?—flicker across the lean, hawklike features, but a wan smile reprieved the blandness of his previous expression and he turned to address Wardieu again.

"As to La Seyne Sur Mer, I believe I passed his party on the road from Lincoln yesterday. He claimed to have some business or other to attend to in town, but I was . . . er . . . pressed to assure you he would be arriving at Bloodmoor before nightfall. A surly, unpleasant fellow, I must say. Very"—a ring-laden hand wafted absently in the air—"enamoured of himself, and not at all friendly to strangers, regardless of their station in life."

"Is it true," Nicolaa asked in her best purring voice, "that he wears a silk hood at all times?"

"As true as sin, my lady," Friar nodded. "An accident early in his youth, I am told, left his face so severely scarred it cannot be looked upon without inciting screams of horror. Queen Eleanor, whom he serves so devotedly, has seen it only the once and was so overcome she ordered hoods of the finest oriental silks to be made expressly so she could enjoy his company without the need of salts or screens. Notwithstanding the hood, however, he has a surly eye and a sharp tongue, neither of which would endear him to a sensible woman's company, I should think."

"Eleanor was never said to be sensible," Nicolaa mused, fondling the mutilated remnants of her pear as if it were living flesh. "Still, I have heard the uglier and more brutish a man is, the more he strives to compensate in . . . other areas. Perhaps our randy old dowager queen has retained La Seyne for more than his ability to merely wield a sword with undaunting chivalry."

Wardieu grinned crookedly. "He does not like straying too

far from his beloved Brittany. I imagine if the queen herself had not issued the command for him to attend, he would be there still, nursing his ill temper and counting his trophies."

"Indeed," Friar concurred gravely, "he wants a stout comeuppance where his boastings are concerned. Do you know he travels with the pennants of every challenger he has met and fought in the lists? Too many to count, I can tell you, and strung on poles like catches of dead fish. I am told" —he leaned forward as if imparting a great secret—"he not only pledges his own armour and gear to anyone skilled enough to split him from a saddle, but his sea of conquered pennants as well! Such arrogance, my lord, begs for deliverance."

"At any other time, I am certain Lord Lucien would rise to the challenge," Nicolaa murmured. "However, since the tournament is being held to celebrate his wedding, he would not want to see his young bride cheated of her nuptial due through a misplaced lance."

Wardieu laid his hands flat on the tabletop and began to thrum his long fingers softly against the linen. It was the custom for tourneys to be staged for formal occasions and celebrations. In the case of a wedding, it was acceptable for the groom to select one of his favoured knights to act the part of his champion, thus saving the bride the humiliating possibility of becoming a widow the same day.

"So," he mused, "this . . . Scourge of Mirebeau wishes to ease the aggravations he has suffered in his journey by paring a few skulls?"

"It was the mood I sensed," Friar agreed guilelessly. "He is, after all, the dowager's equerry, and in his day has unhorsed the best knights in all of France, Normandy, and the southern provinces. But if memory serves, he is well into his third decade; not a young man at all and no longer in his prime. I am certain you could find some eager, robust young varlets bristling to earn their gold spurs by tipping La Seyne's nose into the dirt."

Wardieu's fingers were stilled again. A distinct ruddiness darkened his complexion at the inference he too must be considered past his prime by the bishop's standards.

Servanne risked a quick glance at Friar before leaning back in her chair again. He was saying all the right things, playing on the Dragon's vanity as a champion, pricking his natural envy over a rival's reputation—but why? Why was he goading De Gournay into a match with La Seyne Sur Mer?

"He also said—" The bishop appeared to catch himself and waved the thought away with an apologetic smile. "No, no. I would be speaking out of turn."

"He also said *what*," Wardieu demanded flatly.

Friar glanced along the row of guests seated on the dais as if noticing for the first time they had all become as silent as death. "Why . . . he, ahh, also said something about not wanting to take unfair advantage of a rival who has not appeared in too many tourneys during the past year or two, and who may be . . . er . . . somewhat lacking in form and, ah"—Friar looked into Wardieu's cold blue eyes and swallowed hard—". . . nerve."

Servanne missed Wardieu's immediate reaction, for at that same moment, purely by chance, her gaze settled on the six cowled figures occupying a section of one of the lower tables. Resembling large gray moths, they were garbed somberly, as befitting clerics in the bishop's service. They humbly declined the richer foods in favour of black bread and fruit, and drank sparingly of the watered wine. With their heads bowed and their hoods drawn forward, their features were, for the most part, shadowed and indistinct, but Servanne thought she recognized five of them from amongst the Wolf's men at Thornfeld Abbey. The sixth was Gil Golden.

Another wave of faintness swept through her, the sudden

weakness causing her to lose hold of her jewelled eating knife. It dropped onto the table with a clatter, which might have prompted a neck or two to part company with its skin if it had not occurred the exact instant Wardieu's fist slammed on the wood and sent a volley of buttocks leaping off their seats.

"By the rood," he roared, "we shall see who is lacking in form and nerve! He shall indeed have a match on his hands, and when he finds himself well-spitted and rolling in the dust with his entrails tangled about his ears, we shall also see who suffers the greater mortification!"

A rousing cheer of support went up from the crowded tables. Chairs scraped over the stone floor as knights stood and raised their goblets and their swords in a flashing show of support for their liege lord. The quiet tension of the previous moments burst with a frenzy and there were counter challenges issued, boasts proclaimed, and a voracious round of wagering begun.

Wardieu, flushed with enthusiasm, did not see the look on Friar's face, or the lingering glance that passed between the visiting bishop and Servanne de Briscourt. A toast was made, followed by another. By magic, a pair of tumblers cartwheeled into the centre of the hall and in a blink of an eye, the huge room was vibrating with music and laughter.

Servanne paced away an anxious morning and half an afternoon before the expected visitor was announced into her chambers. Biddy had been dispatched on a series of errands to keep her occupied elsewhere, and Servanne was alone when Geoffrey, the page, escorted Friar into her solar.

In the presence of their young witness, Alaric continued smoothly in his role, conveying his intentions to discuss the upcoming wedding and any fears the bride might be experiencing in regards to her future role as the Baroness de Gournay. Servanne's responses were equally civil, her mood seemingly as genial as she instructed Geoffrey to fetch a flask of wine from the kitchens and perhaps some small sweetmeats with which she could tempt the palate of her exalted guest.

With Geoffrey scurrying away to comply, Servanne and Alaric were left alone, passing the first full minute in heavy silence.

"Are you mad?" she asked finally. "Have you completely lost your senses coming here like this?"

He glanced down at his voluminous black robes and flicked a speck of lint off the long sleeve. "It was a necessary ruse to get inside the castle. I thought I carried the role rather well."

"Gil Golden and the others: Do they feel as comfortable sitting among men who would have their heads skewered on pikes at the first hint of betrayal?"

"Their fates—and mine—rest solely in your hands, my lady. Our lives are yours to do with what you will."

"I do not thank you for the responsibility!" she exclaimed angrily. "You were so sure I would not betray you in the hall?"

"I was hoping you would not."

"That is no answer."

"Then give me an honest question and I will attempt to better it."

Servanne paced to the window. "You take a great deal upon yourself, Friar. *He* takes a great deal upon himself as well, assuming I will not reveal the lot of you to Wardieu."

"Lucien . . . has a great deal of respect for human nature," Friar said easily. "He did not think you were the kind of woman who reveled in blood sport."

"Or revenge?"

Friar gave his shoulders a small shrug. "We had to take the chance."

"Lucien," she said, testing the name on her tongue,

"should not be so sure of himself all the time. It could win him more trouble than he can handle."

"He is already balancing more trouble than he can handle, my lady, although he would be the last to admit it."

"Oh? How so? Has he run out of women to kidnap and abbeys to desecrate?"

Alaric ignored the sarcasm, though its presence was a good sign. "He knew he would have to face his brother one way or another. That is not the trouble he finds himself in, as well you know."

"I know he has a penchant for playing games with people's lives," she said and turned away. "I suspect it amuses him to act the part of a cat in a roomful of mice; to corner each mouse in turn and worry it half to death before discarding it to stalk another."

"He has not discarded you, my lady," Alaric said quietly. "In truth, he has been behaving like a scalded cat from the moment you rode away from the abbey."

"I did not ride away, sirrah. I was sent away. Thrown away, if you will, once I was no longer of any use to him."

"Come now, you do not believe that."

"Do I not?" she demanded, whirling back to confront him. "What would you have me believe of a man who lives and breathes revenge to the exclusion of all else?"

Alaric sighed. "He is a proud and stubborn man who thought his pride and stubbornness should outweigh any softer feelings that might be dangerous to you both if he allowed them to intrude on his emotions."

"Softer feelings? Emotions?" She scorned the notion with a bitter laugh. "He has neither, my lord. He is cold and heartless; arrogant and self-righteous and contemptuous of anything and everything that does not suit his purpose. *I* suited his purpose, but only insofar as my wedding to his brother provided the perfect opportunity to display his cunningness to the world. He has no heart, no soul. He cares for nothing but his own skin and does nothing that does not further his own vainglory! *That* is what I believe!"

Friar drew a deep breath. "Then perhaps you should know a thing or two about him—things he would never tell you himself."

"I already know everything I care to know about him. He is cruel, vicious, and utterly without honour."

"Lucien told me you once asked him why I did not complete my vows to the church," he said quietly.

Servanne held her patience in check, wondering what earthly—or heavenly—connection this had to the subject at hand.

"He would never tell you, but perhaps I should. I was but a few days from making my final vows," he continued, and fingered the gold crucifix that hung from a chain around his waist. "I was assigned to attend the comforts of the bishop who had come to officiate at the ceremonies, and it was in the course of seeing to some minor oversight I stumbled across the bishop and the abbess from the neighbouring convent seeing to a late-night oversight of their own. The breaking of vows of celibacy is nothing new or shocking in either a monastery or a convent; that was not what I found the most disturbing. It was the fact that they were using a young and unwilling novitiate the abbess had chosen for the special occasion, and the fact that when they had finished with her, they intended to carve her up like some sacrificial offering.

"I stepped in barely in time to save the girl's life, but in the process, the knife somehow found its way into the bishop's chest. Before I knew it, I was in chains and being brought to trial for devil worship and murder. It was the word of the abbess against mine, you see. The tribunal consisted of churchmen—none of whom would dare admit to the macabre practices of their bishop."

"What about the girl? You said you were in time to save her; surely she could have testified on your behalf?"

"She was in shock and half dead. It was almost three years before she spoke again, and then only because Lucien spared no expense in finding the best physicians in Normandy to care for her."

"Lucien? He was involved?"

"He was present at the tribunal as the queen's representative. He had no authority over the proceedings, but he watched and he listened, and . . . the day I was slated for final judgment, he came riding in out of nowhere, and slew the half-dozen Knights Templar who objected to his aiding my escape. The queen, whose land bordered the abbey, was not pleased, as you might imagine. But at the risk of his life and reputation, Lucien scoured the countryside, applying his own particular brand of persuasion to tongues that had, until then, remained silent against the bishop's peculiar perversions. As it turned out, there were bodies of other mutilated girls discovered in places the bishop had frequented.

"Solely due to Lucien's efforts, I was cleared of the charge of murder—and mine is not the only such tale to be told. All of the men who follow him—Sparrow, Robert, Mutter and Stutter—all of them owe him a debt of trust and loyalty which can never be repaid. Even Gil, stubborn as she is, would never have been accepted into the band if not for Lucien."

Servanne halted him with a frown. *"She?* Gil Golden is a woman?"

Friar cursed the slip, but after a moment, nodded. "As pigheaded as any man I have ever laid an eye to, but aye, she's a woman."

Servanne was beyond reacting to any more surprises. "So. He saved your life, became the benefactor for a band of misfits and recalcitrants, and lives a life of assured comfort in service to Queen Eleanor of Aquitaine. All applaudable achievements, sirrah, but despoiled nonetheless by his current misdeeds."

"Granted, his methods are sometimes . . . questionable, to say the least, but he is as honest and honourable a man as I have ever come across, and loyal to the death to people who matter to him."

Servanne challenged the softened tone of his voice. "Are you trying to tell me I matter to him?"

"Mock me for a fool if you like, my lady, but I would go so far as to suggest the heartless rogue is in love with you."

"Your jest is cruel, m'sieur," Servanne said, her cheeks flaming hotly. "He is in love with no one save himself. If he were . . . if he were at all *concerned* for my welfare, why did he not send me away from this place instead of handing me over like a platter of rare meat?"

"Why does any man cut off his nose to spite his face? If he kept you with him, he would have had to admit he loved you, and I do not think he was prepared to admit it, even to himself."

"Then how can *you* be so sure?" she demanded.

Friar's grin was self-effacing. "I recognize the symptoms . . . in both of you."

"Both! You *are* mad! I do not love him. I do not even like him! What is more, I doubt it would draw a tear if I never saw him or heard his name—*whatever it might be*—ever again!"

Friar studied the adamantly squared shoulders she presented to him, and scratched his jaw thoughtfully. "Then you will not want to know he will be here, inside Bloodmoor, the day of the wedding."

"He is coming here?" she gasped. "To the castle? But how . . . ? When . . . ?"

"How is not important," Alaric began, but was cut off by an exclamation of dismay.

"Not important! Lord Wardieu has given orders everyone must be stopped, questioned, and his identity verified before being admitted to the castle grounds. You have seen the number of guards who patrol the walls and towers—they have already been doubled since we arrived, and there was talk today of taking even stronger measures to avoid any *unwanted surprises.*"

Friar nodded as if they were all valid arguments he had heard before. "He is counting on La Seyne's presence to see him through the sentry checks. Mirebeau has four score men under his command, a few more will not be noticed."

"La Seyne," she despaired. "Is he as mad as everyone else?"

"Madder," Friar agreed grimly. A short inner debate took place behind the dark brown eyes before he took her hands gently in his and added, "My lady, we have all known, from the instant Lucien learned of his brother's presence here at Bloodmoor Keep, he would not—could not—rest until one or both of them were dead. He is arrogant and proud and stubborn, and when he gets a thing in his head, it is devilish hard to dislodge it or turn him on a new course. Death does that to you, and he came as close to dying as a man can come without touching the hand of God. There is nothing you or I can do to stop this thing from happening. Nothing at all."

Servanne continued gazing up into his eyes for what seemed like an eternity, her own filling with bright, fierce tears of denial. She jerked her hands out of his and backed up several steps.

"La Seyne," she cried. "La Seyne could stop it by killing De Gournay himself."

A second small battle was waged in the depths of Friar's eyes before he answered. "La Seyne will be pleased to hear the Dragon has accepted his challenge, but it will be Lucien who rides onto the field to face his brother."

"What?" Servanne's voice was scarcely more than a ragged breath. "What did you say?"

"La Seyne's business here is with Prince John, and when it is concluded—"

"Business? What business?"

"It . . . is not my place to tell you, my lady. It would not be safe for you to know. Suffice it to say the tournament and challenge will serve to keep the Dragon's attention diverted elsewhere. Already he has abandoned his guests to concentrate on the practice fields, and word of the match has spread outside the castle walls, sure to bring great crowds to the castle—crowds he could no more keep outside the walls than a paper dam could control a tide. Crowds bring confusion, and confusion breeds mistakes."

"Everything has been so carefully thought out, has it not?" she said bleakly. "Even to sending you here in your bishop's robes to warm my heart with promises of love and loyalty. But what if he fails? What if, after all his clever scheming and manipulating, he is no match for De Gournay? What if the wrong man survives to walk off the field? You and La Seyne and your merry band of havoc-makers will ride away and seek other noble horizons to conquer . . . but what will become of those you leave behind? What will become of me?"

"Lucien has already made provisions—"

"Provisions! He has made provisions!" Her mouth opened, closed, then opened again on an oath of incredulity. "*He* . . . has made provisions without even troubling to ask if I wanted them?"

"He assumed . . ." Friar began, his voice trailing off uncomfortably.

"He assumed? When did he start taking it upon himself to assume what I would or would not want?"

Friar's complexion darkened perceptibly.

"I see. Because he bedded me, he thinks he now owns me?"

"No. No, I am sure he does not—"

"My lady! My lady!"

Startled by the outcry, both Alaric and Servanne whirled

toward the door, but at the sight of young Geoffrey's flushed face, Friar's hand slid discreetly away from the handle of the knife he wore concealed beneath his robes.

"Many pardons, my lady, my lord bishop . . . but I was dispatched to inform you Prince John has arrived! He is here, in the great hall, and my lord Wardieu requests your attendance there at once."

Alaric looked deeply into Servanne's eyes, holding steady for several long moments.

"Thank you, Geoffrey," she said softly. "And thank you, my lord bishop, for all your kind words of comfort; you have given me much to contemplate over the next few days."

Alaric set his jaw against the desire to respond, and instead, merely bowed his head and murmured a parting benediction.

19

Servanne de Briscourt, in the company of her late husband, had been presented to Prince John the previous summer, but like her original memory of the Baron de Gournay, his exact image was somewhat ragged about the edges. Yet she had no difficulty in picking John Lackland out from amongst the throng of knights and lords who formed his entourage. The Plantagenet bloodlines, known for producing fair-haired men and women of exceptional beauty, had erred in moulding John, the fifth son of Eleanor and Henry. His hair was black, with shiny tufts of it spreading down his neck and emerging from his wrists to darken the backs of his hands and knuckles. His face was leaning toward fleshiness, a result of his fondness for food, wine, and hedonistic excesses. A wide, smooth brow hinted at nobility, but the sharply pointed nose and black, sunken eyes gave credence to the charges of cruelty and obsessive behavior he was known for.

His hand, when it was extended to Servanne, was long and thin, the palm clammy and the nails gnawed back to the quick. It was rumoured he suffered fits of apoplexy, some lasting days on end when nothing and no one was safe in his presence. Conversely he could lapse into great periods of lethargy when he rarely left his bed or lifted so much as a hand to feed himself. If his moods were erratic, so too was his selection of knights who were regarded with favour from one day to the next. Held high in esteem in the first week, an unlucky knave could find himself thrown in irons the next and left to starve to death for whatever his crime, real or imagined, might have been.

There were few men he feared or respected. William Pembroke, the Marshal of England, was one of those men and possibly the only deterrent to John's bleeding every last coin and copper from England's peasantry. As it was, he increased taxes at every turn, pleading poverty and using the excuse of Richard's crusading ventures to raise financing. As regent, he could and did levy taxes on everything from bread to breathing. His enemies he reduced to penniless vagrants; his friends—of whom there were few—were lavished with rewards and grew as wealthy and influential as John's sense of paranoia would allow.

Servanne had, in the beginning, been both awed and flattered to learn the prince would be a guest at Bloodmoor for her wedding, naïvely assuming his presence would offer a certain decorum and prestige.

More recently—as recent as the few minutes she had taken out in the gallery to compose her racing pulsebeat—she had even toyed with a small hope the prince would respond to an appeal to intervene on her behalf and, if not rescind the betrothal agreement outright, at least postpone the formalities until her plea could be sent to Richard.

Her first sight of John Lackland shattered any idea of approaching him to ask a favour. His eyes had ravished her to the bare bone before her presentation had even commenced; his lascivious grin had told her precisely what manner of payment he would expect in return for the simplest request she might make of him.

Moreover, it had been John's influence over his brother—who could not be troubled himself in arranging such matters—that had won Servanne de Briscourt and her considerable dowry for Lucien Wardieu. Several other suitors had put forth their bids for her hand; some had even been generous enough to cause the prince a second thought. But he had granted the prize to his champion, De Gournay, and there was little hope she could appeal to either his greed or his ambition to win a delay.

Nor was the mood exactly conducive to serious discussions. By the time Servanne and her maidservants had descended to the great hall, a drunken revelry was well under way. Since he was renowned for his carnal appetites, she was not unprepared to see more women than men in attendance upon the prince. Also obvious were his preferred attributes in his companions, for there was hardly a bodice seam not stretched to its utmost and bursting to set its contents free, hardly an unblemished face above the age of seventeen.

It actually afforded the one spot of warmth in the unfolding events, to see the high flush in Nicolaa de la Haye's cheeks. Her bold sensuality was rendered less startling in the midst of so many smooth, clear complexions and bright, avaricious eyes. The surrounding bevy of youth and gaiety had set the aging beauty's teeth on edge and caused more than one shrill reprimand to send a servant weeping from the room.

Servanne was so warmed by her rival's discomfort, she almost missed the sole bowed head in the prince's entourage.

Because there was no distinct fashion for children to wear, they were usually dressed as small replicas of men and women. Thus, the child who stood so quietly between two of John's advisers, wore a gown of blue baudequin styled along the same seductive lines as those worn by the older women. Her straight waist was girded in gold links, her train was long and swirled demurely around her tiny slippered feet. Her wimple fit snugly to chin and cheeks, outlining a face that promised great beauty in the coming years. Sky-blue eyes and pale lashes suggested the child shared Servanne's own fair colouring, enough so they might have been construed as sisters . . . or mother and daughter, since a further inspection placed the child's age at no more than eight or nine.

Faint stirrings of disgust shadowed Servanne's eyes as she saw how uncomfortably the girl stood in the company of bloated, leering men and women. Darker thoughts were confined to the tautness of her lips as Servanne looked at Prince John and recalled stories of his lewdness and debauchery. It was not so unusual for girls of eleven or twelve years to be married off to older men, although the actual consummation at such a young age was hardly considered to be gratifying, or manly. For the prince to keep a child so young by his side, to flaunt her along with his whores left a galling taste in Servanne's throat.

"Ahh . . . lovely, lovely," John said, his wet hands catching hold of Servanne's to draw her attention back to himself. "My Dragon Lord has chosen well. She seems a touch on the thin side, Wardieu," he added in an aside, "but I trust you will have no trouble plumping her up in short order."

The laughter that accompanied John's suggestive caress of his own burgeoning belly caused Servanne to notice how his teeth, green with rot, were overlapped like fangs top and bottom. His breath reeked of wine and what had not found its way down his throat was sprinkled liberally in the forked beard and over the front of his black velvet doublet. As well, he was somewhat shorter than she remembered, and she had to make a conscious effort not to stand too straight to overshadow him.

"You shall sit by me during the meal," John announced, indicating the vacant seats on the dais. And you, Wardieu," he added with a broad wink, "shall endeavour to give me several good reasons why I should not steal your bride away for myself. Come . . . Breauté, Gisbourne . . . sit. Sit! My gut rumbles loud enough to rival the rutting noises of a ram. And where is my pretty little niece? Ahh, the fairest little

princess in all of Brittany . . . I have grown so accustomed
to her smiling face in our presence, I shall miss it sorely
when it is no longer there to greet me at every turn."

His laugh, dry and sardonic, did not affect the child's sombre expression, save for the faint pinkish flush that tinged her
ash-white complexion. The greater effect was noted in the
faces of his closest advisers, one of whom moved hastily forward and murmured a few worried cautions into the prince's
ear.

"Bah! God's chin, what difference can it make now? By
tomorrow, the spiteful little bitch will be on her way back to
Brittany, faster than any gossips can convince anyone she
was ever anywhere else." He paused and belched loudly.
"The game has grown tiresome, Breauté. I have won my
satisfaction; the old milkless teat will know now that I am
not a man to be toyed with. Lock the snipe away if it eases
your bowels any to remove her face from common sight, but
do not spoil my mood! We are come to celebrate the wedding
of my valiant friend. Eat! Drink! Let no man show a scowl
before me this day, lest he crave to see it flayed from his
face!"

A roar of approval went up from the floor of the great hall
as Prince John led Servanne to her place at the long table.
Her legs felt wooden and stiff, her movements so clumsy she
caused the hem of her train to become snagged on the corner
of a bench. While her page was bending over to unpinch it,
Servanne's gaze met Friar's over the head of the prince.

John Lackland had but one niece, and there was but one
Princess of Brittany—Eleanor—named for her grandmother,
the Dowager Queen of England.

But the Princess Eleanor and her brother Arthur were
both in Brittany. Neither had set foot on English soil in the
years since their father's death. The queen had been safe-
guarding them at Mirebeau, wary of John's penchant for
treachery.

What if I were to tell you Arthur and his sister were kidnapped from the queen's castle four months ago?

Servanne felt her mouth go dry as the Wolf's question echoed in her mind. Worse still, she heard her own dismissal of the notion as being absurd and ridiculous, along with the intimation that he had come to England on an honourable mission for the queen.

There are reasons for secrecy and silence; reasons which forbid both Etienne and myself from settling our conflict openly and speedily, and those I dare not tell you, for it would place you in certain danger.

Certain danger?

Servanne's page touched her arm gingerly, indicating her train was freed. She murmured something—she knew not what—and when she looked back at Friar, he was already seated, his face studiously averted.

La Seyne's business here is with Prince John . . . He will be pleased to hear the Dragon has accepted his challenge, but it will be Lucien who rides onto the field to face his brother . . . La Seyne's business here is with Prince John . . . Suffice it to say the tournament and challenge will serve to keep the Dragon's attention diverted elsewhere . . .

Elsewhere?

Certain danger?

Diversions?

Servanne turned her head and stared at the prince.

By tomorrow the little bitch will be on her way back to Brittany faster than any gossips can convince anyone she was ever anywhere else.

My God, Servanne thought, it was true! John *had* kidnapped the children from Mirebeau. He *had* planned to hold Arthur hostage in exchange for political demands. The fact that his plan had been foiled and the young prince had been rescued must have enraged him beyond belief—enough for him to risk the condemnation of every knight and yeoman

man who respected and lived by the codes of chivalry. Holding the princess captive was an unconscionable breach of honour. Exposing her to the decadent behaviour of his puppet court, possibly even forcing her to endure abuse as a victim of his vile and lecherous appetites would rouse the protective ire of every baron and lord not already bristling under John's unpopular regency.

La Seyne's business, therefore, was undoubtedly to ransom the princess back into the care of her grandmother. And the Wolf's mission, as the self-confessed Captain of the Queen's Guard—was it to ensure the exchange went smoothly and peaceably?

Various pieces of the puzzle were falling into place, stripping away Servanne's burden of doubts as they fell. It explained everything—or nearly everything—and so clearly, it was all she could do to keep to her seat and maintain a semblance of normality as the hollow flourish of trumpets called forth a parade of servants.

Heavily strained arms brought steaming crocks of broth and stews, followed by platters of roast fowl, quail, and suckling pig. Noise rose to a crescendo as greedy hands dipped into pots and platters; meat was torn and carved, the half-chewed bones tossed to howling, scrabbling dogs. Chins dripped grease and throats groaned in appreciation of rich and varied presentations of fish, legumes, and meat. Heavily sugared blankmangers—a paste of pounded chicken blended with boiled rice and almond milk—were devoured to the last morsel and bowls wiped clean with thrusting fingers and crusts of fresh baked bread. Wine flowed like water and ale frothed from huge oaken barrels and not surprisingly, a guest or two toppled forward, face down into their trenchers before the final courses of wafers and fruit compotes were served.

By then Servanne's cheeks were well flushed from impatience. She had barely tasted her wine, and her trencher of food sat untouched in clots of congealing fat.

She was quickest to her feet when the men suggested an afternoon of hawking, and the most beguiling in offering her wishes to decline the party in favour of resting for the evening's entertainments ahead. Wardieu regarded her through vaguely curious eyes, especially when she was observed sidling toward the bishop's end of the table, but the combined stimulant of the women's fawning laughter and Prince John's open flattery distracted him long enough for Servanne to whisper a private word in Friar's ear.

"When La Seyne Sur Mer arrives, I wish to see him," she said.

"What?" He looked startled, uncertain of whether he had heard her words correctly or not.

"I want to speak to La Seyne," she hissed again, her eyes bright and defying him to refuse. "I know why he is here. I know what his *business* is with Prince John, and I would speak with him in private before any more mistakes are made." She straightened, bringing the level of her voice up a notch higher as she did so. "Of course, I could wait and speak to him openly in the company of De Gournay and the prince, but I rather suspect he would prefer to keep the subject of *our* business a private matter a while longer."

Friar opened his mouth to protest, but Wardieu's sudden appearance at his bride's side turned the utterance into a tight smile. "Naturally, my lady, I shall see what I can arrange."

"Arrange?" Wardieu asked, his cool gaze narrowing as it went from one face to the other. "What is there yet to be arranged?"

"Oh." Servanne feigned a maidenly gasp. " 'Tis a surprise, my lord, and not for you to know just yet."

"A surprise, is it?" His hand curved possessively around Servanne's waist, his fingers transforming the gesture into a caress. "I am becoming quite fond of surprises, my lady. Quite fond, indeed."

20

"La Seyne does not like surprises," Friar muttered. "He does not like them at all."

"You told him I wished to see him?" Servanne whispered, her voice barely louder than the rustling of her skirt over the stone floor.

"I told him."

"Then it will not exactly be a surprise, will it?"

Friar came to an abrupt halt at the end of one corridor, seeming to mentally verify their position before turning into the musty gloom of another arched stone hallway.

"This is utter madness," he remarked under his breath. "It is nearing midnight. We are as apt to get hopelessly lost and wander undiscovered until morning as we are to stumble across a nest of guards sniffing after trouble."

"Why did you not beg our leave of the company an hour ago—or two, for that matter? Most of the guests were too sodden to have noticed our departure."

"Why could you not have waited until morning to see La Seyne? He has been inside the castle walls but a few hours and is in no temper for entertaining foolish young women."

"I heard he met with the prince's hawking party out on the moor."

"It afforded him the opportunity to decline an invitation to tonight's festivities without appearing to offer insult to either Prince John, or his host—not that such a petty thing as insulting royalty would have stopped him from declining

anyway. But it soured his mood as effectively as if he had
been in attendance. Since you claim to have deduced his
purpose for coming to Bloodmoor Keep, you must also realize his fondest wish is to complete his business and be on his
way."

"Getting the Princess Eleanor safely away from Prince
John is, of course, of some importance—"

Friar halted again, so unexpectedly this time, Servanne
walked up his heels and bumped into his shoulders.

"Firstly," he said in an angry hiss, "the walls have ears.
Secondly, concluding the matter swiftly and safely is of the
utmost importance, my lady. It must be accomplished to the
exclusion of *all else*. Do I make myself clear?"

Servanne bristled at the condescending tone, but in the
next breath, she realized it was fear and concern speaking—
as much for her safety as for the safety of the princess.

"I only want to help," she offered softly. "Believe me, I
know how the little princess must be feeling, and I will do
nothing at all to jeopardize her safe removal from Bloodmoor."

Friar sighed inwardly, refraining from pointing out the
obvious: that she was jeopardizing their safety at that very
moment. Whatever she had to say to La Seyne had better be
damned important to take such a risk. Conversely, La Seyne
should have refused outright to see her—what game was *he*
playing at?

Friar navigated them successfully to the rear portal of one
of the buildings linked to the main keep. It was the exit used
by the servants and it was here Friar ushered her into a tiny
storeroom and mouthed a few choice words as he struck
tinder to flint, finally creating enough sparks to light a small
candle. In the interim between begging her leave of the company in the great hall, and pacing anxiously in her solar until
Friar came to fetch her, Servanne had prudently changed the
ornately embroidered velvet tunic and silk train for a plainer

garment of dark wool. She had removed her wimple as well
and left her hair in a single thick braid trailing down her
back. Now, to further disguise her against recognition by the
guards, Friar handed her a voluminous cloak made from the
same moth-gray horsehair Gil and the others had been wearing.

"A more fetching cleric, I cannot imagine," Friar said
with a comforting smile. "I have already passed through the
sentries once tonight, so there should be no difficulty in gaining the outer bailey. What is more, since the celebrations
have not been restricted to the great hall, there should be
enough noise and revelry outside the keep to cover our
tracks. Ready?"

Servanne nodded and raised her chin so that Alaric could
fasten the cloak properly in place. A final adjustment of the
spacious hood, and Friar blew out the candle. When the
glaring yellow blotches had faded from his vision, he took
Servanne by the hand and cautiously led her out into the
corridor.

The sight of two more cowled figures gave her heart a
momentary start, but when a distant torchlight assured her
she was not seeing double, she nodded a faint greeting to
Mutter and Stutter, and felt safer for their quiet presence
behind them. Two more "monks" joined them outside the
portal, and a third pair, including Gil Golden, fell into step
near the gates to the outer bailey.

The guards at the first barbican tower scarcely paid heed
to the cloaked figures who crossed the footbridge. There
were huge fires blazing in every corner of the common, and
flickering torches thrust into niches every few paces along
the walls. Sentries paced the ramparts up above, but they
were not too concerned with anyone already granted entry to
the inner grounds. There was even the squeal of a woman's
laughter from somewhere high up, showing exactly how interested they were in the pedestrian traffic below.

The second bailey was not quite as brightly lit, but it appeared as if everyone in this tiny, self-contained village was out in force, drunk on cheap ale and anticipation of the next day's events. Alaric's dark cowl and glinting crucifix won them an amiable passage through the gloomy, musty labyrinth of laneways and workshops. Visiting knights had left their retinues of men-at-arms to be housed in the small, crowded barracks that lined the walls, and they had been quick to find the whores who were willing to do the most for the least amount of coin. Goliards and minstrels, practicing for the day of the tournament, put on impromptu shows by firelight and there was singing and dancing in nearly every lane they passed.

It was a far different scene from the image Servanne retained of the day of her arrival at Bloodmoor. These people smiled and laughed, and were not afraid to meet one another in the eye. Even the guards who patrolled the bailey in pairs, stopped to appreciate a daring acrobatic feat, or to sample a taste of sizzling meat roasting on a small grill.

There were heady scents in the air as well. The bakers along bakers' row were bending nonstop over their ovens in hope of meeting the morrow's demand for bread, biscuits, and pastries. In the butchers' quarters, hogs, lambs, goats, and chickens were being slaughtered, skinned, and plucked in preparation for the banquet that would follow the tournament, as well as the feast to culminate the wedding. In the armourers' alley, contrasting the sweet smells, squires had set up booths and pavilions decorated with their lord's crests and pennants. Forges burned and smoked oily fumes into the night air as grease- and sweat-stained smithies worked over anvils, bribed with handfuls of copper zechins into making repairs to horseshoes, lances, or shields. Squires were overseeing the repairs, and would undoubtedly work well into the small hours polishing and oiling suits of chain mail. The loser of each match had to forfeit his armour and horse to the winning knight, and it was a matter of pride that, win or lose, a knight's equipment should bear no spot of rust or broken link of steel.

Servanne was beginning to feel the tension in her legs long before Alaric slowed his pace and lifted a cautionary finger to his lips. They had left the noise of hammers and toilers well behind and entered a darker, quieter sector of the bailey. Servanne had no idea where they were, no idea the grounds were so vast and sprawling. She pressed into the deeper shadows as instructed and wondered how Alaric seemed to know the right twists and turns to make. But then she recalled—the Wolf had grown up within these walls. After fifteen years, if he remembered overgrown forest paths and lost monasteries, he would have no difficulty remembering the nooks and crannies of the place he had called home.

In the gloom, the nook where Alaric had brought her was about as isolated and dismal as it possibly could be—and for good reason. With a small start, Servanne identified the sketch hung on the sign over the door, and realized it was where shrouds and coffins were made for the unluckier castle residents.

"Dear God," she whispered, pulling instinctively away.

"Even God has the courtesy to stay away from here tonight," Alaric said, catching her arm and squeezing it gently for moral support. "It was the safest place we could think of for a meeting. Even so . . . be brief, my lady. Gil and the others will keep a sharp eye out for intruders; I shall wander back toward the psaltery and wait for you there. Go now, and have a care to make some small noise before you reach the door, or you will feel the bite of a knife between your shoulders before you can correct the oversight. Keep well to the deepest part of the shadows . . ."

Servanne drew a deep breath to bolster her courage and crossed the last moonlit patch of ground. Her footsteps crunched over straw and hay and she made no attempt to dampen the sound, chilled by Alaric's warning. She paused before the low-slung door a moment and offered a heartfelt prayer to any saint who might not have already completely forsaken her. She debated knocking, but a further thought saw her simply lift the crude wooden latch and step tentatively inside.

Dust was as thick as fog in the interior of the stone and thatch hut, and it took her eyes several seconds to adjust to the feeble amber light cast by a guttering taper. Another quelling bubble of panic rose in her chest, for the gloom was dense enough to conceal man or beast, and, since she was not certain which of the two she should expect to see here tonight, she did not rush eagerly to meet her fate.

He was there, in the darkest of the shadows, his form slowly emerging from the strangely selective light. He was leaning against the far wall, his arms folded over his chest, observing her calmly and casually, as if it was a nightly occurrence to arrange meetings with noblewomen in a room where mourning shrouds and coffins guarded the silence.

"You wanted to see me?" he asked in a gritty, spine-scratching growl.

"You are . . . Lord La Seyne?"

His response was a long and expressive sigh that warned of little patience for unnecessary questions. He unfolded his arms and Servanne understood why there was a glaring lack of form to give him substance: he was dressed all in black. His fists were gloved in black leather, his jerkin and doublet were quilted out of black wool, studded with tiny silver bosses along the seams and at each junction of the bold squares. His shirt, leggings, and tall knee boots were black as well, and above the band of rolled hide that comprised the collar of his doublet, the gleam of black silk set Servanne's heart fluttering within her breast. At the sight of the mask, despite her resolve to speak her piece, her foot took a reflexive step back toward the door.

"State your *business,* Lady de Briscourt," he rasped. "I have no time for womanly vapours."

"Th-the Black Wolf of Lincoln told me to seek you out if I needed help," she said haltingly.

"And? Do you require help?"

"Help . . . yes. But not for myself."

There was a slight pause before a breath carried a further question to her. "Do you think of me as a charity, offering solace to all the downtrodden?"

Servanne bowed her head for a brief moment, and when she looked up again, her eyes were bright and steady, her voice without tremor.

"I would ask your help for Lord Wardieu. I am informed he plans to take your place on the field tomorrow at the tournament."

"Lord . . . Wardieu?"

"Lord Lucien Wardieu. The *real* Lord Lucien Wardieu. The man who calls himself the Black Wolf of Lincoln . . . and your friend, if I am not mistaken."

"I make a point of having no friends," La Seyne snarled.

"Then you should advise Lord Wardieu of your feelings, for he speaks very highly of you."

The bright glitter of his eyes narrowed behind the slits in the black silk. "*I* was informed you did not believe his story."

"True enough. I did not. Not in the beginning."

"But you do now?" he sneered. "May I ask what brought about such a miraculous change of heart?"

"You may mock me, sir," she said quietly. "And you may scorn a woman's fickle nature, but I assure you, the . . . change of heart . . . as you call it, was not come by easily, nor was it wrought without a great deal of thought to the consequences. You have come to Bloodmoor to rescue the Princess Eleanor. I have come to you in the hope you will also rescue Lord Lucien."

The knight took a deep breath. "Lucien is a capable fellow. He needs not my help to split a bastard brother from a saddle."

"Do you honestly think Prince John would allow him to savour such a victory should it come his way?"

"It is the victory he seeks," La Seyne said slowly. "What comes after . . . is of no importance. What comes after, he will deal with after."

"Alone? In a field surrounded by John's men and the Dragon's paid mercenaries? There will be nothing to *deal with,* my lord, for a single cold command will loose a hundred arrows from a hundred bows, and he will be dead with little of the chivalry and honour he claims to hold so dear."

The pauses were growing longer, the shadowy details of La Seyne's figure were becoming more distinct. Now she could not only see the shape of his mask, but the way the force of each shallow breath caused the silk to swell and recede against his mouth.

"Women should stay clear of war and politics—they understand neither. In the first place, Lord Lucien will not be alone. I have a hundred stout, loyal men of my own to ensure those arrows are not fired."

"De Gournay is Prince John's ally—his champion! He will not sit idly by while a man they both plotted to discredit attempts to prove them frauds and murderers."

"God and the king must judge the weight of John's greed. Lucien's quarrel is with his brother."

"It is a quarrel John will not tolerate in silence."

The silk flared again. "He will if he is faced with the choice of either recognizing Lucien Wardieu as the rightful heir of the De Gournay title, or having his own crime of kidnapping and attempted murder revealed before witnesses. It was Lackland's arrogance to suppose he would be safer making the exchange for the Princess Eleanor at Bloodmoor, surrounded by his most trusted allies. It is that same arrogance which will force him to maintain his silence while his champion is challenged for his crimes. To be sure, he will pretend to be suitably shocked at De Gournay's duplicity, but unless he wants the princess to point an accusing finger at her uncle's royal intrigues, he will support the man who wins on the field tomorrow."

"Are you so sure Lucien will win?"

"Your confidence is overwhelming, my lady," he said dryly. "You do not think he will?"

"I think you are a better match for Etienne Wardieu. You have the trophies and the reputation to prove it."

"Lucien is no mean squirrel in the lists; he has tipped a fox or two out of the saddle before now."

"But not so many as you, Lord Randwulf."

The hooded face turned away for the length of a ripe curse, then looked back. "A man must avenge his honour at any cost," he hissed. "It is the code by which a knight lives. Take it away and he is nothing. Ask another to interfere, and he is less than nothing."

"I am not asking you to interfere, my lord. I am asking . . . nay, *begging* you to save his life."

"How?"

"By taking to the field yourself tomorrow. You could kill Etienne Wardieu with impunity—another challenge, another trophy to add to your armoury. I have seen the pain in Lucien's eyes when he speaks of his brother's treachery. Regardless of the justification, where there was once love, there would be immeasurable guilt should he be the one to take his brother's life."

The Scourge of Mirebeau was silent so long Servanne felt a trickle of sweat form between her breasts.

"You speak as if you care what happens to the rogue," he said with quiet intensity.

"I . . . suppose I do," she admitted in a whisper. "In a way."

La Seyne took a sudden step away from the wall and Servanne, not expecting the movement, flinched back with a small cry of alarm. He was as tall as a pillar and massive with the brawn and muscle of a fighting man. As he walked closer, he flexed his gauntleted hands, and the fingers that crushed the morsel of straw looked as if they could crush her bones with as little effort.

"In what way, madam? Do you care because you now believe his claim and would not want to lose what you so nearly have within your grasp here at Bloodmoor?"

"Lands and titles mean nothing to me!" she insisted.

"No? Is that why you rushed so eagerly to answer the Dragon's summons, barely a month after your husband's death?"

"I . . . had no choice! I was commanded by royal decree!"

"You had a choice in the forest. You could have refused to go with Wardieu."

"I was given no such choice!" she cried adamantly. "Had I been given one, think you I would be here now?"

"I do not know," La Seyne said bluntly. "Would you?"

Servanne opened her mouth to reply, then closed it again, stunned by the echo of her own words. She heard them again, breaking down the barrier of her pride, and the echo grew louder and louder, the words and their meaning pounding within her breast like a smithy's hammer.

"No," she said softly, her eyes filling with tears. "No, I would not be here, monseigneur. I believe . . . I would quite happily have stayed in the forest with him, had he offered me the chance, with no complaint, no second thoughts as to what I would be forsaking. Nay, I would go there with him now, if you could but convince him of his folly. I would willingly follow him to Normandy or France, or any of a dozen foreign countries."

"And what if he does not want your company?" La Seyne

growled, drawing close enough to startle Servanne's heart higher in her throat.

"I—I would follow him anyway," she maintained. "I would content myself just to be near him."

Randwulf de la Seyne Sur Mer stared at her for a long, throbbing moment before breaking the tension with a low, unsteady laugh. "No. No, my lady, by the look of this new revelation dawning in your eyes, I do not think you would be content with anything less than iron chains binding you together hip and thigh."

Servanne returned his stare. His voice had lapsed from its forced gruffness, and the laugh . . . the laugh was familiar enough to raise a spray of gooseflesh along her arms.

Without thinking, she lifted her hand toward the mask, but the gloved fingers were just as swift to close around her wrist and halt the motion.

"I would see your face, monseigneur," she whispered.

"You would not like what you saw."

"I like it less being laughed at and ridiculed by a man too cowardly to reveal his own faults to the world."

The fingers clamped tighter around her wrist, causing a shiver of pain to set the stubbornness on her mouth. But he released her before the pain became too real, and with no further warning or protest, bowed his head and removed the black silk mask.

The light from the taper was on his profile, etching a square jaw with several days' worth of dark stubble blunting it. His hair curled in thick chestnut whorls against his cheeks and throat; his eyes were long-lashed and gray as a turbulent winter sky. There were no scars, no deformities to cringe from. Only a single, partly scabbed slash across one cheek that seemed to add, not detract, from the wild, wolfish beauty of him.

"You!" she gasped, her icy fingers slipping from her mouth to cover the loudly drumming beat of her heart. She could scarcely breathe for the impact he had upon her senses. It struck her like a fist—the realization he was here, standing in front of her, pretending to be someone he was not, listening to her concerns and confessions, mocking the very emotions which had become her only thread to sanity.

"You!" she cried. "How dare you not reveal yourself! How dare you lead me on and goad me into saying things . . . things that were not meant for you to hear!"

The Wolf glanced past her shoulder to the open door. "The rest of the castle is not meant to hear them either," he murmured wryly and moved around behind her to close the creaking wood panel.

She whirled to confront him. "How dare you trick me! Where is La Seyne?"

"He is here."

"Where? Listening somewhere in the shadows so that you might both share a hearty laugh at my expense?"

"It was not my intention to trick you, nor am I laughing at anything you have said."

"Where is La Seyne Sur Mer?" she demanded, stamping her foot to ward off the threat of tears.

The Wolf saw them shining behind her eyes, and, after waging a minor war with what was left of his common sense, he took up her hand in his and laid the black silk hood across her palm.

"You once asked how I could move from place to place without fear of someone recognizing me." He glanced down and enclosed her hand, hood and all, in his. "The mask was an affectation at first. It was necessary for me to earn enough wealth and respect to win back my independence—a disguise seemed the most obvious solution to my problems, since there was still a charge of murder and treason standing against the Wardieu name."

"You . . . are La Seyne Sur Mer?" Servanne gasped in astonishment.

"I took the surname from the small village in France
where I landed amongst the living again. The Christian
name was given me by the physician who swore I should
have died a dozen times in the months I spent recovering
from my wounds. It all seemed fitting . . . the name, the
hood."

"The queen? She accepted you without question?"

The Wolf tilted his head slightly, revealing a faint grin to
the light. "The queen thought it a delicious ruse—her very
words—for a hooded knight to hold her court, and her enemies, in terror."

"And the Black Wolf?"

"Her pet name for me, I'm afraid."

"But what of this . . . this *madness*? Surely she could
not have sanctioned it?"

"The dowager knows nothing of my connection to Bloodmoor Keep, or that I have a personal score to settle with its
master. To her, Randwulf de la Seyne Sur Mer is her trusted
champion, the man she sent to regain her beloved princess's
freedom regardless of the cost."

"La Seyne Sur Mer . . . the Black Wolf of Lincoln . . .
Lucien Wardieu . . ." Servanne shook her head in bewilder-
ment. "Which one of those men is really you?"

"All of them. None of them." He turned fully into the
light and she saw the smudges of weariness under his eyes.
"You should not have come here tonight; it was a foolish
risk."

"Why did you agree to see me? You could have refused."

His gaze was steady, his expression grim. "You are absolutely right. It was stupid of me to worry what kind of trouble you might be in, or that I had promised you help if it was
needed. But no matter, if you are discovered here, the blame
will fall on equal parts on both our heads."

"Alaric and the others are outside. They will give ample
warning of any threat."

The threat is here, the Wolf wanted to shout. It was in her eyes and on her lips. It was steeped in her fragrance and woven into every glimmering strand of her hair. Worse, it was raging white-hot throughout his body, and had been since she had walked through the door. It was all he could do now to force his hands to remain down by his sides and to try to turn his thoughts away from the scent of her skin.

"You . . . have been treated well since your arrival?"

"De Gournay has been very civil, very polite under the circumstances. He asked few questions about you, however, and I am convinced he thinks I know you only as an outlaw, not as his brother."

"He . . . has not touched you . . . or harmed you in any way?"

Servanne looked up into his eyes, wondering how much longer her legs could support her, trembling as badly as they were. "Would you have cared if he had?"

"Of course I would care." He caught the gruffness in his voice and forced it behind a flat grin. "I would care for the safety of your neck, my lady."

"Only my neck?"

His jaw tautened to a ridge of corded sinew and a small blue vein leaped to prominence in his temple. Her hood had slipped back, baring the gleaming gold crown of her hair to the light, and he had a sudden, clear image of it scattered around her naked shoulders, clinging to both their bodies as they lay twined together in the steamy dampness of the grotto.

But it passed in the next instant and a clearer image of a jousting field took shape, and the gold of her hair was replaced by the crimson of spilled blood.

"You should not have come here tonight," he said again, harshly. "I only agreed because I offered La Seyne as a means of protection if you were hurt or required help in some way. Since you look remarkably healthy, my lady, and if, as you say, everyone has been civil and polite—"

"Your brother," she interrupted sharply, "shows even less emotion than you—if such a thing is possible."

She turned her back on him, shielding her outburst behind the cloud of yellow hair that had worked its way free of the braid.

"His expression rarely changes from one hour to the next," she continued bitterly. "Yet I have seen his mere presence reduce a burly man to a mass of cowering fright. The castle is full of fear; the halls and chambers are thick with it, the air reeks of it. To me, he has been polite, yes, but there is a coldness in him, an underlying evil, sinister and cruel . . . traits I might not have seen or looked for had you not planted the seeds of suspicion in my mind. Now that you have, how am I to deal with it? How can I be expected to go through with the wedding, or be the smiling, dutiful wife he has contracted? And if he comes into my bed at night and touches me—"

"There will be no wedding, by Christ," the Wolf exclaimed. "And if he touches you . . . *if he touches you*—" he grasped her by the shoulders and spun her around so that the shadows no longer concealed her features. What he saw, glowing in her eyes, caused the grip of his fingers to squeeze hard enough to promise bruising.

Servanne de Briscourt was smiling. Tears studded her lashes like tiny sparkling gemstones, but she was smiling.

"You do care," she cried happily. "You do. You do!"

His jaw flexed. His hands tightened and the gleam in his eyes flared with anger.

"No," he snarled. "No, you are wrong."

"Am I? Then push me away. Tell me you pray God you never need lay eyes on me again, never need touch me again, never need hold me or feel your body moving deep inside me. Tell me you want no part of this heart that beats so strongly within my breast. Tell me all of that, my lord, with your eyes as well as your lips, and I will walk out the door and never look back. It will be no easy task, for I have only just begun to realize my life will be nothing without you. But I will do it. I will obey your every command to wipe your memory from my heart . . . if it is what you want me to do."

The years of hardening himself, years of conditioning himself to feel nothing, betray nothing, reveal nothing of his emotions, were slipping away with each warm, shiny tear that escaped her lashes. His hands squeezed until he felt bone, and he started to push her away. He started . . . even managed to gain an inch or two of freedom before a pent-up breath exploded from his lungs and he dragged her forward, dragged her into his embrace, into the hungry caress of his lips.

Their mouths came eagerly together. Their arms circled one another, clasping each other tightly, desperate to bring their bodies as close as life and breath would allow. He kissed her deeply again and again, smothering her gasps and sobs, adding his own muffled words of endearment as his hands, lips, and body trembled with further admissions.

"Lucien," she cried softly. "Lucien—"

"Hush," he commanded, and stripped the gauntlets from his hands before lifting them to cradle either side of her tear-streaked face. "You have worked enough of your cleverness on me for one night."

She melted into his kiss, savouring the devouring heat of his lips. When she could bear no more without the threat of a faint, she pressed her cheek into the crook of his neck and surrendered herself to the comfort of his arms.

"Take me away from here, Lucien," she begged. "Take me away . . . now! Tonight! I am so afraid!"

"There is nothing to fear," he assured her, smoothing the blonde wisps of her hair.

"As long as it is your intention to fight tomorrow, I will know nothing but fear."

This time his mouth could win no response and he sighed. "Servanne, I cannot simply walk away from the evil here at Bloodmoor Keep. Perhaps . . . if it were just my own name and honour demanding vengeance, I could happily and willingly forsake it in order to take you away from this place forever. But it was my father who died a traitor's death, starved in his cell like a mongrel, his name spat upon by men who believed Etienne's lies. I can no more walk away from my responsibilities to the memory of Robert Wardieu, than I could turn my back on my most solemn pledge to the queen to see the Princess Eleanor brought back to safety."

Servanne bowed her head and pressed her face against the thickness of his quilted doublet. He was right, of course, and it was unfair of her to think only of her own wants and needs, but it was also suddenly, shamelessly impossible to think of anything else.

Lucien drew his hands away, reluctantly forcing a space between their bodies. He reached up to disengage her arms from around his neck, but she only clung to him more determinedly and raised huge, glistening blue eyes to his.

"You must go back," he urged gently. "You have already been absent from the keep too long."

"Lucien—"

He shook his head and placed a finger lightly over her lips. "And you must not call me Lucien. Not yet. Not while there are a thousand things to betray us."

"Betray us? How?"

"A loose tongue, an unguarded look. The Dragon is keen and clever; his suspicions must not be roused so near the end."

She tightened her arms still further and drew herself up so that their mouths were only a breath apart and elsewhere, their bodies were not even that.

"Promise me," she pleaded. "Promise me this will not be the end for us."

"Has your confidence in La Seyne's abilities gone the way of your expectations for the Black Wolf's success?"

"Promise me," she insisted, ignoring his feeble attempt at humour. "Give me your most solemn pledge, then I know it will be so."

Lucien's gray eyes studied her intently, his body responded to hers despite the armoured strength of his will.

"My pledge, madam," he said softly, "is that when this matter is settled, we will bathe together, and often, in the grotto by the Silent Pool. Moreover, we will discuss this stubborn streak of yours. We will discuss it until you are too exhausted to plague me with it ever again."

Servanne's eyes shone as they drifted down to his lips. "Your word is your honour, monseigneur, and I do not question it . . . but . . . is there no other means of sealing a most solemn vow?"

Lucien was still as a statue; Servanne's cheeks flamed as hot as fire.

"You will be missed—"

"I have spent these past few nights alone, feeling missed by no one," she countered poignantly. "Aching for something . . . I knew not what until tonight."

"Servanne—"

"For you, my lord. I ache for you. I ache with the loneliness and emptiness I feel when you are not near me. I know I dishonour myself in asking, but . . . but I would feel you inside me once more," she whispered haltingly. "I would feel you banish the emptiness, and fill it with some small part of your courage and strength that I might carry it with me through whatever may come on the morrow."

Neither Lucien the man, the outlaw Wolf, nor the vaunted Randwulf de la Seyne Sur Mer knew what to say or do to counter the powerful intoxicant of her eyes. His hands were less than steady as he cradled her face between them; the sight of her tears, flowing in wet shiny streaks to her chin made them even less so.

"There is . . . no time," he said raggedly. "The risk—"

"The risk is that we might neither of us have this chance again. You said yourself, a thousand things might betray us —a slipped tongue, an unguarded look . . ."

His thumbs came tenderly together over her lips to silence her. They parted again, brushing reverently over the damp tearfall, and when they failed to staunch the liquid flow, his mouth took up the challenge, moving over her lashes, her cheeks, trailing lower to collect the salty sweetness that eluded him. A groan sent his tongue plunging helplessly into the velvety recesses of her mouth, and she tasted the curse that brought his lips slanting more forcefully over hers. She felt the tremors in his arms as he gathered her close again, and she felt his desire, rising bold and insistent between them.

"Love me," she pleaded. "Love me, Lucien, that I might know what we shared was not just a dream."

He swore again as the shivered plea rippled through his body. There was no use denying the hunger that raged within him, no use resisting the lithe and supple body that clung to his with a feverish desire. Their mouths came apart and met again, broke apart and met, and he knew he was lost. His fingers searched after the ribbands and fasteners that bound her clothes in place, and the woolen cloak was flung aside, billowing away like a dark sail in the shadows. Layers fell rapidly to the impatience of lips and hands, and when there was only the slippery thin sheath of her linen undergarment between them, he stood back, his eyes burning with passion, growing darker with promise as he pulled and tugged aside his own bulky clothes.

Shivering with the remembered power of all that flesh being laid bare before her, Servanne stepped up when he had

completed but half the task. She ran her hands across the
hard breadth of his chest, her fingers combing through the
storm of crisp, curling hairs. She found the darker islands of
his nipples and a smothered gasp sent her leaning into his
heat. Her lips closed around one of the sensitive aureoles,
caressing his flesh with a hunger that prompted a muffled
hiss of a breath from between his teeth.

He was still flinging aside points, belts, and hose when he
dropped down onto his knees in front of her. His hands
skimmed up her thighs, raising the sheath to her waist, then
her breasts. The last of his patience was expended as he tore
the flimsy garment in two, barely troubling to cast it aside
before his hands were cupped around her flesh and his lips
were feasting on the bared bounty.

Servanne curled her arms around his neck and staggered
against his warm, wet manipulations. She shuddered at each
swirling turn of his tongue and cried out as his lips kneaded
and suckled and worshipped the firm white pillows of flesh
until they were blushing as pinkly as the rest of her heated
body.

He drew her down onto his bended knees and she did not
resist. He guided a snowy white thigh to either side of his
waist and his hands cradled the softness of her hips holding
her against him with an apologetic urgency.

"Yes," she gasped. "Oh yes—!" And the gasp became a
husked cry as he lowered her smooth, yielding flesh over his
straining heat. Groans were wrung from both shocked
throats. She was hot and sleek and moulded to his flesh like a
second, tight skin, and he paused every other heartbeat as he
lowered her, knowing he had never, in all his lusty years of
manhood, wanted or needed a woman with so vast a passion
as he felt now.

One woman, he reflected savagely. *This* woman. Fill me,
she had said; love me, banish the emptiness . . .

He groaned and bent his head to her shoulder, his body

quaking with a fever he feared he would not be able to control. He was all too aware of the subtle, rippling contractions that pulled his flesh still deeper, and of her cries and whispers drenching him in a heat that was almost too much to bear. He shifted his hands to her waist, his fingers rigid with the force of his need. He clenched his teeth against the growing, spreading rings of pleasure that spiraled through him, but he feared it was no use. His arms circled her waist and he groaned aloud, the sound catching like a sob in his throat as he fought valiantly to weather the unholy torment. Servanne shuddered and writhed and he heard her gasped plea, acknowledging it with an even hoarser groan as he gave her hips their freedom to plunder his flesh with their own merciless ingenuity.

Servanne's upper body arched back and her hands clawed into his shoulders. She moved blindly against the hard fullness of him, the rapture engulfing her in waves of heat so intense she continued to quake with shock and pleasure long after she had lost the ability to govern her actions. She had to rely upon Lucien's hands to reclaim their authority, Lucien's arms to bring her to a dazed, quivering halt against him.

Limp and drained, she collapsed into the welcoming comfort of his embrace. Stunned by the depths of her own passions, she panted lightly against the curve of his shoulder and was thankful for his solid presence supporting her. His skin was hot beneath her cheek, and, with the slow return of sensation to her body, she became aware of the pounding beat of his heart against hers, and the fiercely possessive way he held her.

She dared to look up and their eyes met. Incredulously, she felt the wolfish fur at his groin chafing her and the deep, moist pulsations of his flesh sliding, stroking between her thighs.

"I am still there," he murmured tersely. "How, by God's splendour, I shall never know, but I am still there."

He bowed his dark head, his words sounding like oaths where he pressed them against her breasts. Servanne squeezed her eyes closed and a glistening, fat tear splashed onto the back of the hand she curled around his neck and shoulders. Beneath her fingers were the welts of raised scar tissue; beneath her lips the taste of salt, musk, and leather. Deep inside her was the aching heat she had so shamelessly longed for, and she half-laughed, half-cried at her own foolish innocence. He had wanted her as much as she had wanted him and she wept for the joy of it, the wildness of it, the passion that coursed through her veins like rivulets of fire.

Lucien's hands raked up into her hair, scattering the remains of the neatly plaited braid. He dragged the heavy woolen cloak closer and lowered her swiftly onto the padded folds, his body driving into hers with a hungry violence, his mouth eagerly sharing her renewed cries of awe and wonderment.

21

Servanne opened her eyes slowly. She had been oblivious to her surroundings, oblivious to everything but the power and the passion of the man in whose arms she lay. The tiniest shiver of fear chased along her spine when she recognized nothing familiar in the surrounding gloom. Could it all have been a dream again?

No. No dream had ever felt like this. No dream had cradled her body with such contented bliss. No dream had ever provided a shoulder of steely muscle for a pillow, or arms of warm marble for a blanket, or a body of such magnificent textures and essences for a mattress. No dream had ever supported her head when she could not, nor had there been hands half so bold or loving to gently draw her mouth around to his that they might savour the last ebbing shudders of spent ecstasy together. Spent, yet not spent. Drained, yet full to bursting with his life-giving strength.

Moaning softly to express her disappointment as he released her lips, she kept her pale, lovely face level with his. Her hair was spread every which way over her shoulders, with fine, damp tendrils clinging in misty curls to her temples and throat. Strands of it were tangled into the dark mat of hair on his chest. Filaments were tossed over his shoulders and curled around his arms to all but encase them in a gossamer cocoon. And, feeling safe and protected within their golden cocoon, Servanne lowered her cheek and rested it against the hard plane of muscle that breasted his chest.

"I would stay here with you, bound together like this forever, my lord," she whispered dreamily. "Let someone from some future time discover our bones melted together and envy us that we died of such pleasure."

Lucien ran his hands down beneath the silky veil of her hair, but where he should have insisted they at least retrieve their clothes and restore some order to their appearance, he only held her selfishly tight to his loins.

"You are a poor influence on a man's willpower, madam."

Servanne kept her smile hidden. "You are no salvation yourself, my lord wolf's head."

"Still, you have been gone far too long from your chambers," he said gently. "Someone may discover the absence and sound an alarm. Come," he said, kissing her as he lifted her off his thighs, "I will render what clumsy assistance I can to help bring order back to your appearance."

Servanne stood, her long legs as weak and wobbly as those of a newborn doe. Lucien, still on his knees, reached out a hand to steady her, and try as he might, he could not stop himself from drawing her slowly toward him, his sigh almost one of impotent frustration as he laid his cheek against her breast. His arms encircled her waist and for a moment the pain and uncertainty was so stark on his face, it caused a fresh surge of tears to catch in her throat. He was always so sure of himself, so arrogant, so proud and seemingly invincible; the shock of seeing his sudden vulnerability, of knowing she was the cause of it, made Servanne bury her hands in his hair and bow her lips to the chestnut waves.

"I am no longer afraid, Lucien," she whispered. "You have come to win justice and I know now you cannot fail. You will not fail. I asked you to share your strength with me to give me courage, and you have. Ask me for my heart, my love, my life, and I will gladly give them in return; now and forever."

The Wolf's grip remained steadfast a moment longer, then

slowly eased. "Forever is a very long time, my lady, and I am no ordinary man, remember? I have cast my lot with demons and dwarfish fiends. This"—he pressed a kiss into the softness of her belly—"is pure devilry. You should therefore fear committing your soul into my keeping."

"I fear nothing in your arms, my lord. As to my soul, it has not been mine to give these many days now. It was taken in ambush on a greenwood road and no amount of ransom, however dear, will return it to me. I know that now."

The Wolf rose off his knees, his eyes burning with a renewed glow which she had no difficulty in interpreting. She parted her lips for his kiss—a tender mingling of breaths and tastes and promises. Their tongues spoke in a language of their own, invoking emotions so powerful, so potent, it was with some surprise she felt him hold her gently away.

"There must be no more delays," he said firmly. "The dangers are inconceivable, the risks untenable. In this, you must obey me, Servanne."

"Where should I find the strength to obey? Indeed, where shall I find the strength to walk?"

Lucien cupped her chin in his hand. "You shall find it and you shall use it to run, not walk back to the safety of your chambers. There"—he paused long enough to fetch up her gown and straighten it hem from collar—"you shall remain with the door closed and bolted until either Friar or myself come for you."

"But . . . the tournament!"

"Plead illness. Plead injury. Plead whatever it takes to win permission for you to remain behind."

"He will never allow it. Little as I know him, and little as he cares whither I come or go, I know he will want me present in the bower, both to witness his triumph in the lists, and to be on display as his newest possession."

Lucien had lifted her arms, intending to settle the gown over her head, but at her words, he paused.

"A delay then. Beg only a delay and promise attendance to ease his suspicions. He will be eager to leave early for the common and will not have the patience to wait while you change a soiled gown, or retrieve some forgotten bauble from your chamber. Once he leaves, you can stretch the delay into an absence."

"You want me so badly out of the way?"

"I want you safe, well out of harm's way."

"Once before you sent me away when I would willingly have stayed," she said softly.

The Wolf took her hands in his and bent his lips to her cool fingers. "I have blamed myself, cursed myself a hundred times for ever having laid a hand on you. I should have seen the danger and stayed away at any cost, but you were already in my blood and it was too late."

"Why did you send me away? You must have known long before I did, that a word, or a gesture, and I would have—"

He laid a finger across her lips. "You would have stayed with me in the forest? Servanne—I had a score of men at Thornfeld, another eighty or so camped some miles along the Lincoln road. Our task was to get inside Bloodmoor Keep and rescue the Princess Eleanor. You were—"

"A pawn?" she asked, her voice betraying no rancour or bitterness, which only made Lucien's oath all the more self-deprecating as he covered her lips with his own.

"It is a shame I will bear to my grave to have to say we needed the ruse of the wedding to get inside the castle. Without you, there would have been no wedding."

"Surely you could still have ransomed the princess from Prince John?"

"On neutral ground, outside the castle walls, no doubt we could. But then—"

"M'sieur La Seyne Sur Mer would not have been able to challenge the Baron de Gournay to a joust, and Lucien Wardieu would not have been able to fight for his honour and birthright, and there would not have been bowers full of witnesses to bear out your claim."

The Wolf sighed and shook his head in resignation. "I told you once before you were too clever for your own good. Perhaps I *should* have left you in the forest."

"Perhaps I could help . . . ?"

"Do not," he said harshly, his voice changing from velvet to steel in the blink of an eye, "do not even think to interfere or trifle with forces you do not understand. Etienne is a madman—mad with greed and avarice and power. He would not hesitate to swat you like a fly if he thought for one moment you were a threat to him. Promise me . . . swear to me here and now you will do nothing—nothing at all to draw attention to yourself!"

"But how can you ask me to stay away from the tourney when it is my life as much as yours being decided on the field!"

"How can you expect me to concentrate on doing what I must do if every time I look up, I see you seated there between Prince John and Nicolaa de la Haye?"

Servanne had not thought of that. But she did not accept defeat well either, and gave frowning proof of it as Lucien pulled the gown over her head and began straightening the rumpled folds. She continued frowning, and searching so hard for a reasonable alternative, he could not resist a smile.

"Maledictions, madam, I sorely trust each and every decision to be made in the future will not be met with such lengthy catechism. It leads me to believe you have been spoiled too long, and grown too accustomed to having your own way."

"Whereas you, sirrah, have been left in the wild too long and show a marked lack of subtlety and compassion."

"I warn you now, I'll not take well to any attempts to tame me."

"Nor will I," she said, her eyes sparkling with the challenge.

Lucien caught his breath sharply, thinking how utterly beautiful she was at that instant. The pale gold of her hair was like liquid silk against his fingers, her skin like warm satin. Her eyes, luminous and bottomless were as deep and evocative as the waters of the Silent Pool, and he remembered his pledge to take her back to the magical grotto and pleasure her until the forest rang out with their ecstasy.

"Promise me, Servanne," he demanded softly. "Promise me you will stay out of harm's way."

Servanne's eyes grew hooded and a shiver tautened the flesh across her breasts as she felt his hands stroking up her thighs, raising the hem of her gown as they did so.

"I will do as you ask," she whispered. "I promise."

The muscles across his shoulders rippled and gleamed in the flickering light as he lowered her onto their bedding of discarded clothing again.

"Your word is your honour," he murmured, "and I do not question it, but . . ."

Servanne's body ached wonderfully. Her limbs were shaky, but did not falter once on the misty route back to the main keep. Lucien's arm around her waist for most of the journey was more than enough support, and when he reluctantly agreed with Alaric that he dared go no farther, the thrumming, thrilling aftereffects of their lovemaking were enough to see her through the final gates and into the pentice leading up to the second-storey towers.

It was there, when Friar left her at the bottom of the steep, spiraling staircase she had yet to climb, her exhaustion and weariness overtook her. Dragging under the weight of the woolen cloak, she mounted the stone steps to her private chambers one by one, slowing as she climbed higher and higher, her breath rasping and her lungs fighting for air as she reached the top of the darkened spire. She paused on the landing to gather her strength, and was so glad just to have conquered the last obstacle, she did not notice anything amiss as she passed through the outer chamber.

Not until she was halfway across the floor of the huge wardrobe, did she realize the light spilling from the open door to the solar was touching upon tunics and jerkins, hauberks of chain mail, capes and mantles of sky-blue wool . . . Not until the masculine scents of leather and wood musk assailed her senses did she realize she had mistakenly entered the Dragon's private keep, the tower adjacent to her own.

A muffled sound from the inner chamber tore her horrified gaze from the assortment of vestments and weaponry, and fixed it upon the square of bright light shining out of the solar. She dared not move, dared not even back away or retrace her footsteps out to the landing lest a scratch of cloth or a misplaced footstep alert someone to her presence.

What could she do? She could not remain where she was. She could not go forward, nor back; she could not hide or conceal herself until morning even if she had the nerve or the stupidity to do so.

Where were his squires, Rolf and Eduard? Were they inside the main chamber preparing their master for bed? Would they emerge at any moment to find her standing there, frozen into a statue by her fear?

Envisioning what they would see when they found her caused Servanne's heart to miss several more frantic beats. Her hair was a tangle, clotted with bits of straw and dirt. Her gown was wrinkled and caked with dirt from the long walk to and from the shroud-makers. Her mouth felt swollen and tender, her skin was chafed red from the abrasion of dark beard stubble. The warm, slippery residue of their passion had added to her pleasure on the walk back to the keep, but it would offer sure proof of her adultery if discovered now.

And for what other reason would the Dragon assume she had crept into his private chambers at this late hour of the night? She had not been entirely truthful to Lucien when she told him the Dragon paid her little heed. She had seen the growing interest in the pale blue eyes, had felt the increasing speculation in his burning gaze.

No, the Dragon would not hesitate to assume she was come to him for one reason and one reason only: the wedding was but a day away and not worth the frustration of waiting.

What to do? How to get away without being discovered?

The problem was solved for her by the sound of a woman's voice, so close to the door Servanne was not given the opportunity to waste a thought before scrambling to one side of the wardrobe. Crushed up against the coarse folds of a hanging garment, she froze again, fully expecting to feel a rough pair of hands grasp her from behind and haul her into the brighter light.

The hands did not come, however, and inch by cautious inch, she turned her face until she had a partial view of the inside of the chamber.

There was none of the whitewash or painted wildflowers that decorated her own solar. These walls were cold, impersonal stone, dominated on one side by a massive depiction of the De Gournay crest and armourial bearings. The bed, what could be seen of it, was easily twice the size of Servanne's, mounted on a platform three feet high, and shielded by lengths of thick blue velvet draperies. A fire blazed somewhere out of her line of sight, and fully a score of lighted candles added their own extravagant brilliance to the chamber, the sconces lined up on either side of the bed as if to adorn an altar.

"You should try to get some sleep," came the woman's voice again. "It would not do for you to yawn in La Seyne's face."

"I have slept. And I will sleep again—tomorrow—with Mirebeau's pennant beneath my head for a pillow."

The sound of Nicolaa de la Haye's laugh sent Servanne cringing deeper into the folds of cloth. The sheriff's wife strolled out of the shadows and took a seat on the claw-footed chair that perched at the end of the bed, giving her a clear view of the area of the wardrobe Servanne would have to cross in order to effect an escape.

"Well? Should we expect foam and fits from our hallowed regent when we greet him in the morning? I assume you have not been with him all this time discussing his political affairs."

"He was not overly pleased to hear of Lucien's resurrection," De Gournay admitted dryly. "But he was remarkably calm, all things considered. No doubt he had planned from the outset what to do and say if the whole ugly matter came to light."

"He played an equal role in discrediting the Wardieu name. I would have thought his reaction would be much stronger."

"Why? The charges and warrants he drew up were valid; his generosity in clearing Robert Wardieu's name and restoring certain properties would be viewed now as a magnanimous gesture to try to right a dreadful wrong. If my brother rears his vengeful head, our valiant Prince Softsword will simply claim to have been duped the same as everyone else. *Deus volt:* God wills it."

"God help us if he becomes king," Nicolaa muttered, and stretched a delicate foot forward. She was dressed in a sheer, sleeveless tunic, belted loosely at the waist, and the sinuous movement caused the neckline to gape wide, baring the full half-moons of her breasts almost to the nipples. "I waited up for you," she added in a purr. "Are you not curious to know why?"

"You have already advised sleep, so I cannot imagine."

She formed a seductive pout with her lips and blew him a mock kiss. "If you are going to be spiteful, I will not tell you where I spent my time earlier tonight. And I certainly will not tell you what I learned while I was visiting La Seyne's encampment."

"You were in La Seyne's camp?"

"Not in any official capacity, you understand. But I was bored, and thought I might be able to discover a thing or two about our mysterious visitor that could be of some use to you tomorrow."

"I was told his men were as close-lipped as the bastard is himself."

Nicolaa sighed and clucked her tongue. "No man can keep his lips closed under certain methods of persuasion. I found one yeoman in particular who was so engrossed with what I could do with *my* lips, he answered any questions I put to him. Boastings, for the most part, but one could glean a taste of the truth here and there, if one delved deep enough."

De Gournay moved into Servanne's field of vision and she felt sure her gasp would have been audible if not for a timely fountain of sparks bursting in the hearth. He was completely naked, his body a solid, gleaming spectacle of muscular symmetry. There were no scars, no blemishes to mar the sculpted perfection. His chest was hairless and smooth, the powerful bunches of muscle finely delineated by veins that swelled or receded in accordance with the movement required. His belly was flat and hard, his thighs thickened by countless hours on horseback. Shoulders were like slabs of granite, bulked by the weight of heavy armour, sloping down from a proud, bullish neck.

This further evidence of similarities between the two brothers took Servanne's breath away. There could be no two more evenly matched combatants, judging by size and shape. As to strength, she could only stare at De Gournay's unmarked flesh and pray that an unknown physician had indeed excelled in his skills fourteen years ago.

"Well? What have you learned?"

The glistening, jewel-green eyes rose grudgingly from the junction of his thighs.

"I was told La Seyne comes down the course like a black wind from hell, clad in steel, riding a demon-bred rampager. He scorns the use of blunted tips on the lance, and does not hesitate to neglect the niceties of chivalry by aiming squarely at his challenger's visor. Further, in the nine years he has been in the dowager's service, he has never lost a match, never even been jostled from the saddle."

Nicolaa paused and stretched sinuously. "At first I thought this last to be just another case of braggadocio, for even you, my lusty lord, have found the ground beneath you a time or two, yet still gone on to win the match. But no. He has never even been unhorsed."

Wardieu watched her unblinkingly, his only reaction a visible tautening of his lean flanks as Nicolaa's fingers traced lazily across his thighs and came to rest at his groin.

"The yeoman's reluctance to say more required one of my better efforts. He was quite exhausting, actually," she sighed. "But at least it could be said he died knowing no greater bliss."

De Gournay waited, indifferent to the bold exhibit of impatience another area of his body was displaying, and only mildly attentive to the reverent manipulations of her fingers.

"I assume he did say more?"

Nicolaa smiled. She leaned forward and supplemented the actions of her fingers, delaying any further discussion until she tasted an end to his indifference and felt his hands curl around the nape of her neck.

"Apparently"—she released his flesh with a slow, sliding caress—" La Seyne's opponents seldom have an opportunity to place a strike, let alone land it with any effect . . . because he attacks from the wrong side of the list."

De Gournay needed two measured breaths to refocus his attention. "What do you mean . . . the wrong side?"

"It seems he suffers a rare affliction for a fighting man: he favours the left hand."

De Gournay stared, unmoving, and Nicolaa took advantage of his shock to stand and undulate past him, passing so close to the door, her woman's scent assailed Servanne where she stood hidden. Already sorely strained, her heart began to beat in her ears like a drum; it caused her blood to pump through her veins in a heated rush, raising a fever everywhere but in the palms of her hands. They were cold and clammy, adding the coppery smell of salt and fear to Servanne's panic.

De Gournay roused himself enough to accept the goblet of wine Nicolaa handed him. There was a brittle new light in his eyes as they followed her back to the chair, and a deeply etched frown darkening the width of his brow.

Nicolaa sipped her wine and draped a leg carelessly over the arm of the chair.

"Odd," she mused, "how there should be two left-handed men of some considerable fighting prowess, turning up in Lincoln at precisely the same time."

"Christ!"

"Was He left-handed also? I did not know."

De Gournay whirled around, hurling his goblet against the far wall with such force, some of the splashed contents flew back and spattered Nicolaa.

"Christ Almighty! I should have known! I should have guessed!"

Nicolaa gave her leg an agitated swing. "How could you have known, my love? How could you have guessed? Randwulf de la Seyne Sur Mer . . . your long lost, *dead* brother? How could anyone have guessed?"

"I should have guessed!" De Gournay roared. "All these years, living and prospering in Brittany. How very clever of him. The hood, the appointment to the queen's guard . . . how hellishly bloody clever of him!"

"More than simply clever, my darling," Nicolaa pointed out. "He not only waited to use Prince John as a ruse to get inside Bloodmoor, but he managed to distract your attention through the use of your innocent young bride. I would call it brilliant."

De Gournay's hands curled into such tight fists, the knuckles turned white and bloodless.

"I will kill him. By God, I will kill him right now, with my bare hands, and then we shall see how brilliant a corpse he makes!"

He strode toward the doorway, and was almost there, a foot away from Servanne, his back washed in a glow of candlelight, when Nicolaa's voice stopped him.

"Kill him now and what do you gain?" she demanded sharply. "A moment's satisfaction and little else. He has lost his advantage, Etienne. The surprise is no longer his, but weighs heavily in your favour. Wait. Wait and meet him on the morrow as planned."

"I want his blood," De Gournay snarled, halted at the threshold to the wardrobe. "I want to tear his heart from his chest and squeeze the life out of it before his very eyes."

Nicolaa's lips parted around a dry breath and she stood up from the chair. Her eyes glistened with arousal, her finely chiseled nostrils flared as if she could already detect the pungent sweetness of blood. "You will have his heart, my love, and any other part of his body you relish as a trophy, but what harm in waiting a few hours, when you can have so much more?"

"More?" he rasped, his eyes narrowing.

"Kill him now and you bring the eyes of the kingdom frowning down upon you, not to mention the vindictive wrath of the old queen. *Think,* my darling. Randwulf de la Seyne Sur Mer is more than just another name, another pennant to mount on your walls. He is the Scourge of Mirebeau, a knight of unblemished repute and legendary skill. Would it not be better to be known as the Dragon who slew the Black Scourge in honourable contest, rather than a desperate man who slit the throat of his brother in a jealous rage?"

De Gournay's body tensed at the touch of Nicolaa's hands. She laid her palms flat on his back and splayed her fingers, kneading the iron-hard muscles with a sensual reverence that triggered icy shivers of erotic sensation throughout her own voluptuous body.

"He has won his reputation because few have had the training to counter a man guided by the hand of Lucifer. But you, Etienne . . . you learned your own unparalleled skills with him as a sparring partner. You know how he sits a horse. You know the balance, the weight, the strokes he favours. You know the moment he chooses to raise a lance or sword. You know his strengths and his weaknesses. God's love, you benefited from the same knowledge once before; it was only by the devil's luck he survived. Tomorrow he will have no such luck. Tonight, tomorrow, the luck is all ours."

De Gournay breathed deeply, expanding his chest to the limit. "I want him to suffer. I want no quick or easy death for him by sword or lance."

"A well-placed blow will give him into your mercy" Nicolaa assured him, "the mercy of hot irons or dulled knives, whichever you prefer. Once he is carried from the field, he is yours for as little or as long as you want him."

All vestiges of the handsome, golden knight were lost behind a mask of cold fury as he rounded on Nicolaa with a snarl. "You and he made a son together, Nicolaa. Could it be there is some small part of you hoping for compassion? Is that why you argue for a delay?"

"I told you once before, I would have dashed Eduard's

brains out on the first convenient rock had you not stayed
my hand from doing so! I will do it now, here, in front of you
if proof is needed of my loyalty."

De Gournay reached up and clutched two fistfuls of black
hair, twisting and pulling it tight enough to distort the shape
of Nicolaa's cheeks and eyes.

"What else would you do for me?" he asked cynically.
"What else, Nicolaa?"

"Anything! Ask anything, and it will be done."

"Blood, Nicolaa," was the savage response. "I want
blood!"

With her eyes glazing over in the heat of passion, Nicolaa
backed out of his grasp and turned stiffly to a small table just
out of sight beside the doorway. The blade of the knife glittered as she raised it; light from the fire and the candles
flared along the steel as she pressed it to her breast. The
glitter changed from silver to crimson as she carved into the
whiteness of her own flesh and drew the poniard down toward the nipple.

The cut was an inch long and half as deep before Wardieu
cursed and knocked the knife out of her hand. Her cry was
muffled beneath the brutal crush of his lips and the blood
streaming from the wound smeared his flesh as he grasped
the edges of her tunic and tore it from her body. He grunted
as her nails gouged jaggedly into his shoulders, but no
amount of pain or protest deterred him from sweeping her
into his arms and carrying her, naked and thrashing, to the
bed.

Shocked, sickened by all she had heard and seen, Servanne
stumbled blindly out of the wardrobe and ran through the
small anteroom. She was almost clear of the stifling gloom,
almost free of the guttural rutting sounds that followed her
from the lighted sleeping chamber, when her foot caught on
an edge of stone and she was flung headlong into a rack of
polished steel swords.

22

Servanne opened her mouth to scream, but managed no more than a harsh gasp before a roughly callused hand was clamped forcefully over her lips, sealing them. An arm circled her waist, catching her a split second before she made contact with the rack of weapons. Hauled up hard against a man's body, she was partly carried, partly dragged through the outer doors to the square stone landing.

"Make a sound and we are both dead," he advised hoarsely. "Quickly, go down the stairs and wait for me at the bottom."

Servanne nodded blindly, too frightened to even search the shadows for her rescuer's identity. She gathered the folds of her robe and tunic in her hands and fled down the winding corkscrew staircase as if the steps behind were on fire. At the bottom, she spilled out into the dimly lit corridor and sagged against the opposite wall, out of breath, out of courage, out of wits at what to expect next.

He found her there a few moments later huddled against the abrasive, cold stone, trembling so badly he could hear the chatter of her teeth clearly in the hollow silence.

"Come, my lady, we must get you into your own chambers and warmed by a fire."

"Eduard?" she gasped. "Is it you?"

"My lady." He bowed slightly, and when he straightened —when Servanne dashed at the tears blurring her vision—

she could just make out the bold squareness of his jaw and the darkly familiar slash of eyes and brows.

Eduard! The Wolf's son! The discovery was a shock, to be sure, yet somehow she was not surprised.

"Eduard . . . you were in the room? You heard everything?"

The boy's face tensed visibly. "We must not talk here, Lady Servanne. We must get you safely into your chambers."

Servanne offered no resistance as he guided her swiftly and silently along the gallery to the entrance to her tower. He supported her up the stairs and, when he would have hesitated at the outer door, preferring to leave her in the hands of a waiting-woman, she adamantly held fast to his hand and led him through the two smaller anterooms to her solar.

Biddy was there, fast asleep and snoring open-mouthed on a chair by the bed.

"Please," Servanne whispered to Eduard. "Will you add another log to the fire. I doubt an inferno will be able to warm me, but it would help."

Eduard's soft gray eyes flicked askance at Biddy.

"She sleeps the sleep of the dead," Servanne replied, shivering through a slight premonition of dread at her own words.

It took a few fumbled attempts to loosen the bindings of the woolen cloak and cast the bulky garment aside. By then Eduard had selected a suitable length of wood and was bending over the glow of the fire to seat it properly over the burning embers. Servanne moved quietly up beside him, her hands extended to the warmth. For lack of knowing what to say or do next, she studied his features slantwise through her lashes wondering what she could possibly do or say to open the conversation.

If he had been in the wardrobe and had heard what had transpired between Nicolaa de la Haye and the Dragon de Gournay, then he knew Etienne Wardieu was not his father.

Moreover, he also knew Etienne Wardieu *was* Etienne Wardieu and not the man he had supposed him to be all these years.

"I am sorry you had to hear all of that, my lady," Eduard said, his voice forced out of a tautly constricted throat. "I am sorry either of us had to hear it or see it, but most especially you."

"Me, Eduard, but—"

"No." He stood up so suddenly he might have had springs in his ankles. And his face was so gloweringly angry, she could almost see his father standing there in his stead. "No, my lady. Do not feel you have to offer your pity or your sympathy. I have always known I was a bastard. Whether the product of one man's by-blow, or another's, it makes little difference."

"My pity . . . if I were going to offer it," she said evenly, "would not be for you, but for them. And it does make a difference, Eduard. A very great difference as to which man sired you."

"The feared and valorous Randwulf de la Seyne Sur Mer?" Eduard's jaw quivered with tension. His eyes narrowed and glittered brightly for a moment before he averted his face and stared into the fire. "He means nothing to me. I do not even know him."

"In that case, you have something in common, for he does not know you—nor even about you, I would hasten to guess. There the advantage is yours; at least you know he exists."

The thirteen-year-old boy struggled mightily with the sudden burdens of a man and the sternness in his face faltered somewhat. "I . . . have heard he is a knight without equal; a knight whose sword was forged on Satan's anvil, and whose armour was cursed black by the unrepented sins of his forefathers."

"Well, I think the stories are slightly exaggerated—"

"I was in the practice yards when he arrived this morning,

and I caught but a glimpse of him. It is true, my lady: his armour was black, his pennants and crests are wrought in black and gold. It was an impressive sight to behold! And there were maidens swooning everywhere from the dreaded scars they envisioned beneath the black silk mask." His voice trailed away, draining some of his excitement with it. "The mask, my lady . . . ?"

She reached up and laid a hand against his cheek. "The mask conceals a face as handsome and unblemished as your own. It is only fearsome to those who do not know him, and dangerous to those enemies who do."

"The Dragon and his lady seemed duly affected."

"With good reason. The Dragon . . . your uncle . . . stole Lord Lucien's name and birthright. He then tried to murder Lucien, and discredit their father, and . . . and . . ." She faltered under the look of complete incredulity on Eduard's face. "And perhaps I should not be the one telling you any of this."

The young squire's nostrils were white and pinched. "You speak as if you know Lord La Seyne well."

"I know him. I trust him. What is more, I love him with all my heart . . . as you will when you meet him."

"Meet him? Where—on the jousting field? Will I be allowed a brief glimpse of him at the far side of the field while I prepare my lord for the contest? Or if the baron should win, will I be permitted a moment's introduction before they drag his broken and bleeding body from the common?"

Servanne laced her hands tightly together and clasped them against her breast. "But Eduard—"

"I am Lord Wardieu's squire. Because I am no longer his son does not mean my pledge of fealty is no longer binding. Did you think I was the first to ever hear he was unwanted, unloved, and unclaimed? Did you think this was the first time I had witnessed my *uncle's* depravity and brutality, or the first time my"—he gritted his teeth, but the word would not come out—"the first time that *woman* has shown an appetite for cruelty and bloodshed? It is not, my lady, not by any measure. And while it may sicken and anger me, I am still bound by my oath of honour to serve him; to die for him if necessary in my post as squire. Nothing can change that. Forgive me, my lady, but nothing can change that!"

Tears flooded Servanne's eyes as she watched Eduard brush past her and run out of the room. She wanted to go after him—he was just a boy, regardless of how manly he tried to act!—to take him by the arms and shake some sense into him. But she knew it would be to no avail. She felt helpless, caught between the unbreachable honour of the father and now the son.

"Ohhh . . ." She looked for something to break, something to smash into a million bits to vent some of her frustration, and when she turned, she saw Biddy standing a few paces away. The maid had been wakened by Eduard's last heart-wrenching shout, and while she had not been privy to their conversation, she could see the extent of her lamb's pain and fear.

Her chins trembling, she stretched her arms out with an offer of solace, and Servanne accepted gratefully, stumbling forward into Biddy's protective embrace.

"Oh Biddy . . . what shall I do? What shall I do? Why did we ever leave Wymondham? Why did you not prevail upon me to enter a convent and live out my days behind sturdy walls of peace and solitude?"

Biddy pursed her lips. "Because you would always have craved the life outside those walls, my child. Your eyes would always have turned toward the horizon and your heart would have ached to be free."

"It aches now. Almost too unbearably to endure."

"I know. I feared as much. But you must not let the ache cloud your judgment. Nor should you insist upon bearing the burden alone. Tell me what ails you, lamb. A shared trouble is only half so much the worry."

Servanne buried her face in Biddy's bosom. "There is so much," she sobbed. "I do not know where to begin."

"There, there. It cannot be as bad as all this."

"It is, Biddy! It is even worse!"

"Worse than you sending me off on some fool's errand so you could slip away in the company of that scoundrel Friar?"

Servanne choked back a half-formed sob and lifted her head. "You knew? You saw us?"

"I may be old and tending to dribble my soup on my chin, but I am not blind. So now, out with it, missy. Where did you go and who were you with until—saints preserve us, it must be nigh on dawn! And what was all this shouting about fathers and sons and breaking of oaths of honour?"

"Eduard saved me from being discovered in the Dragon's bedchamber. He and I were both trapped in the wardrobe and overheard Nicolaa de la Haye telling the baron that his brother is Randwulf de la Seyne Sur Mer. *And* she called him Etienne, Biddy! *She called him Etienne!*"

"She called who Etienne . . . Eduard?"

"No . . . the *baron*! The baron is Etienne Wardieu, and Randwulf de la Seyne Sur Mer is Lucien Wardieu!"

Biddy regarded her young mistress as one might regard an inmate bound for Bedlam. "And you believe this?"

"Of course I believe it," Servanne exclaimed. "I was with Lucien for most of the night. We . . . we pledged our love."

Biddy used her wimple to dab at the sweat beading across her brow. "First . . . you claim you have been convinced the Black Wolf of Lincoln is Lucien Wardieu; now you say the Scourge of Mirebeau is Lucien Wardieu. Which is it to be?"

"Both. All three are the same man. I know it sounds confusing—it *is* confusing, and must be even more so for poor

Eduard who has just now found out the man he had thought was his father is really his uncle, and the man his uncle intends to kill on the morrow is really his father."

It was too much for Biddy to absorb. Her knees began to wobble and she plumped down heavily on the bench Servanne rushed to place beneath her.

"What shall I do, Biddy? Lucien must be told, he must be warned of the danger now that his brother knows his secret."

"Yes. Yes, child, we will think of something."

Servanne stood for another moment, then sank slowly onto her knees beside Biddy. The older woman cradled the golden head in her lap and smoothed a wrinkled hand over the shiny, sleek crown of waves, feeling very much like her own heart, or mind, or both were about to explode.

"Hush now," she advised sagely. "Another hour and the dawn will be full upon us. We can think then of what we must do. We can think then."

23

Long before the dusty pink clouds tumbled away below the horizon, the tilting grounds bustled with activity. The tournament was to be held on a wide green field that was part of the outer bailey, and overnight silk pavilions in every shade of the rainbow had sprung up like mushrooms in the shadow of the towering ramparts. The lists were enclosed in temporary wooden palisades. A dais had been built in the middle to allow the privileged spectators and guests of honour to watch the activities on the tilting fields or, by a turning of their chair, the archery contests, wrestling matches, jugglers, and tumblers.

Forming a wing along one side of the dais was a second area of tiered seating reserved mainly for the ladies and their serving-women. This was the Bower of Beauty and usually the scene of much amused scandal and gossip, for a knight entering the lists would often pause here to tilt his lance to a favoured damosel and collect his token—a scarf or bit of coloured lace—in returned acknowledgment. By midday, the bower would be filled with ladies who glowed in brilliant tunics and glittered in an array of gemstones, all of them laughing and fluttering amongst themselves like a flock of sun-drenched butterflies.

The De Gournay colours were prominent everywhere, interspersed with flags, pennants and crests of visiting knights and lords. The air was still enough at dawn to render the ocean of parti-hued silks limp and listless, but as the sun rose higher in the crisp blue sky, a salty breeze came in from the sea to whip and snap the flags to attention.

While the guests dressed in their finery and filed into the great hall to break their fasts, the castle's men-at-arms, wearing full protective armour of stiffened bullhide, took up their positions along the borders of the tilting grounds. Earliest to the field, they discouraged children from playing too close to the pavilions, and ominously warned away any persons who had not a specific task to perform in preparing for the games.

Sentries lined up like crows along the crenellated battlements. Each wore full armour, their breasts and backs protected by added plates of steel sewn over the leather. Every tenth man wore chain mail and carried a kite-shaped shield emblazoned with the De Gournay dragon and wolf. They wore swords strapped at their waists and held their crossbows with the casual ease of men trained to shoot first and query later.

The two-ton portcullis gate remained down, although there was a large crowd gathering outside who had ventured from local villages in hopes of watching the spectacle. The Dragon of Bloodmoor Keep had never opened his castle to the general rabble in the past, and probably would not do so today, but they gathered and grumbled anyway, and craned their necks to see through the iron teeth of the portcullis. Enterprising vendors set up their carts to sell cakes and meat pasties, and a second party of minstrels, jugglers, and revelers added colour and sound to the bleak backdrop of the moor.

There were a few admitted to the castle through the narrow oak gates of one of the barbican towers. Late arrivals who could produce proof of an invitation were passed through the heavily armed guards. Minstrels and jongleurs who could win a grudging smile were beckoned through, but only if they were dressed in such a way as to boast success at their profession, and only if they could pay the exorbitant bribes demanded by the sentries.

One pair of minstrels and their diminutive, tumbling companion won particular applause from crowds on both sides of the gates. Twins as strikingly alike as peas in a pod played the lute and viol, while beside them, the peasants were awed by the antics of a curly-haired dwarf who could produce coins from ears and bouquets of feathers from ordinary twigs.

Five crossbowmen thumbed aside the safety latches on their weapons simultaneously and sighted their bolts on an enormous, barrel-chested Welshman who strode through the gates scowling like a hungry bear. He planted his seven-foot frame in the middle of a cleared court and waited until every eye in the crowd was fixed on him. A grizzly smile slashed through the wire fuzz of his beard and in a smooth stroke, he unfastened and tossed his huge flowing mantle aside. As one, the crowed gasped and pressed back. The giant was naked from the waist up, the marbled slabs of muscle were oiled and gleaming under the morning sun. Almost instantly, a second well-greased, semi-naked wrestler stepped out of the crowd to accept the mute challenge, and, spitting voraciously into the palms of their hands, the adversaries dropped into a crouch and began circling.

Squires, pages, and servants belonging to the knights who were slated to participate in the tournament, bustled to and from the pavilions laying out armour and weapons, inspecting all for flaws or defects, and soundly boxing the ears of anyone responsible for a smudge or spot of tarnish.

As the excitement mounted and the spectators' seats began to fill, the jongleurs and minstrels took to the field to entertain their appreciative—and captive—audience. Providing background noises were the whinnies and screams of the destriers who were paraded up from the stables to be groomed and fretted. They would have to look their most magnificent today, bedecked in plumes and silk trappings, their manes and tails plaited and bound with ribbons, tassles, and heavy gold braid. Few stood less than eighteen hands high, none were reluctant to nip at the men and boys who tended them. These war-horses were specially trained to run a course without slowing, swerving, or balking; to respond to the commands given through the rider's thighs, since most knights needed both hands free for weapons. In battle, these beasts would react savagely to the scent of blood, and not even their own masters, if sorely wounded in a confrontation, were safe from the threat of crushing hooves.

Other dangers were minimized as much as possible if the tournament was being staged for entertainment. Lances were blunted and swords sheathed in leather. Such protective measures did not mean to say a man split from his saddle could not break his neck or his back in a fall, or that the impact of a lance striking square in the chest could not crush the ribs inward and pierce through the heart. It was a generally accepted rule in such games to keep the tip of the twenty-foot steel lance lowered and to aim no higher than the shoulder for a strike. Breastplates of twice-tempered iron would usually absorb and deflect the blows, thus preventing serious injury while still sending the unlucky knight sprawling to defeat on the trammeled ground.

Squires stood by to catch the horses. Adjudicators were positioned along the alleys to judge fair or foul play. A win gained through a deliberate foul was negated in the rules, and if the victim died as a result of the foul, his gear—armour, saddle, weapons, and horse—was given to the surviving heirs, not the winner. Few knights who found themselves staring down the lists at a hated enemy cared for rules of chivalric behaviour and gladly forfeited their prizes for the chance to send their rivals to perdition. But for the most part, the entrants were well behaved, and matches set up to avoid pitting known antagonists together.

Naturally, the match between the Dragon of Bloodmoor Keep and the Scourge of Mirebeau was causing the most excitement. The two were undefeated champions on their home terrain and it was eagerly assumed the codes of chivalry would be drenched in gore before the end of the day.

What both men were doing to prepare themselves for the upcoming match was the subject of much speculation, for neither had been present in the great hall for the morning repast.

"What do you mean you cannot find him?" De Gournay asked, his anger causing him to thrust aside the helping hands of the servant endevouring to dress him.

Rowlens, the castle seneschal and chamberlain, swallowed hard and wiped at the beads of sweat trickling down to his chin.

"My lord, he is nowhere he should be expected to be. My men have searched the stables, the baileys, the barracks. He has not been seen at the smithy or the armoury since yestertide. He was not at chapel this morning, nor at table as is his wont early of a morning."

"Well, now that we know where he has not been," Wardieu snarled, "what I wish to know and what I command you to find out, is *where he is now*!"

"My lord, surely another squire could be fetched to assist you—"

"I do not want another squire, damn you!" Wardieu roared, sending a spray of flying crockery against the wall. "I want Eduard! I want him brought here to me, in chains if need be, and I want to see him without any further delays or excuses!"

"My lord?"

The two men whirled to stare at the door. One of them melted instantly with relief, the other clenched his hands into fists and advanced ominously toward the guileless figure who stood there.

"Where" the Dragon seethed, "by God's holy ordinance, have you been?"

Eduard looked calmly from the seneschal to his master, to the raven-haired Nicolaa de la Haye who was lounging close by in a tunic so red it burned the eyes.

"I . . . was at the armourers," Eduard said, glancing back at Wardieu. "I was ensuring your lances were all—"

"Liar!" The flat of De Gournay's hand lashed out and caught the squire on the side of his face, smashing him sideways against the stone wall. "You were not at the armourers! You have not been seen at the armourers since yesterday!"

Eduard straightened, his hand cupped to his mouth to catch the slippery warmth of blood that flowed from his torn lip. He was dazed and reeling slightly; his cheek and forehead had struck hard against the stone, and the flesh was serrated a raw red.

"I will only ask once more," De Gournay threatened. "Where have you been all night and morning? And I warn you now, if you dare another lie, I will have the skin flayed from your body in bloody strips."

Eduard's gray eyes flickered with pain, but did not waver from Wardieu's.

"I was with the maid Glyneth," he said hoarsely. "I . . . *we* overslept, my lord, and I have just been explaining to Mary, the cook, that the fault was mine and Glyneth should be spared a beating."

"You have been wenching?" Nicolaa asked with a wry sneer. "How positively true to the Wardieu bloodlines."

"Nicolaa—have you nowhere else to be right now?"

"My, my," she said, the narrowed green eyes slicing to De Gournay. "We are full of vinegar this morning, are we not? Two servants sent for a flogging because they spilled a few crumbs of bread. A guard railed for a torn tunic and . . .

dear oh dear . . . now a lad knocked half senseless for sharing one of your own favorite pastimes. Is it a simple case of nerves, my lord, or is it due to the glaring tardiness of a certain other yellow-haired insolent?"

De Gournay's teeth appeared in a brief snarl, but a *pat* of blood from Eduard's hand dripped onto the floor and earned a scathing glance instead. "Get yourself cleaned up and fetch the Lady Servanne down from her tower rooms. Tell her I expect her to be ready and waiting to accompany me to the fields within the hour, regardless of her state of dress or undress!"

When Eduard departed, De Gournay turned to the seneschal, who had dearly hoped he had been forgotten.

"Find this wench Glyneth and question her yourself. If she gives you any reason to doubt his story, I want to know it without delay."

"Aye, my lord." Frowning, the seneschal left and Nicolaa arched a brow.

"Rather sanctimonious of you to be so suspicious, is it not? Or is there something you are not telling me?"

"There have just been too many coincidences lately, and I would sooner not be surprised by any more."

Prince John smiled lazily. "I trust you will convey my heartfelt thanks to my dear mother for her . . . generous contribution to the expenses incurred during my niece's visit." He hefted the lid on the small chest of glittering gold coins and equally bright sparks of greed were mirrored in the depths of the squinted, dark eyes. "Ahh yes, very generous."

Randwulf de la Seyne Sur Mer stood tall and silent before the prince, his body clad in various textures of black from linen to leather to the gleaming black silk of his hood. Behind him was a phalanx of armoured knights who stood facing the prince's men, glower to glower, watchful eye to watchful eye.

"The Princess Eleanor?" La Seyne asked.

John stared thoughtfully at the gold for a moment, then flicked a hand vapidly at one of the guards. The knight nodded and turned curtly to a narrow door, opened it, and gestured someone to come through.

The Princess Eleanor of Brittany was eight years old and trying very hard to be brave. Wakened before dawn this morning, she had been helped into her clothes by the coarse-handed, foul-mouthed trull her uncle had assigned as waiting-woman. She had not been told where she was going or what to expect at the end of the anxious, hour-long wait in a small, airless anteroom.

Her thin frame had grown even thinner in the four months since she had been abducted from Mirebeau. She had stubbornly kept her lips firmly shut for all but the barest necessities of food and communication, using silence as her solace and her defense. To her secret pleasure, she had discovered her lack of response and animation riled her uncle John more than any other form of temperament. This, combined with the searingly blue Plantagenet eyes that were never remiss in frosting over with icy hatred when directed at her uncle, made John blatantly relieved to be ridding himself of her.

Eleanor was ushered through the door and stood a moment, blinking to adjust her eyes to the brighter light. She saw the guards—far too many of them for a normal meeting with her uncle—and it took a second fearful look around for her to realize fully half of them wore the colours of La Seyne Sur Mer! Startled, she searched the lines of grim, solemn faces until she saw the one she had hoped and prayed to see all these months of captivity. Sir Randwulf! He had come! He had come to rescue her just as she had known he would!

La Seyne saw the little princess and felt a wave of relief wash through him. She appeared to be unharmed—a trace

thinner, perhaps, and unaccustomed to smiling—but unharmed.

Eleanor darted eagerly forward. One of John's guards
flashed out a hand to bar her path and immediately, from La
Seyne's guard, a score of calloused hands flew instinctively to
the hilts of their swords.

"As you can see," John drawled, "my niece is in perfect
health. She will be given into your care directly, La Seyne,
but first . . . you have no objections if a Jew counts the
gold for me? In these trying times, with chicanery so rife, one
can never be too careful, even when dealing with relatives.
Especially relatives."

La Seyne absorbed the slight with nary a ripple of muscle.
Not so his men, who bristled visibly at this further insult—so
much so that this time it was John's guards who inched their
hands nervously toward their swords.

"I'll not keep you, however," the prince offered gener-
ously. "I know you have much to do to prepare for the
tourney this afternoon, so if you would prefer simply to leave
one of your men in charge—?"

"I will wait." La Seyne scowled, the chill in the fireless
room giving his words a ghostly substance through the black
silk.

John, warmed by his thick velvet doublet as well as well as
his smug self-satisfaction, leaned back and formed a tent
with his gloved fingers, the tips pressed against his lips. "It
should take no more than an hour or two. For a moneylender, he tends to count slowly to avoid any chance of error."

La Seyne crossed his arms over his chest, presenting a
formidable tower of immovable strength. Inwardly he was
thinking: If it was a ploy to unsettle him before the match, it
was a feeble effort at best. Outwardly, he let the silk mask
crease in an imitation of a smile. "I will wait."

* * *

Servanne jumped when she heard the knock on the outer door. Both she and Biddy were standing by one of the tall, arched windows and, as one, they reached for the comforting grasp of each other's hands.

"Who comes?" Biddy called, her voice querulous but remarkably firm. She had had to ponder a great deal in the past few hours—from the Wolf's identity, to the confirmed proof of Etienne Wardieu's duplicity, to the very real possibility they could all be betrayed, beheaded, and their corpses left to rot on spiked poles by way of example to others.

The sight of De Gournay's young squire brought another quailing start to Biddy's breast, a condition augmented by the puffed, split bruises on Eduard's face.

"Eduard!" Servanne gasped, leaving the embrasure to rush to the young man's side. "What happened!"

"'Tis nothing, my lady. It is your welfare, not mine, which concerns me more."

"My lamb's welfare?" Biddy exclaimed, hurrying over. "What do you mean?"

"There is no time for explanations, mistress goodwife. Only know that the Dragon's mood does not bode well for anyone who chooses to cross him this day. He is already in a rampage over the messages my lady has sent to explain her absences at chapel and table this morning. He has been pacing like a caged lion in his chamber all this time, refusing to appear without you by his side. To that end, he has given me explicit instructions not to return to the hall without you."

A small flaring of defiance sent a flush into Servanne's cheeks. "How dare he issue such orders. I am not his chattel. Not yet, at any rate."

Biddy was more practical. "Eduard—what trouble do you anticipate?"

"Too much for any of us to handle alone, but do not fear,

Mistress Bidwell. I will not let the bastard touch a hair on my lady's head; on this you have my word."

Servanne pressed cool fingers to her temple. "It is not for my safety I fear the most. Eduard—we must find some way of warning your father . . . your *real* father; the real Lucien Wardieu. There is no telling what Etienne may do now out of desperation to keep his secret intact. He will set a trap, at the very least—a trap your father will walk into blindly unless he is forewarned."

"You will have to warn him, my lady," Eduard said.

"Me? Willingly, but . . . how?"

Eduard retraced his steps to the door and retrieved a bundle of clothing neither woman had seen him set on the floor when he arrived.

"I brought these—" He shook out the folds of a long-sleeved shirt, jerkin, and buff-coloured leggings, and handed the lot to Biddy. "It was the best I could do in such short order, I am afraid, but even if the disguise is only good enough to get you through to the outer bailey, it will have served its purpose. Beyond there, the confusion and revelry should be sufficient protection."

"You want me to dress in these?" Servanne asked. "Is it necessary?"

Eduard flushed as he allowed himself a bold assessment of the frothing yellow silk gown she wore. "A dead man would sit up and take notice if you passed," he said with unabashed reverence. "Yes, my lady: it is absolutely vital to conceal yourself. Unfortunately, it would not be wise for me to guide you to safety myself, but I have taken the liberty of whispering a word in the ear of your man, Sir Roger de Chesnai. Without revealing the reasons why, I asked him to meet us at the postern of the keep. He should have little difficulty in taking you to La Seyne's encampment, and from there . . ."

His voice trailed away, not quite as confident in finishing as it had been at the outset.

"What about you, Eduard? I cannot run to safety knowing I have left you behind to suffer in my stead."

The young squire's shoulders squared and there was a fierce determination emanating from his eyes.

"Lady Servanne, your safety is all that matters right now. I have borne the brunt of the Dragon's anger before, and I will bear it this time with no complaint if it serves to spare you but a moment's fear or discomfort. I . . . thought about my position a great deal after I left here last night, and I know now my honour would not be compromised by leaving this place and seeking service elsewhere. I . . . hope one day I might meet my real father. But if not, if there is some reason why he would prefer not to see me, or to know me—"

"Oh Eduard, no. No! He will welcome and accept you most proudly, I am certain of it. As certain as I am that you must come with us now. What can you hope to gain by appearing without me? A few minutes' time?"

"A few minutes," he said haltingly, "could make all the difference."

"At what cost?" she asked gently. "And how would I explain to your father that I left you behind? Biddy—fetch our cloaks . . . and the robe over by the firebox. We shall all go together, or not at all."

"Sweet Saint Agnes, we are lost," Biddy cried. But she complied with the order and, in a spurt of conscientiousness, hastened to retrieve her mistress's jewel box from behind the small curtained niche in the corner of the room.

"Our best hope," Servanne was saying, still fighting the look of uncertainty on Eduard's face, "is to seek refuge with La Seyne Sur Mer—the man who is not only your father but the man I love and intend to marry."

"Over my dead and rotting body, madam," came a darkly familiar voice from the doorway of the anteroom.

Servanne blanched and dropped the belt and points she

had been holding. Eduard merely stood his ground as Etienne Wardieu came slowly into the room. A pace behind, her eyes glittering with malice and irrepressible pleasure, was Nicolaa de la Haye.

24

"So," hissed the golden-haired Dragon of Bloodmoor Keep. "The man you love, is he? The man you intend to marry?"

Servanne lifted her chin and held it firm. "I would most surely never marry you, my lord, knowing you betrayed your own father and stole your brother's name and birthright through a cowardly act of murder."

A fine, taut white line of tension delineated the rim of each nostril as the Dragon drew a slow breath. "My brother's tongue seems to have grown looser over the years. He has some proof to bear out these outrageous claims? Or has he merely bewitched you in some way?"

"She says she loves him," Nicolaa said dryly. "One need not speculate too long or too hard over just how this bewitchment was accomplished; I dare say the proof was thrust between her thighs a time or two for good measure."

A warm flush suffused Servanne's cheeks, deepening with the effort it was taking not to glance toward the niche on the opposite wall. Biddy was standing there, half in, half out from behind the thick velvet curtain, her eyes as round as medallions, her mouth gaping open in shock and fright. She had not been seen yet, and instinct as much as fear was prompting her to let the curtain fall back into place, concealing her within the niche. Eduard, bless his presence of mind, moved closer to Servanne, his action steering the Dragon's attention away from the niche.

"Shall I think of a suitable punishment for her, my love?"

Nicolaa drawled. "Or would you prefer to just let D'Aeth use his imagination? He might find her an amusing change from the stable boys he toys with. Why"—her gaze flicked to Eduard—"he could even alternate between the two to keep his interest fully peaked."

The Dragon walked slowly toward Servanne and Eduard. Servanne had not thought it was possible for her to become any more frightened than she already was, but the look in his eyes mocked her supposition and she experienced a cold rush of terror that locked her spine stiff.

"I can well see the benefit to some form of dicipline," he murmured. "But M'sieur D'Aeth's methods are rather harsh, and I would have her able to walk and talk awhile longer yet. At least until after we are wed. After that"—his gaze slid down her body with indifference—"we shall see how penitent she can be before we decide her punishment."

"I have no intention of marrying you," Servanne declared quietly. "Not now. Not ever."

The Dragon smiled. "*Not ever* is rather too conclusive a statement, my sweet. It allows little room for taking into consideration the amount of pain a human body can endure for its stubbornness."

"I will not marry you," she said evenly.

The Dragon clucked his tongue softly to express his sad displeasure. A moment later his hand was lashing upward, the blow catching her cheek and snapping her head sideways in a froth of flying yellow hair. She staggered to one side, but did not fall. The pain exploded in her skull and temporarily blinded her, but even before she could shake the tears free, she saw Eduard leap forward, his hands clawing around the Dragon's throat.

With hardly more effort than it took to swat a fly, Etienne Wardieu sent his fist plowing into the vulnerable hollow just below the young man's rib cage. Eduard's face registered the shocked agony as every last gasp of air was violently expunged from his lungs. He doubled over and staggered back, his legs folding beneath him like crumpled sticks.

The Dragon turned to Servanne. She was leaning against the wall, her face partially blurred by a cloud of hair. He reached out and grasped her by a fistful of the slippery, silken stuff and, with Nicolaa watching on with silent glee, he struck her again, this time bracing her to take the full impact.

"You will marry me, my dear. You will stand before the bishop and repeat your vows like the dutiful, humble bride for whom I contracted. And when the ceremony is over, you will crawl to me on your hands and knees and beg to service me."

"No," Servanne gasped. "Never!"

"There is that annoying word again," he mused. He tightened his fist around her hair, nearly tearing the roots from her scalp.

"You will obey me, madam," he spat, his mouth and breath rasping hotly against the curve of her throat. "You will obey me humbly and willingly, or by the Christ, you will do it broken and bleeding. The choice is yours."

"N-no," she sobbed weakly. "No!"

Wardieu jerked her head back against the stone wall, and when she would have sagged down from the pain and the swirling threat of faintness, he propped her up with the crushing force of his knee, driving it hard and high between her thighs.

Her scream caused Edward to surge forward, ignoring his own pain, but a snakelike hiss of steel marked Nicolaa's shortsword leaving her scabbard and slicing through the air to seek the exposed length of Eduard's neck.

"This is none of your affair, boy," she snarled. "Watch closely and you may learn something about survival."

Servanne was struggling, flaying her hands ineffectually against the looming breadth of Wardieu's chest. He was too strong and wore too many layers of rich, quilted velvet for her to provoke more than a chastising smile. Conversely, Servanne's gown was sheer and delicate, offering little protection from the thigh he ground brutally against her softness, or the hand he insinuated beneath the collar, tearing it down, baring her flesh all the way to the tops of her breasts.

"You used a strong perfume in your bath, my dear, but I can still smell my brother's lust on you. You stink of it!"

Servanne brought her nails up to claw his face, but he caught her wrists and twisted them painfully up and over her head. He crushed her lips beneath his, the kiss brutal, wet, and cruel. Gagging, choking on the sour taste of his rage, Servanne tore her lips free, but he only laughed.

"You will find, my dear, the harder you fight me, the more I want what I am denied. It has always given me the greatest pleasure to succeed where my brother has failed, to take what he cannot have, to know that I possess something he holds dear above all else."

"No," she gasped. "No! You will never have me. My heart will always belong to Lucien!"

Wardieu gouged his hands into her wrists. "But I still have your body, my pet, and in a few short hours, I shall have his too. Perhaps . . . perhaps, as part of a lesson for both of you, we will let him watch. Yes," he mused slowly, his eyes glittering with hate. "That would please me immeasurably to have you naked and begging for mercy—bribing me, perhaps, with what pleasures I desire, while he is forced to stand by and watch. By God, it would indeed be worth sparing his life an hour or two. For that matter, if you pleased me enough with your enthusiasm, you could win a reprieve for days . . . even weeks."

Servanne gaped up at him in horror, her eyes flooding with tears. De Gournay only laughed harder and lowered one of his hands to her breast, scooping it free of the ragged edge of her bodice and squeezing the nipple to a bloodless pink between his fingers.

Servanne screamed again and this time there was an answering roar from behind. The Dragon turned just in time to see the raging blur that was Eduard shove Nicolaa aside and launch himself at his master's back. The glitter of a knife arced downward, aimed for a point midway between the broad shoulders, but the Dragon was able to step aside at the last possible moment, his arm swinging around and throwing Eduard hard against the wall. Releasing Servanne, De Gournay went after his young squire, hauling him to his feet, grabbing for the wrist of the hand that still clutched the steel dagger. Eduard buckled under the pain, but held steadfast to the knife as well as the hatred that blazed from his eyes.

A glance at Servanne brought a malicious smile back to the Dragon's face.

"It seems you have found yourself another champion, my lady. Think you *he* would also be useful in convincing you of the error of your ways?"

Before Servanne could respond, or even react to the loathing in his voice, the Dragon slid his hand farther along Eduard's wrist to engulf the clenched fist. He turned it until the blade was aimed at Eduard's own thigh, then drove it inward, punching the steel through clothing, flesh, and muscle. Eduard screamed with the pain, a scream that was bitten off, crammed back into his throat on a deep gulp of air, then unleashed again as the knife was given a deliberate half twist.

"Stop!" Servanne shrieked, appalled by the sight of the agony on Eduard's face. *"Stop!"*

"No, my lady!" Eduard shouted. "No, do not agree to anything! Do not—*ahhhh*!"

The blade was wrenched again and the spreading stain of blood flowed freely over the two hands clasped around the hilt of the knife. Servanne flung herself away from the wall and clawed at De Gournay's shoulders, her tears blinding her, the terror numbing her to her own pain.

"Stop! Stop! I will do anything you ask me to do, only stop! Stop! Stop!"

De Gournay gave the knife a final twist before releasing it. Eduard's free hand clamped over the one still holding the hilt, and, as he slid slowly down the wall, he used what few grains of strength he had remaining to pull the knife free of his flesh and squeeze his bloodied hands tightly over the wound.

"Eduard!" Servanne dropped to her knees beside him, but was scarcely allowed the opportunity to touch a trembling hand to his ashen cheek before she felt the rough grasp of De Gournay's hands on her shoulders. Dragged upright, she could only stare in horror at the steady stream of blood that leaked between Eduard's fingers and fell in a sickening *pat, pat, pat* onto the floor.

Dimly she was aware of Nicolaa summoning two guards from the landing. Dazed, she watched them pass in front of her and take hold of Eduard under each arm. Helpless, she could do nothing but sob his name as the two grim-faced mercenaries hauled Eduard from the chamber, his leg leaving a smeared trail of crimson in their wake.

"Where are they taking him?" she cried. "What are they going to do to him?"

"They will do whatever I command them to do," the Dragon said wanly.

Servanne looked at him through the scattered tangle of her hair. Her breasts rose and fell rapidly with the need to control her panic; her hands shook visibly where she tried to hold the torn flaps of fabric over her nakedness. She had seen enough wounds in her eighteen years to know the bleeding hole in Eduard's thigh would cost him his life if not cauterized and sealed right away. She knew also, beyond a doubt, the Dragon would not give the command for his leech to do so unless Servanne paid heavily for the request.

"Please," she grated through her teeth. "Help him."

"Why should I? He is nothing to me."

"If he was nothing, you would have killed him outright," she said, her fear giving her more courage than was healthy or wise. Bracing herself for another blow, she felt the blood-slicked fingers curl around the whiteness of her throat.

"It seems the spirit has been bruised, but not yet broken," he mused. "Admirable, but foolhardy. A word from me, and the boy dies; you alongside him."

"Give that word," she countered recklessly, "And see the lands you covet so fiercely slip out of your grasp and into Prince John's coffers!"

The Dragon's eyes gleamed with a speculative fury and Servanne could feel the anger ripple tautly through his body. An instant later she felt only agony as his fingers pinched her windpipe in a cruel stranglehold.

"I like ultimatums even less than I like stubbornness," he snarled, "Especially ultimatums which have no foundation in threat or substance. As I have already told you, my dear, broken or upright, bleeding or whole, it makes no difference to me. Even with your tongue cut out and your eyes scorched black, I could still prop you at the altar and find a score of witnesses to say you repeated your vows willingly and eagerly. Moreover, I have no doubt a further examination would find sufficient evidence of a union having been recently consummated. So you see"—he released her throat with a disdainful sneer—"you really have no choice in the matter. Your fate and the fate of the lands that came into your hands by sheer mischance, was decided long ago. Long before your feeble old husband enjoyed a hearty feast of belladonna."

Servanne's wide blue gaze dared to climb to his level again.

"He was a tough old buzzard," De Gournay added blithely. "I was told it took three times the normal dose to kill him."

Nicolaa de la Haye's surprise mirrored Servanne's. "You clever bastard! You never told me."

"There are a good many things I do not tell you, Nicolaa," he sighed. "For my own sake, as well as—"

His words were cut off abruptly as Servanne threw herself at him, her fingers hooked and hungry for the sardonic grin. He had ordered the death of Sir Hubert de Briscourt! He had had the gentle old warrior poisoned so he could gain back the lands that had once been part of the De Gournay estates. The Wolf had been right again. He had been right in everything!

Servanne's action was quick enough and violent enough to almost succeed. She had the satisfaction of feeling two sharp fingernails fill with scrapings of flesh before her arms were smashed aside and a hard-knuckled fist sent her careening into the side of the bed. Grasped from behind, she was struck again, and flung into a sprawl across the floor, her hands scraped raw in the skidding contact.

The Dragon stood over her, staring in amazement at the blood dabbed from his neck. He leaned over and with one brutish hand, yanked her upright, lifting her so that her face was only inches from his.

"I will kill you for that," he promised. "Slowly. And with a great deal of pain. You and your lover both, side by side, screaming for mercy—"

Servanne reached back into the last reserves of her courage and spat contemptuously in the Dragon's face. The spittle ran down his cheek and gathered into a silvery pendant on his chin, hanging there a moment like a diamond glittering in the candlelight. The same fingers that were dotted with his blood, reached slowly upward and wiped the wetness from his face. He stared at his fingers, then into Servanne's eyes, silently pledging untold agony and cruelty before he smeared the pink stain across her exposed breasts.

"Nicolaa—methinks the lady could benefit from the comfort of her own solitude a while. Have the guards escort her . . . to the eagle's eyrie. She will know, at least once before she dies, who is master here, and who is merely the whore."

He flung her from his side as if she was a sackful of rotted meat. Servanne landed heavily enough to drive another gust of air from her lungs, but she was beyond feeling the pain. Her bruises screamed for mercy, but she never would, and there was no lessening of the revulsion in her eyes as she watched De Gournay stride out of the chamber.

"My my my," Nicolaa murmured. "So there was some spirit in you after all. Sadly misplaced, I must say. Did *he* put it there?"

When there was no answer, Nicolaa reached down and took hold of a fistful of blonde hair, tilting Servanne's face roughly up to hers. There were ugly swellings already rising on both cheeks and threads of blood trickling from cuts to her nose and mouth.

"You should have waited. You would have found your thighs just as slippery for a Dragon as for a Wolf. I know I did. Ahh, but then . . . you never would have been strong enough to match him. This"—she waved a hand in a scornful gesture over the blonde hair and creamy white breasts— "would never have held his attention through the wedding night. He would have had to come to me to find satisfaction."

Nicolaa thrust the pale face away again and, still laughing, walked out to the tower landing to call for more guards.

Servanne, her face and body an excruciating mass of bruised flesh, groped blindly around to see if Biddy was still concealed behind the curtains. A chalk-white face with owlish eyes gaped back at her, stricken with terror, her throat working frantically to contain the nausea churning in her belly.

"Biddy, no!" Servanne gasped, seeing the maid about to rush to her aid. "No, you must go and find Sir Roger. You must tell him what has happened. Tell him . . . tell him to seek out the Black Wolf and warn him. Biddy—"

"There!" Nicolaa commanded imperiously, directing four burly guards to where Servanne lay curled on the floor. "Your liege has dispatched orders for her to be taken to the eyrie and left there to await his further pleasure. Treat her as you would the lowest form of vermin, for if there is any undue comfort or mercy shown her, each of you will suffer tenfold for it."

The guards bent over and pulled Servanne to her feet. One of them accidentally tangled a leg in her frothing skirts and, aware of Nicolaa's venomous gaze, cursed and kicked out viciously with his mail-clad boots. Servanne's leg buckled with the pain and a slipper was lost as she was dragged forward on one knee. Her head lolled and she sagged limply into the coarse hands—hands that were quick to prop her up by breast or thigh as they carried her down the narrow, winding staircase.

Biddy, too horror-struck to move, waited several minutes in oppressive silence, her ears ringing with the echo of her mistress's fading sobs of pain. When she was reasonably certain the chambers were vacant, she gingerly stepped out from behind the tapestry and promptly sagged onto the low seat in the window embrasure. Her heart was pounding frantically and her left arm felt as if a frenzied mob of seamstresses were using it as a pincushion. She rubbed it and cradled it against her breast, but the pain only grew in intensity, spreading up her arm into her chest and flaring into a brilliant starburst of agony.

She slipped helplessly onto the floor, her back scraping against the wall as she slid down. Her neck was arched and rigid as she fought the waves of pain, and her tongue seemed to swell in her throat, making it difficult to breathe, let alone find the air to scream.

She could not afford to be weak or ill right now! Sir Roger de Chesnai would be waiting at the postern gate, and it was Biddy's duty to get to him, tell him all that had happened, and send him to the Wolf for help. The Wolf, who was really La Seyne Sur Mer, who was really Lucien Wardieu . . .

Biddy groaned and clutched at her chest. Her vision clouded and began to fill with exploding black spots. Her heart pounded so fiercely she could feel it slamming against her hands, but then the pain and the blackness overtook her and she felt nothing else. Her eyes fluttered open one last time and she was dazzled by the glitter of gold and jewels . . . dazzled until she saw it was Servanne's treasure box, and the contents were spilling from the window seat onto the floor beside her . . .

Prince John's moneylender dropped the last gold coin into the small mahogany chest just as a disturbance out in the corridor brought a crashing end to the tension-filled silence. The door to the chamber swung violently open and there, in glorious splendour, stood the Baron de Gournay.

"Wardieu?" John frowned and signaled his men to stand at ease. "To what do we owe the pleasure of this unexpected —and unwarranted—interruption?"

De Gournay sent his cold blue gaze around the crowded chamber, suitably impressed by the regal display of Angevin and Aquitaine power. Equally impressive was the sight of the tall, hooded figure in black; a man whose size and presence dominated the room with sinister intent.

"Wardieu!" Prince John repeated the question. "What is the meaning of this?"

The Dragon advanced slowly into the room, a smile of unearthly pleasure on his face. "I thought it time I met the

Scourge of Mirebeau face-to-face. After all, we will be tipping lances this afternoon, and it occurred to me I should
meet the man before I killed him."

The black hood shifted only slightly to show interest. The
gray eyes were more intrigued to note the master of Bloodmoor Keep was unarmed. He was without sword or dagger,
dressed in an elegant midnight-blue doublet lacking the benefit of so much as a breast piece of chain mail beneath. He
was bareheaded and his blond hair fell in glossy curls to his
shoulders. With no forest shadows to cloud the Dragon's
features, the Wolf was able to scrutinize every line and wrin-
kle, every lash hair, every bone and muscle that went into
shaping the contours of his brother's face.

"You have the advantage, sirrah," De Gournay murmured, watching the glinted inspection.

"Our business is almost at an end, Wardieu," Prince John
said irritably. "Could you not have waited a moment or
two—"

"Your business with La Seyne Sur Mer *is* at an end," De
Gournay interjected mildly. "However, if you have some further dealings with the Black Wolf of Lincoln . . . ?"

"The Black—! What are you talking about? Is he here?
Inside the castle?"

De Gournay smiled. "Why, he is right here . . . in this
room, my liege."

John bolted to his feet as if a needle had been thrust into
his buttocks. He snatched the money chest out of the Jew's
hands and shouted for his men to close ranks around him.
"He is here? Your brother is *here?*"

De Gournay's eyes had not wavered from the slits in the
black silk mask. "Apparently, my liege, he has become a
chameleon of many names and guises, the most prominent
among them: Randwulf de la Seyne Sur Mer."

The revelation brought utter, complete silence. No one

moved. No one breathed. All eyes were fixed on the two knights in the centre of the room.

A black gloved hand rose, and for the second time in as many days, Lucien Wardieu removed the silk hood and gave a brief shake to free the unruly waves of long chestnut hair. The expectant—and subsequently disappointed—gasp from Prince John's guard was met by scornfully smug looks from the queen's men, all of whom had known there were no scars or hideous disfigurements to warrant the hood.

"My congratulations," De Gournay murmured. "Your little masquerade almost succeeded."

"Guards!" John cried. "Seize that man!"

The regent's men drew their swords, but gained no more than a few paces across the room before they were met by the flashing steel of their counterparts. The prince scrambled back into the corner, shouting for protection, while elsewhere in the confusion, in a movement so swift only the flickering of an eye caught it, the Princess Eleanor was drawn behind the formidable wall of La Seyne blazons.

"Stalemate?" De Gournay inquired blandly.

A slick whisper of steel brought the Wolf's dagger out of its sheath and the tip nosing up beneath the Dragon's chin.

"Not quite," he said, and smiled.

"Do you think you would leave this room alive if you killed me?"

"One of the main reasons I came back to England was to kill you. Do you think my own survival was ever a weighty consideration?"

"What of the survival of your men? And the Princess Eleanor? Are they of no consideration either?"

The point of the blade was nudged higher. "If the cause is just and honourable, my men are prepared to die—and to die well, taking at least one, perhaps two of your own men with them. Wholesale slaughter within the castle walls might be difficult, even for you to explain to the other wedding guests.

As to the princess, you would not be so stupid as to harm her. The queen sent me to resolve the matter as quickly and quietly as possible—but harm her granddaughter, or kill her, and not only will there be an army setting sail from Brittany on the next tide, but you and your . . . benefactor"—he spat the word, laden with contempt, at the cowering regent —"will rouse the killing instinct in every lord and baron this side of the Channel."

"I claim no part in this," John declared loudly. "The princess is no longer in my care. Whatever happens now lies solely in the hands and at the fault of the Baron de Gournay!"

The Wolf's grin slanted with amusement. "You always did have a knack for choosing loyal friends."

"I have no interest in Princess Eleanor. She is free to leave the castle at any time, as are your men."

"With me riding at the head?"

The Dragon scoffed. "Wrapped in a shroud, perhaps. Surely you would not consider leaving early at any rate. Think of the disgrace: the Scourge of Mirebeau slinking away like a cur with his tail tucked between his legs, his teeth chattering with fright. Your queen would be humiliated; my guests would be chagrined; and my lovely bride— think how distraught she would be at being so slighted."

The steely eyes did not take the bait—not at once—but neither did the Dragon back down from the sudden tautness in his brother's jaw.

"Lady de Briscourt," he mused. "Such a sweet young thing, is she not? Spirited too, yet so refreshingly innocent in her passions. Well . . . perhaps not so innocent as she was before falling into your hands, yet eager enough to make up for her . . . shall we say . . . curiosity?"

The only response was a visible tightening of the already compressed, bloodless lips and the Dragon raised his hand, using the backs of his fingers to push the blade of the knife aside. "I would have thought you had learned your lesson with Nicolaa."

"Where is she?" the Wolf rasped.

"Nicolaa? Why, I believe she is tending to Lady de Briscourt."

"Where is Servanne?"

The Dragon smiled. "She is safely tucked away for the time being. Licking her wounded pride, I would imagine."

"If you have touched her—"

The Dragon's eyes glowed triumphantly. "Be assured," he said viciously, throwing the Wolf's own words back at him, "I have indeed *touched* her. And I will touch her again . . . and again, as often and as inventively as I so choose the moment she becomes my bride."

The Wolf fought to keep his rage in check. His fist closed so tightly around the hilt of the knife, the seams of his gauntlet cracked and split the threads. He had lived by his instincts too long not to sense the jaws of a trap looming in front of him, but until he could determine the exact nature of the trap, and how many other lives were being placed at risk alongside his own, he had no choice but to endure Etienne's baitings.

"You say my men are free to leave. I am curious to hear your terms for such generosity."

"No terms. They are free to go—preferably within the hour, however, so my men will have something other than their own backs to watch. What is more, my guard will be glad to provide an escort as far as Lincoln to ensure they meet no dangers on the road. The forests, as you know, are riddled with outlaws."

The Wolf ignored the sarcasm. It came as no surprise to hear he wanted the queen's men out of the castle. With them gone, there would be no threat of an attack or rescue from within Bloodmoor's walls. Locking them out would also effectively lock the Wolf inside, presumably alone, and here he spared a brief word of thanks for Friar's foresight in insisting some of the men enter the castle as common folk. A dozen stout bow arms well placed gave him a fighting chance—providing there would still be the chance to fight.

"What of our challenge match? Surely *you* are not suggesting we forfeit the contest?" the Wolf asked dryly. "Or is this your coward's way of avoiding a test you fear you cannot win on equal terms?"

The Dragon laughed. "God's love, I would not dream of disappointing our avid audience. They are eager to see blood spilled this day, and by Christ, so am I." His smile faded and his gaze turned brittle. "You should have stayed dead, but since you have not, I would not deny myself the pleasure of killing you again. The match proceeds as planned."

"To what end . . . an arrow in my back if I win?"

"If you live to walk off the field," the Dragon said seethingly, "all of this, including the blushing bride, is yours. If you lose—" He stopped and straightened, curbing his temper before he fell into his own trap. "*When* you lose, you will know it has all been in vain. Your body will be fed to the carrion, and life will go on at Bloodmoor the way it has gone on these past fourteen years without you. No one will mourn your passing, except perhaps my young and passionate bride. Even then, she may cry out your name a time or two in the beginning, but that too will pass, and she will soon learn her proper place beneath me."

The Wolf was taunted by the melodic evil in the Dragon's voice. Images flashed across his mind—images of pain, of watching his own flesh blister under the desert sun, of the physician's knife, and the sound of pitch bubbling sluggishly in a cauldron nearby.

The Wolf continued to stare at his brother, all the while feeling the rage and hatred rise from his soul to flush through his blood and tighten the muscles everywhere in his body until they screamed for some form of release.

When he spoke, his voice was a sheared sliver of ice. "I accept the challenge, and the terms."

The Dragon stood a moment longer, relishing his own flush of satisfaction. In the end, he bowed stiffly by way of an acknowledgment, and with barely a glance at the hunched figure and wide-eyed countenance of Prince John, he left the room. The prince, barking orders for his guards to keep their weapons at the ready, followed with all due haste, and in the silence of the half-emptied room, their footsteps could be heard clanking to the far end of the long corridor.

When the silence became filled with more silence, one of the Wolf's men stepped forward and waited for the gray eyes to shift away from the door.

"My lord, we have no intention of leaving the castle grounds so long as you remain inside these walls."

"On the contrary, Sir Richard, you and the entire guard will leave within the hour, as agreed."

"But my lord—"

"Your loyalty to me is much appreciated, but your first duty is and always was to see to the safe return of the Princess Eleanor to Brittany. She must be taken away from this place at once, before Prince John sees past his initial surprise and begins to consider further possible profits. And for God's sake, do not trust the Dragon's men to lead you to Lincoln. Break away from them at the first opportunity, kill them all, if need be, and take any road that leads in the opposite direction. The queen's ship is anchored at Hull. Be certain it sails within the shortest reasonable amount of time, and do not let your guard down for an instant. Not even when your spurs touch Breton soil. I place you in charge, Sir Richard of Rouen, and entrust the princess's life into your hands. Swear not to fail me in this and your loyalty could not have won a truer test."

Sir Richard stared first at the black gloved hand extended to him, then into the depths of the resolute gray eyes.

"Aye, my lord," he said, locking his gauntleted hand to the Wolf's. "You have my word on it. My life as well."

"My lord La Seyne?" It was a high-pitched, child's voice, and it parted the sea of towering knights like a command on high.

"My lord La Seyne," said the little princess. "Will you be fighting the Dragon?"

"I will indeed, Your Grace."

"You will fight him and you will win, will you not?"

"I shall do my very best, Princess. You have my word on it."

"I require more than your word, my lord," she said, and for a moment, the Wolf's composure was shaken on the memory of another similar challenge.

"What is it you require, Your Grace?" he asked warily.

The little princess raised a finger and beckoned the massive, armoured knight to sink down onto his knee. Without a care for belts or buckles or moulded leather breastplates, she flung her arms around his neck and hugged until her cheeks flushed pink and her eyes filled with tears.

"*This* is what I require, my lord," she insisted. "Both now and later, after you have smote the Dragon from his lair. I—I *command* it."

The Wolf smiled and returned the hug. "Then certainly, it shall be as you command, Your Grace. You have my most solemn pledge."

25

When the Black Wolf of Lincoln had set up camp at Thornfeld Abbey, he had done so with twenty of his best and most versatile men. Both Gil Golden and Robert the Welshman had joined later, along with a few local villagers who had no scruples about where they earned the coin needed to feed their starving and oppressed families. The bulk of Randwulf de la Seyne Sur Mer's men had embarked from Brittany under the capable leadership of Sir Richard of Rouen, arriving in England more than two months after the Wolf had established himself in the forests of Lincoln. This second group numbered some eighty-five of the queen's trusted guard and, like their comrades who had adapted to their garb of lincoln green, would have followed their fearsome captain—the Scourge of Mirebeau—to the edge of the earth without question.

It had been Friar's suggestion to keep the two groups separate, and to have some of the original "outlaws" enter the castle grounds by various means and measures designed to blend them in with the guests and inhabitants of Bloodmoor. The rest of the "foresters" had been instructed to set up camp nearby and to alert those inside the castle should there be any sudden influx of either the sheriff's or the prince's men to the vicinity.

Alaric had also suggested his own disguise, the vestments and trappings acquired from the real Bishop Gautier, who was at that moment a guest in a nearby village. It was a risky

business, shared by the six companions who had assumed the
roles of clerics. Balancing out the danger, however, was the
fact that he would be able to get close to Lady Servanne, and
to remain close in the event of some unforeseen trouble aris-
ing.

Unfortunately it also meant he would be pressed upon to
preside over morning mass for the visiting nobles, and to
remain prominently in attendance in the great hall until such
time as the host chose to depart for the tournament grounds.

Thus, dressed in magnificent black and crimson robes, Alaric was accompanying the Dragon's party to the outer bailey even as the wooden cell door was being slammed and
bolted shut behind the semiconscious Servanne de Briscourt.
He was not concerned. He was, in fact, relieved to see she
had been able to follow Lucien's instructions and persuade
the Dragon to leave the main keep without her.

The rest of the Wolf's men were not so assured by what
they were seeing. They all paused in what they were doing to
stare in amazement at the black and gold crested knights of
Lord Randwulf de la Seyne Sur Mer's guard who filed slowly
out of the massive castle gates. In their midst was a child
with bright blonde hair and regally uptilted chin, but nowhere in the heavily armoured troop of men was there a
sighting of a black silk hood.

"What do you suppose it means?" Sparrow asked Gil.

Gil shook her head, her eyes worriedly searching the four-
abreast riders for Friar's face. She was still in her monk's
robes, her vision tunneled and restricted by the shape of the
hood, but she was fairly certain she had seen all of the
knights' faces, and Alaric FitzAthelstan's was not among
them.

Sparrow, perched on a cart loaded with straw, looked
enough like a pixie in his garishly coloured jongleur's tunic
to draw the eye of several of the grim-faced knights who rode

past. His frowned question drew no answers; a great deal of smouldering anger and frustration, but no answers.

"Something has gone wrong," he surmised sagely. "Have the tents been struck?"

"Nay," said Robert the Welshman, bending to dislodge a pebble from the sole of his shoe. He was passing by the cart, not wanting to draw any more attention to the peculiar sight of a dwarfish imp and a monk standing together. "Nay. I were just by the green and the tents are still in place. Pennants an' shields as well, an' a squire scrubbin' at a bit o' armour. Summit's amiss, though. Ye can smell it in the air."

He moved on, his mantle furling out from his brawny shoulders like the wake after a broad-beamed ship. He strolled casually into one of the small cramped laneways and peered over the heads of others who were vying for grilled bits of rabbit, fish, and mutton.

"Trust Lumbergut to think only of his belly at a time like this," Sparrow muttered.

"If things have gone wrong, we will need Robert's strength," Gil pointed out. "We will all need our full strength and wits about us."

Sparrow gazed past Gil's shoulder and winced at the rusted shriek of the chains beginning to lower the huge portcullis gates back into place behind the last of the departed knights. At a glance, there were at least a score of guards on the gates and towers, all of whom were visibly armed and prepared for trouble.

Sparrow squinted up at the sky, noting the sun was directly overhead. "Aye, well, one of us had best find out what is *amiss*. And soon. Gil, you should not tarry here any longer. Root out Friar and see if his nose has sniffed a change in the wind. I shall tumble my way over to the tourney grounds and see what is what."

"What about us?" asked Mutter and Stutter in unison, poking their heads up from behind the cart.

"Gather as many of our men as you can lay a hand to and wean them on down to the common. Tell them to hold fast and watch for a signal."

"We will be of little use without weapons," Gil advised.

Sparrow nodded and patted the side of the cart. "Tell Robert to move this as close to the field as he dares and to leave a man on guard. And we had best be quick about our business, for unless my ears and eyes are turned inward, those trumpets I hear are heralding the arrival of Prince Gloom at the lists."

As the echo of the blaring fanfare drifted away on the sea breeze, Prince John and the Baron de Gournay took their seats in the spectators' bower. Noblemen and guests of honour—including the Bishop Gautier—filled the seats on either side of their host and the regent, their personal guards, squires, and servants crowded the limited space behind them. Nicolaa de la Haye, assuming her role as high sheriff, sat by the Dragon's side, conspicuously taking the seat allocated for the absent Servanne de Briscourt.

The morning's activities, which had included wrestling matches, archery contests, and demonstrations of skill with swords and quarterstaffs, had attracted only a smattering of interest from the ranking nobles. These events were staged mainly for the entertainment of the castle inhabitants, whose fingers had snapped enthusiastically for each victor, and whose groans and hisses had followed the defeated off the field. As the morning progressed, the excitement and tension swelled proportionately, and as noon approached, the litters and carts began arriving with more and more jewelled and ornamented spectators. The Bower of Beauty teemed with a riot of multicoloured silks and wafting wimples. Targets and quintains were moved to the sides of the field and the wooden palisades brought forward to replace them front and centre.

The jousting matches were by far the most dangerous and titilating events and those who had deigned to forgo the morning activities in favour of extra sleep or extravagant preening, now eagerly craned their necks this way and that to catch glimpses of the preparations taking place at each end of the enclosure. Tables laden with food and ale for the guests were all but deserted as everyone hastened to find seats and points of vantage. The trumpets flared again, bringing a hush over the crowds as the first two challengers appeared in front of their pavilions.

"How many impartial eyes do you estimate?" the Wolf asked, adjusting the metal chausses on his thighs.

"Two hundred guests and nobles at the least," Sparrow replied. "Perhaps twice as many retainers, servants, and folk from the castle village, although most of those have been herded higher on the bailey grounds, away from the field. It is the number of guards that worries me. Like bluebirds they are, perched everywhere. On the walls, roaming the crowds, stalking the pavilions. Robert says he smells trouble and I believe him."

"Robert has a keen nose," the Wolf remarked.

Sparrow plumped his hands on his hips and scowled his disapproval over ill-placed humour. He had found their leader in the least likely place he had anticipated finding him: in his pavilion by the jousting fields. More alarming, he was alone, save for a handful of squires and groomsmen, none of whom Sparrow recognized.

"I expected someone to tell me you were dead," he stated bluntly.

"My apologies for disobliging you."

Sparrow's glittering black eyes narrowed. "We watched the men leaving the castle. You could have told us you had changed plans."

"The change was not at my request," said the Wolf, meeting Sparrow's gaze for the first time. A shocking, indescribable fury flashed in the depths of the normally cool and steely gray orbs, and the sight of it made the breath catch in Sparrow's throat.

"What happened? What has gone wrong?"

The Wolf needed a moment to compose himself. In a half-snarl he related the morning's confrontations, first with Prince John, then with the Dragon Wardieu. "I could not very well refuse his offer to release the Princess Eleanor," he concluded harshly. "Nor could I consider leaving myself until this matter is resolved between us."

"Which he counted upon, of course."

"Of course."

"How did he discover your secret?" Sparrow asked darkly.

"Not the way you think," the Wolf snapped. "And not the way he would have me believe."

"Forgive me, my lord, but are you so convinced of the chick-pea's loyalty?"

In lieu of answering, the Wolf crossed over to the door of the pavilion and snatched the silk flap aside enough for a clear view of the sprawling tilting grounds. He scanned the seats in the main bower, easily identifying the Dragon and his maleficent consort, Nicolaa de la Haye. Seated on the other side of De Gournay was an inordinately subdued John Lackland, and to his left, the Bishop Gautier.

Friar's expression was placid enough, yet it was obvious to a familiar eye that he was beginning to notice oddities and incongruities around him. There were distinctly more guards present in the crowds and on the sides of the field than was usual. And where there should have been discreet placements of black and gold blazons, there were none.

"Our men?" the Wolf asked.

"What few we have are well placed," Sparrow assured him. "They will do nothing without your signal."

"They will do nothing at all. The Lady Servanne's life depends upon it."

Sparrow flinched at the wrath in the Wolf's voice. His own words came back to haunt him: *Who fights the hardest also falls the farthest.* He had been referring to the Lady Servanne's probability of succumbing to the Wolf's powers of persuasion. Never, in his wildest imaginings had he considered the opposite happening.

"Where is she now?"

"I do not know. My guess is the Dragon has her hidden away somewhere within the castle." The Wolf turned from the door and Sparrow's belly plummeted to his feet. "I never should have taken the chance with her life. I never should have let her leave the abbey, never should have met her last night, *never should have touched her!*"

God's rood, he was rambling! Rambling and lovesick, drowning in emotions Sparrow suspected he had blocked from his senses for so many years, he was unable to deal with them. Revenge and hatred had been the cornerstones of the impenetrable wall the reborn La Seyne Sur Mer had erected around his heart. Guilt, love, even feelings of jealousy were as foreign to him as hands on a fish and he was just as helpless to know what to do with them.

Moreover, it was beyond conceivable thought to imagine what his reaction might be if these newfound emotions were found to have no basis in truth. If his love was betrayed or deceived, if his trust was spurned and his loyalty mocked, it would surely destroy him. It would destroy every other living thing around him as well, for his rage, if unleashed, would know no bounds.

Sparrow took a deep breath and forced a calmness in his voice he was far from feeling. "Hidden her away, you say? Even in a castle this size, the walls have ears and the windows have eyes. Someone will have seen where he put her. It is a challenge, make no mistake, but one I will embark upon willingly, if only to save myself the misery of listening to you bay at the moon each night . . . unless, of course, you plan to spare us all the trouble of planning our futures by ignoring the task before you?"

The Wolf flexed and unflexed his fists. His gaze remained clouded and unresponsive, his pain seeking the only outlet it knew: violence.

"Your brother is strong and dangerous," the little man continued, blithely ignoring the bloodlust etched into the Wolf's face. "He did not come by his reputation by chance or by underestimating his enemies. Proof thereof lies in the fact his spies were able to ferret out the identity of Randwulf de la Seyne Sur Mer."

Keep talking, Sparrow told himself. *Do not think of the size of his fists.*

"You have prepared well for this day, but there are always the tinkerings of Luck, Fate, and Destiny to contend with. We shall have to put them out of the way at once by offering them no opportunities to interfere. Smite the Dragon square on the visor, the heart, or the gut. Unhorse him on the first pass and waste no breath on the niceties of honour or chivalry. He will be out to skewer you as clean and sure, make no mistake. Have you recalled all of his weaknesses? Do you remember if he favours aiming for the left or the right side? The shoulder or the chest? The arm or the thigh? One thing to our advantage: Unless he has found himself another left-handed opponent to tilt with him throughout the years, he will be out of practice, whereas you, my lord, will face nothing new or awkward in the list. Is Triton groomed and ready, or has he managed to frighten these blundernoses into adding their own dung to the stable heaps?"

"He is behaving," the Wolf said slowly.

"Good. I shall whisper a word or two in his ear anyway, to be sure he knows his business."

Sparrow's chatter had had its desired effect. The killing

rage had not completely faded from the Wolf's eyes, but at least it was now being channeled in a healthier direction. He thrust aside the flap of the tent once again and fixed his gaze on the Dragon of Bloodmoor Keep, his thoughts focused solely on their pending confrontation.

The bells on Sparrow's collar tinkled as he moved forward and stalked a loose thong he had noticed on the Wolf's hauberk.

"There are twenty matches scheduled for the afternoon," he said, frowning as he checked the laces, buckles, and belts of the Black Wolf's armour. "Three of the early ones are with some lout from Nottinghamshire—Guy de Gisbourne. He will be fighting in place of Sir Aubrey de Vere, who, as we well know, met with an unfortunate accident in the woods. Gisbourne is another dog who strives to lick Jack Lack's backside with admirable energy. He is also skilled and dangerous in the saddle, but I am told he finds the act of thinking too strenuous and prefers not to do it too often. Mark him well anyway if there is trouble."

"*If* there is trouble?" The Wolf dropped the flap back in place. "I admire your gift for understatement."

"Bah! You act as if you hold some doubt as to whether or not you can oust the Dragon from his lair."

"A man without doubts is a fool and could find himself making mistakes."

"Then let us hope the Dragon is as fine a fool as he has proven to be so far."

Sparrow's attempt to bluster his way through a smile faltered noticeably as the Wolf reached down and gripped his slender shoulders.

"She must be found, my little friend. Regardless of what happens here this afternoon, she must be found and removed from this place, for she would not survive a month in his keeping."

Sparrow laid his hand overtop the Wolf's. "We will save

your lady, my lord, or we will all perish in the trying; you have my word on it. Let that be one less worry you take with you onto the field." He paused and gave the matter an extra moment of debate before peering up through his long black lashes. "Does that mean we are bound to rescue Old Blister as well? 'Twould cause a man or two to balk at the notion, I warrant, for she'd be as sour being saved as sullied."

The Wolf almost grinned. "Admit it: You have missed having her around to box your ears and order you about."

"Bah! Poxy trull! I should have drowned her in the pool when I had the chance and saved us all a deal of aggravation."

The Wolf smiled. "Aggravate yourself some more, Puck, and lend a hand with the rest of my armour. I would dress early and enjoy the show a while."

26

The first pair of challengers were announced by the herald and called to horse. Sir Guy de Gisbourne, fighting on behalf of the host, appeared at one end of the lists, his rampager draped in blue and armoured almost as heavily as his rider. The knight wore De Gournay's colours, a sky-blue gypon overtopping oiled chain mail and a breastplate of polished steel. His shoulders, arms, thighs, calves, and knees were armoured by protective steel plates as well, and he carried a kite-shaped shield emblazoned with his own family crest and colours. The helm he wore covered all but a narrow strip across the eyes, which would be subsequently protected when the slitted visor was lowered into place. A towering blue plume danced above the peak of the helm, matching the flamboyant plumes woven into his steed's mane and tail.

Gisbourne's opponent was a visiting knight who had issued the challenge in the hopes of settling a claim over a disputed parcel of land. Mixing business with entertainment was an acceptable way of resolving such matters. The winner would take clear title of the land; the loser would forfeit all future claims along with the customary surrender of his armour and weapons.

After their formal progress around the field, the challengers took up their positions at opposite ends of the list and waited for the signal from the dais. There was a flourish of trumpets while Prince John raised the ceremonial gold arrow above his head; his hand flashed downward and the destriers were spurred into action, charging down the narrow lane, converging at a point midway along the field in a clash of steel and rampaging horseflesh.

Gisbourne's lance struck the challenger's breastplate and unseated the valiant knight on the first pass.

A groan of disappointment rippled through the crowds of spectators at so ignoble a beginning to the afternoon's activities. Wagers grudgingly changed hands and a fresh flurry of excitement began to rise as the defeated knight was helped from the field. The next pair of challengers survived two passes before a victor was declared, the third went the limit of three charges and had to be decided by the panel of impartial judges.

Gisbourne settled his second dispute as effortlessly as the first, and his opponent not only had to forfeit his gear and destrier in the loss, but broke both his legs in the tumble from the saddle. The eighth and ninth pair were unexceptional, prompting the crowd to hiss and jeer at their lack of nerve. Gisbourne took to the palisades for his third and final victory of the day, leaving the field with narry a scratch to armour or flesh.

By this time, the noise and frenzy was reaching a fevered pitch. A cheer swelled and burst as the Dragon de Gournay stood and bowed, his smile promising a good show as he took his leave of the dais. Scarcely an eye was not on his broad back as he made his way to the pavilion to prepare. Those same eyes, alerted by a pointed finger and a gasp of recognition, swept to the black silk tent that stood a little apart from the others. A huge, jet-black beast was being led toward the pavilion, his hooves prancing and pawing his impatience. Caparisoned all in black, it could have been the Devil's rampager save for the startling contrast of the snow-white mane and tail. These were left unbraided and unfettered by bows and feathers, the hair brushed sleek and shiny so that on each toss of the tapered head, it lashed the air like white wind.

Men and women alike watched the remainder of the matches with one eye on the jousting fields and one eye on the far end of the enclosure. When the last pair clashed, tumbled from their saddles, and prolonged their battle on the ground with swords and mace, the spectators grew so incensed by the delay they pelted the combatants with orange peels, figs, and (from the commoners) clods of dung. Hastened into accidentally slitting the throat of his rival, the winning knight limped from the field and promptly broke his sword over the head of a bystander he considered too vocal during the fray.

Hardly anyone noticed this minor drama as a tense hush gripped the crowd. Pennants snapping in the breeze and the sound of a hammer reinforcing a broken length of the palisade were heard as clearly as if the arena were empty of human life. One by one, little murmurs broke the silence, fortified by anxious whispers and frantic wagering. A cheer went up from the crowded hillside as the flap of the black silk pavilion was lifted aside; a corresponding uproar rose from the bowers as red-faced squires cleared a path for the challenger.

At first glance, the Scourge of Mirebeau was well named and no less ominous in appearance than his fiery-eyed steed. Garbed head to toe in black, he drew gasps from all sectors, for even his armour had been tempered a gleaming ebony by some sorcerer's hand. His breastplate, vambrace, and gorget had been hammered with breathtaking precision to mould around the massive musculature of chest and shoulders; his chausses seemed to bulge with the power in his thighs. The visor on his helm was already lowered, sparing the more faint-hearted beauties the necessity of swooning and possibly missing a moment of the excitement.

He was assisted into the saddle of his destrier by two ner-

vous squires and a terrified groomsman. Not a morsel of
food was chewed nor a mouthful of ale supped while the
black knight took up his weapons: a steel lance twenty feet
long and tapered to a deadly spearhead at one end, and a
huge black bat-wing of a shield emblazoned with the snarling
figurehead of a wolf wrought in gold.

On his command, the destrier paced forward, mane and
tail streaming white against the uncompromising black. The
fount of dark plumes on Mirebeau's helm danced up and
down with each prancing step as the ranks of the spectators
melted back, their hands sweaty, their mouths lax with awe.
He completed his progress around the field in total silence,
breaking only once from a stately gait to pause before the
dais and tip his lance in a mocking salute to the regent.
Formalities observed, he then steered his horse back to the
end of the palisades to await the appearance of his opponent.

A second murmur, like a swarm of bees passing over a
meadow, buzzed through the crowd, surging into a rousing
tribute as Lord Wardieu, Baron de Gournay stepped out of
his tent into the bright wash of sunlight. The hearts of the
women fluttered wildly within their breasts as he lifted a
mailed gauntlet in salute. His armour shone like the purest
silver, his raiment was blue enough to rival the colour of the
skies. Bareheaded, his hair shone gold against the bronzed
glory of his tanned complexion, and a swoon or two could
not be avoided as he raised the hood of his mail *coif* and
accepted the polished steel helm from his squire.

With a casual glance toward the waiting black knight, he
mounted his destrier—an enormous beast, as white and
fierce as the driven snow—and took his own weapons to
hand. By the time he had completed his progress, the voices
of those who had been the most raucous and scornful
throughout the long afternoon were struck dumb.

En masse, the crowd leaned forward as the herald, dressed

in a parti-coloured tunic and plumed cap, proclaimed the nature of this, the final contest of the day.

"In the king's name," he declared solemnly, "a test of skill between Lord Randwulf de la Seyne Sur Mer, and Lord Lucien Wardieu, Baron de Gournay. The winner of this bout—"

"The winner of this bout," shouted Prince John from the dais, "will be decided by God's mercy. The fight will be to the death. The participants have waived the limit of three passes, as well as any and all restrictions pertaining to weaponry and tactics. Any foul is hereby declared fair; any rule may thus be broken."

The guests, momentarily too stunned to react, glanced from one end of the list to the other. From his seat on the dais, Friar felt a disturbing prickle of apprehension chill his flesh. A quick glance around the borders of the field—surely the only pair of eyes not glued to the combatants—confirmed his earlier suspicion that all was not what it should be. There were far too many of De Gournay's guards present, and now, acting on some unseen signal, they were pressing forward, forming a solid wall of steel and bullhide around the field. Here and there a familiar face, paled by indecision, looked to Friar for guidance, but he could only warn them against any rash action with a slight shake of his head.

"Further," the regent continued in his most pompous manner, "it has also come to our attention that this is no mere challenge of valour and skill, but a pitting of one man's honour against another. And since a knight's name and honour are those things which he should value most above all else, it has been agreed by both parties that the winner shall take all: trophies of armour and gear, as well as lands, titles, and such wealth as both men have acquired through purchase or battle during their lifetimes. Before God and His witnesses, is it so agreed?"

A flurry of shocked gasps was marked by a general, swirling collapse of delicate figures in the Bower of Beauty.

"I will abide by God's decision," the Wolf said promptly.

"Or die by it," the Dragon declared, and reached up to drop his slitted visor into place.

The herald, an astonished bystander to this point, looked from one end of the lists to the other as the two knights readied themselves for the final confrontation. He started to raise a hand to signal the trumpeters, but reconsidered the gesture as being too flamboyant. He opened his mouth to call the challengers to horse, but since they were already mounted and armed, he thrust his tongue to the side of his cheek and kept his silence. In the end, he slinked back into the lee of the dais and left it up to Prince John to loose the combatants.

The Dragon adjusted the weight and balance of the long, wickedly barbed steel lance he carried, and a keen eye among the spectators launched a fresh volley of wagering. The Dragon couched the twenty-foot shaft of deadly steel on his right side, directly in line with the approach of the opposing rider. The black knight, it was observed with a cry of amazement, favoured the left, making it necessary to angle the lance over the front of his saddle. A wrong step by his charger, a swerve or a veer at the last moment and the tip of the lance would stray wildly off the course.

The Wolf, seemingly unconcerned over the flurry of new speculation swelling in the bowers, affected a last-minute adjustment to the fit of his mail gauntlets. His armour, like the Dragon's, consisted of many plates of steel linked together over a quilted leather surcoat. This, in turn, was worn over a full hauberk of chain mail, and in combination, was like carrying the additional weight of a slender man on his body. His shoulders were covered by metal spaulders, his arms were sheathed in a jointed vambrace. Hammered and molded cuisses, poleyns, and greaves shielded his thighs, knees, and

lower legs, but even though the armour would deflect most
of the potential damage of a combatant's blow, there was
nothing but flesh and muscle to absorb the horrendous shock
of impact. Massive bruising could cripple a man at shoulder,
elbow, or knee even through the layers of link, hide, and
steel, and if an opponent became aware of the weakness, he
could strike again and again at the vulnerable point until his
adversary fell.

Both knights waited, planned, calculated. Their chargers
were still as statues, their armour and silk trappings glinting
in the sunlight.

Prince John stood, the golden arrow raised above his head
for all to see. With his black eyes narrowed against the glare
of the lowering sun, and his face reflecting avaricious delight,
he brought his arm arcing swiftly downward, giving the
command for the two destriers to spring into action.

In a matter of a few heartbeats, the two beasts had thundered to the midway point of the lists, their riders leaning
forward, intent upon the approaching threat. The unblunted
tips of the two lances lifted at precisely the same moment
and converged into a single line of unbroken steel for a split
second before a tremendous crash and scream of metal sent
the horses buckling and the riders staggering to maintain
their balance.

The crowd held its breath, then released it in a long, low
groan as men and horses separated and galloped to the end
of the lists unscathed. Both tossed away broken or splintered
lances and called for new ones. Wheeling their destriers
around, they set themselves for a second pass, and this time
it was the Dragon who reached the halfway marker first, his
lance a notch higher and bolder in its objective to strike for
the blackened visor.

The Wolf had to think and react quickly as he saw the
flash of steel fill his limited field of sight. He raised his own
lance at the last possible moment and hooked it to the inside

edge of De Gournay's, locking the two shafts together, and
creating a fiery shower of sparks from the searing friction.
The Dragon had no choice but to release his grip on the
lance, or risk having his arm torn away at the shoulder.

Furious and cursing, he rode to the end of the list and
screamed for a new weapon. He spurred his horse back into
the cloud of hot dust boiling between the palisades, his rage
launching him like a bolt of blue and silver thunder, back
into the fray. His lance struck a solid blow to the Wolf's
shoulder, gouging through the links of his spaudler and rip-
ping away a goodly chunk of leather and cotton padding
from the surcoat below. On their next pass, he aimed for the
same spot but missed by several inches, the barbed end of his
lance careening wildly off the Wolf's angled shield.

On each successive pass the crowd cheered louder. Each
crash of horseflesh, steel, and raw power sent ribbons of silk
waving madly over heads and pale, trembling hands clutching over hearts. The Wolf warded off devastating blows to his
chest and shoulders; the Dragon shook off crushing thrusts
to ribs, shoulders, and thighs. Neither rode as straight or as
steady as they had during the first run, but neither showed
signs of conceding. They were tiring, however, and weaken-
ing. Even their horses were taking longer strides to turn and
recoup for the next charge.

Three . . . five . . . *seven* passes! Unbelievable! The
crowd was on its feet, stunned by the display of courage and
strength.

The horses converged again, their mouths flecked with
foam and blood, their eyes round and wild with fighting
madness. When the clash came, the lances locked again and
the knights were driven together, neither one willing to give
ground, not even when the animals beneath them reared and
thrashed and pounded the dividing palisade into a heap of
split kindling. Shields hammered into one another and the

two knights abandoned their saddles, eager to bring the fight to closer contact.

Into the choking dust and flying debris was added the deadly glitter of longswords. Within a grinding maelstrom of screaming, pawing horses, their blades hacked and slashed at vulnerable areas of back, neck, shoulder, arm, and thigh. Links were shattered and rivets torn apart; plates of armour were dented, loosened and sliced away by the fury of killing thrusts. Splashes of sweat and blood began to spatter the ground; a thigh was sliced, an arm cut, shields were thrown away and swords gripped in both hands as an end drew inevitably nearer.

The Dragon took a staggering blow to the side of his helm and felt himself reel sideways into a shifting mass of horseflesh. The Wolf pursued and was on him in the next instant, throwing the full brunt of his weight into the effort needed to bring his adversary to the ground. With the roar of the crowd's bloodlust in his ears, he succeeded. He heard the Dragon's breath wrenched from his lungs on a curse of agony as the two landed solidly on the torn earth, then a further curse of outraged disbelief as the Wolf drove the point of his sword into the narrow gap between the Dragon's helm and gorget.

His chest heaving and his lungs scalded from lack of air, the Wolf exerted enough pressure on his sword to convince his brother to freeze where he lay. His wounds stung and his muscles screamed in pain; the scarred flesh of his shoulder, back, and ribs demanded vengeance, swift and sure. Etienne's visor had been jolted loose in the fall, and the wild, pale blue eyes that stared up at him in disbelieving terror were the same cold blue eyes that had once stared down in triumph at the broken and bleeding body he had left to rot in the desert sun.

"Why?" Lucien demanded. "Just tell me why you did it, Etienne!"

The Dragon's mouth opened, closed, and opened again. "Forgive me, Lucien. I beg you, forgive me."

"What? *What did you say?*"

The Dragon gasped, braced for death. "Forgive me. The truth is . . . I am relieved to finally be free of the guilt I have carried with me all these years. Carried it, hated it, loathed the envy and jealousy that drove me to commit such a heinous act. You were my brother, Lucien, and I killed you. I do not blame you for doing this—"

"Blame me?" the Wolf snarled. "*Blame* me? I will die a happy man knowing you do not *blame* me, you soulless bastard!"

The sword moved forward and Etienne sucked a last breath through his teeth. Their eyes were locked together, blue merging with gray, gray with blue until each became a part of the other. Memories, unbidden and unwanted, struck with the swiftness of a second blade—memories of a lifetime ago, of happy times and shared laughter. For one unsettling moment, the Wolf suffered an image of the two of them practicing at a quintain, their youthful arms barely strong enough to lift a lance let alone aim it at the centre of the fixed target.

"You were my brother and I loved you!" the Wolf cried. "I would have shared it all willingly with you!"

"All but the name, Lucien," the Dragon whispered. "Mine would always have been bastard."

The Wolf's fists trembled, but they could not push the blade of his sword the extra fraction of an inch needed to thrust steel and chain and windpipe into a crush of bloodied tissue and bone. A curse, given on a roar of anguish, saw him lift the sword away and heave it across the shattered wall of the list, a bright, cartwheeling glitter of pitted steel and hollow revenge.

"Before God, I cannot kill you," he said hoarsely. "I cannot forgive you, but I cannot kill you either. It will be enough to have the truth come out at last."

Etienne raised himself on his elbow, then onto his knees. His one hand massaged the bruised flesh of his throat, his other shuffled through the dust beside him and grasped the hilt of his sword. Drawing on every last ounce of avarice and hatred he possessed, the Dragon brought the sword up over his head, and, with the Wolf already turned to walk away, he brought the heavy blade down solidly across the base of Lucien's skull.

The Wolf pitched forward, his senses erupting in a blinding sheet of pain. His body went completely numb and would not respond to any command, not even when he felt the presence of Etienne looming over him.

"I did not think you could kill a man who begged your forgiveness" he sneered, "regardless of his crime. Coward! Weakling! You do not belong here anymore. Bloodmoor is mine, and I will not share it with a ghost, however noble he might be."

He lowered the point of his sword, resting the tip just over the steel lip of the Wolf's visor. A brief thrust, a surge of sweet vengeance and it would be over . . . but too quick! *Too quick,* Etienne told himself. There was still the promise he made Servanne de Briscourt to repay her deceit and treachery. It *would* please him to see them die together. To hear their screams. To feel their blood run hot and slick over his hands.

A thrill, carnally delicious in intensity, swept through Etienne and he straightened, raising his voice with the triumph of a conqueror.

"Guards! Seize this man! He is a coward and murderer and has come to Bloodmoor under false pretenses!"

"False pretenses?" Prince John was quick to leap to his feet and feign outrage over De Gournay's actions. "What

manner of false pretenses could justify the arrest of Sir
Randwulf de la Seyne Sur Mer?"

"This man"—the Dragon pointed a contemptuous finger
at the dazed, semiconscious knight at his feet—"has committed crimes against the crown—crimes which include the ambush and murder of honest men, and the kidnapping of my
own bride. All in the name of *the Black Wolf of Lincoln*!"

A roar of disbelief swept through the spectators, rumbling
down to an angry murmur as the Dragon again held up his
hand for silence.

"Further, there is proof he intended harm not only to myself, but to you, my liege!" The piercing blue eyes sought out
the prince and demanded corroboration. "I have reason to
believe he was sent to England to raise his hand against the
very crown itself!"

John gasped, finding it difficult not to applaud the Dragon's performance. "You say you have proof of these charges,
Lord Wardieu—where is it?"

"It begins here." With a boldly dramatic flourish, the
Dragon leaned over and removed the Wolf's black helm. The
crowd gasped, their shock hanging in the air as they recognized the obvious deceit verified by the unscarred, unblemished face that was angled roughly toward them for inspection.

When the silence threatened to linger too long, Nicolaa de
la Haye jumped to her feet beside Prince John. She had to
lean on the rail for support, for she was experiencing the
same erotic throes of pleasure she could see glazing Etienne's
features. Her limbs trembled and her belly spasmed. The
gratification shivered down her thighs as she raised her fist
and incited the crowd to join her screams of: "Treason! Dog!
Arrest him!"

Prince John was given no choice but to nod his head in
complete agreement. "Arrest him. We shall get to the bottom
of this treachery . . . one way or another."

The wall of guards surged forward and swarmed over the fallen knight. Still reeling from the blow to his head, the Wolf was dragged from the enclosure and taken away in chains to the castle donjon.

Friar sat in stunned silence, unable to move, hardly able to believe what he had just seen and heard. There had been no time, no chance to react to Etienne Wardieu's charade, and to a man, the Wolf's knights had stood helplessly by and watched their leader carried from the field in chains. Prince John was already embellishing the lies by speculating over political motivations. Alaric only half-listened; to pay full heed might have been temptation enough to assassinate the gloating regent himself.

He was more concerned over the whereabouts of Gil, Sparrow, and the others. Sparrow had appeared briefly in front of the Wolf's pavilion, but had successfully vanished in the crowd. Robert the Welshman, normally visible by virtue of his height and bulk alone, had melted back into the ring of spectators and either taken cover in the nearby stables, or had been caught doing something reckless—like attempting to rescue the Wolf singlehandedly—and lay dead somewhere with his good intentions spilling out onto the cobblestones.

Friar was no less reassured to see a detachment of guards sent at once to reinforce the sentries on the main gates. Was the Dragon assuming his brother had had the foresight to ensure the presence of a few friendly faces in the crowd? Or was he just taking normal precautions against the sympathy of the general rabble? La Seyne Sur Mer, as the dowager's champion, had been the favorite of the commoners. The Black Wolf of Lincoln, brave, bold, and daring in his exploits against the tyranny of De Gournay and the regent's tax collectors, was more simply put, their hero. To have the two legendary rogues revealed as being one and the same man, had brought upwards of two hundred angry, rebellious bodies crushing against the bars of the iron portcullis gates.

Fear they might break in was ludicrous, therefore it must mean the Dragon was wary of anyone else breaking out.

The guests began to disperse from the field. The ladies departed on cushioned litters, returning to the main keep by the same method they had been carried forth. Some of the nobles rode as well—horses or litters—and took away their flocks of servants and retainers in the process. Prince John was among the first group to leave the dais, but delayed his return to the keep long enough to stop at the Dragon's pavilion and offer his congratulations. There, the castle chirurgeon was busy sewing and bandaging the lord's wounds, plucking out pieces of iron link that had become embedded in cut flesh, clucking and frowning over bruises that had turned the underlying pads of muscle into mush. Most of the injuries were slight; only one caused a flurry of clacking tongues and fingers, and a suggestion to attach leeches to drain off any possible threat of infection.

Friar was one of the last to leave the covered dais. He started to walk toward the rows of pavilions and stared, as he did so, at the empty field, now strewn with garbage, debris from the broken palisades, and clods of uprooted grass and dirt from the horses' churning hooves. He tried to think, tried to place himself inside the Wolf's head to devise a plan for rescuing the captured knight, but nothing crystalized. They were vastly outnumbered. They had been outmaneuvered once and would be again, for without the Wolf's knowledge of the castle grounds, they could search for a week without ever discovering the donjon where he was being held.

And a week was too long by any man's guess.

"My lord bishop—a word with you?"

Friar's attention was startled away from the field by the sound of a man's gruff voice over his shoulder. He turned and could not completely quell a chill of foreboding as he came face-to-face with an armed knight and three brawny guardsmen. The knight looked vaguely familiar with his long, thin nose, deep-set eyes, and coarsely unpleasant features, but for the moment, his blazon of scarlet and yellow eluded identity. As casually as he could, Friar clasped his hands together within the voluminous cuffs of his bishop's robes and nodded a formal greeting.

"Do I know you, sir knight?"

"You might. If you were in the forest a sennight ago and part of a band of rogues who ambushed innocent travelers . . . you might know me."

Friar's right hand inched toward the dagger he had strapped to the inside of his other wrist. The act was concealed by his sleeves, yet the knight detected the movement and grasped a hand around Friar's wrist, knife and all, effectively spoiling the intent.

"I would have a word with you in private, my lord bishop," said the knight again, his voice a low rumble of authority. "You have nothing to fear from me, unless of course, Mistress Bidwell has been duped out of her senses—which I suspect she has—and has asked me to seek help from the wrong quarter."

"Mistress Bidwell? . . . *Biddy*?"

The knight scowled and squeezed Friar's wrist to the point of making the hand swell and turn bright red before he released it. "I gave her my word to seek you out, and seek you out I have. Now, by God, you will come with me or you will die here by your own misfortune."

Friar glanced past the knight's shoulder and shook his head quickly at someone who had stepped out from behind a small, straw-filled cart. The knight, sensing the threat, whirled around, as did the three guards, only to find themselves staring down the shaft of a slender ashwood arrow. The "monk" holding the bow was tall and slim; his cowl had slipped back to reveal a shock of bright copper curls and an even more shocking scar down the left side of his face.

The three guards reached instinctively for the hilts of their swords, but a harsh command from the knight stopped them.

"You," he snarled, staring into Gil Golden's amber eyes. "I know you, by God. You were the one who did this—" Sir Roger de Chesnai smacked his thigh just above the bulge of padding that distorted the fit of his hose. His expression grew blacker as he swept his gaze along the length of Gil's robes. "Aye, 'tis well you hid yourself behind the church's cowl, for I would have scarred the other half of your head for you by now."

"You can still try," Gil said calmly. "Although I stopped your boastings once with ease."

"A lucky shot," De Chesnai growled.

The tip of the steel arrowhead swerved up and held unwaveringly to an imagined target dead centre of De Chesnai's brow. "No luckier than the shot I could use now to send your eyeball out the back of your skull."

"Christ on a cross," Friar muttered. "This is hardly the time for petty vanities. Kill each other later if you have a mind to, but for the moment, could we all set our differences aside and find the answers to some questions? Sir Roger de Chesnai—aye, I have fixed a name to the face—you are one of Sir Hubert's men?"

De Chesnai continued to glower at Gil while he nodded. "Sir Hubert's man, and now the Lady Servanne's."

The feeling of dread that should have dissipated upon identifying Sir Roger had not alleviated in the least, and now Friar knew why.

"Lady Servanne . . . has something happened to her?"

"Alaric—" Gil's voice interrupted before the knight could reply. "I tried to reach you before you took your seat on the dais, but you were so close to Prince John, and there were too many people about."

"Has something happened to Lady Servanne?"

"Not here," De Chesnai commanded coldly. "A dozen pairs of eyes could be on us, and an equal number of prickling ears. And for God's sake, tell this red-haired bastard to lower his bow before we are all done for."

"Gil—" Friar signaled her to put up the longbow, and grudgingly she obeyed. On a further thought, she set both bow and arrow aside long enough to shrug out of the monk's robes, which were now a greater hindrance than a disguise.

"The old woman is hidden nearby," said De Chesnai. "It is best you hear all from her. Come. She may be holding on to life by a thread as it is; we can waste no more time."

Alaric hesitated, wary of a trap. There had been no love lost between the old harridan and the Black Wolf; there was certainly no reason to trust Sir Roger de Chesnai, who still walked with a slight limp thanks to Gil's aim. It could be a ruse, designed to catch Friar and lure out of hiding any others who were taking refuge amongst the castle inhabitants.

"All right," Friar said. "Lead the way. But be advised there are more than a few steady hands pulling back on bowstrings as we wend our way through the shadows."

De Chesnai's eyes narrowed, but he said nothing more. He beckoned his three men to fall into step behind him and started walking swiftly toward the castle's cramped streets of smoky workshops. He followed a twisted route into the heart of the noisy, crowded labyrinth until they arrived at the start of armourers' alley.

As hectic a place as it had been the previous nights, it was all but deserted now. The forges were cold in the smithies, the men all off somewhere celebrating their craftsmanship and skill. De Chesnai headed for one particularly dismal-looking bothy and again Friar paused, acutely conscious of how conspicuous he appeared in his black and crimson robes.

On a command from De Chesnai, the three guards dispersed, strolling casually to take up positions overlooking the approaches to the bothy. Gil had melted into one of the snickleways long ago, but reappeared now to give Friar a reassuring nod.

"There are no eyes but our own watching us," she announced, and smugly arched her brow in De Chesnai's direction.

Bristling at the insult to his integrity, the knight thrust aside the ragged bit of canvas that served as a door. "Inside, the pair of you. And there had best be no tricks, or I will be the first to twist a knife in your gizzards."

Friar ducked through the doorway, followed by Gil and Sir Roger. The bothy was windowless and airless, the stench of raw bog iron nearly as overpowering to their throat and eyes as the tang of animal urine in the filthy straw. What light there was came through gaps in the thatched roof and holes in the canvas door.

Biddy was lying on a pallet in the corner, and at first glance, she was so pale and still, Alaric thought she was dead.

"Biddy?" He dropped down onto a knee beside her and took up one of her ice cold hands in his. "Mistress Bidwell? Can you hear me?"

Biddy cracked open an eyelid. It took a moment for her to bring Friar's face into focus, but when she did, she squeezed his hand with more strength than he would have supposed she possessed.

"What happened to you, Biddy?"

"Not important," she said, straining to form each word. "My lamb is all that matters now. You must find her and take her away from this terrible place."

"Find her? The lady is not in her chambers?"

"I was trying to tell you—" Gil blurted out, halted mid-sentence by the combined persuasion of De Chesnai's grip on her arm and the glowering warning in his eyes.

"The baron's men," Biddy gasped. "They took her away. Dragged her from the tower. He . . . hurt her dreadfully. He . . . struck her . . . again and again!"

Biddy's eyes rolled upward so that only the whites showed from between her shivering lashes. Her breathing was raspy and uneven, and Alaric, at a loss what to do to ease her pain, held her hand as tightly as he dared and suffered silently through the spasm with her.

"She managed somehow to crawl down from the tower and find me where I waited by a postern gate," De Chesnai explained in a murmur. "The effort cost her dearly, but she was determined not to die until I brought her to La Seyne Sur Mer."

"La Seyne?" Alaric looked up.

"Indeed. My men and I barely managed to bring her this far before the talebearers were blazing through the castle grounds with the news of De Gournay's victory. Since her first choice was obviously out of reach, she insisted upon you."

Friar glanced back down at Biddy. Her eyes were open and clear, save for the tears that flowed in a fat stream down her temples.

"He will kill her, Friar," she cried. "He means to torment her first, then kill her; I know he does. The same for poor Eduard—oh, the brave, brave lad! He tried to help, but he was no match for the Dragon. And because he is the Wolf's son, you can imagine how much pleasure it will give the baron to hurt him." A great shuddering sob racked Biddy's body before she added, "I dread to think how much more it will delight him to torture my poor lamb."

Friar shook his head as if to clear it of cobwebs. "Did you say . . . the Wolf's *son*?"

"Eduard. Young Eduard . . . the Dragon's squire. He has been taken away as well but wounded so mortally, I fear he cannot have lived out the hour."

"Do you know where he was taken? Do you know where the Lady Servanne was taken?"

Biddy swallowed hard and ran a dry tongue across her lips. "The boy . . . no. But I heard him tell the guards to take my lady to . . . to the eagle's eyrie. Yes, yes that was what he called it: the eagle's eyrie."

Alaric raised a questioning brow in Roger de Chesnai's direction, but the knight was as much in ignorance of the castle's thousands of chambers and passageways as was Friar. Nonetheless, he had a few questions of his own to ask.

"Is it true what she told me? Is La Seyne Sur Mer . . . your Black Wolf of Lincoln" he said with a faint snort, "the real Lucien Wardieu? And is it also true the man *posing* as Lucien Wardieu is come to the name and title through false means?"

"It is all true," Friar said levelly.

"Have you any proof of this to offer?"

"The proof," Gil seethed, "was there for all to see this afternoon in the lists. What kind of man strikes another in the back, especially when he has just been spared his own life?"

"Indeed," De Chesnai mused. "Your wolf's head fought well today. Better than any forest rogue or political schemer."

"Yet you still harbour doubts to his identity—!"

Sir Roger held up a hand to counter Gil's outburst. "In truth, lad, the only doubts I still harbour are those pertaining to our own abilities. My loyalty must first and foremost be to Lady Servanne de Briscourt, but even I, who would gladly trade my miserable life for hers, cannot see any hope of success in finding her, let alone freeing her, without the aid and knowledge of someone who knows this castle as if he were born to it."

"Lucien Wardieu *was* born to it." Alaric said quietly.

"Then it stands to reason," Sir Roger replied mildly, "we should endeavour to free him first."

"How?" Alaric demanded. "We are still likened to fish out of water here."

"Ahh yes, but the Dragon believes he has captured the biggest fish of all. Will he not boast as much to his guests . . . and his bishop . . . and will it not, therefore, be an easy matter to inquire where and how the villain is being restrained so that one not need fear for the safety of one's neck while asleep?"

"It could be done," Alaric agreed slowly. "There is sure to be much drinking and celebrating in the great hall tonight."

"I have six men at my command," said Sir Roger. "Six who, like me, have no love for this yellow-maned dragon who sits so close to Lackland as to share the same stench of corruption. They will fight, to a man, if we can but provide the wherewithal to fight." He paused and cast an arched brow over his shoulder at Gil. "Is this skinny bag of bones the best you have to contribute?"

"We have a dozen stout men inside the gates, as many more waiting out on the moor." Alaric gave a wry smile before he added, "And I would take a care in how you refer to Gillian—she has a temper as finely honed as her bowstring."

"*She? A wench?*"

"A wench who taught the Wolf a thing or two about the proper use of a longbow. But if you still doubt me, think back to the lesson learned by Bayard of Northumbria, who might have preferred we had a different teacher."

De Chesnai frowned and scratched at the neatly trimmed beard that grew in a point from his chin. "Well, a score of men—and one wench—will have to do, I suppose, at least until we can sniff out a malcontent or two from among the castle guard. There are bound to be some who would be glad to see the Dragon's fire quenched after today's debacle."

Friar shook his head. "There is no time to recruit men from the castle guard. What we do must be done tonight, while there is revelry and celebration to dilute the urgency of the Dragon's purpose. By the morrow, he will be thinking clearly again and know his only safe course lies in the hasty and permanent removal of anyone who poses a threat to his future."

"He will kill your lord, as well as my lady," De Chesnai agreed grimly. "Along with any of us who stumble into his hands."

"Then we shall have to take special care to do no stumbling."

A groan from the direction of the cot sent the men's eyes back to Biddy; a squawk and flurry of parti-coloured vestments and tinkling bells sent them all into a guarded crouch as Sparrow plunged into the bothy. He skidded to a dusty halt when he saw the trio of grim faces and even grimmer weapons aimed toward him.

"Sparrow, for Christ's sake—" Alaric resheathed his dagger and shook off the surge of adrenaline.

"I heard Old Blister was here. Robert said she was hurt—"

"Woodcock?" Biddy's voice scratched out of the shadows. "Woodcock, is that you?"

The round cherub eyes searched past Gil's frame and saw the still figure on the pallet. "Aye, 'tis me. What nonsense is this then?"

"Woodcock?" Biddy stretched out a trembling arm and Sparrow was by her side in an instant to sandwich her hand between his. "Have you heard . . . about my lady?"

"She is not where she is supposed to be?" he surmised grimly. "Aye, Master Wolf had some notion she might not be, although he should have given a deal more concern for his own whereabouts. Know you where they have taken her?"

"Somewhere called the eagle's eyrie," Friar interjected. "Your nose is usually everywhere it should not be: Have you heard mention of this place?"

Sparrow looked offended. "My nose has saved your arse on more than one occasion, Bishop Bother, and will undoubtedly do so again without—"

"*Woodcock!*" Biddy squeezed one of the small, fat hands with enough vehemence to send the little man up on his tiptoes. "I have not flaunted with Death to lie here and listen to children bickering! My lady is in the gravest peril. She must be rescued and *will* be rescued if I have to search every inch of masonry myself for this god-accursed eyrie!"

She started to get up, but thought better of it when the four cramped walls of the bothy once again did a sudden, wild dervish and sent her eyes spinning back into her head. Sparrow bent over her at once, his rancour and crushed hand both forgotten in rush of genuine concern.

"There now, you see what comes of always ordering everyone about? You have done more than enough for one day, you old harridan; leave the rest of the rescuing up to us."

"Woodcock—" She snatched at a fistful of his tunic and dragged him a hand's breadth away from her face. "You will find my lady, will you not? You will bring her back to me safe and sound?"

"I have already given my word to another to do just so," he said. "And I consider his ire of greater consequence to my soul should I fail . . . although—" He tried to swallow through the increased pressure around his throat, and his eyes bulged at the sight of the wickedly sharp knife that had somehow found its way from Biddy's apron to the juncture of his thighs, "I can see the merit of a double promise. Just so. Just so. You have it. I shall happily place her hand in yours myself!"

"See that you do, Woodcock," Biddy hissed. "Or your days of flight are over."

27

The Wolf opened his eyes slowly, careful not to move his lids more than the fraction needed to establish his surroundings. His body ached in a thousand places. He had not moved from where he had been thrown, hours ago, into the dank and musty corner of a stone cell, but he knew by the cautious flexing and testing of muscles in his legs, arms, and torso, that he was one massive bruise. He did not think any bones were broken, but there was evidence aplenty of fresh blood on the mouldy rushes beneath him. He could smell it, and he could taste it on a tongue that was as swollen and furry as the rats who crawled boldly from one fetid cell to the next, sniffing after putrefaction.

As near as he could remember, he was in the donjon beneath the main keep. Even though it had been many years since he had explored here as a child, he thought he recognized the steep, narrow flight of steps that curved around the forty-foot column of block and mortar that supported the floor above. A deep and cavernous chamber of unthinkable horrors, there were cells hewn out of the base of the stone walls, each one deep enough to hold a single man, tall enough to let him sit if he had the strength to do so. Ankles and wrists were chained to thick iron rings embedded in the mortar. Water dripped constantly into slimy black pools on the floor, the echo hollow and prolonged to give each drop a lifespan of several shivering seconds. Rats crouched in the shadows, tearing and chewing chunks of spongy matter that did not bear thinking about. Other dark, huddled creatures who might once have been men, groaned in their private hells, never loud enough to draw the attention of the guards, never quietly enough to tempt death.

The ceiling was lost in the gloom of arched beams, most of them coated in damp and decay. When the huge firepit below was blazing, the smoke floated up and hung there like a thick layer of yellow cream, an unshifting mass whose only escape was time and the odd, errant draft snaking in from the upper corridor.

The fire was a low, paltry thing today, barely hot enough to glow red at the heart. The only irons heated had been the ones applied to the young man strapped on a nearby table. His leg was bare from hip to ankle, and a wound on his thigh had been perfunctorily cauterized to staunch the flow of blood. The lad could not have been brought to the donjon much before the Wolf's own ignominious arrival, for the stench of burned flesh had been pungent and fresh enough to act like strong vinegar in clearing his addled senses.

The Wolf shifted slightly for a better angle of view, grinding his teeth against the expected darts of pain. There had been no sign of movement from the lad and Lucien might have perceived him to be a corpse if not for the frequent inspections given by the sweating, bulbously grotesque bulk of D'Aeth, the castle's chief subjugator. As broad as two men, with gleaming, oil-slicked boulders for an upper torso, D'Aeth had obviously been given instructions to keep the boy alive as long as possible. Now and then a flat, square-tipped hand grabbed a fistful of genitals and squeezed until the lad cried out in pain. Satisfied, the squinted, watery eyes peered speculatively into each occupied niche before he returned to where he was working at a low bench in the corner.

Eight other guards were present, six stationed at the bottom of the spiral staircase, two at the top. The six at the bottom were seated at a small wooden table playing at dice. Occasionally one would glance at D'Aeth and wince over a particularly gruesome tool the subjugator was cleaning and sharpening with such dedicated reverence.

The Wolf leaned back and choked back an involuntary groan as the wound at the base of his skull scraped against the stone. The Dragon had caught him with the flat of his sword, saving his neck from a swift detachment from his shoulders, but leaving him with a lump the size of a man's fist. His armour, surcoat, and mail hauberk had been removed, and if not for other, more pressing concerns to occupy his thoughts, he would have noticed how cold he was, dressed only in an open-throated shirt and torn hose.

One of his main concerns was to hold on to his sanity. Pain was his biggest enemy at the moment, and he knew he had to conquer and master each individual wave of agony before he could block it from his mind. To help his concentration, he isolated and identified the incessant dripping sounds, the muffled groans, the scraping whinny of tools and whetstone, the furtive scuffling of rats in the rushes. He chose one sound and closed his eyes, forcing himself to see past the pain, to envision each drop of water as it formed, swelled, stretched, and finally fell into an inky puddle below. Another drip, another source of pain was numbed. He worked his way through his body like a navigator charting and marking known landfalls, using methods taught to him years ago when he had wept for madness or death to claim him. Now he prayed only for a chance to survive and lay his hands on a sword or a dagger . . . a bow . . . anything! Just once more. And just long enough to get within reach of Etienne Wardieu.

A sound that did not fit into the malevolent breathing pattern of the donjon caused the Wolf to open his eyes again. It had only been a fleeting thing, a scrape of cloth where there should have been only air and wafting smoke, but

weeks of training his senses to become alerted to misplaced
footfalls and snapped twigs in the forest, made him angle
himself forward against to see out of his niche.

The weak orangy glow from the torches barely lit the cressets they were propped in, much less the vaulted gloom
above, but the Wolf stared up into the darkness, waiting for
the sound to recur and be identified.

His gray eyes flicked once to the recessed enclave where
D'Aeth worked. They scanned briefly past the sentries dicing
at the bottom of the stairs, then followed the spiral upward
to where a faint smear of light provided the vague outline of
the door to the upper corridor. The guards posted there were
mere shadows, occasionally clinking a bit of armour to prove
they had not turned to stone. There would be more guards
stationed farther along the corridor, and at every junction of
the honeycomb of storerooms and ale cellars that comprised
the vast underbelly of the castle keep. A second flight of
stairs led up through more guards and emptied into the
square, ivy-drenched courtyard where Servanne had first
been struck with the enormity of Bloodmoor Keep. From
there, one climbed an enclosed pentice to gain entry to the
great hall, or passed through low, well-patrolled laneways
which led to the kitchens, pantries, and gardens.

The Wolf could see it all with remarkable clarity. Indeed,
his knees and shins could recall better than his mind's eye
every stair and endless mile of winding black corridors he
had been hauled along during his descent into the lowest
level of the labyrinth.

What he could not envision, as he gave up on his unidenti-
fied sound and lay back in his cell, was the solemn group of
figures dressed in gray robes who were making their way
through the upper alleyways into the courtyard.

The sentries were in the process of explaining to the lost
monks where they had erred in making a turn, when the

clanking footsteps of a small patrol approached the court from the direction of the barracks. The captain of the patrol was ill-tempered, declaring he had been interrupted in his evening meal to comply with new orders to double the sentries posted around the main keep. He then demanded to know, in his best Draconian mien, why the guards had left their post and why the court was swarming with a nest of scurvy, lice-ridden acolytes.

The first two sentries should have looked more closely at the face behind the steel nasal, for by the time it occurred to them to question why the captain's voice sounded odd, there were blades slashing through the darkness, ending their curiosity for all time.

Sir Roger de Chesnai quickly ordered his handful of men to hide the bodies and assume the posts of the dead guards. The "monks" hastened forward, spilling across the courtyard and shedding the cowls that would hamper them in the close confines below. All but one were dressed in leather armour and blue surcoats borrowed from the guards' barracks on an enterprising raid conducted earlier in the evening.

"That was too easy," Alaric worried, his neck craned back, his head swiveling to scan the sheer stone walls rising above them. The only windows were high up on the third storey, and on the twin towers that rose above the turreted roofline. Most of the guests would be in the great hall, where the Dragon was undoubtedly reveling in his triumph, but there were guards everywhere and every shadow was suspect.

"Come," De Chesnai said urgently. "Give me your hands so I can bind them."

"Loosely, damn you," Friar muttered, thrusting out his wrists and watching as a length of twine tied them together.

"There must be hundreds of chambers below the keep,"

Gil protested in an angry whisper. "How can we possibly search them all?"

"One at a time, if we have to," De Chesnai grunted. "And a fat lot of good *that* will do"—he glanced wryly at the longbow she carried slung over her shoulder—"in a place where the longest corridor is half a turn more than the shortest."

Gil opened her mouth to offer a retort, but staunched it on a warning glare from Alaric. She did not completely trust the knight, nor did she like the idea of using Alaric as bait. It was the only logical way they could hope to gain entry to the cells below, yet it caused a quickening in the blood and a pounding in her heart to see Alaric without sword or armour.

"Christ's ribs," spat a disgruntled Robert the Welshman. He had squeezed his broad frame into one of the confiscated surcoats and looked like an overstuffed pasty about to burst its seams.

"Your own fault for swelling to the size of a bullock," Sparrow hissed from the seat of the makeshift sling suspended from the Welshman's broad shoulders. A dwarf would have been difficult to explain to an alert sentry regardless of his disguise. Dressed in his own forest clothes and riding Robert's back, Sparrow could pass for just another bulge of muscle . . . providing he stopped squirming for better balance in the sling.

Mutter and Stutter snickered in unison and adjusted the angle of each other's helm.

"Ready then?" De Chesnai asked. "We'll not have a second chance. You, lass, if you are as good a shot as the bishop says, get by my elbow and stay there. Aim for the throat to cut off any sound of alarm."

"I know full well how to kill Normans," Gil replied tautly. "See to your own skills, Captain."

De Chesnai prodded Alaric toward the door. Both men

had to duck to clear the archway, then climb down the short flight of steps single file in order to reach the guard's station below. There, three of De Gournay's men stood instantly alert, their hands clasped around the hilts of their swords.

"Rest easy lads," De Chesnai barked gruffly. "Just another bit of amusement for my lord D'Aeth. Caught him trying to empty the kitchens of venison, and right under the prince's nose."

The guards chuckled and eased their hands from the swords. A bat of an eye later, one of them was crumpled on the floor, unconscious, and the other two were pressed flat against the wall, their eyes bulging with the pressure of the cold steel blades thrusting into their necks.

"The Black Knight," De Chesnai asked the closest. "Where is he?"

"Where you will never get to him," the guard spat.

Sir Roger sighed and shook his head. He gave his hand a jerk and the blade of his knife plunged forward, slicing through cartilage and bone like a cleaver splitting through a joint of mutton. Blood and air bubbled through the gaping wound and, before the guard had finished choking and twitching himself into a tangle on the floor, De Chesnai was approaching the second man and waving Gil aside.

"Now then. I shall ask again. Where is the Black Knight being held?"

"B-b-below," the guard stammered. "In the main donjon."

"Lead the way, there's a good lad. Oh"—he raised the dagger and rested the point on the guard's cheek, letting him feel the warm wetness of his comrade's blood—"and if you attempt to cry out a warning, or sound an alarm of any kind, you will feel the bite of this up your buttocks, my friend, and I promise you, the sensation will not be a pleasurable one."

The guard blinked, swallowed, and nodded jerkily.

"Move," De Chesnai ordered.

The guard reeled away from the wall and stumbled ahead of them along the dimly lit corridor. De Chesnai, Alaric, and the others were close behind, leaving three of their own men to replace the guards on watch.

Two more posts were broached and cleared, with De Gournay's men bound and gagged—if they took the suggestion peaceably—or the bodies hidden and the vacancies filled with erstwhile foresters. At the third guardpost, there were four men playing a game with dice and pebbles. Boredom caused one of them to inspect the new prisoner with more care than usual, and to wonder why the sentry from the main post was sweating rivers in the chilly air. He was on the verge of shrugging aside his suspicions when the sling around Robert's waist snapped, bringing Sparrow down with a yelp of pain.

Gil wasted neither thought nor action, but raised her bow and fired an arrow into the guard's throat before he could cry out a warning. De Chesnai's dagger tasted blood again, buried to the hilt in a man's belly, while Robert accounted for the third and fourth guard by grasping them around the necks and cracking their heads together with enough force to send their eyeballs squirting out of the sockets.

In the sudden eruption of violence, the sentry who had been their hostage darted ahead into the gloom of the corridor. He did not get very far before an iron bolt from Sparrow's crossbow thumped his flesh like a hatchet striking into wood and sent him sprawling forward into the wall. He grabbed for a chain hanging nearby and tried to use it to hold himself upright, but it was no use, and he slid slowly down onto his knees, his mouth moving in soundless agony.

Alaric discarded the ropes from around his wrists and bent over to arm himself from one of the dead guards. They were standing at a junction where the corridor branched off in two directions, each hazy and poorly lit. The guard had been running toward the one on the left . . . because it was the closest? . . . because he knew there was help within reach? . . . or because he was hoping to lead them away from their true goal?

"In a week," De Chesnai remarked dryly, "I've not yet met one of De Gournay's paid louts who can claim a brain bigger than a pea. He would have been after saving his own neck, methinks, by giving M'sieur D'Aeth the pleasure of chewing upon ours."

"To the left then?"

"Aye. The left."

They did not waste the time to hide the bodies, but ran swiftly along the low-ceilinged corridor, pausing where lit torches marked the entrance to a storeroom. There were no doors and no guards blocking them, and thus were deemed by Friar to be of no importance. After several more sharp turns along a route that took them deeper and deeper beneath the belly of the keep, they were drawn by the smell, rather than the dull light, emanating from a doorway up ahead.

This one was guarded.

Two arrows released simultaneously from Gil's bow and Sparrow's harp-shaped arblaster, struck the men-at-arms posted on either side of the iron-grille door, killing them with only the faintest of thuds to mark their passing.

Gil was the first to sidle up to the entryway and edge an eye around the stone frame. When she saw the vast, sunken maw of a pit that yawned beneath her, she recoiled back against the wall again, needing a moment or two to brace herself for a second look.

"Christ's mercy," De Chesnai murmured, the bile thickening in his throat at the sight of the hooks and ropes and chains that dangled over tables, benches, and wooden racks stained dark with blood. Iron tongs, pokers, and pincers were suspended like cooking utensils over the firepit—different sizes for different purposes. Cauldrons of oil and pitch sat cooling beside the grate, steam from the surfaces drifting lazily upward to blend with the sulphurous miasma above.

"I can only see two guards," Friar said tautly. "But there must be more . . . listen."

The sound of voices and the rattle of dice seemed to be coming from around and behind the base of the central column. As much as half of the huge room was effectively cut off from view.

"Alaric!" Gil's voice, whispered in his ear, urged him to follow her pointed finger to a table almost directly below them. A young boy was stretched out, bound hand and foot in a spread-eagle position. His eyes were open and he was staring directly up at the door, but there was no change in his expression to indicate whether he had seen them or not.

"Eduard," De Chesnai said unnecessarily. "You were right, Bishop. Tomorrow would have been too late."

Alaric's gaze flicked back to the two guards he could see at the bottom of the stairs. They would be easy enough to deal with, but he did not like going in without knowing how many more were inside, out of sight. Nor did he like the size or location of the huge bronze alarm bell. It looked big enough to bring down the walls of Jericho if struck with any force at all. Of equal concern, suddenly, was the chain attached to the bell pull. It climbed all the way up the wall and disappeared into a small, neat hole in the ceiling rafters—undoubtedly connected to another bell located in the soldiers guard station above, and possibly to a third and fourth on storeys higher up.

Alaric stiffened, remembering the guard they had shot back at the junction. He had died reaching for a chain, and the chain had slipped several links before drawing taut in his death grip.

"Christ! The alarm is already given! Gil, Sparrow: the guards!"

The two archers stepped into the doorway and without

questioning the order or the unexpected savagery, fired down on the two visible sentries. The arrows both struck the same man an inch apart, and while Sparrow gaped up at Gil and fumbled another bolt from his quiver to rearm his crossbow, Gil swore and nocked another of her longer arrows, catching the second, startled guard squarely in his opened mouth. The cry of warning was strangled short, but given nonetheless and a scramble of heavy boots, chain mail, and the scrape of crossbows being armed reached the top of the stairs.

Alaric and Sir Roger were halfway down the flight of steps when the first guard stepped out from cover and fired his weapon. Sparrow was ready for him, releasing a bolt that pierced De Gournay's mercenary neatly through the heart. Almost immediately two more guardsmen appeared, one kneeling to shoot, one discriminantly diving behind a table the instant his bolt was loosed. Both shots were wild but Gil's returned fire sent an arrow furrowing halfway up the length of one man's arm, expending its force in an eruption of bloody tissue at the elbow. The guard screamed and spun sideways with the agony of his shattered arm, landing close enough to the man crouched behind the table to splatter him with gore. The latter wiped away a hot splash that had landed on his cheek and, with his weapon rearmed, fired triumphantly at a much larger, much broader target who leaped down the stairs two at a time, bellowing Welsh oaths on every step.

Sparrow aimed for the guard, but his bolt struck the wooden face of the overturned table. He slung his bow over his shoulder and with a hop and leap that appeared to take him flying out into empty space, he grabbed hold of a crossbeam and swung himself into the jungle of wooden arches. Several more swinging leaps carried him halfway across the ceiling rafters, and while Gil kept the guard pinned effectively behind the table, the little man unslung his bow, nocked a bolt, and settled the matter with a definitive whoop of satisfaction.

Unfortunately the whoop was followed instantly by a yelp of dismay as he lost his balance and felt his remaining bolts fall out of his quiver and clatter to the floor below.

The last pair of guards rushed Alaric and Sir Roger at the bottom of the stairs, their swords glinting in the murky half-light. Alaric disposed of his adversary with a vehement cut and slash, but De Chesnai wheeled his blade again and again, taking pleasure in driving his opponent into a far corner before delivering the death blow.

Mutter and Stutter ran down the steps and, obeying Alaric's sharp commands, cut the ropes lashing Eduard to the table. They were helping the boy carefully to his feet even as Alaric was answering a summons from the chained occupant of a nearby cell.

"You took your bloody time getting here," the Wolf said, grinning through the blood and grime on his face.

"There is gratitude for you," Friar remarked, cursing fluently over the discovery of locks on each of the fetters chaining the Wolf to the wall. "Keys?"

"You want keys?" asked a coarse, gritty voice from the shadows. "Come. Take them from me."

Alaric whirled around. The bald and glistening, half-naked monument of sinew and muscle—D'Aeth—stood a few paces away, his one fist closed in a crushing grip around Sir Roger's throat, his other wrapped around the end of a length of heavy chain. De Chesnai's sword was gone. His eyes bulged and his lips were turning blue, his face was florid and his fingers were scratching desperately at the five-pronged slab of iron D'Aeth called a hand.

"Throw down your sword or this codpiece dies," D'Aeth snarled.

Out of the corner of his eye, Alaric could see Gil creeping slowly down the stairs, but it would take her several seconds to reach the floor of the donjon—several seconds longer than De Chesnai's neck would bear the strain. Mutter and Stutter had laid aside their weapons to help Eduard to his feet, and Sparrow was somewhere up in the vaulted gloom, but without his quiver of arrows his bow arm was useless.

"Let him go," Alaric said, laying aside his sword with exaggerated care.

D'Aeth grinned, displaying two rows of teeth filed into wickedly sharp points. He gave Sir Roger's neck an additional squeeze before flinging the knight aside, then with a sneer of malicious delight, he slashed out with the length of chain. The end snaked across the floor and found Alaric's ankles; a jerk of the trunklike arm pulled the chain taut and swept Alaric's feet forward, bringing him crashing to the stone floor.

The Wolf strained against his own chains, but they were anchored well and only caused the iron rings to gouge deeper into the flesh of his wrists. Friar's head had snapped back in the fall, landing hard on the stone and he was momentarily too dazed to defend himself as the chain curled outward again and cut him across the tops of his thighs. His hose was torn as the links bit into his flesh; blood smeared across the floor as he rolled in agony and tried to avoid the third whiplash of iron.

Mutter and Stutter ran forward, but the direction of the chain was easily changed, slashing them both across the chest and hurling them against the rack that held an assortment of curved pikes, metal starbursts, and clawed pincers. Mutter landed harder than his brother, striking the side of his head against a protruding iron bolt.

Gil rounded the base of the pillar but was so shocked by the sight of Alaric crawling through his own blood, that she released the arrow without allowing for D'Aeth's reflexes. She saw the shaft streak past his head, killing nothing but a block of wood, and with a cry, she turned the bow in her hands, intending to use it like a club. Once again the chain lashed out and gleefully tore it out of her grasp, the force spinning her brutally into the wall.

Screaming, Alaric dove for his sword the same instant a small shrieking form came sailing down out of nowhere, arms and legs splayed wide to break his fall as he swiped across the path of the charging D'Aeth. Sparrow landed hard, plastered flat against the bulwark of chest muscles, knocking more air out of himself than out of D'Aeth, but before he was swatted aside like an annoying insect, he managed to plant his stingers—two glittering knives—one in each side of D'Aeth's massive neck.

Alaric was on his feet, the sword gripped in both hands as D'Aeth lunged forward. The first cut barely creased the rock-hard mountain of flesh, the second carved a deep welt of gore from shoulder to ribs, and still he came on. Alaric backed up, hacking and slashing at the grinning monster. He was pressed into the corner, his sword red the full length, and D'Aeth was there in front of him, the chain raised in one hand, a leather-shanked battle-ax in the other. The first swipe of the axe broke Alaric's sword in half, the second would have sheared his head from his shoulders if both the axe and arm were not halted midstroke by the arcing fury of a steel morning star. The rounded, spiked club tore a swath through flesh and muscle, bone and sinew, opening a raw gash from the top of D'Aeth's skull to the base of his spine.

D'Aeth's ugly face registered surprise, then shock, then an incredulous horror as his legs folded beneath him and he pitched forward like a felled tree. He was dead before he struck the ground, a torrent of blood gushing out of the hideous wound, some of it spattering a wall ten feet away.

The morning star was clotted with shreds of flesh and bone right up to the handgrip as Gil sank onto her knees beside Alaric. They were both winded and badly shaken, but there was no time to do more than exchange wry grimaces of pain to assure each other they were not mortally injured. After a moment, Alaric groped at the fallen behemoth's waist for the ring of iron keys, while Gil went to extricate Sparrow from the tangle of hooks and barbs he had been flung into.

The right key was found and fitted into the padlocks at the Wolf's wrists and ankles. The two men helped one another to their feet and took toll of the wreckage surrounding them.

De Chesnai was alive, but breathing with difficulty through a partially crushed windpipe. Sparrow was complaining—a good sign that the blood leaking from his arm was not critical. Mutter was dead, the spike still jutting from a small, bloodless hole in his temple. Gil was unharmed but for a few bad bruises and scrapes. Robert the Welshman, forgotten in the general melee, was the second unexpected casualty, a man whose courage and fighting strength they could ill afford to lose. He had been struck in the chest by one of the guards' bolts, and while not quite dead of his wound, would most certainly be if he tried to move.

Together, Gil and Sparrow propped him more comfortably against the stone cistern, then turned to their leader for guidance.

"We are almost certain an alarm has been sounded," Alaric advised. He hurriedly explained about the guard and the chain, and added unnecessarily, "Our men will put up a good fight and delay them as long as possible, but they are sure to break through."

Lucien clenched his fists, still numb from having watched his friends fight and die for him. "The price of vengeance . . . was too steep this time, I fear."

"Tell that to your son . . . and to the Lady Servanne, if and when we find her."

The burning gray eyes moved slowly to Friar. "What did you say?"

"Lengthy explanations and formal introductions will have

to wait for a more prudent moment, but for now—" Alaric nodded toward the trembling but steadfastly upright young squire. "Here is your son: Eduard. Nicolaa de la Haye birthed him, but I trust you will not hold it against him. It seems he gave a good account of himself trying to step between the Dragon and Lady Servanne."

The Wolf's eyes flicked up from the wound on Eduard's thigh and turned to Alaric. "Servanne . . . you know where she is?"

Friar glanced up at the arched doorway, his neck prickling with an unmistakable warning. "We were, ah, hoping you could tell us."

"*What?*"

"According to Biddy, she was taken to something called the *eagle's eyrie.* Do you know what it is, or where it is?"

The Wolf frowned. "The eagle's eyrie? The eagle's—" A gasp of shock cut the words short. "That bastard! How could he do such a thing to her? I will kill him, by God. I swear I will kill him if it is the last thing I do!"

"Yes, well, we would be more than willing to help you fulfill your vow . . . providing we solve one small problem." He gazed pointedly at the stone walls, the crisscross of solid beams overhead, and the single door representing the only way out. "Unless of course, you think we have a good chance to fight our way past a blockade of guards?"

"Was that your plan?"

"My plan was to get us in. Since I did not think we had a hope in hell of succeeding, I must confess, we made no contingency for getting out again."

The Wolf barely heard him. "The monk's wall," he murmured. "I wonder—"

He searched the row of cells until he came to the one he thought served memory best, then crouched in front of it. "The story goes . . . a monk was once imprisoned down here and used his crucifix to wear away at the mortar in his walls. His cell was next to the shaft of an old well that went dry, and when it rained, he could hear the water leaking down. Mind you, it was a long time ago that I found the loosened stones. They could have been discovered by others since then and resealed."

The men exchanged a glance, then looked up at the doorway as the sound of fighting grew distinctly clearer.

"We will not know until we look," Alaric said, plucking one of the torches out of a wall sconce and following the Wolf into the small, slimy cell behind them. At first there was no noticeable difference in the feel or texture of the mortar, but as the Wolf began scraping and scratching the seams around the middle block with one of D'Aeth's iron pokers, it began to crumble and fall away. In no time at all they were able to shift the stone and drag it forward to the centre of the cell.

The Wolf took the torch and thrust it through the opening. Bits of broken mortar were pushed inward and fell a long way into utter blackness before rewarding the two worried faces with a distant splash of sound. Craning their necks upward, there was nothing to see beyond the glare of the torchlight except for more blackness.

"An enterprising monk," Alaric muttered. "I presume his bones lie at the bottom somewhere?"

"No. No, he escaped. He escaped up the well and, by God, so shall we. Look there . . . and there, above!"

Alaric slid his hand up the wall over their heads and felt the step carved into the hard surface. In the flickering torchlight, he could see the shadow of another step above, and another above that until it climbed into darkness.

"The damned fool must have been mad! It would have taken months to cut such a ladder into the stone . . . years!"

"What else had he to do with his time?"

"True. But where does it lead?"

"Up," the Wolf said succinctly. "Which is all I care about for the moment."

They backed out of the cramped cell and hastily explained the escape route to the huddle of wounded men. Gil and Sparrow exchanged a dubious look, but Sparrow, being the smallest and nimblest, agreed to at least see where the ladder went. He was back in a trice, coughing and spitting up dust through an impish grin that stretched ear to ear.

"Never shall I call a monk a fool again for wearing out his skirts in holy pursuits. The ladder leads up to a grate, and the grate covers a hole in the garden overgrown with bushes and hawthorn. An easy climb too, if you think to keep your back braced against the wall as you are going. Easier" he said to Gil, "than clambering up a tree, even with one wing damaged!"

"I will take my chances here, Puck," Gil said grimly. "I prefer to die with a bow in my hand, thank you, not wedged up some tunnel like a frightened rat."

Alaric was about to join the argument when three of the Wolf's men who had been left on guard in the corridors, came staggering through the door. All three were badly wounded and out of arrows. Helped down the stairs, they gasped a warning that De Gournay's mercenaries were in the cellars and closing fast. There were only three, perhaps four men left between the donjon and the tide of murdering guardsmen, but how long those men could last before they too had to retreat, was anyone's guess.

"That settles it then; we use the shaft," Lucien said, and reached to arm himself. A crossbow was thrust into his hand and he found himself staring into eyes as gray and brooding as his own. The boy had gathered the guards' weapons and quivers of bolts without being ordered to do so, despite the terrible pain of his wound.

"Do you think you can climb, lad?"

"I think so, milord. Yes milord, I can climb."

"Good. Sparrow, off you go again. Take the boy with you and if you value your scrawny neck, you will not let him fall."

"Aye, lord, and good luck to you too."

"Gil—" The Wolf turned to the master archer and the look in his eye warned against any further arguments. "You and Sir Roger are in charge of the wounded men. Use ropes if you have to, but get them up that shaft and yourselves after them."

"What about Robert?" she asked quietly. "He needs more than ropes, and he cannot make the climb."

"Robert can bloody take care o' himself," the Welshman gnashed through his teeth. "I need no flame-topped wench keening after me. Now go! Do as the laird says, or by the saints, I'll not only show ye how swift I can climb, but I'll do it kicking yer backside up ahead of me!"

When Gil had moved away, the Wolf dropped onto his knee beside the burly Welshman. "Robert—"

"Do not trouble yerself, laird. I am almost dead now, and surely would be long afore ye could think of a way to winch me hand over heel up a wee tunnel. At least here, I can still be of some use to ye. Give me weapons—arm as many of the poxy crossbows as ye can set beside me, an' I'll keep the bastards honest as long as I can."

Lucien grasped the Welshman's big paw of a hand. "You have been a loyal friend, Robert. I have envied you your courage and your laughter, and have been honoured to have you fight by my side."

"Bah! The honour was mine in knowing there are still men who fight for what is good an' just. As for courage—ye have all that ye need and more . . . and still more waiting for ye in some godforsaken place called the eagle's eyrie. Save her, laird. She'll help ye laugh again, see if she does not."

Alaric had come up beside them and his attention was

split between listening to their exchange and listening to the sudden, ominous silence coming from the top of the stairs.

"I do not think there will be any others joining us," he said tautly as the Wolf joined him in staring up at the dimly lit archway.

"Did you get the wounded away?"

"Aye. Sir Roger argued to remain behind, but I threatened to throttle him myself if he did not start climbing. Lucien . . . the other prisoners cannot be moved. Most of them . . . have no hands or feet."

The Wolf's gaze followed Alaric's to the row of low, dark cells that lined the walls. For a long moment he stood in stony silence, his face expressionless, yet more ominous than a gathering storm.

"I put the worst of them out of their misery," Alaric said softly. "That leaves only the three of us and—" He tilted his head meaningfully toward the workbench where Stutter sat cradling his brother's head to his heart.

"Go," the Wolf said tersely. "We will be right behind."

"God be with you, Robert," Alaric said quickly, touching the brave man's shoulder before he too was gone.

"Stutter, you are next. Off you go."

"I . . . cannot leave Oswald," said the desolate twin. He lifted a face that was wet with tears and appealed to Lucien forlornly. "I would not know what to do without him."

"You could live," the Wolf insisted. "It is not a new or uncommon notion, and I am certain your brother would have wished it."

"No." Stutter shook his head sadly. "We made a pact, my lord. To live and die together. We swore it."

"Well . . . unswear it, damn you, and get into the shaft. We can argue honour later."

"My lord . . . no. Even if I wanted to . . ." He glanced pointedly at his leg and the Wolf felt a further sinking in his breast as he realized the blood pooled on the floor was not

Mutter's. Stutter's leg had been broken in the fight; he had been thrown by D'Aeth and had landed awkwardly on the stone, twisting his leg and breaking it with enough force to drive the splintered ends of the bone through the flesh.

"Oh God," the Wolf murmured, sitting heavily on the edge of the bench.

Stutter shook his head. "You must not linger any longer to worry over us, my lord. Robert and I . . . we shall keep one another company, and together . . . we shall endeavour to keep the bastards honest. I am not nearly as good a shot as Robert, but I can keep the bows armed . . . and besides, you need someone to push the stones back into place behind you, or the Dragon's men will just climb up after you. This way, perhaps they will be confused enough to have to think on it a while."

"The lad speaks sense," Robert admitted. "It would work in your favour for the bastards to find no answers here. And they'll not find any, laird, not live ones. That I promise ye."

Lucien Wardieu looked from Robert to Stutter, and it was one of the hardest things he had ever had to do, to nod assent. "If I thought there was the slightest chance—"

"There is no chance for us, laird, an' well we know it. But there is a chance for you to lead the rest o' the men to safety, and by God, I'll not be the reason any more good men give their lives! Go now, laird, and God be with you."

"God be with you," said the Wolf, clasping hands in a reluctant farewell.

He helped Stutter to the door of the cell and squeezed himself through the hole in the wall. He stood there in the darkness, clinging to the damp stones, listening to the harsh scrape of the blocks being nudged and cajoled back into place. His heart was pounding in his chest and his brow was clammy cold. The taste of rage was strong and bitter in his mouth—rage at his own helplessness; rage over the loss of the valiant men they were leaving behind.

28

"The eagle's eyrie," said Lucien bluntly, "is about the most inaccessible place he could have found to put Lady Servanne. Two guards with a ready supply of arrows could hold off an army until hell froze over."

Alaric and Gil exchanged a glance before she lowered her head and continued to bind a minor but annoyingly leaky cut on her arm.

The pitifully small group had taken refuge in one of the overgrown orchards flanking the keep, where they had an excellent overview of the castle grounds. For the time being, all was relatively peaceful, but the Wolf was certain, when the general alarm alerted the castle to the escape, the guards would be thick as fireflies, poking their torches and their swords into every nook and cranny. The orchard would not be safe for very long, nor would the routes that led to the outer walls.

As for the eyrie . . .

"Thank God for Biddy," Lucien said grimly. "In truth, I never would have throught of the eyrie until after I had searched every tower and chamber within the walls."

He finished tying up a makeshift sling for Sir Roger's arm, studiously avoiding Alaric's startled glance as he did so. De Chesnai had been carrying his shoulder at an odd angle and it was not until after he had stumbled and fallen that they discovered the joint had been dislocated. Lucien and Alaric had managed to reseat the shoulder, but the arm was swollen and immobile.

"*Within* the walls?" Alaric queried. "Are you saying this eagle's eyrie is something other than a tower or a spire?"

"It is a single cell, built to hold a single prisoner . . . but I thought it had been abandoned for that purpose years ago."

"Which was probably why the Dragon put her where he did."

"Nonetheless it was a brave thing Biddy did, and she deserves more than just my thanks." He glanced up from under his brows and found where Sparrow was hunkered down in the shadows. "Perhaps I will make a gift to her of young Woodcock."

Sparrow's tousled cap of brown curls jumped as he whirled around. "You would do that to me?"

"If I thought the challenge of clipping your wings would help her recover sooner, aye. Gladly." The Wolf's grin faded and he looked at Sir Roger. "You are certain she is safe enough?"

"She is safe," De Chesnai nodded grimly. "You would be disturbed to know how many of the castle's inhabitants care naught for the name of Lucien Wardieu."

"A situation we shall do our damnedest to rectify," the Wolf promised tersely.

"You can start by telling us exactly where this eagle's eyrie is," Alaric said, his brow knitted in a frown. "The longer you delay, the more my neck itches and tells me I should have remained a Benedictine."

"The eyrie is on the cliffs, my lord," Eduard volunteered. "Halfway down to the sea. The cell itself is no more than a crack in the rocks, and the path leading down is scarcely wide enough for one man to pass another. Of course"—he overcame a tremor in his voice and squared his shoulders manfully—"I have climbed down several times and will do it gladly again for the chance to help rescue Lady Servanne."

Lucien strained to see the boy's face through the shadows, wondering again at the madness and hatred that had conspired to bring them all to this point in life. Eduard was his son. A man nearly grown and him not even knowing there had been a seed sown.

"How is your leg, boy?"

Eduard smiled lamely, feeling his pulse quicken at the sound of the Wolf's voice. This tall, fearsomely bold knight was his father—a stranger, yet one who brought a calming, deep-felt peace to a heart that had always reviled in the notion of carrying the Dragon de Gournay's blood.

"M'sieur D'Aeth unknowingly did me a service by plying the hot iron to my wound. The bleeding was stopped and the flesh sealed. I can use the limb, my lord, and will do so as required."

"What is required," Lucien said slowly, "is a quick way out of here. We have men camped nearby in the woods—men with strong bow arms and tempers frayed from inactivity."

"If they could be gotten to," Sparrow contributed eagerly, "they could certainly put a burr up the Dragon's arse and distract his attention away from our true purpose."

"And let us not forget the rabble outside the gates. They were strongly in favour of Randwulf de la Seyne Sur Mer and could easily be roused into keeping the guards on the walls looking out to the moor."

"My lord?" It was Eduard again. "I think . . . I mean, I am convinced there is a way to get out of the castle unobserved."

All eyes turned to the young squire, who wiped his cuff across his mouth to dry the sweat beaded on his upper lip. "There is a small, seldom-used gate in the east wall which opens out onto the lower slopes of the sea cliffs. The fishermen sometimes use it when they need more fish than the seneschal allows them to catch, and it gives access to smugglers too, those who cannot gain entry by the main gates.

The keeper can be rendered deaf, dumb, and blind for the proper amount of coin, and since he knows me well enough, he would not ask too many questions, nor look too closely at any companions I might have with me."

Lucien regarded the boy with a steady eye.

"It would be dangerous to move the wounded out that way," Friar said quietly. "But better than waiting to be picked off here like overripe fruit."

Sir Roger de Chesnai, cradling his injured arm, stood up. "My shoulder makes me near useless as far as wielding a blade or a bow, but my legs are strong enough to carry me all the way to Lincoln if need be. I will take my chances with the gatekeeper's sight, but I hesitate putting the same faith in your men—if and when I find them—or to count upon them holding back their arrows long enough for me to explain why they should trust me."

A long, drawn-out sigh of exasperation drew attention to Sparrow. *"Mor dieu!* 'Tis true, they will skewer him sooner than ask his name. Moreover, they have learned too well how to hide in the greenwood; it will take a kindred eye to find them."

The Wolf arched a brow. "Are you volunteering?"

"Certainly not! You need me here to help rescue your little dove from her cage."

Lucien smiled the kind of smile that boded ill will for the recipient. "Let me put the question to you another way: It must be well past midnight now; how soon do you think you can find the men and return?"

Sparrow threw his arms up in the air, decrying the Fates who were obviously determined to remove him from the hub of the excitement. "Very well, no need to beg. I will go. After midnight, you say? Then dawn at the earliest—assuming I get through the gate, and assuming the faeries do not turn the moor into quicksand by moonlight."

Lucien and the others looked up at the sky. A bank of

heavy black clouds scudded across a faintly lighter, star-splashed backdrop, bringing a sharp salty tang to the air. The moon would be full and bright when it reached its apex but for now was still too low on the horizon to do more than hint at the speed and mass of moving cloud. There was likely a storm somewhere out at sea—a blessing for those who would need the darkness for safety, a curse for anyone trying to feel their way down a narrow path etched into the side of a cliff.

"Sir Roger . . . do you think between you and these four —Cedric, Sigurd, Gadwin, and Eduard—you could manage to buy or steal a cart from the villagers outside and have it down the coast a mile or so, before dawn?"

Sir Roger de Chesnai, hardly renowned as a cart-stealer, puffed his chest and glowered past Eduard to the three wounded foresters he had already helped haul up the escape shaft. "I would have to have a damned good reason for doing so!"

"The reason, my lord," said Lucien, "is that I do not know how well or how poorly the Lady Servanne has fared. Regardless, we certainly cannot expect her to run across a moor after all she has been through."

Chagrined not to have thought of it himself, Sir Roger's chest deflated and he nodded solemnly. "Tell me where you want the cart and it shall be there."

"My lord—" Eduard was flushed warmly with a mixture of anger and impotence. "My leg may be a hindrance for running, but my arms are scarcely bruised. As I said, there is an inlet where the men go to fish, and in that inlet are boats. They are sturdy and agile, and if one knows the currents—as I do—one can slip in behind the breakwater and bring the vessel close to shore near the base of the cliffs. If you know the way to the eagle's eyrie, then you must also know the small bay of which I speak."

"I recall sneaking out at night and doing my fair share of

fishing there as a boy," Lucien said evenly. "I also remember currents that could smash a boat straight up against the rocks if the oarsman chose to follow the wrong one."

The boy stood, and to the surprise of no one, was nearly as tall as the Wolf, and possessed the same uncompromising tilt to his jaw.

"You need another avenue of escape, my lord," he reasoned. "Sparrow could drown in a quagmire, Sir Roger could run his cart right into the hands of the Dragon's mercenaries. I know the currents. I will not choose the wrong one."

"I could break your arm as a deterrent," the Wolf said with equal logic. "Then you would not be able to row at all."

"No, my lord. Nor would I make a very good squire to you with a game leg and a crooked arm."

Lucien returned his son's unwavering stare for a full minute, then had to lower his gaze to control the pride tugging at his lips. "Very well, if you are determined. But you will not go alone. Gil!"

Gil Golden looked up, startled. "No! You need me on the cliffs!"

"I need you below," Lucien said firmly.

"There is nothing wrong with my arms or my legs," she protested, looking from the Wolf to Alaric. "My bow can be of more use here, protecting your backs. You know it can!"

Alaric chewed his lip savagely, and after a glance from Lucien, took Gil by the arm and led her several feet away into the deeper shadow of an ancient apple tree.

"I want you to go with Eduard," he said softly. "He cannot handle a boat alone."

"But—"

"I do *not* want to argue, Gillian. This has nothing to do with my wanting to send you out of the castle to keep you safe—God knows, I would despair of calling anywhere safe at this moment. Nor has it anything to do with you being a woman, for you have shown the courage of ten men since this whole thing started. No, the plain truth is, we need you *and* your bow arm down below. God willing, if we should somehow succeed at freeing Lady Servanne, and if we should survive the descent to the beach, I would rather know your bow was waiting for us at the bottom instead of taking the risk of having it silenced at the top."

Gil's mouth opened to protest, then closed again as a tremor passed through her chin.

"Besides," he added gently. "You know yourself, you are terrified of heights. You can scarcely climb a tree without turning as green as the leaves. The cliffs drop six hundred feet straight down, with the darkness and the wind there to hamper our every step. You would never make it down."

"How did you know?"

"It was one of the smaller things that gave your secret away," he said, smiling as he tenderly laid his hand against her cheek.

For once Gil did not pull away from his touch. She bent her head forward and rested her brow against his chin, and her sigh was like a chorus of angels' voices in his ears.

"Such a foolish weakness," she whispered.

"Nothing . . . absolutely nothing about you, Gillian, is foolish or weak," Alaric stated flatly. "And if we come through this . . . *when* we come through this, I intend to prove how much I love you, and to prove how much stronger we both can be if we share our pain and our love together."

Gil tilted her face upward at the urging of his lean fingers and their mouths came together, lightly at first, in a kiss so fragile it took her breath away. A sob of surrender saw them clinging more hungrily to one another, mouths, bodies, hearts binding together until the sound of an apologetic cough forced them apart.

"Forgive me," Lucien said, "But by the sound of it, they

have broken through to the donjon. We must move quickly to reach the gate before the avenues are sealed off."

Alaric smiled briefly. "The matter is settled. Gil will go with Eduard."

Gil backed away, a sudden glimmer of light reflecting off the brightness welling in her eyes.

"I guess this leaves just you and me, my friend."

Alaric winced. "I was never very fond of heights myself, you know. I suppose it would be too much to hope there were a few ambitious monks confined in the eyrie at one time or another?"

"Sorry, no. Only one way down. But look you to the bright side: At least we know we have three ways to get away once we have made the rescue."

Alaric watched Eduard limping his way out of the orchard, followed by a grumbling dwarf, a half-throttled knight cradling a useless arm to his breast, three bleeding knights wearing the garb of their enemies, and a slender, long-limbed woman who had steadfastly refused to abandon her longbow despite the danger and awkwardness of carrying it.

"How" he murmured, "can we possibly fail?"

"How could they have gotten out of here? Where could they have gone?"

The Dragon stood over D'Aeth's gored body and the rage sent his blood running cold through his veins. His gaze touched upon each of the dead guards with a detachment that only considered the loss of life in terms of loss of manpower—and inconvenience.

"Fools!" he spat. "Not one of them with the sense to ring the alarm bell. This travesty could well have gone undiscovered until morning if not for a sound mind elsewhere."

Nicolaa was crouched over one of the guards. "This one is

still alive. He has lost enough blood to be dead twice over, but he is still alive."

The Dragon skirted quickly around D'Aeth's body and stepped over another to get to where Nicolaa stood. The guard was huddled at her feet, a mass of quivering agony. A long, slender ashwood arrow was still embedded in the length of his forearm, the fletching stuck out from between his fingers, the steel tip dripping blood from his shattered elbow.

"What happened here?" the Dragon demanded.

"A-attacked, sire," the guard gasped.

Etienne Wardieu's patience snapped and he reached down to grasp a fistful of the wounded man's hair, jerking the bloodless face upward.

"I know you were attacked, you simpleton fool! What I want you to tell me is how they got in here, how many of them were there, and how in blazes did they get out again?"

"Th-the wall, sire. Th-they went through the wall."

Etienne's fist tightened and pulled the man upward, jarring the injured arm and wresting a groan of unbelievable pain from the guard's throat. His eyes rolled back into his skull and the Dragon was forced to release him, kicking out at the unconscious man with a curse of contempt. Straightening, he looked around at the row of shadowy cells. Some of them held even shadowier occupants; half-broken creatures D'Aeth had kept alive for his amusement.

"Anyone! Anyone who can tell me what happened here is a free man!"

The silence was deafening and oppressive. Water dripped and the embers hissed in the firepit, but otherwise, the Dragon's generous offer was met with utter silence.

Furious, he crossed over to where the bodies of the three rescuers had been found behind the stone cistern. One of them was as big as a bear, stuffed into a hauberk and blazon several inches too tight. The arrow jutting from his chest had left a wide, red stain on the front of his tunic, but that was not what had killed him. A gash, delivered by his own hand, went from ear to ear, the wound so fresh the blood was still steaming where it hit the cooler air.

The other two bodies were like children by comparison, reed-thin and identical in features. So identical, even in death, the Dragon paused to take a second look, noting the spike in the one man's temple and the crossbow bolt in the other's. His gaze rested briefly on the hands of the twins. One had died holding fast to the other as if to ensure their journey through eternity together.

The Dragon drew an impatient breath and started to turn away, stopping when he noticed the pattern of blood smears on the floor. The giant and one of the twins had apparently been responsible for putting up a last defense against the massed guards. Admirably, they had killed or wounded more than a dozen men before their supply of arrows had run out. The twin's broken leg accounted for most of the blood leaked around the pile of empty quivers, it being dragged behind him as he loaded and armed the bows. But there was one streaky swath leading back toward the cells that gave no immediate explanation for its presence.

"A torch," Etienne barked, holding out his hand.

The smoking, pitch-soaked light was thrust at him and the Dragon lowered it to concentrate its illumination on the bloodstained floor. He followed the trail to the far wall of the donjon, then ducked down to examine the scuffs and crumbled mortar that covered the floor of the cell.

"Look," Nicolaa gasped, stabbing a finger at where the light flickered on the back wall. Four central blocks had been hastily replaced but not pushed flush against the surrounding squares.

The Dragon threw the torch aside and began clawing at the loose blocks. They moved easily enough and within seconds he had the hole opened again and was reinacting Alaric's and Lucien's discovery of the steps carved into the side of the shaft. A scrap of burning jute from the torch was scraped loose and fell down into the blackness, and, as his predecessors had done, he tracked the depth of the well shaft as the light was swallowed into the void below.

"You!" he shouted over his shoulder for the closest guard. "Climb up this bloody thing and see where it leads."

The guard stared into the cold blue eyes for a moment and decided it would present a greater peril to refuse. "Aye, lord. And when I do . . . find out where it leads, that is . . . what then?"

"Well," Etienne ground his teeth beligerently. "If you get to the top and find no one else there, you might consider shouting for your comrades and letting them know you are still alive. If you find company at the top, it will hardly matter, for you will be screaming all the way down again."

The guard swallowed hard and disappeared through the hole in the cell wall.

"Did you know this was here?" Nicolaa asked.

Glaring his response, the Dragon turned and addressed the rest of the guards. "I want the sentries doubled on all the gates and the inner bailey completely sealed. They cannot have gone far, nor moved very fast with wounded men in their midst. I want every inch of these cellars searched in case we have been fed a false clue; overturn every barrel, move every board, scour the towers and keeps from top to bottom. I want the bastard found!" he screamed. "I want his heart in my hands, and God have mercy on the man who lets him escape again!"

"Calm yourself, Etienne," Nicolaa murmured, laying a hand on his arm. "He may have slipped his chains and gained his freedom temporarily, but he will not go far. Not while you still have something he wants very much."

"Wants—?" The Dragon whirled on her, the madness in eyes clouding his reason.

"The girl, Etienne. Your brother will not leave the castle until he has found the girl."

"But he will not find her, because you and I and the guards who are standing watch over her are the only ones who know where she is hidden."

"We have underestimated him once already. Perhaps we should not be so eager to do it again."

"How can he know what he cannot know?"

"How? Because he is not human, he has proven that already." Nicolaa moved an intimate step closer. "But *she* is. She is quite human—soft and fragile—the perfect bait with which to catch a wolf . . . alive or dead."

The need for violence was in the Dragon's jaw, clamped shut with the effort it was taking to contain his anger. Nicolaa waited, her eyes glistening, the nerves in her belly fluttering with anticipation as she detected the first glints of sadistic pleasure in his eyes.

"Perhaps you are right," he murmured thoughtfully. "Perhaps the least obvious place will be the most obvious choice after all. Yes . . . yes, he will know she is in the eyrie and he will attempt to go to her."

"We can have fifty men on the cliffs waiting for him!" Nicolaa cried eagerly.

"No. No, by God, we will do nothing to interfere. If he is so desperate to rescue the fair maiden, who are we to stop him? After all, where can he go? Where can he take her except down?" Etienne indulged in a wry smile, noting Nicolaa's macabre arousal and feeling a similar response stirring in his own loins. "That is where we shall have our fifty men, my dear. And that is where we shall snare ourselves the last black wolf in England."

29

The drop from the castle to the eagle's eyrie was every bit as hair-raising and suicidal as Eduard had described. The path may once have been wide enough for two to pass safely, but wind and weather constantly buffeted the sheer wall of the cliffs, eroding the rock inch by inch leaving nothing to prevent a misplaced foot from skidding over the crumbling edge. From there, a body plummeted to a violent death, smashed on the crush of rocks and frenzied seas below.

Conquering the steeply declined path in daylight was proof enough of anyone's mettle. Attempting it by sporadic moonlight, without a torch or the comfort of familiarity to guide each footstep, was sheer and utter madness . . . or so Alaric kept shouting, each time his heart was not in his throat and he could be heard over the roar of the waves below.

The Wolf kept a tight rein on his nerves—admittedly not as steely as he would have liked them to be on this wind-ridden night. He forced himself to look at the path not the void beside it. He fought to ignore the constant lurching of his stomach and the feel of cold sweat running in torrents between his shoulder blades. Instead, he concentrated on placing one foot in front of the other, and on trying to remember the exact layout and approach to the eagle's eyrie.

As a reckless young boy, he had taken special pride in exploring every dangerous and forbidden area of the castle grounds: the donjons, the high catwalks surrounding the ramparts, the darkest heart of the forests where pagans worshipped and druids offered sacrifices to Herne the Hunter. The cliffs had been a particularily satisfying challenge, for the only weapon he could use against his fear of the wind and the terrifying height was his own courage.

The eyrie was a fluke of nature, a ripple on the face of the rocks where the path widened briefly to form a large, flat ledge. In poor weather a fire could be built on the eyrie to warn away ships that were straying too close to shore, but in the years since the Dragon had become Master of Bloodmoor Keep, no doubt it was considered more profitable to let the ships wander where they may and spew their cargo up on shore. The currents were fierce and ever changing, as able to suck an unsuspecting vessel into the reefs and boulders and reduce it to kindling, as to deliver a boat into the narrow sheltered cove that was tucked like an armpit between the outer reef and shore.

Lifting his face to the gloomy sky, Lucien tasted the strong bite of salt on his lips. The wind was sharp and cold, strong enough to gust against the rocks and snatch at the folds of the monk's robes they wore. The ruse had worked once, Alaric had reasoned, and it might make a difference of a few precious seconds while the sentries were deciding whether to fire their crossbows or not. Besides which, the first cart Sir Roger had spied, not fifty yards outside the castle walls, had belonged to a brace of holy brothers who had camped there in the hopes of attending the wedding in the morning.

Precisely why two monks would be found climbing down a perilous path on the side of a cliff in the dead of night, Alaric had not yet fathomed, but if nothing else, the warm woolen garments gave them some protection from the cold and kept their teeth from chattering an alert to the guards ahead. Hopefully the sentries would be too cold and miserable themselves to be watching the path.

Making their way to the gate and bribing their way through it had cost precious time. Sparrow had been the first to disappear into the darkness, having the farthest to go and the most to accomplish before dawn threatened the sky. Sir Roger had thought the business of stealing the cart a tad anticlimactic, but the holy brothers had not been wont to squander their alms on sturdy wheels, and the route Lucien scratched into the dirt would take several hours to cover. Eduard and Gil had set off cheerily enough for the fishing boats, and it was not until they were long gone that Alaric noticed fresh blood stains in the scuffed prints Eduard had left behind.

Robed and cowled, Friar and the Wolf had followed the base of the castle wall looking and feeling much like two ants crawling around the base of a giant oak. What breath they had left at the end was taken away by the wind and the awesome view of the sea so far below. Black and oily, the surface glistened with pewter-coloured troughs. The moon was two, perhaps three hours above the horizon, and it would travel several more before the two men had finished picking their way down the cliffs. Alaric had stared at the sea, at the ridiculously narrow mouth of the path, and at the tall shadowy figure who stood silently beside him, his hood flown back off his head, his dark hair streaming back in the wind.

"I should have pushed you off then," Alaric shouted, battling a mouthful of woolen cowling, "and jumped after you. This is madness! Utter madness!"

"We have come more than halfway," the Wolf countered. "And if you shout any louder you will have them shooting at us from the castle walls!"

"How much more than halfway?" Alaric asked after a moment.

"See there . . . where the path widens?"

Alaric craned his neck to see around the Wolf's shoulder

without having to lean too far out from the wall. He could see nothing but a black void below them, but he nodded anyway, trusting Lucien's keener eyesight.

"Just around that curve, it widens and flattens into a ledge. Another few minutes we should be able to see a glow from their fire, if they have one. We have made good time, all things considered. It would do no harm to stop here and rest a few minutes."

Alaric sagged gratefully against the wall of rock. But his respite was short-lived, and voluntarily so. Out of the corner of one eye he could see the silhouette of Bloodmoor's ramparts rising black and evil into the night sky above them. Out of the other he could see the face of the Wolf, and for a moment, he did not know which of the two terrified him more.

"We can rest in hell, old friend," he said. "Let's go."

Lucien checked the balance of his sword and unsheathed two razor-sharp poniards from his belt, tucking one into each sleeve.

"You had better let me go first here on in," Friar advised. "And for the love of God, keep your hood up and well forward to shadow your face. The Devil might welcome such grisly fierceness, but I doubt any wary Christians would see comfort there."

Lucien cursed the delay, but drew the hood forward. So far this night, others had done his killing for him, and he was more than ready, willing, and eager to draw blood.

They inched downward another fifty paces in cautious silence, then with a deep breath drawn to stop his pulse from racing away from him, Alaric raised his voice and called for help.

"Ahead! Ahead! God love us, is there anyone ahead!"

He scraped, stumbled and scuffed his way around the last curve of rock and was not surprised to see several grim-faced guards braced in a crouch, their crossbows armed and aimed at the two monks who came spilling out of the darkness.

"Oh thank God, thank God!" Friar cried, moving onto the ledge and hugging the rock as if he had no intentions of letting go ever again. "Holy Father in Heaven, 'tis a wonder, a *miracle* we are here at last!"

"By the rood, who are you and where have you come from?" demanded one of the guards.

"Why . . . 'tis only me, Brother Benedict, and my companion, Brother Aleward. We have come from the castle on Lord Wardieu's command . . . though God knows how he expected us to bring our souls down this mountain without aid of light or guidance. Oh, we had a torch, but it gave up its life nearer here than the way back and we had no choice but to come ahead . . . not that we would have turned back too eagerly in any event. No, no. I should rather have faced any peril than return to the baron without his orders obeyed. Are you all right, Brother Aleward? Dear me, the poor man has no stomach for heights, you see. Twice he lost it on the way down and I dread the thought of having to nurse and coddle him the way up again, but at least it will be dawn soon and we will have God's light to guide us back."

"Why have you come?" demanded the guard, his eyes slitted warily, his hands still taut on the grip of his crossbow.

Lucien kept his face averted, marking the positions of the guards who stood between them and the cell door. There were four sentries all told, two men-at-arms with bows, two mercenaries in mail armour with longswords drawn and ready for trouble.

"In truth," Alaric replied, spreading his hands wide to discourage any hint of a threat. "I did not question Lord Wardieu's command. I merely assumed, because it is to be his wedding day, he is offering his bride every opportunity to confess whatever sins may be tormenting her soul, and to offer prayer and counsel as a means of redeeming herself in the eyes of the Lord."

The knight who had issued the challenge laughed gruffly and resheathed his sword. "Prayer and counsel? Give us free rein with her and she would be as docile as a lamb. A little worn between the thighs, perhaps, but knowing how to give proper thanks when and where it is due."

The four guards grinned and exchanged a glance between themselves, giving Alaric the distinct impression they had already drawn lots to see who among them would be the first. He knew also, by the sudden stillness of the figure behind him, that Lucien had arrived at the same conclusion.

"A pity," Friar sighed, almost to himself. "We might have been able to spare your lives."

Lucien's hands disappeared into his sleeves for a split second and when they emerged again, there was a flash of steel and the two men-at-arms were doubling over, clutching at the hilts of the poniards jutting from their chests. Friar was on the first mercenary before he was aware of the danger, his blade slashing through the firelit darkness and severing the man's hand from his wrist before his sword was fully drawn. The knight grunted and held out the bleeding stump in disbelief; stunned, he staggered too close to the edge of the promontory and, with a scream that was torn away on a gust of icy wind, vanished into the misty darkness.

Lucien had engaged swords with the other knight, a man whose skill might have been laudable under any other circumstances. But he was driven by duty, not passion, and though he fended off one savage thrust of the Wolf's blade after another, he was clearly outmatched. Fear took him back beneath the overhang of rock, and desperation saw him reach into his baldric and slash out with a shorter, sharper-edged dagger. The Wolf lunged, locking hilts with the guard's sword and pinning it against the stone while his free hand grasped for the knife and twisted it inward, slicing it down across the man's exposed throat and nearly separating the head from the shoulders.

He let the body slump to the ground and reached for the rusted iron bar that was slotted across the door to the cell. The door itself was crudely fit to the shape of the fissure opening, and so low he had to duck to clear the stone arch. Alaric was right behind him, thrusting a lit torch through the entryway.

At first, Lucien saw nothing past the searing flare of burning pitch. The rage boiled over in his blood and he was about to curse his brother's further deceit when a movement in the corner—a pale splash of yellow against the blackened stone —sent his gaze to the deepest recess of the cell.

"Servanne?"

Round, frightened eyes, blinded as much by fear as by the sudden light, lifted to meet his. He pushed back the hood of the monk's robe and saw the terror give way slowly to recognition.

"Lucien?" she gasped. "Is it . . . really you?"

"Name another man fool enough to chase after you on a night such as this," he said, his grin belying the pounding pressure in his chest. Dear God, her face was bruised and swollen, her lip torn and caked with dried blood. Her arms were blue, scratched in too many places to see in one glance, and her gown was torn at the throat, the whiteness of her flesh violated by further bruising and scratches.

"I . . . thought you were dead," she whispered. "When no one came . . . when I heard nothing . . . I thought you were dead."

"Did you think you could be rid of me so easily?"

Her eyes flooded with tears, Servanne flung herself across the width of the cell and felt the long, powerful arms sweep her into a crushing embrace. The blood-slicked poniard dropped forgotten onto the ground and his hands raked into the tangled mass of her hair, holding her against him, turning her lips up to his for a kiss as passionate as life itself.

"Lucien!" Alaric hissed from the doorway. "Can you not celebrate later when we have the time and leisure to do so?"

An oath that was more a promise tore Lucien's lips away from Servanne's, but the taste of her, the feel of her drenched his senses, almost blinding them to the urgency in Alaric's voice.

"My lady," said Friar, his smile shaken as well by the extent of Servanne's bruising. "Are you well enough? Can you walk?"

"I shall run as fast as the wind if need be," she replied without hesitation, her own beautiful smile shining through her tears.

Lucien took her hand and led her out into the brisk night air. Was it only his imagination, or was the sky growing lighter overhead? To be sure, the wind was picking up speed and energy, gleefully plucking at the flimsy silk of Servanne's tunic. Quickly he divested himself of the gray woolen robe and handed it to her.

"Here, put this on. We have a way to go yet, and—"

"Lucien! Come quickly!"

The Wolf ran to where Alaric stood on the lip of the upper path. A grim line of bobbing orange dots could be seen spilling out the postern gate at the base of the castle wall; a dozen guards carrying a dozen torches were making their way down the side of the cliff, lighting the way for a dozen more armed with swords and crossbows.

"Go," Alaric shouted, ridding himself of the bulky robes. "I'll loose a few arrows their way to discourage them long enough for you to get Lady Servanne below."

"There are too many of them!"

Alaric fetched the crossbows and quivers of bolts from the dead guards. "You said yourself, a man with a ready supply of arrows could hold off an army until hell froze."

Lucien hesitated, the desire for blood and revenge warring with his need to see Servanne to safety.

"In God's name"—Alaric had to shout to be heard over the roaring of the waves and the rising winds—"we have not come this far to lose to them now! Go! I will join you in a trice. Have no fear—I have no more intention of perishing on this godforsaken eyrie than I have intentions of walking the way back to Lincoln!"

Knowing there was no time to argue, Lucien grabbed Servanne's hand again and picked up the path on the other side of the ledge. It was no less steep and treacherous than the upper half of the descent; if anything, the closer it came to the sea, the more the path degenerated to a mere lip of crumbling stone. They were forced to walk singly and to keep one arm and hip pressed painfully against the rough stone. Servanne's boast of being able to run like the wind was mocked at every gap and broken toehold that reduced their pace to a snail's crawl. Her one slipperless foot seemed to find every sharp needle of rock on the path. The monk's robe weighed her down, snagging on brambles and crevices, twice jerking her back and needing to be torn from the grasp of the greedy talons of rock.

The moon was well behind the mass of the cliffs, casting a dull glow over the surface of the water, but sparing nothing for the path. Lucien seemed to be guided by instinct and, on those occasions when the blackness erased all trace of solid footing, prayer.

Back at the eagle's eyrie, Alaric waited patiently for the lead guard to come within crossbow range before he leveled the bow and released the trigger, loosing a bolt with a re-sounding *thwang*. He struck his target dead centre of the De Gournay blazon, sending the wearer into an almost graceful arc out over the lip of the cliff and into the foaming wash of the sea below. He fired the second weapon, already armed and waiting by his side, killing the next man in line while he was gaping after his fallen comrade.

Calmly, Friar braced the heavy bow nose down while he loaded another quarrel onto the firing shaft. He drew back the string to arm it, raised the ungainly weapon to chest level to fire . . . and saw that De Gournay's men had already begun a hasty scramble back up the cliff. There was no return fire. Not even a testy challenge by a guard farther along in the rear.

It had almost been too easy.

Alaric rubbed the skin at the back of his neck and glanced upward at the silhouette of the castle, its shape growing more distinct as the false dawn gave way to the spreading stain of pale gray along the horizon. Even in this uncertain light and at this considerable distance, he could see the heads of the guards patrolling high up on the battlements. If he could see them . . .

Alaric straightened and whirled around to stare at where the path resumed on the far side of the ledge. There was only the one way down, only one place to go, and, if the Dragon had been alerted to their presence on the cliff, what could be easier than to set a trap at the bottom and simply wait for the Wolf to walk into it? The Wolf, Servanne, Gil, Eduard . . . !

"Christ!" he swore and ran for the path. Without the need to guide and steady a frightened woman behind him, he moved much faster than the Wolf and Servanne, arriving at breakneck speed at the base of the cliff just in time to catch a glimpse of their two shadowy figures rounding the last curve in the rocks.

The fleeing pair was soaked in sea spray when they finally stumbled down onto the beach. There, to Servanne's surprise and relief, she could see the glittering swath of a small bay. Though the air continued to vibrate with the thundering roar and crash of the sea, the inlet was nestled behind a breaker of huge boulders and the water was calm enough for a small boat to have maneuvered to within twenty feet of the shore.

The last stretch of their flight was made over a bed of sharp, cutting shale. Lucien, hearing Servanne's involuntary cry as the first steps drove a shard of glasslike stone into the pad of her bare foot, swept her into his arms and, without missing a step, plunged into the knee-deep water. A shout and the sound of a second pair of boots crunching across the shale brought the wolfish grin back to Lucien's lips as he turned and saw Alaric swerving away from the shoreline to follow them into the surf. He was shouting something, both to Lucien and to the occupants of the small boat, and Lucien's smile vanished. Dawn was in full bloom, the orange and red flare of the verging sun caught and reflected in the glint of conical steel helmets lined along the shore.

They were trapped! The Dragon's men had been waiting on the beach; they had allowed the boat to enter the bay unmolested and they had bided their time until their quarry had run straight into the ambush!

Water began to plop and spout on all sides as a hail of crossbow bolts arced out over the beach. Lucien commanded every ounce of strength he possessed into his legs, but the water, now waist deep, hampered him, and even though the breaker of rocks helped to cut the force of the sea, there was still a wicked undercurrent that pulled and shifted the sand beneath every footstep.

Less than ten yards from the longboat they went down under a slapping wall of silvery water. Coughing and sputtering oaths, Lucien struggled upright again, managing to maintain his grip on Servanne, sodden clothes and all.

Eduard, ignoring Gil's cry, vaulted over the gunwale and began plowing through the waves in an effort to reach the labouring couple. Gil, an arrow clenched between her teeth and another already nocked to her bow, began to return the fire of the guardsmen, who were now running in the open, in a parallel line along the shore. As they knelt to fire and rearm their heavy weapons, Gil was able to pick her targets carefully and with startling accuracy. Many of them heard the singsong hiss of arrows streaking out of the darkness toward them and did not rise from the shale again. Others ran back into the cover of the nearby rocks and dove behind them, assuming—and rightly so—the supply of steel-tipped arrows was not endless. But they were still well within the ideal range for firing their own weapons, and they did so continually, their rage fueling and improving their aim.

Servanne heard a cry and glanced over Lucien's shoulder in time to see Alaric careen sideways into the water, an iron quarrel embedded in his upper chest. Lucien shouted and released her, shoving her toward Eduard before he turned and started running back to where he had seen Alaric go under. Servanne's scream of warning went unheeded. A mercenary running along the shore took aim with his bow and fired, the bolt flying straight and true, tearing a ribbon of flesh from Lucien's temple.

Stunned, the Wolf heeled to one side, the pain and blood blinding him even as his legs continued to churn toward Alaric. The knight armed his weapon a second time, but before he could sight along the shaft, he heard a graceful hiss and felt a punch of steel and ashwood pierce cleanly through his leather breastplate.

The dead knight was no sooner swept into the foaming wash of the surf than another took his place, seeming to rise like a golden-haired Goliath out of the receding fingers of mist.

Servanne screamed again, this time to beat away the determined arm that had snaked around her waist and was dragging her toward the longboat.

"No! No, let me go! Let me go to him! Lucien! *Lucien!*"

Eduard's arm remained like iron around her waist even though she kicked and writhed and fought to be set free. Salt water was in her eyes, blurring her vision, her hair was a drenched, tangled mass wrapped around her throat, choking her. Her hands, flailing wildly around, tried to strike away the force that was carrying her away from her love, her life, and smashed instead into something solid and wooden—the boat! A streak of white-hot pain lanced up her arm, causing her to temporarily cease her struggling and go limp in Eduard's arms.

He strained against the current and the violently rocking boat to try to lift her over the side. His leg was crushed against the keel by the undertow and he grunted in pain, feeling his wound reopen to the searing fire of salt water. Servanne felt his grip falter, saw him claw desperately for a hold on the gunwale . . . lose it, and begin to slide under the rolling waves. Instinctively she reached out to help him . . . and screamed again.

It had not been the side of the boat her hand had struck. Rather, she was the one who had been struck, and not by a wooden plank but by a twelve-inch-long crossbow bolt. The iron head had split through the padding of flesh between her thumb and forefinger and buried itself in the wood planking, pinning her helplessly to the boat.

A wave washed over her head, filling her eyes, nose, and mouth with salt water. Without the strength or ability to resist, she was carried along with the tiny vessel as it was pushed relentlessly toward the waiting danger on the shore. The sandy bottom fell out from beneath her feet and she was dragged down by the current, down into a void of muted sound and roiling darkness.

Nicolaa de la Haye was a few short paces behind Etienne Wardieu when he stepped out from behind the shield of rocks, and she raised her voice with his in calling for the guards to put up their bows and swords. The trap had worked perfectly. The wolf was caught in the snare and it only remained for the Dragon to have the pleasure of dealing the killing stroke himself.

Nicolaa's excitement had been growing to a fever pitch from the moment the sentries had confirmed seeing two men on the cliff. She had insisted on accompanying Etienne and his guard to the beach and she had spurred her horse with equal vehemence, carving up the shale and sand, galloping through still tidal pools with the fury of vengeance shooting plumes of spray ten feet in their wake.

Within a hundred yards of the sheltered cove, he had reined in his horse and positioned his men among the rocks and boulders lining the beach. They had not had long to test their patience before the low, black shape of a longboat had slid around the reef and sidled into the shallower water. Recognizing Eduard on the oars had only reinforced the Dragon's rage and hatred; hearing the boy cry out and dive heedlessly into the surf to meet his father had altered the Dragon's face into a mask of murderous malevolence.

Nicolaa could have laughed out loud at the ludicrous attempt Lucien Wardieu had made to outwit her glorious Dragon knight. The girl was drowning, the other two would-be rescuers were going nowhere fast. The Wolf had struggled to his feet in the knee-deep water and now stood facing his brother, their two profiles etched in black against the blood-red sky. The fifth participant in this most enjoyable farce was floundering against the force of the waves, fighting the pain and nausea to reach one of the dead guards whose sword lay temptingly within his grasp.

Striding toward him, Nicolaa drew her own short falchion and arched a raven brow in mild surprise.

"Well, well, well. Bishop Gautier . . . we were wondering what had become of you."

Gil Golden knew she had no time to waste on subtlety. Servanne was helpless, pinned to the side of the boat, and

Eduard was using all of his remaining strength just to keep his nose and mouth above water. With her lips moving around a silent apology, Gil reached over the gunwale and took hold of the end of the crossbow bolt. She snapped off the feather fletching and, praying the salt water had already numbed the wound beyond any additional agony, she jerked Servanne's hand back, sliding it off the broken end of the shaft.

The boat lurched onto a sandbar, stranding the three in shallow water as the wave receded. It was then, as Gil braced herself to keep from falling headlong into the surf herself, that she saw Nicolaa de la Haye stalking Alaric. He had managed to crawl to a dead guard and had retrieved the man's sword, but as he started to haul himself upright, Nicolaa kicked his legs out from beneath him and he went down hard. He clutched his upper shoulder as he rolled with the pain, his fingers splayed on either side of the protruding arrow shaft.

Gil stared long and hard at the woman she had loathed with every breath of her being for the past five years. Nicolaa and one of her lovers had been attending the Lincoln Fair, where Gil's father—an expert bowyer and fletcher—had set up a booth to display his wares. Because Gil had looked pretty enough to earn a wink from the handsome soldier, Nicolaa had ordered her arrested and accused her of thievery. Gil's father had come to her defense, and for his trouble, had been slain on the spot. Gil's mother and two sisters—the latter barely in their tenth and eleventh years—had been taken to the guards' barracks for the amusement of the sodomizing bastards until none had had the strength or will left to plead for mercy.

Nicolaa had saved Gil to the end, teasing her just enough with the hot irons to know that when the screams of her mother and sisters stopped, hers would begin in earnest. By sheer luck, one of the dungeon guards had been a friend to

Gil's father. He bore the screams of the women as long as he could, then one night, after another poor red-haired lass was dragged dead from the barracks, the old man had put the body in Gil's cell and had whisked her out in an empty ale barrel.

Gil had survived, but she could hear her sisters screaming still, in her nightmares, just as she could hear Nicolaa de la Haye laughing and goading the guards to another round . . . and another . . .

"No," she gasped, seeing Nicolaa raise her sword above Alaric's head. *"No!* By God, you will not take the life of anyone else I love!"

She jumped out of the boat and screamed Nicolaa's name. Too late, she realized she had set aside her longbow to pull Servanne's hand free, and, for lack of any better weapon to use against the falchion that turned eagerly in her direction, Gil paused to scoop up a fallen crossbow. She released the trigger only to hear a wet snap as the string refused to respond. Nicolaa's fleeting moment of panic gave way to grinning delight and as the slender, red-haired archer ran closer, she clasped her shortsword in both hands and drew it back for the killing stroke.

Something black, salty, and gritty struck her stingingly across the face. The muck was in her eyes and in her mouth, and Nicolaa was repulsed into breaking her stance as well as her grip on the hilt of the sword. Alaric threw another handful of wet sand, but by then she had turned away, cursing and scraping the stuff from her face in time to see the blurred fury that was Gil Golden slam into her chest and send them both crashing into the surf.

Alaric doubled over onto his elbows and knees, his head bowed forward with the pain. Gil and Nicolaa became a rolling, thrashing mass of arms and legs beside him; Lucien and Etienne stood a dozen paces away, their swords unsheathed, their footsteps bringing them together in an ever-decreasing circle of crouched wariness. Nicolaa's falchion lay in an inch of water, a body length away, but before Alaric could drag himself over to it, a mail-clad boot kicked it a hopeless distance away. Almost too weary to expend the energy to do so, Alaric looked up, seeing his death in the eyes of the mercenary who braced himself to deliver a hacking blow across the back of Alaric's neck.

Fff-thunck!

The mercenary stiffened, his back arched against the brutal force of a six-inch arrow fired from an odd, harp-shaped arblaster. Two longer, thinner ashwood arrows, tipped in steel, fired simultaneously from raised longbows, thudded into the guard's back and shoulder, skewering through leather armour and Damascan chain mail as if it was soft cheese. The knight toppled forward, his arms spread wide, his sword splashing harmlessly into the shallow water beside Alaric.

Sparrow's gleeful cry brought a wall of black and gold clad knights surging out from behind the tumble of boulders. Calmly, coolly, half of them dispatched a spray of arrows into the ranks of De Gournay's surprised mercenaries; the rest, led by Sir Roger de Chesnai and Sir Richard of Rouen, poured out onto the beach, their throats roaring an unmistakable challenge.

The Dragon saw his men falling back, retreating under the onslaught of flashing swords.

The Wolf smiled and felt a resurgence of energy burn away the fatigue and despair that had nearly claimed him.

"And so, it comes down to just you and me, Etienne," he said in a low, controlled voice. "With honour as our judge and God our witness."

Etienne's blue eyes glittered his response and, in ankle-deep water, the Wolf and the Dragon brought their blades slashing together. Lucien, his black shirt and leggings shading him like a dark wraith against the sparkle of the sea, lunged and spun away, his hair shedding bright droplets of salt water into the breaking sunlight. Etienne blocked the thrust and countered with a strength-shattering one of his own, the muscles across his back and arms bulging beneath the quilted blue silk of his surcoat. Steel bit into steel, the swords screaming as loudly as the gulls who spiraled down from the roosts on the cliffs, attracted by the fresh scent of blood.

Each driving stroke of arms and legs was evenly matched. Both men had suffered bruising and earned wounds in their earlier meeting on the tournament grounds, but this was a new battle, the final battle, and neither spared a thought or grimace for the aches or fatigue. They attacked like rampant lions, blow upon mighty blow staggering first one, then the other. Their swords slashed and hacked without grace or deliberation, each cut searching for a hidden weakness, probing for an unguarded flaw—some imperfection in skill or speed that could reward a bloodthirsty blade.

They fought their way onto the sand where the footing was not sucked out from beneath them, but where the weight and drag slowed their turns and lengthened the time needed to recover. The droplets sprayed from Lucien's hair were tinged red from the wound on his temple, and the front of his shirt became splashed with sand and gore. Etienne's arm and thigh were gashed, the links of his mail unable to withstand the tremendous power behind each of the Wolf's blows.

The two crashed together, locking swords, their eyes blazing at each other over the crossed shanks of steel. Lucien saw nothing in the icy blue gaze to jar the memories of happier times that had softened him before; he saw only hatred and twisted jealousy, and the arrogance of greed and unchecked corruption. He saw more. He saw his father's face and the agony of the betrayal he must have felt knowing his son had condemned him to a traitor's death. He saw Eduard lying spread-eagle on the torturer's rack, and he saw Mutter ar

Stutter, Robert the Welshman, and all the faces of all the good men who had given their lives over the past twenty hours. And he saw Servanne . . .

Lucien surged forward with a roar, breaking the tension in Etienne's arms. The Dragon fought to retain his balance, doing so at the last possible split second, and was able to angle his sword down, ready to block the anticipated stroke his instincts screamed would come at him from the right. He committed his sword and his eyes followed the stroke . . . *but it came from the left,* not the right, and the enormity of his error flickered across his face even as Lucien's blade carved into the exposed rack of ribs and sliced its way through silk and leather, mail and muscle, flesh and sinew and wildly beating heart.

The Dragon sagged forward, a groan of incredulous agony pulling him down onto his knees. He dropped his sword and reached frantically for support, but Lucien had already taken a broad step back, his chest heaving, his hands clenched into fists by his sides. The Dragon looked down in disbelief at the blood gushing onto the sand. He clasped his hands over his chest as if to keep any more from spilling from the wound, but he was already dead, and he fell facedown, his flaxen hair glittering against the crimson sand like tarnished gold.

Lucien barely had time to collect his senses before a woman's piercing scream drew his gaze to the shoreline. He spun around just as Gil, her hands gripped around the hilt of a knife, thrust her weight forward to plunge the blade deep into Nicolaa de la Haye's chest. The scream was cut short as Nicolaa's body went rigid with the pain. Her green eyes blazed wide through a moment of shocked recognition as Gil Golden's face turned into the sunlight, but the only sound that came from her lips was the gurgle and hiss of a dying breath.

Servanne, trembling like a leaf in the heart of a storm, stood in the midst of the carnage, her wounded hand cradled to her breast. She saw Gil run over to kneel by Alaric's side, and she saw Sparrow leap into the surf with several other men to retrieve Eduard before he was dragged out to sea again. Sir Roger and another tall, noble-looking knight were talking to Lucien but he gave them only the briefest of acknowledgments as he cast a swift, smouldering glance along the beach and found Servanne.

He seemed to need a deep breath to steady himself before he started staggering slowly toward her. His gloriously handsome face was streaked with blood, his shirt was cut in a dozen places and clung to his flesh like a wet black sheath. But he had never looked more wonderful to her. Servanne had never felt such happiness, such love, such pride before in her life.

He stopped within arm's reach, his eyes a paler gray than ever she had seen them, and filled with more emotions than she would have dared hoped or dreamed. He stared at her for a long moment, his gaze moving over her soft curves, pausing at every scratch and bruise as if offering a silent pledge to atone for each and every one. There was a breathless little silence between them and her knees turned to jelly. She knew if he did not say something soon, or take her into his arms, she would melt into the sand and be washed out to sea on the next tide.

They must have been sharing the exact same thought at the exact same instant, for her half-sobbed cry was lost beneath the heartfelt oath he murmured as his mouth came crushing down over hers. His arms went around her, clinging to her so tightly she became moulded to the muscles of his body. His kiss was deep and ravaging and might have frightened her with its demanding intensity if her own lips were not just as eager, just as frantic to become a part of him.

"Ahh-hem."

The discreet cough behind them made no impression.

"Ahh-*hem*. My lord?"

Sparrow happened by and chuckled dryly. "I warrant you would have better luck winning a response from a tree trunk, Sir Richard of Rouen. These two shall not move again until hunger, thirst, or body needs lay them by the heels."

Lucien's mouth lifted from Servanne's with a grudging sigh, but he made no move to release her from his arms.

"Sir Richard . . . were you not supposed to be well on your way to Hull to rendezvous with the queen's ship?"

"There is gratitude for you," Sparrow chirped, earning a scowl from Sir Richard in return.

"As it happens, my lord, as soon as we were out of hailing distance of the castle, my men lost patience with the louts sent to escort our troop to Lincoln. We laid them by in short order, then set off in the direction of Hull, but bedamned if my steed did not pull up lame and require the services of a farrier. In all conscience I could not risk the safety of Princess Eleanor over such a trifling matter, and so I sent her on ahead with the bulk of the men, retaining only a few good lads to, ahh, aid me in my search for a smithy."

Lucien's gaze had not broken from Servanne's, nor had the heat in his body grown any less threatening to her composure.

"And? Did you find a smithy?"

Sir Richard ignored Sparrow's rolling eyes and nodded quite seriously. "Aye, my lord, but by then it was broaching dusk and so misted on the forest roads we could scarce see our hands before our faces. Imagine my surprise when the road we took brought us back to the moor instead of away to Hull."

"Imagine," the Wolf mused, his embrace tightening around Servanne, the movement rippling along the muscles 'n his arms and chest.

"And then the further surprise of stumbling across the mp occupied by our own men! We were naturally pressed lodging there the night and—"

"And just happened to still be there when I arrived," Sparrow interjected, "although I am sure, had I been a wink later in gasping my way out of the moor, Sir Richard and his men would have departed for Hull."

"No doubt they would," the Wolf murmured, his mouth lowering to Servanne's with a warm, devouring passion. "Well, my lady? What do you think of such a tale?"

"I think it heroic and brave," she whispered. "Sir Richard has obviously been in your service long enough to have learned by example."

"The devil you say, madam."

"The devil you are, my lord," she sighed, and stretched up on tiptoes to ensure he did not speak again.

EPILOGUE

Servanne ran the palms of her hands reverently over the warm bulge of male flesh beneath her. Discovering the two raised beads of his nipples, her lips formed a moist pout and leaned brazenly forward to claim their prize. Lucien groaned and raked his fingers into the silken mass of her hair, but that was a mistake too, for it freed her hips to move at their own impudent pace, and he could feel himself being drawn deeper and deeper by muscles that were becoming just too damned proficient at undermining his authority.

He skimmed his hands down to the firm, pearly skin of her breasts and took some satisfaction in hearing a faintly rasped warning. She was just as close as he was, but twice as determined to squeeze every delicious shudder of pleasure from his body before she relinquished the reins of passion.

Bowing to the demands of chivalry—not to mention the sharp nip of her teeth—Lucien moved his hands away. He curled his fingers tightly against the rivers of heated sensation her swirling, suckling tongue and lips were drawing from his flesh and pressed his head back into the soft pillow of moss. Staring up at the phosphorescent greens and blues that sparkled on the ceiling of the grotto, he watched the eddies of steam whorling above them and wondered if either of them would have any skin left on their buttocks, backs, and knees. Probably not, he grinned. Why should this excursion be any different from the dozens they had taken before? day spent in the secluded privacy of the Silent Pool and

the grotto usually left them both so chafed they were forced
to sleep on furs for the next few nights.

Lucien closed his eyes and tried not to think about her
hot, sliding flesh, but that was like not thinking at all. Not
breathing. Not living . . .

Servanne felt the powerful shudder that gripped his body
and she slowed the rhythm of her hips to hardly more than
an insistent throb. She pushed herself upright and saw the
gray eyes open a sliver, but she only smiled and trailed her
fingers down onto his hard, flat belly, marveling that she
never failed to discover new areas of sensitivity. The chiseled
beauty of each muscle and sinew was branded into her mind
and on her body. The texture, taste, and scent of him was as
much a part of her as her own skin. He was her love and her
life, and even after six months of wedded bliss, their hunger
for each other was as insatiable as it had been the first hour
after their rescue on the beach.

Bloodmoor was Lucien's now, but there were too many
memories haunting the gloomy towers and battlements to
keep a smile on his face too long. He had destroyed the cell
on the eagle's eyrie and scorched the donjon to the bare walls
before sealing the cavernous death chamber behind block
and mortar . . . but it was not enough. The Wardieu crest
was emblazoned everywhere with its depiction of the dragon
and the wolf locked in eternal combat. Lucien had proudly
reclaimed his name and birthright, but there was too much
of Etienne in every room, every court, every uncertain eye
that followed him from hall to bailey.

Moreover, Prince John—who had been only too eager at
the time to put his seal to the documents Lucien had handed
him at the point of a bloody sword—had had those same six
months to stew over his embarrassment and humiliation.
Having to admit publicly to Etienne Wardieu's duplicity and
declaring Lucien to be the rightful heir of the De Gournay
titles and estates had sent the regent away from Bloodmoor

in a state of mortified rage. Sooner or later he would exact his revenge. The fact he had even waited this long before showing signs of doing so was a credit to the lords and barons who had come forward in Lucien's support. Their names were undoubtedly marked for future consideration as well, but for the time being, they were King Richard's men and safe enough from John's machinations.

Servanne had suspected something was afoot when Lucien had sent Alaric and Gil to Brittany two months ago, ostensibly to check on his lands and estates in Normandy. The glowing reports of prosperity had come swift on the heels of letters from Queen Eleanor, who thought it churlish and disloyal of him to remain in a country that had treated him so badly. For his part in winning the safe return of the little princess to Brittany, the dowager had rewarded him with a barony in Touraine, and was anxious to know what further bribes he would demand of an old woman's heart before he deigned to return to her court, where he belonged. Sir Richard of Rouen made a fine captain of the guard, she added, but she missed her black wolf's sharp wit and brooding strength.

A second clue was Eduard's sudden interest in geography. He had recovered—some said miraculously—from his wounds, and now served Lucien as squire. He grew more and more like his father every day, in appearance and in manner, causing more than one startled head to turn and gape after them in awe. They made a breathtakingly handsome pair of rogues together, and had grown close enough in their relationship to make anyone doubt they had ever been strangers. In another few years, however, Eduard would be seeking ways to earn his own gold spurs, easier done from Brittany with its ready access to the richest tournaments in France and Italy, than from a remote and wind-swept castle on the English coast.

Biddy was her fiery, imperious self again. She had, by one

means or another, convinced herself she had been responsible for the way everything had turned out . . . which was, of course, vastly different from Sparrow's interpretation of the events. At least once a day Biddy could be seen chasing the diminutive aggravation about the halls of the castle, a broom or fire poker in her hand, and at least once a day, she found her cap swiped off with a flying arrow, or her apron pinned to a wooden door.

As for Lucien, his visible wounds had healed rapidly enough, adding but a few more scars to a body that already boasted far too many to count. He was healing inwardly as well under Servanne's tutelage, and, as Robert the Welshman had predicted, had begun to laugh again. He could easily remain at Bloodmoor Keep, he reasoned, and face the wrath of Prince John . . . but to what purpose? He had already fought one dragon and won his right to peace and prosperity; John was England's dragon and it was up to her to find some way to defeat his greed and ambition. Lucien had no regrets about leaving. Brittany had become his home and he could return there quite happily to grow very old and very sedate with his beautiful new bride by his side.

"The only thing I will truly miss is this place," Servanne murmured, her eyes gazing dreamily around the grotto. "Have they anything half so . . . inspiring . . . in Touraine?"

Lancets of fire were bursting in his loins, fragmenting his senses, making it difficult for Lucien to think, let alone speak through the increasingly violent shivers.

He managed to nod, however, and gasp out an assurance. "We will find one, I swear it."

Servanne sat straighter and the undulant motion of her hips caused the curling ends of her hair to sweep and drag across the tops of his thighs. She lifted her hands off his belly and smoothed them over her own, smiling at the burgeoning evidence of the new life growing within her.

"Sparrow says our child will be charmed. He is convinced these magical waters cannot help but have aided in conceiving a man of some great future destiny. He feels so strongly about it, he says he may have to take the babe under his wing to insure he learns how to make the most of his powers."

"Madam . . . there is only one thing I feel very strongly about at the moment."

"Oh? And what might that be, my lord?"

Lucien reached up and brought her mouth down to his for a plundering caress. His lips and tongue silenced her soft laughter as effectively as the proud thrust of his flesh brought about an explosive end to their sensual odyssey. He held her and braced her as the heat of ecstasy flared along the length and breadth of their bodies. He surged within her, again and again, blinded by the fury of their passion, humbled by the consummate purity of their love.

Beyond the wall of lush green ivy, the sweeping boughs of the mighty oaks began to rustle and sigh with envy. The sun danced in a more sprightly way over the surface of the Silent Pool, keeping tune with the bubble and gurgle of the tiny stream that chuckled its way over the rocks and drew the attention of a curious doe and her fawn. Soft, velvety ears pricked forward, for there had never been such a chorus of sounds in the sunlit glade before. It was as if a spell had finally been broken and the forest had come alive again, teeming with life, and hope, and joy.